OF STARLIGHT
AND PLAGUE

BETH HERSANT

Matador
9 Priory Business Park,
Wistow Road, Kibworth Beauchamp,
Leicestershire. LE8 0RX
Tel: 0116 279 2299
Email: books@troubador.co.uk
Web: www.troubador.co.uk/matador
Twitter: @matadorbooks

ISBN 978 1800462 632

British Library Cataloguing in Publication Data.
A catalogue record for this book is available from the British Library.

Typeset in 12pt Adobe Jenson Pro by Troubador Publishing Ltd, Leicester, UK

Matador is an imprint of Troubador Publishing Ltd

To Amelia and Matthew, and my Richard — you are my stars.

Also a thank you to Eleanor and Deborah
for listening to me prattle on about this.

"I will love the light for it shows me the way,
yet I will endure the darkness for it shows me the stars."

Og Mandino

ACORN

It is said that terrible omens preceded the outbreak of the Black Death in medieval Europe. Frogs, serpents and scorpions fell from the sky. There was thunder and lightning and then fire rained down from the heavens. It's a dramatic image — but obvious nonsense. Big events are not heralded by a rain of toads. They have simple beginnings and we often find the germ of great horrors in the ordinary and the small. There is the tiny air bubble in the vein, the microscopic not-quite-alive strand of viral RNA that causes Ebola, that last shot of Captain Morgan before getting behind the wheel. After all, mighty oaks from little acorns grow. This was the case with our own Great Plague. And so our story begins with a little girl and a small red rubber ball.

Rachel Pickman sat in a shady spot where the concrete wasn't too hot and played Jacks. It was a sweltering August day and she looked longingly at the bright blue water of the swimming pool. She wasn't allowed to go in by herself. She was not a confident swimmer and so either her father or Mrs. Williams had to be present for her to take a dip. It was Mrs. W's day off and, well, she knew better than to ask her dad. And so she fetched the game that her babysitter had given her as a treat. It was a cloth bag containing ten bronze-colored jacks and a ball. The aim, apparently, was to toss the ball into the air, scoop up the jacks and then catch the ball all with the same hand. To Rachel this seemed impossible. She could not pick up the little metal spikes before the ball ricocheted away from her.

One such bounce sent it flying into the large rhododendron bush that lined the yard's fence.

"Boogers," she sighed.

It was going to be impossible to find among all those flowers. A part of her was tempted to just forget about it. It was a cheap thing, after all — a little bit of rubber the color of a cherry-flavored gumball with the word CHINA stamped onto it. She could probably replace it with the few coins she had in her piggy bank. But it had been a gift from Mrs. Williams, and therefore important.

Sighing again, she began to shake the branches and pick her way through the bush — carefully in case there were spiders. That was when she heard the growl.

"Rufus?" Forgetting all about the bugs, she squeezed behind the rhododendron to welcome her best friend. Rufus was a small Jack Russell Terrier who belonged to Mrs. Winslow, the old lady next door. Her dad said that Mrs. Winslow had something happening to her brain that made her confused and forgetful. And so Rachel had started feeding the dog, just in case Mrs. Winslow forgot. This was accomplished through the "Doggie Door" — a hole in the wooden fence that separated the two properties. Rachel had widened it to allow Rufus to sneak through and she would meet the dog there, screened from view by the pink flowers of the bush. She didn't have any dog food to give to the animal, so she saved bacon from her breakfast and chicken from her sandwiches at lunchtime. As you can imagine, Rachel and Rufus were great friends.

Today, however, Rufus did not welcome her with a wagging tail and a belly ready for scratching. The dog hung back and squinted at her through puffy eyes that were little more than slits. His muzzle was wet with thick, white strands of drool. His legs trembled.

"Are you ok, boy?" the child asked.

Rufus answered her with a low growl.

"Hey," Rachel cooed to him. "Maybe you'll feel better when you've eaten." She fished the napkin containing morsels out of the pocket of her shorts. "I get grumpy when I'm hungry too."

Her eyes were not on the dog now, but on the napkin as she extracted a strip of bacon, careful not to drop it onto the loose earth at her feet.

"Here…". She looked up as she held out the treat.

2

Rachel froze. A terrible change had come over the dog. His eyes were now wide, crazed and so, so angry. His teeth were bared and they seemed really big for such a small animal. With a snarl, the terrier lunged forward and bit. Rachel yelped and jumped back as Rufus staggered sideways and fell face-first into the wooden fence. He lay there snarling — a wet, choking sound that modulated from a low growl of fury to the high keening of an animal in distress. The sound drove the child from her hiding place behind the bush. His terror was infectious — that awful cry brought out goose pimples on her arms and made her heart pound wildly in her chest. She ran sobbing, not so much from pain, but from fear and the shock of betrayal. Rufus, her friend, had turned on her.

Once in the cool, dim shadows of the house, she stood there sniffling and debated what to do. She wanted to run and tell her father what had happened, but decided not to. He had become increasingly impatient with her since her mother's death. The last time she hurt herself, he got really mad at her. She'd been playing swamp — a game in which the floor of the living room was a deadly marsh filled with piranha, leeches and alligators. To make it to safety, you had to jump from the couch to the big chair to the footstool to the piano bench. It was at the piano where it all went wrong. The bench tipped; she fell and whacked her head on the corner of the coffee table. A gash in her forehead bled all over the carpet. Summoned by her wails, her father had cleaned her up and put a butterfly bandage on the cut; but as he did so, he yelled at her for the mess, for the interruption, for her stupidity.

Therefore she went to the downstairs bathroom and cleaned the wound herself. The bite was not large, nor was it deep, but it had broken the skin on the fleshy part of her arm above the elbow. At eight years old, she was used to dealing with skinned knees, brush burns and the odd cut. So she washed the bite with soap and water, put a dab of Neosporin on it and applied an unnecessarily elaborate array of Band-Aids. (The Disney princess ones her mother bought for her were still in the medicine cabinet).

The wound healed and she forgot all about it. And then three months later, when she came down with what seemed like the flu, she did not connect the illness with the dog bite.

Rabies, once introduced into the body, foregoes the blood stream where it may be detected and attacked by the victim's immune system. Instead it creeps along the peripheral nerves at a rate of three millimeters per hour. The virus traveled along the radial nerve of Rachel's arm to her central nervous system finally reaching her brain. This marked the visible "beginning" of her illness, essentially the moment she first displayed any symptoms.

It was now two weeks shy of Thanksgiving and the children of Abraham Lincoln School were already busy sharing the autumn's crop of germs. There were runny noses and sore throats enough to go around. Therefore when Rachel presented with a low-grade fever, headache and cough, her father (a doctor at Eastern Maine Medical Center) did the only logical thing. He gave her Children's Tylenol, kept her fluids up and installed her on the couch to watch *Bugs Bunny*.

Five days passed, then seven, and she didn't get any better. Disturbed by the flashing lights of the TV, Rachel retreated to her bedroom. Her body ached and her throat felt as if shards of broken glass were lodged there. They seemed to cut her every time she swallowed. She was even hurt by light. Her bedroom was a bright, south-facing room that her mother had decorated with white furniture and pastel accents. It was a beautiful room but now the sun, glaring off all that white, stung her eyes and made the pain in her head pulse with every heartbeat.

In his novel, *When the Lion Feeds*, Wilbur Smith described the headache that accompanies rabies as "a hundred hobgoblins doing a cossack dance around the roof of my skull." The hobgoblins drove the girl from her bed. She slid underneath it and used her pillows and a big plush dog named Bo to block out the light.

Bo was a huge stuffed animal, luxuriously soft, with big floppy ears and a nose fashioned out of brown leather. It felt cool so she pressed her burning forehead against it and lapsed into an uneasy sleep. She dreamt that she was in the backyard watching the rhododendron bush twitch and shake as if a large animal was hiding behind it. The garden had always been safe and yet she was afraid. Whatever lurked just behind the long green leaves and clusters of pink flowers had *teeth*.

Then it leapt. Bo came at her out of the hedge, his white fur streaked with dirt. His big floppy paws landed on her shoulders, driving her to the ground. And then that great body was on top of her and she couldn't see and she couldn't breathe and she'd die. She knew she'd die there in that smothering darkness. The scream she couldn't give voice to in the dream finally tore itself from her tortured throat.

"Rachel?" Her father was there. "What are you doing under the bed?"

The child wept and clung to him as he pulled her out. Her head, from her eye sockets back to the base of her skull, pounded out beats of pain that made her stomach roil. As she gagged, her father managed to fetch her wastepaper basket to her before she got violently sick. Vomiting, oddly enough, often brings people some relief. The physical act of regurgitation releases endorphins which are the body's natural painkillers. But Rachel cried out hoarsely, "It hurts!"

"What hurts?"

The child grabbed her throat and wept in loud, shuddering croaks. He scooped her up and ran for the car.

Rachel Pickman was admitted to the Eastern Maine Medical Center with a high fever, severe vomiting and loss of muscular coordination down her right side.

Outside her room on the isolation ward, her father stood at the nurses' station, leaning against the counter for support. Dr. Edmund Brubaker, Head Consultant for Pediatric Infectious Diseases, put a reassuring hand on his friend's shoulder.

"It's not time to panic yet," he said gently.

Aaron Pickman nodded. "But what is it?"

"My best guess is encephalitis." He studied her chart for a moment. "Let me just verify her medical history. She's had all her vaccinations? Her MMR?"

"Absolutely."

"And there has been no sign of vaccine failure? No indication of measles or mumps?"

"No."

"When was the last time she was out of the country?"

Pickman shook his head, "She's never been abroad."

"All right. I've already ordered blood tests to rule out EBV and look for any autoimmune response. The blood work should also give us an answer about measles and mumps."

Pickman was reading over his shoulder now. "You've ordered a lumbar puncture," he said quietly. "You're looking for?"

"Rabies."

The girl's father tried to laugh that suggestion off, but he only managed a sharp exhalation of air. "That's ridiculous. There are — what? — two cases a year?"

Brubaker nodded, "And most of those are contracted outside the U.S. I'm just being thorough. You know that in half of our encephalitis cases we never get to the bottom of what caused it in the first place. I'm just trying to cross everything I can off the list."

Pickman drew in a juddering breath. "You've started her on antivirals?"

Brubaker nodded again, "Acyclovir."

"And…"

The old doctor held up a placating hand. "… and corticosteroids and a sedative and I've ordered anticonvulsants to be kept on standby in case of seizure. We'll monitor her respiration around the clock and get the test results back asap."

"I know you're doing everything you can…"

"The thing to remember is that there *is* a lot we can do. Encephalitis is rarely fatal, especially among the young."

While Dr. Brubaker attempted to reassure her father, the Head Nurse in Pediatrics, Edith Creighton, tended to Rachel. With thirty years experience on the ward, she'd been there longer than anyone and during that time had earned the nickname "Sybil" among the doctors. Like her fictional counterpart, the woman seemed to display at least three distinct personalities on the job. There was "the machine": a tireless, relentlessly efficient worker who ran on a steady supply of coffee and Hershey's chocolate. She kept the department running like clockwork. And then there was "the dragon" — the scourge of sloppy interns and condescending specialists alike. Once, when she misheard Dr. Naseby and ordered a PET scan instead of a SPECT scan for an epilepsy patient, he threw his stethoscope at her yelling, 'Are you stupid or something?'

She informed him that no, she was in no way stupid, and if he ever spoke to her like that again, she'd make him *eat* that stethoscope. This pronouncement was delivered calmly and quietly, but in a tone that made the man take a step backward.

For all the efficiency of "the machine" and all the ferocity of "the dragon," Edith Creighton was — to the children in her care — a veritable

Mother Goose. She was soft and warm and funny. And it was this person who sorted out Rachel's catheter and IV drip, all the while talking to her quietly in gentle tones.

"There, I think you're all set for now," she said.

"Where's dad?" Rachel croaked.

"He's just talking to your doctor, honey. He'll be along soon. Do you want me to stay until he comes back?"

The girl nodded.

Edith looked at her watch. She was supposed to be on her break now. She sighed. "Would you like a story? Something to take your mind off of how yucky you feel? The boy who was in this room before you had me reading to him every night. It was a really funny book. Hang on."

She nipped out and was back in a jiffy. "Here it is: *My Big Fat Zombie Goldfish.*"

She showed the cover to Rachel and the girl smiled at the picture of a big orange fish with crazy eyes and pointy teeth. Edith looked at it with her head cocked to one side. "The fish kinda reminds me of the nun who taught me Math," she said drily. She settled into the chair next to the bed and fanned herself with the paperback. "It's warm in here!"

The child twitched away from her. The movement was so sudden and violent that Edith stopped short. She had helped Dr. Brubaker perform the lumbar puncture on the girl shortly after she'd been admitted to the ward. The doctor, she knew, had ordered the test to rule out rabies. But no one really believed that that was the cause of Rachel's illness. And yet…

She waved the book again. The child recoiled from the breeze, jerking her head away, her eyes squeezed shut, her mouth agape.

"Honey," Edith said softly, "I'd like you to try something for me." She helped the girl sit up and brought her a plastic cup of water.

At the sight of it Rachel became agitated. As Edith brought the cup toward her, the child started to shake and pant heavily. Her breaths came in a steady stream of exhalations ("Hu, hu, hu, hu"), her chest heaving and shoulders bouncing with each hitch.

"Ok, ok, no water." Edith backed up and leaned out the door, glancing down the hallway. She desperately wanted to talk to Dr. B, but he was still deep in conversation with Aaron Pickman. She'd wait.

Returning to her patient with a warm, practiced smile on her face, Edith settled once again into the chair and began to read: "Yesterday my big brother Mark turned into a real-life actual EVIL SCIENTIST..."

They did not get far into the story — they had not even met Frankie the goldfish yet — by the time Aaron returned. Edith vacated the chair for him. As she left, she caught Brubaker by the sleeve and gently tugged on it. Her face was so grim that he followed her out into the hall.

"What is it?"

"Not here." She led him to an empty room and closed the door behind them. "It's rabies."

"What?"

"Rachel Pickman."

"How ... how do you know?"

"She's aerophobic and you should have seen her reaction when I offered her some water."

The old doctor sank down to sit on the vacant bed behind him. His eyes were fixed on the floor.

"We need to tell her father..."

"No," the doctor interrupted. "Not yet. I'm not going to diagnose rabies until the test results are in."

"But he's a doctor himself!" Edith protested. "If I can pick up on the signs by spending fifteen minutes with her, he sure as hell can!"

"Yes, he'll see it. But he won't *know* it. If you're right, Edith, these are the last moments of hope he has left."

Aaron Pickman sat and watched his daughter sleep. She was a beautiful child. She had her mother's heart-shaped face, crooked smile and dark hair that fell in waves to her shoulders. But now her cheeks were sallow, her hair hung limp and dark brown patches underscored her eyes. It wrung his heart to see it.

He admitted to himself that he had trouble connecting with her. He didn't really understand her — kids in general were ... hard for him to comprehend. But he loved her. And he was so, so afraid.

Meanwhile Dr. Edmund Brubaker slumped at his desk with his head in his hands. After a moment, he straightened up, put his wire-rimmed glasses back on and read the report again. He'd called in a favor from

Malcom Wallace at the CDC in Augusta to give the test top priority. The results came back in a matter of hours: cerebrospinal fluid tested positive for lyssavirus antibodies that could only be present as the result of infection. The child had rabies.

"I'm getting too old for this," he muttered. But he stood, straightened his lab coat and put his game-face on. He now had to go tell a friend and colleague — a man who lost his wife in a hit-and-run accident six months ago — that his eight-year-old daughter was going to die.

Upon hearing the news, Aaron Pickman ran to the nearest men's room and threw up. Brubaker leaned against a sink and waited for his friend to stop retching.

"It can't be," Pickman gasped. "I just lost Mary."

"I know. Aaron, I am so sorry."

"What about PEP?"

"Post-Exposure Prophylaxis?" Edmund shook his head. "It's too late for that. PEP requires five injections over twenty-eight days and ..."

"... and she'll die long before that."

"Yes."

"Then *what*?" Pickman shouted. "What can we do?"

"We have two options. We can provide her with palliative care. Basically, we drug her up and keep her as comfortable as possible."

"Or?"

At that moment the men's room door swung open and an orderly walked in, whistling.

"Out!" snarled the doctor.

Wide-eyed, the man spun on his heel and left.

Brubaker took a long, calming breath. "Or we could try the Milwaukee Protocol."

"Milwaukee ..." Pickman muttered to himself. "I remember reading an article about it, but I can't ..."

"I've got all the information back in my office. Come on." And with a hand on Aaron's shoulder, Edmund guided him out.

"The Milwaukee Protocol was devised by Dr. Rodney Willoughby at the Children's Hospital of Wisconsin," Brubaker read from an open file on his desk. "He used it to treat Jeanna Giese. She contracted rabies from a bat bite and had not had any of the shots. It's based on the theory that rabies doesn't actually kill the brain. Instead it disrupts communication between the brain and the central nervous system. Essentially, the brain can no longer regulate autonomic functions such as heart rate or respiration. That's why most rabies patients die of suffocation. Without instructions from the brain, the body just shuts down."

"And so?"

"And so he placed Giese in a medically-induced coma. Machines kept her alive in order to buy her immune system time to fight off the infection."

"With the help of antivirals."

"Yep. Ketamine, Amantadine, Ribavirin — combine it with a range of sedatives and you've got quite a chemical cocktail."

"And she lived?"

"She now has a BA in Biology, is married and gave birth to twins."

"That's wonderful!" Pickman stopped short. "What's the catch?"

"The Milwaukee Protocol has been attempted thirty-five times."

"How many survived?"

"Six. That's a seventeen percent survival rate. Other studies put the survival rate as low as eight percent. It's a bad bug, Aaron. Of the six survivors, one died of pneumonia and three were left with," he read from the report, "profound neurological disabilities."

"But there were two success stories."

"It would appear so." The doctor looked old and tired and infinitely sad. "They're not great options, Aaron. Either we drug her up until she slips away or we fight and hope for our own little miracle. But understand that if you decide to see what's behind door number two, you are rolling the dice."

Rabies, from the Latin *rabidus* meaning furious or raging, is thought by many to be the worst way to die. After the initial (or Prodromal) phase of flu-like symptoms, the disease progresses to the Excitation Phase. The victim experiences high levels of anxiety, confusion, delirium and aggression. She will have seizures and lose muscle control. She will be hypersensitive to everything: touch, breeze, light, sound. And despite her terrible thirst, she will be unable to drink. Attempts to sip a little water (even the mention of the word *water*) can induce agonizing spasms in the muscles of the throat and larynx. These spasms are not only accompanied by intense pain, but also by great fear. Hence the name hydrophobia, the fear of water. When Charles Lennox, fourth Duke of Richmond and Governor-General of Canada, contracted the disease in 1819, he could not stand the thought of remaining in a house near a river. The sound of running water and, I suspect, just the knowledge that it was there upset him so much that he asked to be moved further inland. Unable to drink or swallow, the victim literally "foams at the mouth" as saliva accumulates and dribbles over the chin.

It wouldn't be so bad if the virus addled your mind with an all-encompassing delirium and left it there. But this is not the case. While Hamlet was afraid "to sleep, perchance to dream," rabies patients must dread the moment of awakening. Despite all the ravages, all the hell of the disease, it pauses for moments of terrible lucidity when the victim knows exactly what is happening. She is fully aware that she will suffer and then die.

It was during one such clear-headed moment that Dr. Brubaker spoke with Rachel. Rabies is a public health concern and he had to find out where she had contracted the virus and who else might be at risk.

"Were you bitten, honey, by a dog or a cat or something else?"

The child nodded. "But that was a while ago, before school started." Her voice was raw and weak.

"Over the summer?" The doctor asked and the child nodded again. "Can you show me where?"

Rachel pointed to a small, light scar on her arm.

"It broke the skin? It bled?"

"Yeah."

Listening to this conversation, Aaron cast his mind back over the events of the summer. And he remembered: the missing dog flyers that had been posted around the neighborhood. Each bore the picture of a perky-looking Jack Russell with a snow-white body and chestnut-colored patches of fur over his ears and each eye. Rufus. Knowing how Rachel loved the dog, he'd said to her at the time, 'That's a shame about your friend. Have you seen him around anywhere?' The girl, who had been playing with her Barbie dolls at the time, didn't even look up. 'Nope.' He'd looked at her curiously. Something about that response wasn't right — she should have been worried and upset. But then the fatigue, the fugue he'd been in since Mary's death settled over him again and he'd retreated back to his work.

"Rufus bit you, didn't he?" he asked.

Tears welled up in Rachel's eyes.

"Where was Mrs. Williams when this happened?"

"She wasn't there."

"She left you alone?"

Rachel shook her head. "It was her day off."

Oh my God, he thought. *I was there. This happened on my watch.* "Why didn't you tell me?"

"I was afraid you'd get mad."

"Why the hell would I get mad?" he snapped.

The child began to weep and he knew. He was always mad at her — mad at her for interrupting him, mad at her for piling extra responsibility on him when he just needed peace and distraction and time. Mad at her for the noise and mess she generated, for the loss of control he felt in his own house, in his own life. Mad at her for looking at him with Mary's eyes — but these eyes held no love for him. The only thing he saw in those implacable eyes was *her* need, a need that was tyrannical, insatiable and left no room for him to fold into himself and there, in the quiet, to mourn. *Well, the house will be quiet now, won't it?* But it would not be quiet enough to stifle his thoughts. He was a doctor — a fucking doctor — and his only child was dying a stupid, senseless, preventable death because he had not been paying attention. He could make all the excuses in the world about the grief and trauma of Mary's death, about his own pain and the importance of his work, but the bottom line was that he had utterly failed her. God, if he could just stop thinking, just retreat into other thoughts and escape this...

Rachel stopped crying abruptly. Her right arm jerked spasmodically, followed by convulsions that shook her tiny body. Her eyes rolled back in her head and her spine arched off the mattress. Her face and hair were wet with tears and sweat and foam dribbled from her lips. A warning beep sounded nearby — her heart monitor.

"200 bpm. She's tachycardic," Edith said as she tried to hold the child still.

Rachel shrieked — a harsh, guttural sound that sliced through everyone in the room.

"It's decision time, Aaron," Dr. Brubaker announced, "because this is only going to get worse."

Doctor Aaron Pickman watched his daughter writhe and knew that he was a short hop from madness. "We'll roll the dice."

Rachel was heavily sedated and hooked up to machines that would run her body for her. As she sank under the influence of the Midazolam, the word went out on WABI5 that the rabies virus had reared its head in Bangor. Brian Sullivan introduced the story in the studio and then cut to a segment with Taylor Kinzler standing in front of the hospital. Brubaker had asked her to graphically describe the disease so that no one would harbor any doubts about the seriousness of infection. A picture of Rufus followed with a warning issued: anyone who had come into contact with the dog (or who had been bitten by an unknown animal) should contact the Maine Center for Disease Control and Prevention.

That was the key: prevention. *Infected bites we can deal with. But if you ignore even a small transdermal bite (a bite that breaks the skin), you risk an agonizing death. We see it again and again in countries with large populations of stray dogs.* There was one outbreak of the disease in Angola in 2009 that killed ninety-three children in three months. They died either because of a shortage of the vaccine or because they sought medical help too late. No one thought that Bangor, Maine would turn into another Angola tragedy. Most pets were vaccinated against the virus. But still Brubaker was afraid. How many more kids had come into contact with Rufus over the summer? Of those, how many had believed that the bite was not serious enough to cause a fuss? How many more children would he see convulsing and foaming at the mouth? How many more parents would look at him with that mixture of terror, anguish and insanity — just as Aaron Pickman was looking at him now?

Writer Tony Cleaver once said that "Desperation is the best innovator." As Dr. Aaron Pickman sat by his daughter's bedside, he was certainly desperate and now turned his mind to what he would change — what he would fix — if he was given a second chance. He'd take time off work at the hospital and stop hiding in the book (*Case Histories in Neurosurgery*) that he was writing at home. The thought of the book tugged at him. He wanted to be there now — in the quiet sanity of his study working on it. *No. Stop it, stop hiding.* He needed to change: he'd talk to his daughter and, more to the point, he'd listen. He'd play *Candy Land* with her and they'd go for walks in the Bangor City Forest nearby. He could put it right, he knew he could, if he was just given the opportunity. He begged God for this as he sat and stared out of the window at a November sky heavy with clouds and dark with rain.

Sometimes, however, that crucial second chance is not offered and sometimes when you pray, the answer is "No." Rachel Louise Pickman, eight-year-old daughter of Mary and Aaron Pickman of Bangor, Maine, died two days later. She never regained consciousness.

When a parent has to bury a child, it is the most gut-wrenching of stories. Unfortunately, it was not the story's ending.

PART ONE

MIGHTY OAKS

CHAPTER ONE

MOURNING

"I had begun life with benevolent intentions, and thirsted for the moment when I should put them in practice, and make myself useful to my fellow-beings. Now all was blasted: instead of that serenity of conscience, which allowed me to look back upon the past with self-satisfaction, and from thence to gather promise of new hopes, I was seized by remorse and the sense of guilt, which hurried me away to a hell of intense tortures, such as no language can describe."

Mary Shelley, Frankenstein

"Many parents who lose their child ... experience post traumatic stress similar to that experienced by Veterans of war."

Cindy Dix, RN, "Depression After Losing a Child"

Aaron Pickman stood, eyes closed, face tilted up to the sun. After a month-and-a-half of solid rain, it did feel good. The breeze was cool and the clear turquoise of the Caribbean stretched out before him. It reminded him of those rare summer days when Mary had coaxed him out of his study to come and sit by the pool. She would serve up daiquiris and plates of sliced watermelon and they'd lounge in the shade of the big umbrella and watch Rachel diving for rings in the shallow end.

But it was that memory — the association of Rachel with water — that snapped him out of his reverie. By the end Rachel could not take a drink or even hear the word "water" without bursting into terrified, convulsive screams. So no, he did not have the time, nor the right, to stand here admiring the view. He had work to do. He turned on his heel and went back into the lab.

It was patently awful. After the immaculate facilities he'd enjoyed at Massachusetts General and the EMMC, this place was a nightmare of rusting grey metal and cracked beige concrete. An old English air base traded to the American government as part of the 1940 Lend-Lease Agreement, its original purpose had been to protect a petroleum refinery on the tiny island of Cáscara. But in 1942 a German U-boat bombarded the coast destroying the aircraft hangar and the oil tank farm nearby. In the intervening years, nature had crept in to cover the worst signs of devastation, blanketing the craters and twisted wreckage with tree ferns, lobster claw heliconia and wild mamey fruit trees. Thick foliage pressed close to the remaining buildings and roots wormed their way through the old runways reducing the concrete to grit. All, however, was not lost. The barracks, mess hall and command center still stood and these Pickman had converted into labs, animal quarantine rooms and living quarters.

While the outside of the facility was a ruin being reclaimed by the jungle, the interior was all diffuse fluorescent light, rusting cages and the stink of animals in the hot, close air. And the sound was like nothing of this earth. The dogs weren't barking or howling — they were screaming. It was a wrenching croup-like yowl and the most eloquent expression of utter desolation Pickman had ever heard. As human beings we rely so much on language, but nothing expresses what it means to be hopeless and tortured and damned as effectively as a rabid dog. Aaron hastened into the lab and made a beeline for his noise-canceling headphones.

How a prominent neurosurgeon could end up having to jerry-rig a research lab in the ass-end of nowhere is a saga in and of itself. It began in the spacious living room of the house he used to own in Maine. He'd sat there with the lights off and the curtains drawn, surrounded by flowers and sympathy cards and with a refrigerator full of casseroles from well-meaning friends and neighbors. And he wished he was dead. It was just too much. First he'd lost his wife Mary to a hit-and-run driver. He'd had to identify her body and you know, at first he wasn't sure it was her. The left side of her face was a bloody pulp from the road rash. The coroner had attempted to mask the depressed fracture where the left side of her skull had caved in, but Pickman's practiced eyes knew exactly what he was looking at. She hadn't stood a chance.

The right side of her face, however, was largely unscathed. It was his Mary and the room seemed to lurch to one side and he had felt cold and afraid. And so he hid. He topped a sixty-hour work week by devoting the lion's share of his free time to writing his book: *Case Histories in Neurosurgery*, by Dr. Aaron Pickman. And he used that to blot out the image of Mary lying on a slab in the morgue.

And when that didn't work, he'd tell himself that at least her death was quick. She wouldn't have suffered, the coroner said, and that was true. From Mary's perspective it had probably seemed like someone had just come along and turned out the lights. No pain, no fear, no awareness. Just oblivion. But Rachel … he kept seeing her tiny body writhing on the bed as she screamed and screamed. And that was his fault; *he* had caused that. And how, exactly, was he supposed to know that and live? What was that line from the Robert Frost poem? Something about having no pride in the past and no hope for the future? Because that's what the death of a child is: the negation of all future hopes. Wayne Loder, a man who has spoken movingly of his own loss, pointed out that children are supposed to be our legacy, our contribution to this world, a part of us that will survive after we've gone. Now there was nothing left. No family. His work — the grand distraction that enabled him to ignore the child — was tainted by her death. The house? That was just a beautiful memorial to the life he should have cherished. And there was no future. The world held nothing for him.

The coffee table in front of him was littered with pamphlets that a nurse at the hospital had given him. They had titles like: "Be Gentle With Yourself While Grieving" and offered advice about looking after your health and nurturing your soul. But that was all beyond the point. First of all, he didn't deserve to get over his grief because he was the cause of all this hell. If he suffered, surely that was natural justice and any pain he felt did not hold a candle to what Rachel had endured. And let's, just for the sake of argument, suppose that he could heal through the liberal application of prozac and counseling and kumbaya moments in the local church — then what? He was done.

How do you even continue to live in a world in which random disaster lands on you out of nowhere? Rabies? Are you fucking kidding me? This isn't medieval Europe or deepest Africa or India where packs of wild dogs prowl. This is peaceful, orderly Bangor, Maine. But that doesn't matter, does it? The world is a fucking war zone and you get to wonder when the bullet with your name on it is going to nail you.

Rabies. Until Rachel, he'd never seen a case of it. He didn't really know that much about it. He rose from the couch and retrieved the laptop from his study. He wanted to see this prick. Soon he found an image of the disease: tiny, bullet-shaped (of course it was), with fine cilia covering its body. So that was the culprit. He began to read. He read how rabies, known in medical circles as the lyssavirus, eludes the immune system by bypassing the blood stream and traveling directly along the peripheral nerves. Of course, if Rachel had had the vaccine during that interval (when the virus was still in transit), she'd be alive. But once the disease reaches the brain, it's game over. Hence rabies kills 55,000 people a year.

That can't be right. He read on. In India the mortality rate is nearly 21,000 deaths per annum — that is a third of all cases reported worldwide. And do you know how much a course of the rabies vaccine costs in India? 1800 rupees. That's $27.12. He would have paid more for Rachel's jabs — the American health system would have bled him for about $400, but it was still a small price to pay to prevent all this. He would have given every penny he had. He continued to scroll through the articles…

… The vast majority of victims are children…

…The incubation period varies depending on the distance from the bite to the brain…

…The virus is heavily present in the victim's saliva. The inflammation of the throat, the inability to swallow, the victim's fear of water — all allowed the virus to maximize its concentration in the animal's spit. When Rufus bit Rachel, it was certain that he'd pass on the disease. And the dog had no choice but to bite because the virus ramps up aggression. This is hailed as an excellent example of how a pathogen can modify its host's behavior in order to reproduce…

…Throughout history rabies has been a symbol of madness, excessive violence and unstoppable plague…

… Spanish neurologist, Juan Gómez-Alonso, has theorized that rabies is actually the origin of the vampire myth — that the idea of a bite that could steal your soul and make you prey upon your loved ones is founded in mankind's experience of the disease…

…Only twenty-five percent of all human victims actually bite another person. People make really poor vectors for the disease; therefore, scientists now believe that we are not the virus's primary target. We constitute the collateral damage — the unintended victims of a pathogen that is targeting dogs, foxes, skunks and bats as the means to spread quickly. Human deaths are just a needless side-effect…

…And it is never going to stop. Having gained a foothold in wild animal populations, rabies can never be eradicated from the earth. Furthermore, they are not even working on a cure for patients like Rachel. The vaccine that halts the disease before it reaches the brain is deemed to be good enough. Why? Because every year 8.2 million people die of cancer; 1.2 million succumb to TB; 719,551 will be killed by malaria; and 230,615 women will die in childbirth. The rabies mortality rate of 55,000 a year isn't high enough to warrant further investment of time and money into a cure for patients in the final stages of the illness — not when those resources are needed so urgently elsewhere. Charles Rupprecht, head of the CDC's rabies unit, cited this as an example of the "cycle of neglected diseases"…

And if, hypothetically, the money were to become available, is a cure even possible? He read on through the night.

CHAPTER TWO

MEANING

"If this most ancient of viruses can never be eradicated from animals, molecular biologists have hit upon the next best outcome: they are harnessing its uniquely diabolical properties in an attempt to resolve one of our thorniest medical problems. Rabies still knows how to infect us, but at the molecular level we have learned how to infect it."

Bill Wasik and Monica Murphy, <u>Rabid</u>

"...take something designed by nature and reprogram it to make it work for the body rather than against it."

Dr. Alice Krippin, 2007 film, <u>I Am Legend</u>

It turns out that the current research being done on rabies focuses not on finding a cure, but on using the virus to treat other ailments. The human brain is protected by the blood-brain barrier, 400 miles of capillaries that supply the organ with oxygenated blood. These threadlike capillaries are so densely packed around the brain that they form a sort of helmet that keeps out many infections. Unfortunately if a virus or bacterium does get into the brain, it is effectively inside the fortress, protected by the very walls that were meant to keep it out. It can then wreak havoc at will. Our immune systems and our medicines cannot reach it to fight it off. That is, in fact, why we can't do a damn thing about rabies once neurological symptoms present.

But innovators like Priti Kumar of Yale Medical School are working on an interesting idea. Rabies is very adept at slipping past the barrier and entering the brain. So why not turn this deadly trait to our advantage? Why not genetically alter the virus, essentially removing its harmful content while retaining its structure? Pickman imagined the result as an empty bullet casing designed to hit a target that used to be out of reach. That empty shell could be used to deliver a payload of our own design — gene therapies, medicines, you name it. As Dorothy Crawford suggests in *Invisible Enemy: A Natural History of Viruses*, "Why not use a ready-made parasite with generations of experience in penetrating cells [as a] 'magic bullet' approach … to treat killer diseases?" So here is the question: could rabies be used to cure rabies? Could the hollowed-out virus be used to deliver a remedy to an infected brain?

Dr. Aaron Pickman puzzled over the logistics of that question for the next month and the epiphany, when it came, was like that scene in *Young Frankenstein* when Gene Wilder declares, "It. Could. WORK!" He had found it: the thing he could do with his blighted life. He had a mission. It's not all that surprising, really. Many people cope with tragedy by taking up a crusade. It is a way of proclaiming: 'See! Something good *can* come out of this!' It allows us to take all that anger and pain and despair that might otherwise destroy us and funnel it into something positive. Doris Tate, mother of murdered daughter Sharon, founded COVER (the Coalition on Victims' Equal Rights). Candace Lightner, whose thirteen-year-old daughter was killed by a drunk driver, started Mothers Against Drunk Driving. Whether we start movements or establish scholarships and memorial funds, we all try to find some silver lining in that grief-laden cloud. "In some ways," Viktor E. Frankl wrote, "suffering ceases to be suffering at the moment it finds a meaning." Pickman, surrounded by printouts and hastily scribbled notes, sat back and took a long, deep breath. Just think of all the thousands of lives that could be saved — all because Rachel had brought him to this fight.

When Shakespeare wrote "The course of true love never did run smooth," he did not know that it is a frolicking jaunt in a meadow compared to obtaining funding for most research projects. Pickman first approached the Eastern Maine Medical Center about the possibility of conducting clinical research there. His colleagues nodded along to his proposal, but as he spoke he began to feel distracted and flustered. They weren't listening, not really. And he began to wonder what was going through their minds at that moment. They felt sorry for him — that was clear from the sideways cock of their heads and the somber earnestness of their expressions. But there was something else: a reticence or a judgment? Before them stood a brilliant, highly educated doctor whose daughter had died a wholly preventable death. That placed a question mark over any professional assertion he made. And now, here he stood trying to make it all better by grasping at straws.

Undeterred, he submitted his proposal to his alma mater, Harvard Medical School. After an interminably long wait he received their response...

> Dear Dr. Pickman,
>   Thank you for your interest in conducting your research with us. As you know, Harvard Medical School has a reputation for producing groundbreaking research in a variety of medical fields and your proposal to broaden the scope of Priti Kumar's work is intriguing ... Blah blah blah.

He scanned through all the formalities, certain that he would soon be moving back to Boston, until he encountered the word "unfortunately." Unfortunately, they could not sanction his work at the school. They had grave concerns about his proposed methodology. Apparently it relied too heavily upon animal testing. The letter reminded him that Harvard maintains full AAALAC International accreditation for excellence in its treatment of laboratory animals and its commitment to the three "R's":

1. Reduce the number of animals used for testing,
2. Refine procedures to minimize distress to the animals, and
3. Replace live test subjects with computer simulations wherever possible.

His proposal would, frankly, burn through a large number of rhesus macaques, standing in direct violation of the Animal Welfare Act. The letter thanked him again for his interest and invited him to enquire again in the future if the parameters of his research changed … blah, blah, blah.

He sat there stunned. Couldn't they see the importance of what he was trying to do? Children all over the world were dying in agony. How could they so glibly ignore that fact? But then they hadn't sat in that room with Rachel and watched… He took a deep breath. No, they hadn't. They could not understand the full rip-your-guts-out horror of watching a child die of rabies. And so he could excuse their ignorance and short-sightedness. He'd simply find somewhere else to go.

He applied to another university — Tufts, thinking they might be a little more tolerant of his methods. Online, he'd found a 2016 article entitled "Modern Day Frankenstein" by Yasmin Jeffery. It outlined the work of a Dr. Levin, who apparently had created a range of monstrosities at Tufts including six-legged frogs and tadpoles with eyes on their backs. As grotesque as that may seem, Levin insisted these experiments were merely steps on the way to the primary goal: "to one day be able to restore the function of damaged or missing sensory structures" — lost eyes, damaged ears. Pickman received another letter and another lecture on the "3R's" as well as a reminder that Dr. Levin's work was on tadpoles and *not* non-human primates. They further asserted that Pickman's procedures did not conform to the Tufts Refinement Initiative, which sought to protect the welfare of test animals and implement non-harmful alternatives wherever possible.

He got the same response again and again. So he cast his net further afield. The Caribbean Primate Research Center (CPRC) had a Laboratory of Virology conducting research into new vaccines. But any proposal to them required approval by the Institutional Animal Care and Use Committee — which adheres to the Animal Welfare Act and around we go again. The bottom line was that the proposed experiment stood in violation of every law and ethical guideline that regulated medical research. No reputable lab would touch it and the National Institutes of Health would not fund the project. Even the shoestring labs that ignored the law in favor of profits weren't biting because, frankly, animal testing was unlikely to produce a marketable (FDA-approved) drug. Cure cancer in mice all you want, it doesn't mean that that product will ever be effective on human beings or available on your prescription plan. Simply put, they couldn't see any money in it.

He began to look at poorer countries with different laws and even that proved problematic. Bioquark had just had its "ReAnima" project booted out of India when the local government halted its research on the reanimation of dead human brain tissue. They would be moving their operation to "an unidentified country in Latin America." That's what it boiled down to. Controversial research had to go underground. It had to be self-funded and hence, it was going to be conducted in some jerry-rigged "lab" in the middle of nowhere.

Pickman's frustration mounted. People were so stupid, so short-sighted. We fight wars over land and politics and religion, but shed a little blood to actually *save* lives and you're Attila the Hun. But that's ok. He'd manage it on his own. He'd find the answer he sought and Rachel's death would not be in vain.

He liquidated all of his assets and sold the five-bedroom house on Reinzo Lane. He cashed in his shares, savings plans and pension fund and poured every last dime into his laboratory on Cáscara. And it was there, as he prepped the latest round of slides, that he happened to glance at the clock. His assistant was late again — probably sleeping off last night's bender. Like the lab, the island, and the situation, Travis Montgomery was yet another thing Pickman had to settle for because he couldn't get anything better.

CHAPTER THREE

IGOR

"*The possibility of physical and mental collapse is now very real. No sympathy for the Devil, keep that in mind. Buy the ticket, take the ride.*"

Hunter S. Thompson, <u>*Fear and Loathing in Las Vegas*</u>

"*How did I get here? Somebody pushed me. Somebody must have set me off in this direction and clusters of other hands must have touched themselves to the controls at various times, for I would not have picked this way for the world.*"

Joseph Heller, <u>*Catch-22*</u>

"*Contrary to the myth of pure evil, one does not have to be at all evil to cross the line. Once one has done so, there are powerful forces that sweep one along into greater acts of cruelty…*"

Roy F. Baumeister, <u>*Evil: Inside Human Cruelty and Violence*</u>

Travis Montgomery woke up with the mother of all hangovers. He was naked and lying on a rough wooden floor next to a full ashtray and empty bottle of tequila. *Oh God, the tequila.* His head swam.

He'd told the girl last night that, according to connoisseurs, you should choose an añejo tequila that has been aged for at least a year in an oak barrel. This should be enjoyed while following strict "sipping protocols" (she'd giggled at that).

"First," he said when he'd stopped nibbling on her ear, "you pour an ounce into your glass and inspect the color." He demonstrated, pouring a measure into a Flintstone's jam glass that had Fred and Dino etched on the side. He cocked an eyebrow as he surveyed the liquid's hue. "It looks like a normal urine sample," he nodded. "I declare the patient healthy!"

The girl collapsed against him in fits of laughter.

"Next, you swirl the tequila." He did so. "Apparently it's supposed to cling to the side of the glass creating a string-of-pearls effect... Huh. I see no string of pearls; that's disappointing."

The girl reached for the glass.

"No, no," he said. "You take a small sip and swish it, kind of like mouthwash, so that it bathes every part of your tongue."

"Estás jodidamente loco!" She grabbed up the bottle and took a big gulp.

"You know I don't speak Spanish."

"You are fucking crazy!" She translated and then she was on top of him and he wanted her so urgently he could barely get his hands working to unbutton her dress.

As always it was ... what? The word "incandescent" sprang to mind and he congratulated himself on his grasp of advanced vocabulary at this juncture of the morning. The word fit, though. With Clarita he could forget about everything else and just be there with her, listening for the little catches in her breath that signified real, not pretended, pleasure.

The girl was gone now ... and so was his wallet. It was not the first time, bless her, and so he'd bought a collection of cheap wallets from a souvenir shop and each evening he'd put in enough cash to cover her fee plus a little extra because he really did like her. Her departure signaled the end of all things good and he was now left with the morning after the night before.

First of all there was the taste. There was a woody, I've-just-chewed-on-a-leaf-and-for-some-strange-reason-my-mouth-is-on-fire taste. That was the tequila. Then there was another flavor, further back in his throat, that tasted just the way gasoline smells. That was the coke. The two made for a rancid combination and he groped blindly around him for his pack of Marlboros. They had gone the same way as his wallet. This too was not a new development and so he crawled over to the bed and dug a spare pack from its hiding place beneath the mattress. He lit up, took a long drag and let the comparatively mellow flavor of tobacco mask the piquant, battery-acid astringency of drugs and booze.

Even though he just woke up, he felt like he hadn't slept. His head pounded, his nose was sore and stuffed up, and he should have been at work an hour ago. Luckily, he had the cure. Recommended by a friend and fellow pharmacological enthusiast, the magic antidote to a cocaine-tequila hangover was … (drum roll please) … Gazpacho soup. (Don't ask. No one knows why). And because you eat Gazpacho cold, he could keep it in a Tupperware bowl in the mini-fridge in his room and didn't even have to go down to his landlady's kitchen to nuke it. Awesome. You have to appreciate life's little gifts.

He ate, downed four bottles of mineral water, took a hasty shower and was soon guiding his old, beat-up Jeep along Highway 11, the coastal road that led to the lab.

It wasn't raining this morning and so his view of the sea was stunning, even if it was over-bright. This glimpse of sunshine in the middle of the island's rainy season should have cheered and lifted him. But as he approached the lab, his mood darkened and his shoulders hunched over the wheel. *I could just turn around*, he thought, *skip work today, crawl back in bed with Clarita and hide.*

He pulled the jeep over and stared in the rearview mirror, looking back the way he'd come. This was not the first time he'd sat on the hard shoulder and had this debate with himself. The reasons to quit this job were many and he'd recited the list often enough to know it by heart. And to stay? There was only one reason — something that happened shortly after he'd arrived on Cáscara.

At first he'd been so grateful for the opportunity. A research position. On a Caribbean island with golden sand and clear water and bikinis. And no human patients. That was the thing. Although he'd been a surgeon in Chicago, he could not bring himself to touch another human patient. Not after Joyce Sheldon. The mother of four had come in for a keyhole procedure to remove a tumor from her adrenal gland. He'd done it a hundred times before. But after a heavy night on the flake, he'd fucked it up. He clipped the wrong vessels and cut off all blood supply to her liver and gut. She was dead in less than twenty-four hours.

Yes, he'd messed up, but he was not an animal. He felt that he should pay for what he had done. He was going to tell the truth and let her family sue his ass for malpractice. But then his dealer called with an excellent shipment of Mexican Panda — only $300 a gram! — and he realized: that money had to come from somewhere. He had to be able to work and so he told the medical review board that he must have been disoriented by the angle of the camera during the procedure. He thought he was clipping one blood vessel when unfortunately he was clipping another. It was a fatal mistake, but not malicious and anyone who'd had to orient those tiny cameras knew how easy it was to misinterpret what you were seeing. They labelled the incident "an unfortunate accident" and he thought he was home free …until he had to pick up a scalpel again. It was for a routine appendectomy — surgery 101 — and he couldn't bring himself to make the opening incision. His hand trembled, sweat got in his eyes and he actually fled the operating theater.

Sitting on cold steps in the stairwell, he worked it all through in his head. He was dangerous — he couldn't deny that. He could not kick the habit. Frankly he didn't *want* to kick the habit. And so he would continue to use. If he used, he couldn't be trusted with other people's lives. But he was a doctor and that was kinda part of the job description and so what could he do? Then the answer came to him like a shaft of light from heaven. Research. Clinical research where the greatest harm he could do was to kill a rat or a monkey. No human patients.

And so, here he was: working in a dump of a lab on Cáscara. But if he thought that he'd finally escaped to a job that wouldn't prick his conscience, he was very wrong. The environment he had to work in, the things he had to do there — it was killing him. That's why he tried to self-medicate through an afternoon of particularly grim labor. And that is why he OD'ed. He should have seen it coming. One by one all the classic symptoms emerged. As he worked to obtain a sample of infected brain tissue (which required him to drill a hole through a live beagle's skull), his mood fluctuated wildly. One minute he was euphoric, sure that he was working at the top of his game and he was going to crack this problem, find a cure, and be a hero. The next he felt crushed by a sense of utter despair. He was certain that there was no point even trying because it was impossible. Then *that* just pissed him off. Next it got really hot in the lab and he couldn't seem to get a good breath of air. His head thudded. A tremor jerked his hand at the wrong moment and he thought he'd nicked himself with an infected scalpel. In a panic, he inspected his gloves for tears, wondering if he'd just fucking given himself rabies, but the latex was unbroken. He took a break to go be sick. Then one more line of coke in the bathroom and the seizure hit. It was accompanied by almost total blindness as his retinal vessels went into spasm. As he hit the floor he thought, *Nice going, meathead. You've finally killed yourself.* And then there was nothing.

He awoke in a strange bed with Pickman sitting nearby. "It's alive," Aaron said wryly.

Travis's voice was a dry rasp. "What happened?"

"You OD'ed, you fucking idiot."

"Where…"

"I put you in my bed."

It was true. Travis was lying in a spartan room that held a bed, a chair and a dresser. There were other things too: a heart monitor, a crash cart, a stand laden with IV bags. He blinked and let his eyes focus so he could read the labels: Saline (for hydration), Lorazepam (to calm him), Nitropusside (to lower his blood pressure).

"Why am I wet?" he croaked.

"I had to pack you in ice. Your temp was so high I was afraid you'd spontaneously combust. The good news is, that despite your best efforts, you're going to live. Your kidney and liver function are normal. Your cardiac evaluation wasn't stellar, but your heart didn't explode so … *yay.* What on earth were you thinking?"

Travis was quiet for a long time but Dr. Pickman did not move. He just sat there, looking at his patient intently. It was clear that he wanted an answer and he wasn't going anywhere until he got it.

"It's this place," Travis said quietly.

"What? The lab?"

Montgomery nodded. "How can you stand to work here, to live here, doing what we do?"

Pickman nodded and sat back in his chair. "It's grim, painful work, I know. But it's necessary work. Your problem is that you get too emotionally attached. You need to stop treating the monkeys like they're your pets."

Travis glared at him. "I'm not the problem here. My feelings aren't the problem here. Those animals…"

"Those animals are vital for the research. What will it take to convince you? You have Nobel Laureates like John Gurdon and John Walker asserting that, and I quote, "primate research is still critical for developing treatment for debilitating illness." Emeritus professors of medicine at Oxford insist that there is a strong scientific and moral case for using primates in medical experiments. Eighty percent of all drugs for the treatment of Parkinson's are tested on marmosets. Rhesus macaques have been used to develop vaccines for rabies, smallpox, polio and AIDS. Animal testing has allowed us to treat Zika and Ebola…"

"I know!" Travis cut him off, the effort of the exclamation making him feel dizzy. "I know all of that. But the conditions here…"

"Are all I can afford. You asked me why I came here and I explained to you that we are doing research that no one else cares about and no one else will *fund*. I've sunk everything into this — my house, my car, my savings, my pension. There isn't any more that I can give. This is it." He gestured to the room around him and Travis looked again at the sparse furnishings, the lack of comfort. There was no decoration to brighten up the place, no items that made it feel like home.

"I *know* that the lab is bad," Pickman continued, "but what of it? Hell, I've read about labs with worse violations than this that still passed USDA inspection!"

"It goes beyond a few AWA violations," Travis insisted. "What we're doing here is grotesque!"

"I know it's hard on the animals…"

"That's a fucking understatement."

Pickman looked at him placidly. "The animals suffer not because I'm cruel, but because *nature* is cruel. I didn't invent rabies; I'm trying to cure it so that no one ever has to suffer like that again."

"But we have a vaccine, isn't that enough?"

"That is *not* enough!" Pickman hissed. "You think you just suffered because of your little overdose? That was a cakewalk compared to dying from rabies. When Rachel went down…"

"Hang on, who's Rachel?"

And then it all came pouring out. Travis, mind still raw and body weak, absorbed it all. The terrible shock of Mary's accident and how

32

Pickman withdrew into his work in an effort to cope. The neighbor's dog. And the full horror of Rachel's death. She had died because her father had messed up (and Travis was again painfully reminded of his own fatal mistake). Pickman related the whole sorry tale in minute detail, but that is not what spoke most eloquently to Montgomery. It was the change in Pickman himself. The usually sardonic, emotionless man paced and wept. People say that some things come out all in a flood and that cliché is wholly apt. The story tumbled out of him in a ceaseless flow of horror and agony that brought tears to Travis's eyes. *Is this,* he wondered, *the first time he's ever talked about it? Holy shit.*

And then Aaron handed him a photo of the child and she was beautiful. She had a heart-shaped face framed by shoulder-length brown hair clipped back in a butterfly barrette. She was smiling for the camera — a mischievous grin. He thought he would have liked her. Anyone who can smile with that mixture of innocence and devilry promised to be a lot of fun.

Pickman had stopped talking and was sitting back down with his head in his hands. After a long pause, he spoke quietly. "I'm sorry. I shouldn't have unloaded all that on you. But understand this," he looked up, "the work will continue because honestly, if I don't keep going with it I might as well eat a bullet. Stay if you want." He rose and left the room.

Travis lay there and cried. He cried for Pickman and the girl and for himself — all of them little more than wreckage in this junkyard world. But then he took a long, calming breath and … Lo! He could breathe! Dr. P had done a fantastic job of bringing him around and that first easy, unhindered breath was a small taste of paradise. God, the relief of it. Gratitude and sympathy combined in that moment to bind him indivisibly to Pickman. And the experiment, which had seemed like something demons would conduct in hell, now gave him purpose. If they succeeded, then no one would ever die like Rachel again. Hence, they had to succeed. God, all the people they'd save! Surely rescuing 55,000 a year from certain death would atone for his one mistake.

Thinking back on that night, on the reasons for the research and how it offered them both one last shot at redemption, Travis started the Jeep and headed toward the lab.

When he arrived, he found Pickman hunched over an electron microscope.

"You're late," he mumbled.

"Sorry."

"Never mind. So what shirt is it today?"

Travis brightened at the question. When Raoul Duke and Dr. Gonzo embarked on their trip in *Fear and Loathing in Las Vegas*, the former insisted: "right … we need the car and after that, the cocaine. And then the tape recorder, for special music, and some Acapulco shirts." It was a packing list that made eminent sense to Travis Montgomery. But "Acapulco shirts" were by nature garish items and not designed for a man of taste. In order to wear one with panache, you had to own it, to embrace the ugliness and love it for that reason alone. So, since moving to the Caribbean, he had set himself a personal challenge: to find the most hideous Hawaiian shirt on the planet. It had turned into quite an amusing game and even Dr. P., with all his professionalism and unwavering focus, had been drawn in by the quality of Travis's finds.

"Oh I think I've found the winner. This is something special," he drawled.

Pickman turned around and gaped at him.

Travis performed a little catwalk strut. "Today's offering, fresh from the Paris fashion houses, comes to us in a jaunty shade of baby-shit yellow. Notice the word "Luau" is included throughout the pattern in fluorescent orange and that gives us a cheeky little hint about the raison d'être of this gorgeous design. It is all things luau, darling. Grass skirts in pea green and ukuleles in a blue so bright it actually sears the retinas. And don't forget all of those luau pigs just waiting to be roasted on a spit. Marvelous. But the pièce de résistance is the clever rendering of a hand dipping two badly-drawn fingers into a bowl of poi."

Pickman couldn't breathe he was laughing so hard. "That is fucking vile."

Travis beamed at him, "I know!"

It felt good to laugh, but the moment was short-lived. The smile faded from Montgomery's face. "First inoculation today?" he asked quietly.

"Yeah, and cages A, B and F need to be cleared."

Cages A, B and F had to be cleared because they contained dead animals — dogs who had died in the night. In and of itself, it was an awful job: hauling the carcasses away to be burned and then scrubbing out the soiled cages. But it was the live animals that really unnerved him. Every dog in the room had rabies and the full spectrum of infection-based behaviors was on display. One large German shepherd bit down on the bars of his cage and rattled the door so violently Travis feared that the catch wouldn't hold. Another dog, a black Labrador, had bone-in-the-throat syndrome in which it clawed at its own mouth trying to dislodge an obstruction that wasn't even there. It rolled around and around its cage, raking at its face with its dewclaw. A beagle, thirsty but unable to drink, dug at its water bowl in frustration and then broke into a repetitive rasp of coughing until it vomited up dark bile. A fox terrier was fly-snapping at invisible insects and the rest of the hounds were baying like the doomed, damned wraiths they were. However one dog, a mutt with odd fennec-like ears, was quiet and still. He fixed Travis with an odd glare that was at once vacant and full of meaning. The dog's mind was all but gone, but the virus was still calculating whether to make one more lunge in the man's direction. The dog staggered and fell over on its side, its legs twitching as if he was trying to run. Travis glanced up at the label. Cage H. He'd be clearing that one out tomorrow.

He retreated from the room of the damned to a place where there still lived some hope. The next animal housing area contained the rhesus macaques. The facilities here weren't any better, but at least the animals were healthy ... for now.

Pickman had devised a series of potential cures for full-blown neurological rabies and he'd managed to hollow out the virus itself and turn it into a vehicle that would deliver the treatment directly to the brain. He'd named the resulting combination "Compound 606" after Paul Ehrlich's magic bullet cure for syphilis. His newly recombined, bullet-shaped virus would be his gift to the world.

However it had not been smooth sailing. The first protocol, Compound 606.1, had no effect whatsoever. 606.2 caused fatal grand mal seizures in the second batch of monkeys; 606.3 sent the animals into a coma from which they never awoke, and on it went. But now there was a real sense that they had turned a corner, that they were on the cusp of success. Compound 606.25 had taken a long, long time to engineer — but every attempt, every failure had rewarded Pickman with new insight and understanding. This, he assured Travis, was the one. This would save the unsavable.

But before this miracle could occur, they had to inoculate the latest batch of macaques with the rabies virus. Inoculate. That was such a benign word for the procedure. They would anaesthetize the monkeys with chloroform, strap them down and trepan a hole in their skulls. Then they would take infected brainstem tissue from one of the poor bastards yowling in the next room and place it directly onto the healthy monkey's dura mater — the connective tissue that covers its brain. Inoculation? Try execution. They were deliberately infecting the animals with a highly virulent, quick-to-incubate, form of a fatal disease. In just over a week, the monkeys would be raging.

The thought made him nauseous. He had performed the procedure 384 times before and it had never been easy. But this time it was worse. During the first twenty-four rounds of testing, the animals came and went so quickly. But Compound 606.25 had been a long time in development. And every day he'd fed and looked after this latest batch. He'd been amazed at how diverse their personalities were, how intelligent they were, and how affectionate. He had come to know them, to care about them, and yes, to name them. Pickman was right: he was a fucking idiot.

There were eight cages in the room to house two occupants each (although three monkeys had died already). The first was injured in a fight with his cagemate when Travis had accidentally put two dominant males in together. That one had to be euthanized. The second, a small big-eyed creature, had tried to escape from his pen. He wriggled through a narrow gap in the door and sliced himself up on a sharp bit of exposed metal on the door frame. He'd gotten halfway through, got stuck and remained there, bleeding and distressed, for hours. The shock killed him. The third had sickened a few days ago and died. Travis didn't know what the actual cause was. That left thirteen test subjects for Compound 606.25.

He'd named them after characters in Mad Magazine, issue #488. Its tag line read: "MONKEYS! MONKEYS! MONKEYS!" and in it they claimed that, due to a decline in standards, they had replaced their entire editorial staff with monkeys who obviously could do a better job. These provided the monikers for this latest batch of animals and so they had names like Mister Jingles, T. Worthington Snoots and Baron von Whoopsie. That issue of the magazine had been dedicated to "the late, great J. Fred Muggs, the first monkey contributor to MAD (issue #38, March 1958) who bravely paved the way for those of us who humbly follow in his paw-steps. EEK! EEK!" Travis walked over and stood in front of Muggs's cage.

"Hey buddy," he said softly.

The macaque came immediately to him and grabbed his finger with tiny simian paws. He barred his teeth at the human — a look not of aggression, but of submission. You know how a dog will roll over and show you his belly? Well, a toothy display is the monkey version of that. Next he cooed at Travis.

"I know you're hungry," he said. "But you're nil by mouth before the procedure. I'll bring you some nice apple slices when you wake up though."

He backed up from the cage and spoke to the room in general. "I'm sorry about this, guys. We're going to make you sick for a while. But we're going to fix you. It'll work this time, I know it."

He'd procrastinated as long as he could. It was time to pick the first animal. He looked again at J. Fred Muggs — he couldn't take him first. He just couldn't. Bumble McDaniels in cage 8 was a short-tempered little bastard; he could go first. Knowing that this monkey bites, he put on a pair of thick gauntlets and removed the animal from his cage. Even though he disliked McDaniels, Travis still hesitated, quailing at what he was about to participate in. He looked at a picture he'd Blu-Tacked to the wall. It was the photo of Rachel that Pickman had handed him on the night of his overdose. He'd hung it there so that he could keep reminding himself why this was necessary, why he had to carry on. *It is,* Travis reminded himself, *the Utilitarian Approach to medical ethics. The right course of action is the one that maximizes the amount of overall benefit or happiness for the greatest number of people. Hence, it is acceptable to sacrifice animals to preserve human lives.* He shaved a small bald batch on the squirming monkey's head and carried him to the operating theater.

The job was done. The monkeys were infected and Pickman was whistling to himself as he sterilized the instruments. Aaron really didn't seem bothered by any of this. Part of it, Travis guessed, was due to his obsessive focus on the goal. But it had to be more than that, surely. He wondered if Aaron's capacity for pity had been burned out of him by all the trauma he'd endured. Whatever suffering surrounded him at the lab was nothing compared to what he'd already been through. And Travis suspected that the good doctor was hanging on to sanity by retreating again into a world of pure, sterile logic, just as he had done after Mary's death. But that was a losing game. In the words of G.K. Chesterton: "The madman is not the man who has lost his reason. The madman is the man who has lost everything except his reason." You can't deny your nature; you can't turn yourself into a robot that doesn't hurt anymore — not without doing yourself real damage (his addiction was case in point). And you could not do what they were doing without feeling *something*.

The only indication that the work might be getting to Pickman was the growing collection of empty scotch bottles in the dumpster. Aaron already had another one lined up: a bottle of Teacher's and two empty glasses on the desk. *Oh hell,* Travis thought. *I can't stay here drinking with him tonight.* He had to get away from this lab and so he finished clearing up and beat a hasty retreat to Clarita.

CHAPTER FOUR

ABBY NORMAL

"The end cannot justify the means, for the simple and obvious reason that the means employed determine the nature of the ends produced."

Aldous Huxley

Dr. Frankenstein: Igor, would you mind telling me whose brain I did put in?
Igor: And you won't be angry?
Dr. Frankenstein: I will NOT be angry.
Igor: Abby… someone.
Dr. Frankenstein: Abby someone. Abby who?
Igor: Abby… Normal.

Gene Wilder and Marty Feldman, <u>Young Frankenstein</u>

J. Fred Muggs began to display symptoms of the rabies virus on day 7 of the post-inoculation period. Travis offered him apple slices (his favorite), but the monkey would not take them. Donning the gauntlets, Montgomery opened the cage and reached for Muggs. Usually the animal would come to him enthusiastically, savoring the affection and contact he got from the man. Today, however, the macaque huddled at the back of his pen and would not come when called. Travis reached for him and

Fred's mouth formed the large, round "O" of a severely pissed-off monkey. He screamed shrilly at Travis and sank his teeth into the gauntlet.

The animal was running a fever and a lumbar puncture revealed that his system was flooded with lyssavirus antibodies. Muggs was infected. Strapped down to the operating table, the animal screamed and writhed against the restraints, but Montgomery could not anaesthetize him yet. If he put the monkey under too soon, then Muggs might wake up mid-procedure and that was too horrible to contemplate. And so, while Pickman prepared for the operation that would deliver Compound 606.25 right to the subject's brain, Travis tried to soothe the animal.

"You are going to be so famous," he said gently, "just like your namesake." The monkey stopped screaming. He recognized and loved that voice. He looked at Travis and waited for him to make more sounds that were gentle and friendly and good.

"You know the first J. Fred Muggs was a big TV star back in the 50s and everybody loved him. Children asked for dolls and puppets that looked like him for Christmas. My dad even had this old, beat up board game in the attic: *J. Fred Muggs 'Round the World Game.'* Can you believe it? That monkey was once loved by my old man and I didn't think he was capable of loving anything. That's how good Fred was. And you..." he slipped a gloved finger into the monkey's restrained paw. Muggs squeezed it. "... You are going to be even more loved. You will show the world how people can be saved."

The monkey, who had been watching Travis out of the corner of his eye, tried to turn his head to look the beloved man full in the face. He couldn't. The muscles in his neck seized up and the macaque whimpered in pain.

"What's the matter with your neck?" Travis asked. He let go of Muggs's paw and was about to examine him when Pickman came in to start the procedure.

All thirteen monkeys had now received the antidote and were sitting in restraint chairs to keep them from scratching at their stitches. Muggs looked particularly bad, sitting in a perspex box, his toes dangling through the bars that comprised the cube's base. This would allow urine and feces to fall through rather than collect around the animal's haunches. His bandaged head protruded from a hole at the box's top and slumped to one side. The unconscious monkey's tongue lulled out of its mouth.

"Now we wait." Pickman poured them each a scotch.

"So when will we know for sure?"

"It's difficult to say. Death from the rabies virus would usually occur within ten days. But that's variable. We'll just have to monitor them and see what happens."

Travis nodded and held his glass out for a top-up of *Grant's*. He was not a big whisky fan, however he was pleasantly surprised by the effect it had on him tonight. The first sip had burned his lips, but they tingled a little now. And the liquid smelled dark and warm — a warmth that spread all the way down and calmed his stomach. He could eat, he decided. And he and Pickman threw some frozen pizzas into the oven.

Later on the bottle of *Grant's Blended Scotch* was all but gone. The pizzas were burnt, but consumed anyway and the men were drunk. Travis was teaching Aaron a drinking song which, he instructed, you sing to the tune of "Tie Me Kangaroo Down." Across the courtyard in the lab, Fred's eyes flickered open. The lights were low, but he could hear the others breathing slowly somewhere nearby and underneath the antiseptic, he could smell them. He could barely move and he hurt. Normally, that combination would send a monkey's stress levels through the roof, but he was too weak to feel distressed or afraid. His eyelids slipped shut. No, he really couldn't engage with the full horror of the head wound, the box he was in or how bad he felt. Somewhere in the distance, a man — his favorite man — was singing: "Bestiality's best, boys, bestiality's best (shag a wallaby)." The words meant nothing to Muggs, but the high, slightly hysterical tone of the voice made his eyes snap open again. The man was laughing, but he was not happy. The man was distressed. And that fit. It fit with the lab and the box and the pain in his head and the certainty. As the animal finally lapsed back into unconsciousness, he was sure that there was danger here. And something in him was very, very wrong.

Three rhesus macaques died within twenty-four hours of inoculation with the cure: Protocol 606.25/test subjects 1, 2 and 10 (otherwise known as Mister Jingles, T. Worthington Snoots, and Captain Zippy). That left Pickman with ten viable subjects to monitor for the cure. They were all fading fast — all except J. Fred Muggs who seemed to be gaining in strength as the days ticked by. The monkey's temperature had returned to normal. He was eating and drinking. His eyes were bright and aware.

But something had changed. It was subtle at first — Muggs was just a little stand-offish with Montgomery. He would still accept food from the man, but he would not tolerate any physical contact. Travis mentioned this to Pickman, but the doctor shrugged it off.

"We've put him through a lot and he doesn't understand any of it. What you're seeing is probably the psychological impact of the experiment."

The following day a small female macaque named Hoops slipped her fingers through the bars of the neighboring pen in a gesture that Muggs was familiar with: she was asking for the leftover bits of fruit that littered the floor of his cage. He held up a slice of brown banana and offered it to her. She reached in as far as she could until the bars on her side prevented her from closing the gap any further. She flashed him a toothy grin to say please. He went to pass her the morsel but then at the last moment jerked it away. His head darted forward instead and he bit her. Hoops screamed and withdrew, but not before J. Fred Muggs had taken two of her fingers. He was feeling very hungry now and looked at the banana in his hand. He threw it aside and ate the fingers instead.

Travis Montgomery was coming unglued. The conditions the animals were kept in were bad enough. The experiments they were subjected to had left him clinging to sanity by his fingernails and now this.

"*I mean, what the fuck?*" he ranted. "What the hell is happening?"

"Travis, calm down," Pickman soothed.

"No! I can't do this anymore, Aaron."

"But it's Day 8 and I still have ten subjects alive. We're so close! Can't you see?"

"You think you've cured them?" Montgomery laughed. "You have nine sick monkeys and a cannibal. Congratu-fucking-lations. I'm done."

Pickman surveyed him coldly. "Then what the hell did you do any of this for?"

"What?"

"You watched generation after generation of lab animals suffer and die. You've helped perform experiments that were tantamount to torture. And *now* you're done? *Now* it's too much?"

"This has to stop," Travis whispered and Pickman was surprised to see tears in the man's eyes.

"But if it stops before we find the cure," Pickman said quietly, "then you tortured those animals for nothing. All our work will just amount to senseless brutality. How can that possibly make you feel any better? We've gone too far. The only thing that will redeem what we've done here is to find the cure and let the lives we save atone for our sins."

"You mean *your* sins."

"*Our* sins, Travis. You were right here with me every step of the way and it is too damn late to walk away with a clear conscience."

Travis was openly weeping now. Pickman put a fatherly hand on his shoulder. "I know it's awful. But I'm not a monster and neither are you. We're trying to save human lives here — just as we've done every day since med school, just as I did for you."

And there it is, Travis thought. It was masterfully done. Remind him of his guilt and offer absolution if we soldier on and reach our goal; appeal to his altruistic side because of course the goal is good and noble and think of all the little Rachels out there who could be saved if Travis tortures another monkey. And then Pickman played his trump card: "*I saved your life so don't you forget that you owe me.*" Travis looked at him. *Next, he'll make peace and try to counsel me through this.*

He didn't have to wait long for the olive branch. "Come on, I've been working you too hard lately. Let's get you out of the lab for a bit."

They drove along the coastal highway and stopped for lunch at a lechoneras on the outskirts of town. A good meal of chicharrones de pollo and trifongo and Travis calmed down significantly. And all the while Pickman talked. His logic was unassailable. If they were going to be anything more than a couple of criminally negligent Dr. Mengeles, then they had to continue and actually get a positive result from all of this. And it was worthwhile — Pickman showed him footage (available online) of a small boy in the throes of rabies. The child writhed and struggled on the bed. Finally, he managed to wriggle out of his restraints and then, quick as a shot, he was on his feet. He jumped on the bed to gain some height and then smashed his naked fist through a high window. Another jump and he was up, dragging his body over the jagged glass in order to escape the isolation ward.

Through all this Aaron Pickman was so kind, so understanding, so human that Travis actually started to feel guilty for threatening to bail on him. He said he'd stay and Pickman clapped him warmly on the back and called him a "good man." Then the doctor, fatherly as ever, slipped Montgomery some extra cash and told him to take the rest of the day off.

Once back in the village of Carite, Travis stopped to look at the wad of bills Pickman had handed him. How generous. There was enough there for the tequila, for the girl ... and for the coke.

CHAPTER FIVE

ON THE RADAR

"It was as if all the pain in the world had found a voice...in spite of the brilliant sunlight and the green fans of the trees waving in the soothing sea-breeze, the world was a confusion, blurred with drifting black and red phantasms, until I was out of earshot of the house."

H.G. Wells, <u>*The Island of Dr. Moreau*</u>

"...there burst the most appalling and demoniac succession of cries that either of us had ever heard. Not more unutterable could have been the chaos of hellish sound if the pit itself had opened to release the agony of the damned, for in one inconceivable cacophony was centered all the supernal terror and unnatural despair of animate nature."

H.P. Lovecraft, *"Herbert West — Reanimator"*

While the two men were out, there were three fatalities and one further injury at the lab. Pickman walked slowly down the line of cages, inspecting the condition of the animals and recording his observations on a dictaphone as he went.

"Protocol 606.25/test subjects 7 and 10: deceased and have, presumably, succumbed to the rabies virus. An autopsy will confirm.

Subject number 6 was bitten on the leg by her cagemate Hoops (where the hell does Travis get these names?). The bite is not life threatening, but will require a few stitches. Subjects 3, 4, 5 and 8 show no change. They remain weak and lethargic and ..."

He stopped in his tracks. He had reached the final occupied cage in the row — the one shared by test subjects 12 and 13 (simians Travis had named "Zappy" and J. Fred Muggs). The whole interior of the cage was red. Blood covered the bars and the back wall and dribbled out from under the door to pool on the concrete floor below. In the center of the pen sat Muggs, placidly chewing on what looked like a piece of meat. Subject number 12 (aka Zappy) had had his throat torn out, his right hand gnawed off and a chunk torn from his right thigh. He looked like he'd been attacked by a shark.

Pickman's mind leapt into action. He'd just brought Montgomery back around. If Travis saw this, he'd quit for sure and the project had already suffered too many delays. So damage control: tranq the little bastard, clean out the cage, and have your story in place when Travis staggers in here around lunchtime tomorrow. Stress-induced psychosis. It happens like this:

- Put intelligent primates in restrictive cages under artificial light,
- Give them no stimulation or opportunity for enrichment,
- Provide no chance to express natural behaviors,
- Subject them to painful and invasive tests,
- And surround them with bars and concrete instead of trees and sunshine...

...and you can literally drive the animal insane. Monkeys suffering from lab-stress have been known to frantically spin around in circles in their cages. They bite themselves and each other and sometimes they'll rip out their own fur.

And it's not like he'd be telling a lie. Lab psychosis *was* the most likely explanation. And best of all, it didn't affect the research one iota. Muggs was getting better — he was surviving a full-blown neurological rabies infection and it didn't matter a bit if his life at the lab had made him unstable. All he had to do was keep breathing.

What Dr. Aaron Pickman did not know was that the altercation in that cage had been a noisy one. Zappy's petrified screams had been heard through the lab's open windows by two tourists hiking in the nearby Soledad Nature Reserve. Pale and frightened, they were on their way back to Carite and the local sheriff.

By nine o'clock that night Travis was already passed out on Clarita's lap. She looked at him curiously. He didn't even want to fuck tonight, he just curled up with his head on her thighs and his arms tightly hugging her around the waist like some little boy. She gently stroked his hair to soothe him whenever he twitched or cried out in his sleep. He mumbled something about a fredmug — but that didn't make sense in any language.

"You crazy American," she murmured. "You don't need a *prostituta*, you need a mommy."

As she slipped out of his grasp and headed back out onto the street, Sheriff Abran Manolito was just pulling up in front of the lab.

Pickman, a crystal tumbler of scotch in his hand, came out to greet him. "Hello, Sheriff."

"Doctor," Abran nodded. "I suppose you know why I'm here."

"No I really don't." Aaron's face stiffened. *The coke.* "Is Travis ok?"

"Your man Montgomery? Yeah, as far as I know. I'm here about the screams."

"What screams?"

"Two tourists this afternoon heard some terrible sounds coming from your lab."

Aaron shrugged, "They must have heard the dogs."

"What dogs?"

"Test animals."

"And why exactly would they be screaming?"

"They're rabid. I'm studying them."

"Dr. Pickman ..."

"Look," the scientist interrupted. "You already have rabies on this island both in your stray dog and wild animal populations. I'm not breaking any laws by studying them."

Sheriff Manolito pulled a folded sheaf of papers from his pocket. "Technically no. But are you familiar with the fact that we're governed here by Puerto Rican law?"

"No."

"The Puerto Rican Legislature has passed Law 154, a very clear, very *binding* animal protection act." He handed Pickman the sheets outlining *Classifications of Crimes* and *Maximum Penalties*. "For your information."

"Thank you," Pickman smiled, taking the papers.

"As you can see, the penalties are severe — up to $20,000 in fines and fifteen years in jail. Today, Dr. Pickman, some terrible allegations were made about this lab and so," Abran smiled slyly, *"for your legal protection,* I'm going to drive out here more often to keep an eye on things. But you should know, if *I* hear anything that sounds like," he flipped open his notebook and read from it, "'an animal getting torn to pieces' then I'm going to shut you down."

CHAPTER SIX

UNPRECEDENTED

"I made a thing of pain and fear, and left it bound up to heal... Monsters manufactured."

H.G. Wells, <u>The Island of Dr. Moreau</u>

"I beheld the wretch — the monster whom I had created... I ardently wished to extinguish that life which I had so thoughtlessly bestowed."

Mary Shelley, <u>Frankenstein</u>

Day 21 of the post-inoculation period and the lab was uncharacteristically quiet. The dogs in the first animal containment room had died and had not been replaced with new specimens. In the next room four monkeys remained alive.

The doctor hailed it as a success. "That's a 30% survival rate, Travis! That beats Willoughby's Milwaukee Protocol by 13%! It's unprecedented!"

Yes, Travis thought, *it is*. But unprecedented didn't necessarily mean *good*. The monkeys were damaged. Before, they had been unique living creatures, each with their own personalities. They'd had souls. Neuroscientist Antonio Damasio noted that "Feelings form the basis for what humans have described for millennia as the soul or spirit." And

49

these animals definitely had had feelings. They joked, they got scared and hurt and pissed off and they recognized him and showed him affection. But not now. Now when he walked into the room, they threw themselves against the bars of their cages in an effort to get at him. And they didn't stop. They just kept flinging their tiny bodies against the metal until they split skin and broke noses and shattered teeth. And when they couldn't bite him, they bit themselves. The floor in front of their pens was constantly slick with blood. He tried immobilizing them for their own good, strapping them into restraint chairs. And then they would just sit there and look at him with blank eyes. There was not a hint of recognition or personality or *life* in those eyes. Their hearts still beat — the monitors told him that — but those animals were dead. There was no one home and something else — something diabolical now occupied the empty house like a ghost.

Yes, congratulations Dr. Pickman, you've achieved the unprecedented. And it is grotesque. A line from one of his favorite books, *Night of the Living Trekkies*, came to him then: they "hated it when the unprecedented happened, because there was always the chance that it could quickly morph into something horrible. Something that could never ever be allowed to see the light of day."

But internal ranting and quotes from zombie fiction were not going to solve this problem. *Let's look at this logically,* he told himself. *Analyze it like a puzzle, devoid of all emotion.* He sat down at his desk and began to type:

Profile of Remaining Test Subjects:
1. Protocol 606.25/Test Subject 13 (J. Fred Muggs) — alive. The subject's temperature, heart rate and blood pressure are normal. While physiological symptoms appear to be wholly absent, behavioral changes associated with the rabies virus are clearly present. The subject displays a high level of aggression whenever I enter the room. Tests to determine the cause have so far proved inconclusive.
2. Protocol 606.25/Test Subject 9 (Hoops). After an initial and sharp decline in the subject's condition, number 9 has rallied and displays the same physical and behavioral characteristics as subject 13. Note: Hoops was bitten by Muggs.

3. Protocol 606.25/Test Subject 6 (Little Miss Coconut). Former cagemate of and bitten by subject 9. Following the same pattern as 9 and 13.
4. Protocol 606.25/Test Subject 3 (Sir Wobbly). Same physical and behavioral characteristics as the other survivors. Temporarily housed in the same cage as subject 6, during which time sexual contact was observed between the two animals.

It seems highly improbable that the subjects' behavior is a symptom of stress-induced psychosis as Dr. Pickman claims. Simply put, it is unlikely that all four survivors — despite being placed under identical stresses — would go crazy in precisely the same way. It all started with Muggs. And then it — whatever it is — was passed from one animal to the next along the chain. That means it's communicable and it spreads through fluidic transfer — through bites and sexual contact.

The Tom Lehrer song, "I Got It from Agnes" was now stuck in his head. He hummed it as he worked through the night trying to figure out just what the hell was wrong with those monkeys.

While Travis burned the midnight oil, Aaron Pickman got quietly hammered on *The Famous Grouse*.

"What did you do to get so famous?" he enquired of the russet bird depicted on the front of the bottle. "No, I'm serious. What contribution did you make? What disease did you cure? *I cured rabies*," he slurred.

But that was not even remotely true and he knew it. By the time Travis was done digging, he would know it too. And that would pretty much be the end of everything. He knocked back another dram and, unable to face the quiet loneliness of his bedroom, fell asleep in front of the TV in the lounge.

The television was tuned into Travis's favorite satellite station, Syfy, which was currently airing Stephen King's *Pet Sematary*. And throughout Aaron's uneasy sleep, lines from the movie filtered in. He heard someone say: "Don't go on, doc. No matter how much you feel you have to, don't go on to the place where the dead walk." He half-heard, half-dreamed this and in his dream it was Travis who spoke. And there was Rachel, walking toward him as the four monkeys staggered along beside her. His daughter was grey and gaunt, with a thin film of white over her eyes. She grinned at him and her teeth were covered with bloody froth. He'd wanted to undo his mistake and, my God, he wanted her back … but not like this. He screamed.

Pickman flailed and fell off the couch. He was trembling and crying. And that old actor (the one who used to play Herman Munster) was saying, "Sometimes dead is better."

At ten a.m. the next morning, Travis found Pickman sitting in front of the TV watching *Bats: Human Harvest* and drinking scotch straight from the bottle.

"Klebsiella," he said.

Pickman didn't look at him. "Yep."

"You knew."

"For a few days now."

"Why didn't you tell me?" Travis demanded.

But Pickman did not answer; he just sat there watching Pollyanna McIntosh run away from carnivorous bats. With one swipe of his hand, Travis sent the old TV crashing to the floor.

"Now that I have your attention," he said quietly, "tell me what you know about the Klebsiella."

"About a week ago," Pickman began, "I ran another round of blood tests and took a lumbar puncture from each of the surviving animals. They all had viral antibodies present in their systems — that was to be expected as a normal immune response to the rabies. But I also detected an elevated NK count."

"Yeah, Natural Killer cells, indicating a bacterial infection. I found them too."

"Then you'll know from the blood work that one of the monkeys — most likely Muggs — had contracted a Klebsiella infection."

"Yes, but where the hell did it come from?"

"Our monkeys have been in other labs, any one of them could have picked it up and brought it here."

"But they showed no sign of infection…"

"The macaques used for protocol 606.25 didn't, but what about 606.24 or .23 or .5? This experiment has utilized four hundred monkeys — the infection could have hitched a ride in on any of them. And didn't one from the latest batch die of unexplained causes?"

"Yes."

Pickman nodded. "Yeah. So Muggs picks it up and develops bacterial meningitis, a secondary infection you get from Klebsiella. It would explain the anomalous symptom you mentioned."

"The stiff neck."

"Right again. Every other symptom looked like rabies — all except for the fact that the damn monkey couldn't turn its head."

Travis let out a long breath. "And so his brain was infected with both the rabies virus and bacterial meningitis when we delivered our cure."

"Give that man a prize!"

Travis rubbed his temples; he was brewing a colossal migraine. "I get all of that. I've *seen* all of that under the microscope. What I don't understand is what the hell happened next. Why didn't he just die?"

Aaron took another long drink from the bottle. "Well, that's the thing," he said, swaying slightly. "Our clever new, geneticalisticly …"

"Genetically," Travis corrected.

"Right! Our new gen-net-ick-ly engineered cure did something unexpected."

"What?" Montgomery hissed.

"It acted like a bacteriophage." And with that pronouncement, Pickman toppled forward and passed out on the floor.

Bacteriophages are viruses that attack and consume bacteria. The new cure didn't eradicate the rabies, it attacked the meningitis. Travis was still fuzzy about what that would accomplish. And so he let himself into Pickman's office and snooped through his computer files. It didn't take long to find the document which read…

"I cannot, with the equipment I have on hand, precisely chart the neurological changes wrought by the bacteriophage. I do, however, know this: phages alter a bacteria's genes. Joe Pogliano, Professor of Microbiology at UC San Diego, recently published a study asserting that 'a virus can instruct a bacteria to create a structure more complex than either' — so complex in fact that it resembles the cells that make up all plant and animal life on earth. Some evolutionary biologists believe that that is how life on earth got started in the first place. A virus attacked a bacterium and they made something unprecedented. I must have made a mistake when I altered the virus and now our little phage has made something new. Under its influence, the test subjects survived rabies.

They continue to live, but *they are still infected.* Furthermore, the rabies virus itself appears to have mutated into a highly virulent strain whose properties I cannot yet fathom. I haven't cured the disease. God help me, I've created the *Néos Lyssavirus,* the New Rabies."

CHAPTER SEVEN

EL CHUPACABRA

"... a monster has been terrorizing Veracruz and the nearby villages... The locals call him El Chupacabra... I saw him with my own eyes ... he walks on two hind legs; he is covered with thick fur, has the face of a hideous monkey... Double lock your doors, say your prayers and whatever you do, don't go outside!"

Scooby-Doo! And the Monster of Mexico

"Fly, my pretties, fly!"

The Wicked Witch of the West (commonly misquoted),
The Wizard of Oz

There are many clichés that refer to the prevalence of bad luck in this world. Murphy's Law advances the theory that if something can go wrong, it will. There is, of course, the stoical and ever-popular "Shit happens." And then there's the meteorological: "when it rains, it pours." That one is fairly apt in describing the next misfortune to befall Aaron Pickman. Due to the unconquerable nature of the human spirit, the good doctor was not ready to admit defeat. He still believed he could salvage a cure out of the four demented, slathering creatures that shrieked at him from their cages. And so they were alive and raging when a category 3 hurricane hit the island on the twenty-eighth of November.

The Cáscarans had seen this all before; and after Hugo devastated Carite in `89, they had rebuilt their village to withstand the yearly onslaught. However the same could not be said for the dilapidated airbase on the north east corner of the island. One felled palm tree was all it took to cave in the roof and take out an exterior wall. J. Fred Muggs picked himself up and surveyed the devastation. His cage lay on the floor on its side and one gentle push of his hand revealed that the door had snapped off its hinges. He was free. He could see the rainforest lying just beyond the strewn cinder blocks of the collapsed wall. For a brief moment it captivated him. Trees — tossed by the storm, yes, but *trees*. When had he last seen one? As beautiful as that moment might have been, most of the consciousness that could have appreciated it was gone. He was aware primarily of hunger, of the need to run and hunt and feed. A cry snapped his attention back to the other cages. A female was rattling the door of her pen. Muggs calmly opened it — opened them all — and together they slipped out into the night.

The storm did not linger over Cáscara, but pushed on to the north leaving clear skies and pleasant temperatures. It also left power outages and localized flooding. The phone on Sheriff Manolito's desk was ringing. He picked up the receiver, ready to hear a complaint about another impassable road or looters sniffing around the flooded houses on the waterfront.

"Abran, it's Sebastian." Sebastian Garcia, who bred chickens on a farm just north of the village, was an affable, talkative man. This abrupt greeting made the sheriff sit forward in his chair.

"Hi Sebastian, everything ok?"

"No. Something got into the coop last night and killed the chickens."

"Ok, we can deal with that," Abran said soothingly, imagining half a dozen dead birds. "How many did you lose?"

"All of them."

"What?"

"All of them," Sebastian's voice shook. "All 200."

"I'll be right there."

The large outbuilding that housed the chickens was hot and the air was close. Dead birds lay strewn all over the floor. Donning a pair of gloves, Manolito stooped to examine one of the bodies. Its feathers were matted with blood from two ragged bite marks — one on a wing and one on its throat.

"They're all like that," the farmer said quietly.

"It must have been wild dogs."

"No," Sebastian shook his head. "I've seen what stray dogs can do — they'll just rip a chicken up. Whatever did this just bit a few times and then moved on. And there's something else…"

"What?"

Sebastian grew terribly pale and the sheriff noticed he was trembling. "These chickens are my life, Abran. I don't just let them run around unprotected at night. Before sundown, they each go into their own cage here in the barn."

Manolito inspected the cages — they were all intact. There was not one hole in the chicken wire, not one loose nail or splintered bit of wood. "Somebody opened the cages?"

"It's the only explanation."

"That means it was a person. But those aren't human bite marks on the chickens."

"Now do you see why I'm so freaked out?"

The sheriff was nodding. "Yes I do."

The attack on Garcia's ranch was only the beginning. Backyard chickens were slaughtered in their coops. Hector Osvaldo lost half a dozen goats in one night; the carcasses were not only covered in bite marks, but were also dismembered and partially devoured. Small pet dogs vanished and some larger canines came limping home with terrible injuries for the local vet to sew up.

Between the disruption left by the hurricane and the spate of animal killings, the inhabitants of Carite were already on edge. Then one night, as Alondra Ruis drove home from her shift at Café Lechero, something leapt out in front of her and was caught, transfixed, in her high beams. She slammed on the breaks. It sat in the middle of the road, no taller than her infant son, Jorge; but unlike her one-month-old baby, it stood confidently on two feet. Its patchy fur made her think of mange and its long, boney fingers were hooked into claws. The thing turned to look at her. It had a simian face … sort of … but it had lost all the fur from its cheeks and nose and forehead to reveal the wrinkled, gray skin beneath. Grinning at her, it flashed a mouth full of jagged teeth. And then, quite suddenly, it was gone.

Alondra sat there for a moment breathing heavily and then finally hit the gas pedal. Nothing happened; she'd stalled the car. Kicking it into neutral, she turned the key and thanked all the angels above when she heard the engine turn over and catch. As she pulled forward, something else darted out of the woods in front of her and this second shock tore a scream from her throat. Again she slammed on the breaks to avoid hitting it. This time, however, it was a man — he'd come into the Café a few times... the American who'd taken over the old airbase. His clothes were muddy, his hair disheveled and his eyes were wild. In one hand, he held a gun of some sort. And then he too was gone, running off in the same direction as that *thing*. Later, when she told her friends and neighbors what she'd seen that night, the myth of the Cáscaran Chupacabra was born.

For the second time Sheriff Manolito paid a visit to Pickman's facility. And for the second time, the doctor met him outside. *He doesn't want me to come in,* Abran thought. *What the hell is he hiding?* He did not voice these suspicions, only whistled as he surveyed the damage to the lab.

"You got hit *hard*."

"We did indeed."

"That's an awful shame," Manolito said, although he didn't sound too upset about it. "You must be very busy, what with the clean up and all the repairs. That's why I was a little surprised to hear you were out hunting last night."

"What?"

"At nine o'clock at night, through a waterlogged forest, with a dart gun! What were you hunting, Dr. Pickman?"

"Monkeys."

"There are no monkeys on Cáscara ... unless you were keeping more than dogs in that lab of yours."

"They're mine," Pickman said quietly.

Manolito nodded, swallowing back his anger. "Let me guess, they escaped during the storm and are now loose on the island."

"Yes."

"And what did you say you were working on here? Rabies? Are they infected?"

Dr. Pickman would never know quite why, but in that moment he opened his mouth and the word "No" came out. He could have said yes. There was already rabies on the island; a couple of infected animals more or less wouldn't make any difference. But he said no. His instinct was still to protect the project and if he told the truth — the whole truth — about what those monkeys were carrying, then he'd discredit everything he'd worked for. Every advance in technique and understanding would be dismissed as the ravings of a mad scientist, a Jekyll, a Frankenstein.

"Dr. Pickman?"

Aaron looked up, startled. "I'm sorry, what did you say?"

"I said: I think you're lying. There is no reason to keep monkeys here unless you are using them in your tests. Are you working on anything *other* than rabies?"

"No."

"You damn well had better not be, because ..." Aaron tried to interrupt here, but Abran's hand shot out and grabbed the doctor by his collar. "*Because*," he hissed, "those escaped animals are scaring the hell out of you. Why else would you be idiot enough to chase them through that forest at night? What do they have?"

"Just rabies!"

"Tell me the truth!"

"It's just rabies, I swear!"

Abran released his grip and the doctor staggered backward.

As the officer turned to go, Pickman shouted after him: "Sheriff, please! Could I get them back alive?"

Manolito paused with one foot in his cruiser. "I'm going to kill every last one of them, doc. And then I'm going to run you off this island."

On the other side of the village, Juanita Pimental let her German Shepherd, Manso, out to do his business. Her backyard was fenced in so she could leave the dog to sniff around the hibiscus and bauhinia shrubs, knowing that he'd scratch on the door when he wanted back in. She washed her supper dishes, pressed tomorrow's work clothes and was about to curl up with a book when she remembered that the dog was still outside. That wasn't like him. He never stayed away from her for very long. The way he followed her from room to room, she should have named him "Sombra" (shadow) instead. And lately it had gotten worse. Ever since he tangled with some mongrel in the park, he'd been very clingy. For a breed used by the military and police, he was such a big baby.

She opened the door and was surprised to find Manso standing there, staring at the house. His bandaged front paw quivered beneath him and she made a mental note to give him one of his antibiotics from the vet once she got him in and cleaned the mud off his paws.

"Manso, ven." The dog didn't move. "Venga! Come on!"

Manso, so named because he was gentle and meek, growled and bared his teeth.

The woman was taken aback. Her dog never growled. For heaven's sake, he let Juanita's little niece dress him up for tea parties. The poor thing would just sit there with a look of long-suffering patience on his face.

"Manso, what's wrong?"

And that is when he came at her. Juanita hopped backward and tried to slam the door. She almost made it, but the dog managed to get his head through the gap and in one quick movement sank his teeth into her arm. The woman screamed and slammed the door on the dog's neck again and again until he finally withdrew. As her beloved pet attacked the shuddering door, Juanita dove for the telephone. With shaking hands, she dialed 911.

Sheriff Manolito had had a hard night. The call from Juanita Pimental had come in before he'd managed even a bite of his dinner. He was running solely on coffee which gnawed at the lining of his stomach. He'd had to shoot the dog, which was just horrendous, and then drive a hysterical Juanita to the clinic to get stitched up. Based on the circumstances, the doctor prescribed a course of rabies shots. And there it was again: rabies. He was on his way home when the second call came in — another domestic animal attack. And on it went — four in all and one of them quite serious when a family's Labrador mauled a five-year-old child.

Morning found him standing over Travis Montgomery's bed with a bucket of water. Rosemalia, the owner of the boarding house, had let him in and helpfully provided the pail. He'd kicked the hooker out despite her pleas to be allowed to stay and watch. The girl found the situation hilarious.

"One for the money," he sloshed the bucket. "Two for the show, three to get ready and four to ..."

"Aargh!"

Abran smiled down at him. "Good morning, Mr. Montgomery."

"What the *fuck?*"

"We need to talk. Now." He threw the spluttering man a towel and sat down in the room's one chair. "It doesn't make sense."

"What?"

"What's happening on Cáscara."

Travis groaned and sat up.

"Rabies was already here and it didn't cause much of a problem. Then your boss comes here to study the disease. Four monkeys — rabid monkeys so I'm told — escape and now all hell is breaking loose."

"What's happening?"

"There's been a spate of attacks on pets and livestock. And now four cases of family dogs attacking their owners... That's four cases in *one night*."

Travis gaped at him.

"Now you're going to tell me what the hell is going on."

Montgomery's mind was reeling. *New Rabies, he'd called it the New Rabies. And it's out now — in the animal population and in ... people? Could it be passed to people? No cure. Fuck. No cure no no no no...*

Travis leapt from the bed and grabbed a waste paper basket as a wave of nausea swept through him. There was nothing in his stomach and so he dry heaved for what seemed like an eternity. By the time it stopped, he'd broken out in a cold sweat and his chest and left arm hurt. At first he thought it was just muscle cramp from the violence of the retching, but then it hit. The pain. It felt like a giant hand had reached into his chest, grabbed hold of his heart and squeezed.

"Mr. Montgomery?" the sheriff was saying, but he sounded very far away.

Travis heard Manolito swear and then everything went dark.

"When it rains, it pours," the sheriff muttered as he stood by his cruiser later that day. Manolito had gone out to the lab, not only to inform Pickman of Montgomery's heart attack, but also armed with a search warrant. He was going to find out what the doctor was up to once and for all. When he got there, however, every remaining building of the old airbase was on fire. He'd called it in, but there was no way the town's only fire engine (manned by scattered volunteers) could reach the scene before it all went up. Pickman had neatly covered his tracks and now appeared to be missing.

He got back on the radio. "Miguel?"

His deputy answered, "Yes boss?"

"I want you to contact every pilot and boat owner on the island and tell them that Dr. Aaron Pickman is not to leave Cáscara."

"Will do."

He might be able to hide for a while, but Manolito was going to get him yet.

Cáscara is a small island with one village (the town of Carite) nestled around La Herradura Bay, so named because the inlet is shaped like a horseshoe. Behind the village, the land rises in gently sweeping hills dotted with small farms and one large coffee plantation owned by Juan Valdez (and yes, he took a lot of ribbing over the name). Why the hell would his parents name him after a character in an American coffee commercial? It was an act of cruelty. Anyway, having driven out to check on his crops, he was pleased to see that the bushy plants were now taller than him as they stood in neat lines across the hillside. He walked in a few rows and stopped to inspect the crop. The "cherries" that held the coffee beans were densely clustered on the vine, but they were still pale green and small. They would not be ripe for picking for another few... Something moved nearby. It wasn't much, just a rustling of leaves spotted out of the corner of his eye.

Normally, he wouldn't think anything of it, but there had been quite a few dog attacks in the village lately and some damn fools were insisting that it was really the work of El Chupacabra. Which was bullshit. Nonetheless, he did not relish the idea of a course of rabies shots. He backed out and away from the high plants that obscured his vision. All was quiet and suddenly Juan felt silly. It was probably a bird or something, and here he was picturing Cujo. He turned back to his truck and stopped short. A small monkey sat on the hood.

"Hey, where did you come from?" he asked.

The animal's mouth formed an exaggerated "O" that Juan misinterpreted, thinking that the creature was blowing him a kiss. He laughed and blew a kiss back and that is when all hell broke loose. Enraged, the animal shrieked and flung itself at him, attaching itself to his face. Juan staggered backward and tripped over something that had not been there before — another damn monkey. He fell hard. As he struggled to tear the animal off his head, he felt a sharp pain on his ankle and then one on his arm. Managing finally to pull the creature from his face, he saw for the first time that three other monkeys were on him now, holding on like grim death, and biting. J. Fred Muggs wriggled free of the man's hands and leapt again, this time burying his teeth in Juan's throat. His jaws closed on something tough and he shook his head to tear at it. He was rewarded by a warm, dark flow of blood that tasted better than any banana or apple slice. Valdez, his eyes wide with shock and horror, clutched at his throat as he bled out. As he lay there twitching, the monkey drank.

CHAPTER EIGHT

COMING HOME
TO ROOST

"Our lives are never free of grief ... [when] a pestilence of terrible ferocity has come into our midst like a great rage."

Llywelyn Fychan, writing on an outbreak
of the Black Death in England

"There are universal laws at work, even here. The Law of Attraction; the Law of Correspondence; and the Law of Karma. That is: like attracts like; as within, so without; and what goes around comes around."

H.M. Forester, Game of Aeons

Sheriff Abran Manolito was exhausted and, for the first time since the hurricane, he took a night off to relax. In the two weeks since the storm, he'd managed to coordinate the clean up operation, kill three of the escaped monkeys (and he was pretty sure he'd hit the fourth) and enforce a cull of every stray dog on the island. There had been no more livestock killings, no more missing pets and no further animal attacks on humans. In doing so he'd calmed the near-hysteria that greeted the news of how Juan Valdez had died. Once again his town was peaceful.

Tomorrow would be busy: the twelfth of December was the Feast Day of Our Lady of Guadalupe and there would be church services in the morning followed by the Festival de la Madre Sagrada. The main street of town would be all noise and music and pageantry. The locals would wear vejigante masks — hideous creations, really, that represent all the demons of hell that challenge the reign of Our Lady. Carried in the procession, towering placidly above them all, you will see the statue of the Virgin in a deep green robe bedecked with stars. It is a strange and wonderful spectacle that draws in many tourists and hence many needed dollars for local businesses. And it had almost been canceled. Rattled by recent events on the island, Manolito was worried about public safety. But Louisa Gaultiero, the Mayor of Cáscara, convinced him that if they could cull the stray dogs, then it was right to go ahead. The town, she said, had had so much anxiety. It needed something positive, something *fun* so that it could settle back down to normal.

And so on the twelfth of December the festival went ahead. Many faces were obscured by masks made from gourds and coconut husks and papier-mâché. Enormous work had gone into these facades to make them as intricate and colorful as possible; and pale-skinned tourists laughed and shrieked whenever a local came up and nudged them with one of the mask's many horns. Watching the parade, Juanita Pimental wiped the sweat from her brow. It was a mild day and yet she was burning up. Well, that was just the cherry on top of the whole rancid sundae that was her life right now. She grieved for Manso as if she had lost a human friend. But he was such a vital part of her life. She had no husband, no children; she was shy with her co-workers and Manso was the one living, breathing thing that made her feel connected to this world. And now he was gone. She'd stormed into the veterinary clinic and demanded to know why the hell the dog's rabies vaccinations had not protected him. Her vet could only guess that, because other animals were similarly affected, the island must have received a bad batch of the vaccine. He was going to sue the pharmaceutical company that made it, he said, and get compensation for his customers and the damage done to his business.

Juanita swayed a little on her feet. She really did not feel well, but then that was normal, right? The doctor at the hospital had started her on a course of Imovax rabies shots and the leaflet on Imovax said that she might experience headaches, dizziness, nausea and muscle pain — all of which she had. It was better than getting rabies, though. She shuddered at the thought.

At that moment a man in an orange and yellow mask ran up to her and gave her a gentle nudge with one of his horns. She'd been lost in thought and so it startled her and she gaped up into the face of a demon. It had the standard array of horns and tusks, but what disturbed her was the blank chasm of its eyes and the mouth full of wickedly sharp teeth. That is what she had seen in Manso that night. Nothing behind those eyes — no mind, no soul. But his fangs had dripped white foam. The man danced away from her and she followed him.

"Manso? Venga!" She was convinced now that she was looking at her dog. But those eyes and teeth — he was infected! He was dangerous! No! She had to stop him, to get him by the scruff of his neck and drag him home.

He approached a blond tourist wearing a faded Rip Curl t-shirt. Afraid that her dog might bite someone else, Juanita leapt on him. She was a small woman, but her momentum bore him to the ground. And that triggered it. The pursuit, the leap, the contact of bringing the man down and she was clawing at the mask, knocking it aside to expose bare flesh beneath. It was Pablo Vasquez, her handyman, but she did not recognize him as she bit into the rough skin of his cheek. Pablo screamed and threw Juanita from him. She did not even pause. Back on her feet, she lunged at the blond tourist, who threw her hands out defensively in front of her. Juanita bit her on the hand. The woman's boyfriend intervened and Juanita raked her nails along his arm like an angry cat. Then she was running, dashing through the crowd of visitors, biting and scratching.

Having used a festival mask to walk unrecognized through the village, Dr. Aaron Pickman watched it all unfold. He noted the bandage on Juanita's arm and the similarity between her behavior and that of the infected monkeys. It was proof of zoonotic transfer. The disease could be passed to humans. *No.* His mind rebelled at the concept. *No.* The woman was crazy; she needed a shrink and maybe some anti-psychotic meds, that's all.

But whatever the cause, the blood-streaked wretch was bearing down on a small child, a little girl with dark hair and big, startled eyes. Pickman's arm shot out, his fist connecting with the side of Juanita's head. As the child's mother scooped her up and ran off through the crowd, Pickman swore and shook out his hand. He was not a brawler and he'd made the fist wrong, curling the fingers over his thumb. Distracted by the pain, he did not see the woman hop to her feet. In another instant, she'd bitten him on the forearm. Then Sheriff Manolito was there, tackling her to the ground and Aaron Pickman slipped away unseen.

Nine tourists and one local man were treated at the hospital for bites and scratches. The physicians there gave them each a course of antibiotics and a tetanus booster. Juanita Pimental, clad now in a straight jacket, lay sedated in a private room under guard. Doctors had ordered a psych evaluation for nine a.m. the following morning.

While Abran Manolito took statements from the victims, Aaron Pickman snuck up the back steps of Rosemalia's Boarding House and let himself into Travis's room. With Montgomery still in intensive care, this was the best place to hide until he could bribe a local fisherman to ferry him off the island.

He surveyed the room: it was a mess. The sheets were hanging off the bed, the place smelled of booze and stale cigarettes, and on the floor in the general vicinity of a clothes hamper lay a mound of hideous Hawaiian shirts, cutoff shorts and sweaty Y fronts. But at least it was quiet. He walked to the ensuite bathroom and ran his injured arm under the cold tap. Then he dumped a whole bottle of hydrogen peroxide on the bite.

"Fuck shit fuck," he hissed as the solution foamed and burned.

He patted his arm dry and then sat down at Travis's desk to dress the wound. On the wall in front of him was a canvas picture of one of Banksy's paintings. In it a monkey stood with hunched shoulders and fingers hooked into claws. Its face was inscrutable, you couldn't make out its eyes, but it wore a sandwich board sign on its chest that read: "Laugh now, but one day we'll be in charge."

CHAPTER NINE

BEGINNING OF THE END

"...vice has degraded me beneath the meanest animal. No crime, no mischief, no malignity, no misery, can be found comparable to mine. When I call over the frightful catalogue of my deeds, I cannot believe that I am he whose thoughts were once filled with sublime and transcendent visions of the beauty and the majesty of goodness. But it is even so; the fallen angel becomes a malignant devil."

Mary Shelley, _Frankenstein_

"Here, truly, was something that, in Melville's fateful words, 'stabs us from behind with thought of our own annihilation.'"

Caspar Henderson, _The Book of Barely Imagined Beings_

A clatter in the room woke him. Travis Montgomery jolted awake to find Pickman dragging a chair up to his bed.

"Sorry, tripped over the chair," Aaron mumbled as he collapsed into it.

"What's going on?"

"Oh, you know, the usual..."

"That bad?" Travis said wryly.

"You were the only one I … I … could talk to. You can … yeah … you you can fix this."

Confused, Montgomery switched on the light. He stared at Dr. Aaron Pickman — if indeed it was him. The figure in front of him was thinner and a filthy Hawaiian shirt hung from his bony frame.

"You shaved your head?"

"I'm in disguise," the thing in the chair laughed. "On the lamb from our good sheriff, Maa…" He stumbled over the name for a full minute and finally settled for "whatshisface."

"Ok…" Montgomery continued to stare in disbelief. The skin on his boss's face was a dingy grey that clung to every bulge and cleft of his skull. The terms came back to Travis from medical school: the zygomatic bone of the cheek, the mental foramen of the chin, the sphenoid bone of the temples — all stood out in horrible, skeletal relief. And his eyes, underscored by the heavier grey of dark circles, were utterly blank. *They're the open eyes of a dead man*, he thought, *or the eyes of a Thing, an It*. Why did his mind seize on those words? The form in front of him, though emaciated and sick, was undeniably human. He knew this man. But still, the word "thing" asserted itself. Montgomery could not shake the feeling that Pickman was no longer Pickman. He'd been hollowed out somehow and the fact that he still in some ways looked like Pickman made it all the worse. That terrible collision of the familiar and the wholly alien unnerved Travis and made his exhausted heart race.

"I need…," the Pickman-thing paused to wipe a line of drool away from his lips with the back of one bony hand. "I need you to do something for me."

"Aaron, what's going on?"

"The New Rabies — people can get it," Aaron whispered and held up his bandaged arm.

"*What?*"

Pickman handed him a notebook. "It's all here. You have to stop this."

"What … wait," Travis stammered, but the doctor was already tottering for the door.

"Please, Travis. Stop this." Then he was gone.

Travis examined the journal and realized that it was his. The cover was black with a message emblazoned on it in white block capitals: "Dear

Scientists, thank you for giving the world Levitra, Viagra and Cialis. Now could you stop playing with your dicks and give us something for cancer?" Yeah, it was his notebook all right, but now it was a bulging, tatty mess and page after page was filled with text. He glanced at the clock. It was three a.m. He started to read…

I was bitten today by a woman who had gone berserk and was attacking people on the street. While I do not know what her mental health status was prior to the incident, she was probably suffering from nothing more remarkable than a psychotic break. The odds that the episode is linked to the escape of test subjects 3, 6, 9, and 13 are minute. Hence, I'm not even sure why I'm recording the incident here.

Perhaps it is just a way to fill the hours. Sheriff Manolito's interference has barred all possible exits from the island and necessitated the destruction of the lab — there were enough evident violations of Law 154 there to get me five to fifteen in a Puerto Rican jail. I cannot afford it. It is vital that the work continues. Yes, the four remaining test subjects are erratic and violent, but THEY ARE ALIVE. They were infected with rabies and yet they live. I am convinced they hold the answer I've been searching for and, when I find it, the tens of thousands of lives saved will vindicate the methods I used to develop a cure.

Edward Jenner gave James Phipps the cowpox virus believing that it would render the boy immune to a more deadly smallpox infection. Then, to test his theory, he inoculated that eight-year-old child with smallpox over twenty times. He exposed a human child to a deadly pathogen to test his vaccine and is hailed as the "father of immunology." I, on the other hand, am stuck hiding here in Montgomery's flophouse because I experimented on a few monkeys.

So yes, the work will continue. The capture of the escaped test subjects is paramount, and I have set Travis's alarm clock for 4:30 tomorrow morning so I can get up and resume the hunt. In the meantime, I will consolidate all research data that I collected before I destroyed the lab. The USB hard drive taped to the back cover of this book holds all information available on the development of the Néos Lyssavirus, the New Rabies…

Travis flipped to the back to find a thin memory stick taped there. That was good. It should contain all the information he'd need. The

70

journal then went on to cover what Montgomery already knew: the purpose and methodology of the experiment, the many failures, and the unprecedented results they achieved with J. Fred Muggs. The next entry reads:

3 a.m.
Can't sleep. My head was buzzing with all the logistical problems I'll face once I've got the test subjects back. Mind you, I don't even need them all; Subject 13 (the one Travis calls J. Fred Muggs) would be enough to continue the work. Furthermore, one small rhesus macaque would be easier to smuggle off the island.

I think the stress of the situation is finally catching up with me. My head is pounding. I don't get migraines, but I imagine this is what one feels like. The pressure behind my eyes is incredible and my head seems to throb with every heartbeat. I took aspirin and Tylenol and washed them down with scotch. But that hasn't helped. My throat is so sore that choking down the whiskey felt like swallowing broken glass. I've been working nonstop and I seem to have run myself into the ground. I've picked up a bug. Friggin typical. I don't have time for this — there is still too much to do.

11:30 a.m.
Slept through the alarm — God, I'm so tired. The headache and sore throat are worse and I'm now running a fever of 103°F. It's making me nauseous. I've finally decided that it's time to admit defeat and just acknowledge that I'm sick. There won't be any hunt for Muggs today and so I'll crawl back into bed.

4:30 p.m.
Dozed for most of today, but was aware of the pain and the fever even in my sleep. I'm more tired now than I was before. But I'm restless too. I feel anxious although there is no immediate or discernible cause. It's a good thing Travis isn't here. He worries too much and would be banging on right now about the possibility of zoonotic transfer. No. One woman's psychotic outburst does not indicate that New Rabies has jumped into the human population. I'm run down, yes, and sick. But it makes sense after that cold, wet hunt through the forest. I must

71

*be getting better, though, because as I write this I seem to have more
energy. I feel I need to go do something. I'll sneak out for a while.
Maybe some fresh air and a little food will help.*

Travis groaned aloud. It was a phenomenon he'd encountered often but
could never quite understand: the stupidity of smart men. Why the hell
didn't Pickman seek help? Yes, the sheriff was gunning for him and yes,
jail time was a distinct possibility for them both. But New Rabies is a
disease we know nothing about and for which there is no cure. And still
the man, *a doctor*, did not ask for medical assistance.

Was it guilt or denial or just that he could not bring himself to
abandon the research? That was it, wasn't it? Travis had tried to set the
world record for how much coke a man could snort before his heart
exploded, but Aaron was the true addict. Aaron Pickman would continue
using his drug of choice — his work — even as he lay dying from it. It
was an intensity of vision that was at once awe-inspiring and frightening.
It could produce great things. Writer Ashley Stanford noted that a man,
obsessed, would "push harder, longer, and with greater devotion…it
is the person with the obsessive personality who is going to make the
great discoveries." And Travis had believed that it *would* produce great
things and they *would* find the cure. How could that white-hot focus not
reach its goal? But Pickman had become focused to the exclusion of all
else. He couldn't assess the risks he was running or see how needlessly
cruel his actions were. He was so hell-bent on finding the answer that
he didn't care what rule, what law, what life he had to crush underfoot
to reach it. This wasn't inspiring devotion to a noble cause, this was a
relentless pursuit that ground everything in its path to dust. Travis had
once believed that his boss was, in the words of Lovecraft, a "benevolent
fanatic." But he wasn't. He was a monster, a ghoul. And that thing, (to
quote Lovecraft again) that "shivering gargoyle" that came and sat here
and handed him this notebook was just the final, physical manifestation
of an inner madness that had been there all along.

Travis's head started to spin and his breath came in ragged gasps. He
was getting too upset. He needed to calm down and view the problem
with a clinical detachment. Only then could he figure out how to proceed.
He took several minutes to quiet himself and then read on.

11 p.m.
Things are spiraling out of control. today I ...

Let's start's where I left off and take the sequence of events chronologicly. Maybe then I can make some sense of it all.

My walk through the village today was stupid. What was I thinking? There was nowhere I needed to go and yet to risk exposure and arrest ... why? and it is clear now that I am not well enuff for even that level of exertion. First of all, to be walking around in this heat and the glaring carribbean sun with a fever was madness. I couldn't stand the light. It hurt and made me angry and so I darted down a shadow-y alleyway and right in front of a car. the blare of its horn hit like a sledgehammer. And I found myself crouching by a dumpster being violently sick. It was the kind of vomiting that I hate when you just can't stop and have lost all control over your body and feel in that moment like you're gonna to die. It was time to head back, but my feet wouldn't work. All movement has become clumsy, spazmodic and I found I could only make any real progres if I slowed down and inched my way along. even then I kept tripping over curbs, over nothing at all and this hurt my head more and made me more agitated. i collapsed onto a bench near a bus stop and sat there panting and, if you can believe it shivering in the heat.

But it was good to sit down and rest. I was so tired I could have wept. I watched the peeple go by. it was I guess an everyday scene just another street in another small town on a planet full of towns and streets like this. Why then should it suddenly apear so alien to me? These were people who had gotten up this morning and brushed there teeth and dressed 4 the day and gone off to their jobs and i could not fathom what it was like to be them. I could not see the point. Nor could I see the point of all that activity the cars, the buses, the buildings full of peeple who ran around talking, talking endlessly to each other, to their fones. It meant nothing. theres a illness I think — i read about wear everything is seen as froth — no substance n no meaning. Is that whats happening to me? i don't feel part of the world.

and the people were so strange. They appeared to me all as bits and peaces. The slap of a shoe on pavement, a wolfishly hairy arm, a painted red mouth. They all seemd disjointed, grotesque. And I hated them and they hated me too. there eyes were staring and wary.

I knew my perseptions were skewed. i could remember thinking and feeling differently and I could not figure out what happened to change things. maybe I jus needed to Make a connection. talk to someone. I got up and shuffled over to a newsstand I picked up today's edishon of Verdad newpaper.

"Do …" i found suddenly that, while i knew what i wanted I didn't have the words to expres it. "Past. Past Eds"

"Past editions?" The man asked.

I nodded.

there wuz that look again on the man's face. looking at me like I'm the one who's crazy. "Let me check." he disapeard into a van parkd nearby and came out with a small stack of paypers.

I gave him a $50 bill into his hand snatched the papers and walked away.

"Your Change!" He called after me. "Señor, your change!"

I ground my teeth as I stumbled away why was he yelling at me about change? I'm not the one whose changed. The world had unraveled or maybe it was nothing that dramatic. Maybe it had always been this stoopid and meaningless and only now i was seeing it.

The scailes had finaly fallen from eyes. And so when a woman colapsed nearby in the street i saw it for what it was — nothing. The people who scrambled to hold her still while she convulsed on the pavment would soon forgit about her The world would forgit about her because her life amounted to nuthing. Lives never do. you struggle and suffer and die and are forgotin. what does it matter? And then the ambulenc arrived with a blaring siren and that mattered very much. I felt like a swarm of bees were in my ears stinging and stinging. and a man brushed passed me, knocking me on the arm and my skin prickled and hurt at that and he didn't even stop and say sorry and I followed that man. i wanted to tell him sumthing. He turned into a quiet street and realized finaly that I was there because turned around and said What? And i … i couldn't find words. My hands fluttered in meaningless gestyures and suddenly he wasn't a hole person, just skin smooth skin a browned golden shade. my stomach growled.

What? he asked again.

I found a word and it was a good word, the only one that really mattered. Hungry

The man sighed. "I don't have much change, but you canhavewhat I've got." he began to dig in his poc-kets.

Then everything went red.

I'm back at Travis's now sitting at his desk wearing his close. my ones were two bloody after the thing that happened. i'll hav to get rid of them sumhow.

It is the New Rabies i have all of the symptoms — the violance, the aggreshon. blood pressure is 170/96, pulse 167 bpm, respirtion hindered by spasmz in the muscles of th throat and larinx.

I should be horrified but honestly I don't have the enirgy that is one of the mercies of being sick you reach a point whare you are too sick to care. I feel so

5:32 a. .

i woke up on the floor [something unintelligible followed, and then] think a seizure.

I feel a little better now. I can breathe easier I am fully lucid. that Is a bad, bad thing. Because with lucidity comes knowledge and with knowledge comes guilt.

Yesterday I killed a man. I don't know why. it just felt like being on fire and their's a lake, rite in front of you, and all you have to do to stop the pane is jump in. I had to do it. i needed to. And so I jumpd on him and bit. I must have fastend on his karotid becaus he bled out so fast. Blood spirted from the wound onto my face and I should have been horrified but Godhelpme, I was at piece. The sense of release when I bit down on him ekstasy i crave that release agin.

I am not the only one. I've been looking through the newpapers and there have been atacks here on the iland — peple biting peeple. u could find a plawsible explanashun for each attak. But I no better. With rabies infections you woulld get maybe 25% of your patience actualy biting another person. I think — no, I kno that 100% of those who get the new rabies will bite some body else. And they will do it becaus the dizease takes away who you R.

Think you are a nice persun? A good persun? Think that u would never stoop to acts of barbearity or cruwelty? think agin. because once

75

this infectshun is in u it seems to croud everythin else out. I am an absolute prick i am a failure as fathur an a husbund and I have dun terible things for my work but I am NOT a fucking murderer i don't rip peoples throats out and revil in the act. I wanted to save lives But im disapearing n going quik. in a little while, there will be nothing of Aron Pikeman left. this demonvirus will ware me like a soot and I'll hurt more peple and thayll hurt more peple and on and on and i didn't just kill some man I met on the street I think I mite have killed the world.

and so it is 4 u Travis to set things rite Take this put it into the rite hands and stop it here while u still can.

And no that i am so so sorry.

Your frend, Aron.

Travis hastily grabbed a tissue from the bedside table and dabbed the page to keep his tears from smudging the ink. While that was Pickman's goodbye, it was not quite the end of the journal. On the subsequent pages, Aaron had pasted a couple of articles he'd printed off the internet. The sheets of paper were ragged and torn (the Doc had had trouble with the scissors) and he'd taped them into the book with all the skill of a kindergartener. The first article, entitled "Bill Gates: Pandemic Disease Threat Could Kill 30 Million People in Just 6 Months," had run in *Newsweek*. Pickman had highlighted the following passage with an unsteady hand: "Gates compared the risk of a pandemic disease outbreak to the challenges of preparing for a massive war and argued that we've fallen behind in readying our public health system for an epidemic."

Travis flipped to the next article. This one, from *Time Magazine*, bore the title: "Why America Could Become Vulnerable to the Next Major Pandemic." The article highlighted our current state of "global hyper-connectedness" in which "a deadly germ can travel from West Africa to North Texas before we even realize the threat exists." We learned this lesson from Ebola and since its first appearance, the U.S. had become a global leader in finding, monitoring and treating diseases before they became pandemics. Now however, with the CDC facing budget cuts of up to 80%, our capacity to carry out this vital work is hamstrung. We are no longer prepared to spot and stop new diseases before they land on our doorsteps. According to journalist Liz Schrayer, "the sneeze on the other side of the world" just got "much more dangerous."

As Travis frantically stabbed at the red call button to summon the nurse, he had the old nursery rhyme running maniacally through his head…

Ring-a-ring o' roses,
A pocket full of posies,
A-tishoo! A-tishoo!
We all fall down.

Dr. Emmanuel Malavé nodded as Travis ranted on about viruses and secret labs and a coming pandemic. He glanced again at the man's chart — cardiac arrest resulting from prolonged cocaine addiction. He looked at Montgomery: yes, that fit. The bloodshot eyes, the hyperactivity and agitation, the emaciation — all signs of an addict. Travis had stopped talking and was staring at him.

"So will you take a look at it?"

"What?"

"The journal! It's all here. You need to know what you're dealing with!"

Malavé could see the words "playing with your dicks" on the journal's front cover. He'd had enough of this. "Look, you need to get some rest and I need to get back to work…"

"This is your work! Because you are going to see more and more people admitted with this virus!"

"Ok." The physician addressed his next comment to the nurse. "Lorazepam — 2.5 milligrams."

"No! You have to listen to me! Talk to Sheriff Manolito. He knows. He knew that something was wrong at the lab! Fuck OFF!" He batted the needle out of the nurse's hand. "I don't need a shot! I need you to listen to me!"

But then it was a chaos of orderlies and restraining hands and a needle in his arm. As he writhed, Travis began to cry and this made it really hard to speak. He had to tell them, he had to …

There was pain. It was as if a bony fist had just punched him in the chest. He couldn't catch his breath. The beep of his heart monitor sped up and was swiftly followed by an alarm.

"He's arresting..."

There was a flurry of movement around him and in the chaos, the journal slid to the floor.

PART TWO

`ROUND THE WORLD WITH J. FRED MUGGS

CHAPTER ONE

NEW ORLEANS

"By the pricking of my thumbs,
Something wicked this way comes."

William Shakespeare, <u>Macbeth</u>

"There is a dark foreboding ... that augurs a new downfall."

Hartley Coleridge, <u>Prometheus</u>

Tammany Lanuit got home just as the paperboy was delivering *The Times-Picayune*. It had been a hell of a night. The arthritis in her knees had reminded her of roman candles that shot spark after spark of pain through her joints. By morning, she knew, they'd be swollen and warm to the touch. It was just one of the many delights of getting old. Her bladder leaked whenever she laughed or sneezed, and gravity was getting to be a problem — honestly, if her boobs sagged any more she'd soon be tucking them into her socks. And so yes, growing old was a bitch. But it was also a privilege denied to many.

She was doing that whole 'count your blessings instead of sheep' thing when the phone rang at three a.m. A voice choked with sobs asked, "Mambo, can you come?"

It was her friend, Nola Hudson. She was a sensible woman and wouldn't call at this hour over a trifle. And so within half-an-hour, Tammany was seated at Nola's kitchen table, trying to make sense of what the woman had to say. It all came out in a jumbled rush. Otis (Nola's husband) was missing. But there was also some hurried mention of work and Ragu and cigarettes. The mambo rubbed her temples. It was three-thirty in the freaking morning and this woman was ranting about spaghetti sauce.

"Honey," Tammany interrupted. "I'm not firing on all cylinders yet. Please ... take a breath." Then, with the practiced calm of years as a voodoo healer and the quiet interjection of a few questions, Tammany managed to piece together the details.

Otis Hudson had left for work (he was an overnight stocker at Whole Foods Market) at nine-thirty Tuesday night. He'd made it to work ok, but his boss said that Hudson had been off kilter the whole evening. He'd put Pampers on the Wonder Bread shelf and knocked over a display of Ragu Traditional. He was clearly still suffering from the flu that had knocked him down over Christmas. And so his boss, surveying the red scene of carnage in aisle eleven, had ordered him to take a break. If he didn't feel any better after that, he should go home to bed. Otis stepped out for a smoke; he never came back in. That was at one o'clock Wednesday morning. It was now four a.m. Thursday and Otis was seven hours overdue for his insulin injection.

Nola was calmer now and making sense. "The doctor has him on a basal injection that would have covered him for twenty-four hours."

"What happens when he goes more than a day without his insulin?"

"Well, by now he's probably hyperglycemic and getting quite ill. Within the next day or two DKA will set in."

"DKA is ..."

"Uh, I can never say it right." Nola closed her eyes, her fingers gripping the bridge of her nose as she concentrated on the term. "Diabetic Ketoacidosis. It's the downward slide. Tam," she clutched the old woman's hand, "if he doesn't get his meds, he'll die."

"Right," Tammany was rummaging in the huge red purse she carried everywhere. "How much time does he have?"

"A few days. A week at most."

"And the police?"

"Are looking for him."

Tammany had extracted an old, battered deck of Waddington playing cards and was shuffling them. "How was he before he left? I mean, other than the bug. Did you guys have a fight? Was he upset about something?"

Nola sighed wearily. "He's low … ever since Pascal Construction went under and he had to take the stock boy job. And he hates the late hours at Whole Foods. But he has an interview tomorrow."

"For what?"

"Foreman. With Landis Construction." Nola paused watching Tammany shuffle the cards. "The loa will know where he is, right?"

"Let's see what they'll tell us." She waved her hands at her friend. "Now shoo for a few minutes so I can concentrate."

Without a word, Nola rose and left the room.

Tammany sat quietly for a moment and breathed steadily. As a mambo, she was a servant of the loa, the spirits. These are like the saints who can be called upon in times of trouble and she called on them now. She prayed to Papa Legba, who helps us find what is lost and asked Azagon Loko, the one who sees far, to give her clarity of sight. And as she continued to shuffle the cards, she asked again and again: where is he?

The cards, once dealt, would form three columns — one for the past, one for the present and one for the future. Each column would contain three cards, all clues about the problem at hand. She turned over the first: the King of Hearts indicating a good-natured, affectionate man. That was a fair description of Otis and a good sign that the loa were directing the cards to answer her question. Next, she laid down the Jack of Diamonds. This confused her because it added another person to the equation, probably a young man or teenager, and a bringer of bad news.

"Nola, who's the young man?" she called.

Nola appeared at the doorway. "What young man?"

Tammany gestured to the cards that lay face up on the table. "I don't know. Someone who's had a negative impact?"

Nola was shaking her head, then her eyes went wide. "The fight."

"What fight?"

Five days before his disappearance, Otis Hudson had stood on the loading dock at the back of Whole Foods Market, surveying the inventory sheet on his clipboard. They were supposed to have received an order of paper towels. Where were they? He looked wearily at the boxes stacked around him. Tissues, diapers, baby wipes ... no paper towels.

"Why am I here?" he muttered. Try as he might, he just could not care about paper towels and whether they were displayed attractively on a shelf. He stood there in the silence and told himself yet again that this was temporary, just to keep the money coming in. There was an opening at Landis Construction and he could do that job with his eyes closed. He just had to nail the interview...

The small, tinny sound of an empty soda can rolling across concrete interrupted these thoughts. He walked to the edge of the loading platform and peered out into the back lot. At first he saw nothing and then, as his eyes adjusted to the dim light, he made out the dark shape of a man — just standing there, swaying on his feet.

"Hello?" Otis called.

The man's head jerked up.

"Listen, pal," Otis began, "a lot of trucks will be in and outta here tonight. It's not really safe for you to be here."

A shudder went through the stranger and Otis could hear him breathe — a ragged panting like an overheated dog.

He's drunk ... or high, Otis thought. *Great.* "Come on, I'll show you the way out. Maybe call you a cab?" he said as he hopped down and placed a hand on the man's shoulder to guide him.

And that is when the stranger lunged. Hudson tried to push him away but the guy's scrabbling fingers closed on the strap of his Whole Foods apron and held on.

"What the —" Otis gasped as his attacker's head darted forward, teeth snapping shut close to Hudson's throat.

Otis was a big guy, powerfully built and, although he was in his early forties, he had not yet gone to seed. One punch from him would likely put most men on the ground. And indeed the man's knees buckled when Hudson's fist connected with his jaw. But he would not relinquish his grip on the apron strap which was proving to be the sturdiest piece of cheap fabric Otis had ever seen. In a tangle of flailing arms and legs, the stranger knocked Otis off balance and both men went down. Then the man was on top of him and was actually trying to bite at his face. Again Hudson's strength held him in good stead and those teeth never met flesh; but for the first time he was really afraid. It was like trying to fend off a frenzied animal — a wolf or a shark. Panicking now, Otis lashed out with his fists, his feet, with his own teeth to get this lunatic off him and make him stop.

He only just managed it. As the stranger lay in a crumpled heap, Otis pulled himself up onto the platform and hit the switch to bring down the big loading bay door. He stood there in the bright fluorescent light, trembling. There was blood all down the front of his shirt and it took him a moment to ascertain that it was not his own. *That's right*, he thought, *I bit him.* His stomach lurched and his mouth began to water as if he was going to throw up. He had to wash that blood off him and get the coppery taste of it out of his mouth.

It was then that his eyes fell upon a box marked "Bounty — the Quicker Picker Upper." Laughing somewhat hysterically, he ripped opened the box, grabbed a roll of paper towels and hurried to the washroom.

By the time the police arrived the stranger was gone and, due to the unprecedented excitement, all work at Whole Foods had ground to a halt. As his coworkers looked on, Otis tried to communicate just how disturbing the encounter had been. However, the only wound he could find on himself was a brush burn on his elbow from where he hit the macadam.

"Please don't underestimate this. I had real trouble fighting him off." He drew himself up to his full height to illustrate that he was a head taller than the cop who was taking his statement. "The guy was crazy and if it had been somebody else — someone old or frail or some poor woman walking home from the bus stop, you wouldn't be dealing with a skinned elbow right now."

Tammany listened to this account trying to figure out how it was connected to Otis's disappearance. Did the attacker come back?

"Thanks, Nola," she mumbled as she went back to the cards.

Nola left her to it.

The third and last card in column one was the Nine of Spades. That suggested bad luck or illness. Tammany frowned. It wasn't enough information. Otis was definitely ill because he'd missed his last insulin injection, but what about his attacker? His behavior didn't exactly suggest good mental health. Why the hell was he trying to *bite* Otis? Mug him? Sure. Pull a knife or a gun? Yep. But bite his face? What on earth was that all about?

She dealt the first card of column two to clarify the present state of things. The King of Spades — a dark man, not to be trusted. Did this suggest the addition of yet another negative figure? *No, she thought, I don't think so.* She looked for a long time at the two kings that lay side by side in front of her and could not shake the idea that the second king corresponded to the first not only in position (they were each the first card in their respective columns), but also in meaning. The King of Hearts in column one clearly represented Otis. What did it mean that the King had now gone dark? The two were polar opposites: one red as lifeblood, one black as ash; one looking left, the other right; one with empty hands, the other grasping a sword. If both kings represented Otis, past and present, then what did it mean? A change in the man? A fall from light into darkness?

And why? Because he lost his job and had to take another that was below his skill set and pay band? Because he was battling his diabetes and probably sleep deprived from all the shift work? Because then some drugged-out asshole jumped him in a parking lot? It was bad, but was it bad enough to alter the pattern of the man's life?

Next card: the Two of Spades for separation and the breakdown of a relationship, possibly infidelity. Tammany shook her head. She couldn't imagine Otis cheating. He and Nola were the "old marrieds" of the neighborhood, always together. Every week he strolled into *Tommy's Flowers* over on Dumaine to buy her a bouquet of the white and purple stocks she loved. And the way he looked at her...

She quickly turned over the last card in column two. Eight of Spades — temptation, misfortune or danger. The reading was just getting worse.

Column three and she turned over the first card, hoping to see another king (of clubs perhaps) to suggest that Otis would come through his troubles in the future. It was the Queen of Spades. A divorced or widowed woman. Which? Next came the Ace of Spades for death or a bad ending. And finally the Four of Hearts for travel or a change of home.

Tammany rested her head in her hands. It was a grim message that foretold the dissolution of a marriage either by illness and death or by infidelity. And she was going to tell Nola none of it. She might be wrong. The loa know all the affairs of men, but that didn't mean that Tammany's interpretation was correct.

"Well?" Nola was peeking in through the kitchen doorway.

Gathering up the cards Tammany said, "You're right to be concerned. If I'm correct, then he is ill and not thinking very clearly, but he's alive."

"But *where* is he?"

"Honey, I don't know. There are other things we can try, though." She dropped the pack of cards into her purse and fished out a notebook and pencil. "I need to go home and get a little sleep. Come on over to mine at ten-thirty. In the meantime, I need you to pick up a few things." While she spoke she made a short list which she tore out of the notebook and handed to Nola.

The woman read it aloud: "St. Anthony's candle, sage incense …"

"… if they don't have that, then cedar or sandalwood incense would do just as well. Just hand the list to Marie over at *Carmel and Sons*. She'll sort you out." She gave Nola a tight hug and headed home.

By the time Tammany got there and fished her newspaper out of the bushes, she was tired and cranky; and while she was about to go to sleep, the purpose of the nap was not to rest. One of the truest forms of communication with the loa was the act of dreaming. Contrary to Freudian theory, vodouisants believe that dreams do not come from the mind of the dreamer. They express no subconscious wish nor do they grapple with the impulses of the psyche. Dreams come from without, from the loa who use the dream-space as a middle ground where pure spirit and human mind can meet and communicate. Furthermore, dreams are not seen as a separate realm of experience that can be fictionalized as nonsense and dismissed. They are considered to be as real and as relevant as anything encountered in waking life. Adam M. McGee described this beautifully in his 2012 article, *Dreaming in Haitian Vodou*: "Vodou is ultimately a dreamed religion, lived half in dreams and half awake — in much the way that a halved symmetrical object, placed against a mirror will be uncannily made whole, although half of it be immaterial."

While these dreams could come spontaneously any night of the week, in urgent cases there were things you could do to help them along. Tammany pushed her old iron bed aside and with a groan knelt on the bare floorboards beneath. Her knees immediately lodged a protest and so she tried to work fast, taking a handful of cornmeal and sprinkling it onto the floor. She sat back and surveyed her work. It was unsatisfactory. The cornmeal was supposed to have formed the sign of the crossroads, essentially looking like a neat plus sign. But while the vertical line which represents the realm of the loa was straight, the horizontal one (for the world of men) was on a downward slant and the crucial point of intersection was smudged. She wiped out the design and started again. With the crossroads finally clearly depicted, she struggled to her feet and pulled the bed back into place.

Next she hobbled into the kitchen and took a purple candle and a bottle of greenish-brown oil from the cupboard. Onto the candle she carved the word "Yah" for Yahweh.

"You must never forget to center God in all you do." Grandma Eula, who had taught her about the loa, had repeated this crucial rule many times. It is a part of the faith that few outsiders comprehend. Voodoo is like gumbo, a great mix of different things. And central to it is its connection with the Bon Dieu — the Good God of Moses, who led his people out of slavery. While some are uncomfortable with a melting-pot religion that sees African spirits and Catholic saints on the same altar, still many vodouisants identify themselves as Christian. Marie Laveau, the Voodoo Queen of New Orleans, had been a devout Catholic and that was a good thing. There is great power in the spirits and great influence over the community. It should only be wielded by someone who loves the Light.

With the rough letters carved into the candle, she unscrewed the stopper from the bottle. Her nose was hit by a heady blend of spices: the warm, sweet smell of cinnamon, the nutty aroma of cardamom, a hint of licorice that was in fact anise and the lemony smell of coriander. These had been added to a jojoba base to form "Aunt Sally's Dream Oil." She anointed both the candle and her own forehead with it.

As she placed the candle on her nightstand, she murmured, "The Lord is my shepherd; I shall not want. He maketh me to lie down in green pastures…" When finished with this recitation of Psalm 23, she lit the candle and prayed to God to show her where Otis was and what had happened to him. She lay down and within minutes the exhausted old woman fell asleep.

Tammany is at Temple.[1] It is a huge hall that is obviously run by some powerful and influential mambo. She herself was never "big-time" enough

---

1   Vodouisants always recount their dreams in the present tense.

to have a place like this —large and ornate and filled with followers and initiates. She is a "home-grown" mambo, who learned in her grandmother's kitchen and tends only to her friends and neighbors.

Inside, initiates are dancing to a rolling drumbeat that is pitched low, rumbling like distant thunder. The white-clad bodies move in unison around the center post, the potomitan. Every body, whether young and lean or old and ample, moves lithely to the drum and it is beautiful to see. But there is one island in this sea of motion — one who is not dancing. Sitting on the floor in the corner is Zeline, a woman who lives three doors down from Tammany.

She's harmless but not the mambo's favorite person in all the world — too frivolous, too concerned with her clothes and makeup and nails. There's always too much of it all. Eyeshadow and lipstick applied with a spatula, her skirt and jacket a bright pink, and too much bling — gold rings, gold chains, gold bracelets. It always made Tammany want to open a dictionary in front of her and point out the meaning of the word "subtlety" in the hope that she might take the hint. But there is nothing subtle about Zeline. As the local gossip, she opened every conversation with the phrase, "Have *I*. Got *news*. For *you*."

But today Zeline looks different. Her glad rags have been replaced with denim overalls and her intricate coiffure is squashed under a straw hat. Instead of her normal choice of eye-wateringly high stilettos, she is barefoot. Incongruities such as these are common in dreams. You see someone you know, but they are different somehow. They are dressed differently or act out of character and you know that that is really a loa who stands before you. They may appear in the guises of your friends or neighbors, but they always give you clues to their true identity. An outfit, an item they carry, a way of talking, a mannerism — they can employ all of these things and more to make sure you know exactly who you are talking to.

In this case it is Azaka, a loa of farms and agriculture, who sits before Tammany in his dungarees though he'll speak through Zeline's mouth. Indeed she is an apt choice of cheval (literally the "horse" the loa rides). Azaka is a gossip too. *Good*, the mambo thinks, *he knows everybody's business. He'll know where Otis is.*

"Good morning, cousin." You must always address a loa politely.

Azaka makes no response.

Tammany kneels down beside him and wouldn't you just know it: her knees are killing her even here in this place.

She asks, "Would you like some?" As is possible in dreams, Tammany's hands are suddenly full. She is holding a tray laden with coffee and corn cakes smothered in cane syrup — all Azaka's favorites, all presented as an offering.

Zeline sadly shakes her head but says nothing.

The mambo is suddenly uneasy. This is not right. Azaka never turns down a meal. Ever.

She tries again. "Zaka, you know where Otis is, please —"

The loa throws up a hand to silence her. Tammany is surprised to see that it is trembling. Zeline's face is uncharacteristically pale, her mouth drawn into a tight line, her eyes glazed and staring. She mumbles, "Just … just go dance with the others."

Tammany is deeply troubled by this. A hungry, talkative loa who will neither eat nor speak is highly unusual, but a frightened, visibly distressed one… What the hell could frighten pure spirit?

She has so many questions, but Azaka has told her what he wants her to do. Obediently, she struggles to her feet and steps onto the dance floor.

The song is *Po' Drapeaux* with two drums that manage to beat steadily while also rolling in syncopated snatches of rhythm. An asson rattle shakes in time with the drums, occasionally accelerating to sound like an angry rattlesnake. Female voices sing in harmony, then in dissonance. And this mix of fluctuating sound should be a cacophony, a mess impossible to dance to. Yet it all fits together and sounds right. Tammany steps to the beat, shoulders pulsing in time. She and another woman (Mabel from the Post Office) bend and the mambo's right hand clasps the woman's left. They lift these and twirl — now back-to-back, still holding on, they shimmy. They unwind, embrace and dance away from each other. Giving herself over to the dance, Tammany closes her eyes and moves. Somehow she manages not to bump into anyone in the crowded room, but she can smell them all around her. Human sweat and Florida Water cologne — a mix of roses, lavender and jasmine with the heavier, muskier smell of vodka that goes to her head as if she'd been drinking it. She is starting to feel good: young, lithe, and happy. She is here, with her neighbors, dancing for her loa.

But then the drumming falters. The tight rhythm loses its cohesion as the song begins to unravel. Tammany's eyes snap open. Around her the dancers jerk awkwardly. At first she thinks that they're trying to keep time with the stuttering drums, but soon she realizes that they're convulsing. Mabel is holding her head as if in great pain. Dropping to her knees, she pulls the white scarf from her head and clutches it in trembling fists. She is changing. Tammany watches in horror as the woman's eyes roll back in their sockets and her features shift. Her wide, flat nose juts forward into an animal-like muzzle. Her full lips shrink back into a thin, grimacing line. And her beautiful mahogany skin grows livid and pale. It takes a moment for the mambo to identify the animal that now writhes before her. A bobcat.

"What the actual *fuck?*" she hisses as she backs away.

She bumps into someone else: a man, but not a man, a fox that fixes her with hostile, vindictive eyes. All around her they are changing. Into wildcats, coyotes, alligators — predators all. And Tammany is running for the Temple door as teeth snap and claws reach for her.

Tammany woke up drenched with sweat. She ran her hands over her quilt to reassure herself that she was back, safe in her bedroom, and not still in that horrible place. For the first time since she was a little girl she had dreamt of the Baka. The Baka were demons from local folklore and were a bit like werewolves. They could be anyone, any smiling friend or neighbor that you met on a daylit street. But at night they changed into animals and their animal nature did not know you. They'd rip you to pieces.

Unlike the loa, however, the Baka *weren't real.* They were bogeymen, the stuff of children's nightmares. So why on earth was she seeing them now? Why wouldn't Azaka eat the food she offered or answer her questions? And what good could she hope to do in the face of something that frightened a loa? As her thoughts began to spiral downward, she suddenly got very angry. She hated that hopeless voice that whispered, *It's too big. Don't even try.* Frankly, it pissed her off.

She rose, washed her face, and got ready for Nola.

The rest of Tammany's morning was spent in the living room of her tiny shotgun house. There she had an altar to the loa — a beautiful old dresser with ample space on top for whatever a ceremony required and plenty of drawers beneath to store supplies. She installed Nola in her comfiest chair with a cup of tea and then got down to work. The mambo tried everything she could think of to find Otis. She lay a recovery spell and then another designed to make a man come home. She used St. Anthony's Oil with its good, wholesome scents of coffee and sugar and rum and prayed to the saint because he, as the orison goes, was "ever ready to speak for those in trouble." When the work was done, she sent Nola home with a hug and collapsed into the chair.

It was still warm from her friend and this, unfortunately, was not the only thing of Nola's that lingered. Tammany felt her friend's torment as sharply as if it was her own. That awful mix of fear and confusion, the sense that a well-built life was crumbling to pieces, the loneliness and the questions … it was too much. Grandma Eula had warned her many times about being too empathetic: "You can help them," she'd said, "and pray for them and support them. But if you suffer with them, child, you will go crazy." She was right, of course, and so Tammany rose, shook her head to clear it and turned her mind to what she needed to do next.

There was a lot of food on the altar, an offering to Papa Legba so that the old man of the crossroads would permit the loa to come and help with the work. She'd lined up his favorite foods: grilled meat and vegetables as well as chocolate and coconut treats. Having missed her breakfast, she was hungry and looked longingly at the plate. But this food was not for her. The only proper way to dispose of it was to give it to someone in need. So she packed up the meal, headed down Dumaine Street and cut across Louis Armstrong Park. There she found George, an old homeless man, singing for change at his regular spot near the Buddy Bolden Statue. He was in his groove with "I Ain't Superstitious" so Tammany caught his eye, held up the paper bag and placed it on the old man's coat. He gave her an elaborate, flourishing bow of thanks.

The rest of the mambo's day was filled with a stream of clients who needed advice in matters of love or help finding a job. She had a few home remedies to prepare and what amounted to a counseling session with Twyla White, who came to her in tears when her monthly bleed signaled the failure of her IVF treatments. As she ushered the last of them out the door, she noticed a handsome young white boy sitting on her front stoop.

"Can I help you?"

"Sorry. I don't have an appointment, but I was wondering if you could fit me in today?"

Tammany looked at her watch and sighed. "All right, come on in."

She led him into her kitchen and started rummaging around in one of the cupboards. The young man looked on with great interest, wondering what voodoo paraphernalia she would use as part of the session. Words cannot describe his disappointment when she pulled out a packet of Fig Newtons.

She popped one into her mouth. "Want one?" she asked with her mouth full.

"Uh, no thanks. Is ... is this how most voodoo readings start?"

She took a big drink of milk and shook her head. "Only the ones I have to do when I'm tired."

She sat down at the table and beckoned him to do likewise. "So what's your name?"

"Daniel Wade."

"Hello, Daniel Wade. What can I do for you today?"

"I was hoping for a general reading."

"For?"

"What do you mean?"

Tammany shrugged. "Is there a particular question you have or a problem you need help with or..." she paused and looked at him. He sat there smiling at her and it was an open, friendly smile. But there was a guarded expression in the young man's eyes. He was dubious about all this. "Or is it a test?"

He blushed.

The mambo's response was good-natured. "What exactly are you looking for? Proof that this works?"

"I'm a writer. I am working on a book on Voodoo in the United States and in order to fully understand it, I thought I should have a few readings done."

"Fair enough. So you just want me to — what? — tell you about you?"

"Yes, please."

"Ok," she said as she shuffled the cards.

She explained the configuration: the columns for past, present and future and then flipped over the first card.

"Seven of Spades. It usually indicates loss." Another card. "Seven of

Clubs suggesting business or financial success, but perhaps difficulties in love. You said you're a writer. Most writers I know are dirt poor. You the exception?"

"My first book — it was on modern day vampire culture — did very well. A New York Times bestseller," he nodded.

"Is there a Mrs. Wade? Someone to share all that success with?"

"No."

"That's a shame." She turned over another card. "Yeah, see? The Jack of Hearts for a warm-hearted man." She gestured to the three cards lying face up on the table. "All the cards can tell me about your past is that you suffered some great loss …"

"So has everybody." The friendly smile was gone.

"It's the first thing the loa have to say about you. It is a defining loss. And my guess is that, while it doesn't stand in the way of your commercial success, it does interfere with your relationships. Do you know why that is?"

"You tell me."

"Sweetheart, it's a deck of playing cards, not an all access pass to your brain. I just figured that a lot of people have trust issues after they've been burned."

Daniel was on his feet. He was so angry, so outraged it brought tears to his eyes. "Well, you've obviously read about *that*!"

"What?" she asked.

"About the … the fire."

"Daniel, I didn't know you were coming to see me. I had no time to prepare for this session. I don't read the gossip columns and I haven't googled you. Until two minutes ago, I'd never heard of your werewolf book…"

"Vampire book…"

"Whatever. If you don't trust me, we don't have to continue with this."

"You really didn't know?"

"Child, my best guess was that you'd been jilted. If I'd known that there'd been some terrible fire…" she sighed heavily, "I never would have used the word 'burned.' If you want to go, please do. But if you want to stay, I'll finish the reading free of charge."

He looked at her for a long time. He'd encountered and exposed many charlatans and liars in this business. But if she was willing to continue without payment … well, it was a sign she might be on the level.

"I'm going to make a cup of tea." She rose and busied herself at the counter. "Want one?"

"Why would you continue without payment?"

"That look on your face just now. If I could ignore that, I wouldn't be a mambo."

She carried a tray over to the table and poured him a cup. "Did you drive here?"

"No, I took the bus."

"Good," she said and added a generous measure of bourbon to his mug. Settling back into her chair she said, "Now. Do you want to talk about the fire? Or should I just carry on with the cards."

"It's not like it's a big secret…"

The house had been a wooden two-story colonial in the historic district of Kennett Square, Pennsylvania. The family was in bed and the Christmas tree glowed with those old string lights with replaceable colored bulbs. That's where the blaze started and it was hungry. It licked at the carpet and consumed the sofa which emitted poisonous dark smoke. And then the fire was at the walls and the door and up the stairs.

If the family — which was now wide awake thanks to the high-pitched shrieking of the smoke alarm — had gotten out then … well, Daniel had tortured himself with the what ifs for years. *If* he, as a four-year-old child, had run to his parents' room instead of hiding from the fire. *If* his panicked father had stopped to look under the mound of teddy bears in the closet where he hid. *If* they'd remembered to turn the damn tree lights off in the first place. All such little decisions, little omissions that became so big in consequence.

Firefighters hauled them out — all three of them — and the Chester County Press reported that paramedics worked feverishly to save them. Joanne Wade was pronounced dead at the scene and Franklin R. Wade died on his way to the hospital. The article was accompanied by the picture of a child, sitting in an ambulance, wrapped in a blanket. His face was a mask of black smudges and streaks of gray ash. His whole world had just imploded and this certainly warranted a good howl. But he was struck dumb. He sat there in such unnatural stillness that he looked more like a mannequin or a doll, than a living breathing boy.

That boy, now a grown man, was sitting in Tammany's kitchen, the effort of telling even this truncated version of the story making him nauseous.

"It must be a hard time of year for you," Tammany said quietly.

"It always starts after Halloween, when all the Christmas decorations appear in the shops and there's the Black Friday sales and fucking snow."

"What starts?"

Wade shook his head. "I don't even have a word for it."

The silence that followed was long and heavy and Tammany knew that he needed a nudge to get him talking about what was on his mind. She turned over another card. Ten of Hearts.

"What does that mean?" he asked.

"Success after difficulty," she paused, "or maybe because of it."

"How do you mean?"

"I just wondered whether or not you found the writing to be therapeutic."

"It is. When I'm working, I'm just away. I'm somewhere else."

"And some*one* else?"

"No, I don't have the burden of *being* anybody. At its best, it's like the book writes itself; it just flows through me and I'm in another world."

"That's probably why you've done so well."

"Yeah, but then I have to stop or someone talks to me or asks me a question and then my brain — it's like having spontaneous Alzheimer's. I'm just not all there." Daniel leaned forward, keen to explain something he'd never articulated before. "I can work on the book for ten hours straight and be surprised when I look up and see what time it is. But at my worst, I can't pay attention to what someone else is saying to me for more than ten minutes. Because by then, I realize I'm back in reality and it *sucks* and I get this sick, empty feeling as if someone has reached into my gut and just ripped out my stomach and my lungs. And all I have left is this gaping black hole. And I'm afraid and there is nothing to be afraid of and that's worse because it is so vague. It is a fear of nothing and everything — a whole world of terrible possibility. And then I don't sleep and I feel like I'm losing my mind. But I'm sane and I'm smart. And yet I look at the calendar and can't remember the day, the actual *date*, my parents died. It was the single most significant day of my life and I can't remember."

"You can't remember, child, because that's a common symptom of PTSD."

"What?"

"Joseph Turnbull, Wanda's boy from the grocery store, came back from Afghanistan with it. He has trouble remembering too." She pushed the cards aside and took hold of his hands. "You don't need a card reading, Daniel. You need counseling so someone can guide you through this. They say that, um, CBT — that Cognitive Behavioral Therapy — is meant to be real good."

She fished a clean tissue out of her pocket and handed it to him.

"I'm sorry," he mumbled, drying his eyes.

"No need."

He made a brave attempt at laughter. "I was supposed to be here learning about voodoo."

"But Daniel," she gave his hand another squeeze, "you just did."

They parted as friends with plans to meet up again in a day or two. He wanted to interview Tammany about Voodoo and life as a mambo. She was about to put the cards away when she realized that she never did finish his reading. Out of dumbness, she turned over the last two cards in column two: the Six of Hearts for a stroke of good luck and the Queen of Hearts for the appearance of a good-natured woman, a motherly figure. She chuckled. The loa knew her too well. She was always collecting strays and people in trouble and there was no way she could listen to that man's story and not want to help him.

The future cards in column three, however, wiped the smile off her face. There it was again, the Nine of Spades for illness and bad luck. The Eight of Spades came next with its warning of danger and finally another of the same suit, the Ace. Those three cards had also come up in Otis's reading, and to see them twice in one day was yet another bad sign in a day filled with omens. There was clearly danger here for Daniel Wade and she resolved to do something about that.

But first, she needed a break. And so she went through her daily unwinding ritual. This one, however, did not involve burning candles, anointing with oil or praying to the spirits. No, it consisted of a nice crisp newspaper, her Lazy-Boy New Hampshire Power Recliner Armchair, and an ice-cold bottle of *Grace and Grit* beer. That's a craft beer distilled by the Great Raft Brewing Company and Tammany bought a couple of cases of it every summer when it went on sale. She took a swig, savoring the earthy dankness with its hints of pineapple and mango. But then she opened the paper and choked on her drink.

The headline read: "Local Man Found Dead" and all Tammany could think was "Don't be Otis, don't be Otis, don't be Otis…" She quickly scanned the article: a local man, identified as Alan Tisono (*oh thank Christ!*) was found tangled up in the cattails along the bank of the London Avenue Canal. A spokesman for the NOPD announced that Mr. Tisono had been the victim of a violent attack and appealed for any witnesses who were in the area on Wednesday morning between two and six a.m. Tammany exhaled loudly and waited for her heartbeat to slow back down to normal.

She turned the page. Next there was an article about a teacher at Benjamin Franklin High who was hit and killed by a truck. Witnesses claimed that, in the moments prior to the accident, she had not only looked "unwell" but had deliberately stepped out in front of the vehicle. A source at the school noted that Miss Emily Hardy had been off ill from her post since returning from a short holiday to the Caribbean. The coroner was expected to hold an inquest into the apparent suicide and the police were particularly keen to locate her boyfriend, a Mr. Nicholas Durand, who has been missing since Monday night.

Below this was an article entitled, "Trouble in Paradise," detailing a series of disturbing events on a tiny island called Cáscara:

> "To stand on the cliffs and look out over the glittering blue of the Caribbean is to stand for a moment in paradise." So reads the holiday brochure inviting visitors to Cáscara, "an oasis of calm in a busy world." However, this quiet little island off the coast of Puerto Rico has recently suffered a catalogue of problems threatening its vital tourism industry.
>
> Since the disruption caused by Hurricane Hildy late last month, Cáscara has been hit by an alarming rabies outbreak among wildlife and local pets alike. Local veterinarian, Carlos Báez, is pursuing legal action against Lyndo Pharmaceuticals who manufacture the vaccine he administered to the island's pets. "It was obviously a bad batch,"

he said, "because so many animals who received that vaccine have contracted rabies. These are not stray, neglected dogs. They are beloved members of many families. It has been heartbreaking to see."

The outbreak has resulted in many attacks on people who report that their docile animals "just turned on them." A spokesman for Cáscara General Hospital confirmed that they have treated an elevated number of animal-related injuries, including a case in which a child suffered 'life-changing injuries' after being mauled by her family's pet. The most shocking incident, however, was a wild animal attack on local coffee grower, Juan Valdez, who died of his wounds. This has led to an island-wide cull of stray dogs and cats and a program to revaccinate all pets. However, it is as yet unclear as to whether these measures have finally tackled the problem.

And it would appear that the animals are not the only ones falling ill. A strange flu-like epidemic has recently hit the island. While some locals suspect that this may be the result of contaminated drinking water after the hurricane, Mayor Louisa Gaultiero has dismissed this, citing the rigorous safeguards they place on their water supply. She has, however, arranged for the CDC to come and review the situation. In the meantime, the local hospital has been inundated with patients complaining of fever, sore throats, headaches and, in some cases, seizures. Among the stricken is prominent American neurosurgeon, Dr. Aaron Pickman, formerly of Bangor, Maine…

CHAPTER TWO

CÁSCARA

"Even a single outbreak … can go global. In addition, although the zombie plague is only spread through biting or other fluidic transfers, the infection rate is 100 percent. Even powerful disease vectors like smallpox or influenza have infection rates that are considerably lower. Because the zombie contagion is so powerful, its cross-border spread is a near-certainty."

Daniel W. Drezner,
Theories of International Politics and Zombies

"Time is of the essence. We must act now if we are to have the maximum possible opportunity to contain a pandemic."

Margaret Chan

Dr. Edwin Caldwell stared at his patient in open-mouthed disbelief. As a field investigator for the CDC, he thought he had seen it all: Ebola patients bleeding from the eyes, the buboes of a plague victim bursting at his touch, and spontaneous miscarriages brought on by Lassa fever. But he had not been expecting this. The initial report, passed to him by the EOC, had cited a suspected outbreak of H1N1 on the island of Cáscara. The working case definition he'd been handed had read:

100

Clinical Case Definition
An illness presenting with fever, persistent cough, sore throat, muscular
pain, shortness of breath, headache, chills, dizziness, loss of appetite,
nausea and fatigue. Current H1N1 global mortality rates suggest that
the infirm will be less likely to recover from the disease and generally
succumb a few days after the onset of symptoms.

Laboratory Criteria for Diagnosis
A positive respiratory sample (nose and throat swab).

Therefore, he'd headed off to the Caribbean ready to implement the same
protocols he'd used in Northern Ireland in 2009. He had doctors on hand
to care for the critically ill; he had flu shots ready to protect the local
population with special emphasis on vaccinating new mothers and the
immunocompromised. All he needed was a positive set of lab results and
he could run with the plan. But the best laid plans of mice and men often
go awry.

On his tour of Cáscara General Hospital, he had indeed seen people
with the flu-like symptoms described. Then Dr. Emmanuel Malavé had
taken him to see "the more advanced cases." One, Pablo Vasquez, had
slipped his restraints and was pacing around a room that the nurses now
refused to enter. Standing at the door, Caldwell peered through a window
streaked with blood and bile. He knelt down to peek through a clear
section of glass and saw Vasquez, bare-chested and wearing a soiled pair
of jeans. Clawing at a bleeding wound on his cheek, the man babbled and
screamed. He caught sight of Caldwell and charged at the door, slamming
into it with enough force to make it rattle on its hinges.

"Why didn't you include the behavioral symptoms in your report to
the CDC?" Edwin asked quietly.

"Originally, everything we saw looked like swine flu. And then…" Dr.
Malavé paused and cleared his throat.

"And then?"

"When the infected became aggressive, Mayor Gaultiero decided to
get a CDC diagnosis before making the facts public."

"Why?"

"Oh come on, doctor. With the current climate in the U.S., would
you want to release footage like this?" He gestured at the door. "Just more

crazy Hispanics and bad hombres, right? They'll take one look at our friend in there and think it's drug-related. And it's not. The toxicology report on ninety percent of the cases came back clean."

"And nasal swabs did not test positive for H1N1."

"No."

"So that leaves us with the $64,000 Question: just what the hell is it?"

The real detective work began with a detailed history of every one of the infected and a list of the people they'd come into contact with during the last two weeks. It appeared that the disease had already produced multiple generations of victims. The latest group of infected (Generation Four) all had contact with the earliest human cases. These interactions ranged from sexual contact to breast feeding to violent altercations, but in every instance the newly infected had received some fluidic transfer from a carrier of the disease. These were essentially the victims of victims. The story behind Generation Three chilled Caldwell to the bone. Each of these patients had previously been treated for an animal bite. As the island was in the grip of a rabies outbreak, each of them had received the standard Post-Exposure Prophylaxis that would have protected them from developing full-blown neurological rabies. And yet each had developed the flu-like symptoms and aggression of a lyssavirus infection. He ordered lumbar punctures across the board. If they came back positive, then the rabid dogs were clearly Generation Two. A trawl of the veterinary clinic's records confirmed that each of the infected dogs had been brought in for stitches after tangling with some unknown vector, a wild animal and presumably Generation One.

As a CDC physician, Caldwell could quote its *Principles of Epidemiology* chapter and verse. In it, in Lesson 6 to be precise, you will find the guidelines for identifying possible bioweapon exposure. The two criteria that stood out for him at the moment were: 1) "Unusual disease presentation" and 2) "Unusual pattern of death or illness among animals that precedes or accompanies illness or death in humans." There was a clear link here between the sick animals and the sick people. And while high levels of aggression were common in cases of human rabies, the behavior he was witnessing on Cáscara was off the charts. He had never seen human beings respond this violently to the pathogen. Every patient was in a frenzy of unabating rage. Many of them should, by now, be too ill to continue and yet they showed no signs of slowing down. It wasn't natural. It was just ... all wrong.

But was it bioterrorism? The locals certainly thought so. Rumors flew of the gringo's "secret lab" where he was apparently brewing up some doomsday virus. The gringo, Dr. Aaron Pickman, was unavailable for comment. He was currently lashed to a bed in the isolation ward, screaming.

Caldwell was about to pursue this line of inquiry when Sheriff Abran Manolito requested an urgent meeting. He was a harried-looking man in his early forties, with dark circles under his eyes; and he was quite clumsy — probably, Edwin guessed, due to stress and fatigue. The sheriff, his arms full of brown folders and lugging an old cooler, left a trail of paper down the hall behind him.

"Take a minute, Sheriff, to get organized," Caldwell said as he gathered up the errant paperwork.

"Sorry, things have been crazy."

"So I gathered." The doctor led him to an empty office that had been set aside for his use and Manolito went immediately to the desk to sort the sheets of paper back into their respective piles.

"Right," he said. "Have you heard of a Dr. Aaron Pickman?"

"I've seen him."

"Then you know he's beyond the point where he can give us any useful information."

"Yes, but what information *did* he have? I've heard all kinds of wild rumors, stuff straight out of Frankenstein. Does he or does he not have any bearing on this outbreak?"

"I think he's the cause of it."

"You think..."

"This," he handed Caldwell the first folder, "is all of the information we have on his immigration status and the rental agreement he signed with the U.S. military for the old airbase on the north side of the island."

"Why was he renting an airbase?"

"It's derelict. He turned it into a medical research lab, although we did not know that initially."

"Right."

"This," Manolito handed him a second folder, "is the first time he appeared on my radar. It is a report filed by two tourists at the end of October who heard terrible screams coming from Pickman's facility."

"Screams?"

"Animal screams."

"Did you search the premises?"

"Two hikers hearing a noise in the rainforest isn't enough to get a search warrant. So I drove out there, spoke to Pickman and acquainted him with our animal welfare laws."

"What did he say?"

"That he kept rabid dogs at the facility. He said he was studying the disease."

There it was: rabies again. It emerged that the recent rabies outbreak on the island occurred after the hurricane damaged Pickman's lab. Manolito was rattling through the facts quickly now: the four escaped monkeys, the fire that gutted the lab and the hunt in which he managed to kill three of the four escaped animals.

Caldwell eyed the cooler. "Please tell me that's one of the monkeys."

"Not one of the first three. Those we incinerated because we were still working under the assumption that they were merely rabid. This is the fourth monkey. I found the carcass today down by the docks."

"Do you know what killed it?"

"No, but when we found him, he looked like this." Manolito handed him a photo of a dead rhesus macaque in the early stages of decomposition.

"He's chewed up," Caldwell murmured.

"We think rats got at the body post-mortem."

"Rats," Caldwell could not keep his voice from rising. "Rats down by the dock. How many ships have left here within the last couple of days?"

Sheriff Abran Manolito looked at him with haunted eyes. "My deputy is compiling a list right now."

Edwin placed the island under quarantine and four U.S. frigates were en route to patrol the coastline. Cáscara, however, was only part of the problem. He had a team working with the sheriff's department to trace every boat that had left the island within the last two weeks. And now he turned his mind to the tourists. The Caribbean had just come out of its hurricane season and hence visitor numbers had been down. However, with the *Our Lady of Guadalupe Festival* and the *Festival de la Luz* over Christmas, tourist numbers had increased during the outbreak period. He now had to track every single one of them down.

Not only had a significant number of people dispersed from Cáscara, but information was leaking out as well. A colleague at the EOC forwarded an article to him from the *dailymail.co.uk*. It sported the headline: "Wounded man with gaping facial wound appears to be 'possessed by the devil' as he terrifies hospital staff." It was accompanied by a grainy picture of Pablo Vasquez, stalking around his room with that weird backward-leaning gait of his. The vacant, almost soulless look on the man's face was so pitiful that it was almost mesmerizing.

A soft tap on the door startled Edwin out of these thoughts.

"Sorry to disturb you," his assistant Janine entered and handed him a file.

"The preliminary lab results on the monkey?"

"Yeah," she said, "but we still don't have the full picture."

"Thanks." He flipped through the papers. It *was* rabies. And it wasn't. The RNA strands of the virus included too many lines of genetic information. The pathogen had been greatly altered. Dr. Pickman seemed to have given it an upgrade and, in the process, created something entirely new.

"Possible criteria for bioterrorism, number three," he muttered. "'Unusual, atypical, or genetically engineered strain of an agent.'"

He glanced again at the Daily Mail article. Vasquez looked horrific. His skin was waxy, his foam-covered teeth were bared and his eyes were a black nothingness. He *did* look like a demon from hell. Or a zombie.

"This, ladies and gentlemen, is the face of the new outbreak."

CHAPTER THREE

NEW ORLEANS

"I pray you all give your audience,
And hear this matter with reverence,
By figure a moral play —
The Summoning of Everyman called it is,
That of our lives and end shows
How transitory we be."

Medieval Morality Play, <u>Everyman</u>

"Hippocrates introduced the case history, a description of the natural history
of disease…but they tell us nothing about the individual and his history; they
convey nothing of the person as he faces, and struggles to survive, his disease."

Oliver Sacks, <u>The Man Who Mistook His Wife for a Hat</u>

Emily Hardy's body lay on a table in the morgue while the coroner examined her injuries and recorded his findings onto an audio file. The cause of death in this instance was hardly a mystery. The occipital bone at the back of her head was the only bone in her skull left intact. Her skull had been fractured in a dozen places and the resulting brain damage was too complicated to fully catalogue.

"List the cause of death as catastrophic trauma to the brain. The neck is broken at the second cervical vertebrae. A preliminary scan of the torso and limbs shows massive bruising and a wound, partially healed, on her right hand. It appears to be a human bite mark."

As the autopsy continued, he identified internal injuries and broken bones. The catalogue of damage was so severe and so extensive that he paused and took a deep breath. Usually he could remain wholly detached during a post-mortem, but this was just relentlessly grim. And she'd done it to herself.

"What on earth were you dealing with that prompted you to choose *this?*"

Emily Hardy had sat on the old battered couch in her apartment and watched the clock. She had a hell of a fever. A moment ago she'd been so hot, she could not abide even the weight of her nightgown on her skin. Now she was freezing and had wrapped herself in an old fleece blanket. Her throat was on fire and her thudding head made her feel nauseous. But she had bigger problems than a case of seasonal flu.

It was two o'clock in the morning and Nick hadn't come home yet. He never stayed away from her like this. But then, they were doing a lot of things they had never done before. They were snapping at each other and fighting over nonsense. She'd gotten so angry with him earlier that she actually took a swipe at him. She had hooked her hand into a claw and slashed it across his arm. It landed about four inches below the other gouge, the one from that crazy lady on Cáscara. The woman had darted from the crowd at the Guadalupe parade and had sunk her teeth into Emily's hand. Nick had stepped in, pulled the woman off her and had gotten clawed up in the process. And now Emily was lashing out at him? Horrified and ashamed at her behavior, she'd run to her bedroom and cried herself to sleep. When she awoke, Nick was gone.

Where was he? She grabbed her phone and flipped through her contacts. Would he have gone to any of their friends? Or hit a bar? *Or met someone?* The insidious little voice that whispered that gem was also new. She'd never been afraid of him cheating on her before. But now she could not shake the feeling of distance between them, of strangeness. And with these thoughts swirling around and around in her head, she eventually drifted into an uneasy sleep. In her dreams, she was surrounded by people she knew (mom and dad and cousin Toby and her history teacher from high school), but she didn't really know them, did she? Because there, before her eyes, they were changing into animals and monsters and she ran and ran, all the while knowing that she was never going to be able to run far enough.

Nicholas Durand had walked away from the apartment building, and from Emily, as quickly as he could. His arm was still bleeding from where she scratched him and he was so angry that he literally shook with rage. If he didn't get away from her, he was going to pound her through the wall. He stopped abruptly. Where the fuck did that come from? He had never hit a woman in his life — *would never* hit a woman — and yet, God, he wanted to. This wasn't him. He was a good man and proud of that fact and so he picked up the pace, putting as much distance between himself and his girlfriend as he could.

He dove into a bar, *The Chart Room*, but it was so hot and crowded that he bought a Budweiser and took it outside. The scattering of tables under blue awnings were all occupied and so he sat down on the curb and took a long swig of beer. His throat instantaneously rebelled and passersby gave him a wide berth as he choked and spluttered. God, his throat hurt. He really did not feel well and had just made up his mind to go home. And that was when he saw the girl.

She was wearing a pair of painted-on blue jeans with a series of rips down the front that showed a hint of brown skin. A tight white shirt (no bra) was tied at her waist and her hair was piled up in a carefully constructed "do" that was meant to look casual and a little sloppy. She was smiling at him. He got up and went over to talk to her.

The talking bit did not go so well. Nicholas found that he was uncharacteristically tongue-tied. He kept losing words and having to stop and search for them before completing his sentences. Luckily the girl, who'd been drinking since three o'clock that afternoon, wasn't particularly eloquent herself. The two, however, did manage to communicate one essential thing to each other and they swiftly made their way down a side alley. They had barely gotten out of sight before Nick was fumbling with the button of her jeans. After a lot of frustrated tugging, he managed to peel the denim off her.

"You're eager," she laughed.

Then, without a kiss, a touch or a caress, he was inside of her. She'd dated a guy like this before — the type that just barrels in and so she shifted beneath him, drew her knees back and finally got him where she wanted him. And it was like fucking Tarzan. He was more animal than man and a group passing the alley laughed and applauded as she screamed and pulled him to her.

That scream and his own climax brought a moment of clarity to Nick. He looked at her, unsure of how he'd gotten there: physically inside a stranger in a back alley. *Emily. Oh my God, Emily.* He had just cheated on her and that was something else he thought he'd never do.

He rose quickly, pulled up his trousers and, without a word to the girl, walked away. He paced the streets, angry (again) but this time at himself. What the hell was wrong with him? Why all of a sudden was he being such a dick? And, dear God, why did he want to jump on every woman he passed on the street? The sight of an old dirty bag lady gave him a hard-on and he quickly crossed the street to avoid her because he didn't think he could stand the temptation.

What Nick did not, could not know in that moment was that he was infected with New Rabies. Unlike the old virus, it would not kill him, but it would treat him to all of the classic symptoms including aggression and hyper sexuality. According to the literature, the virus can kick the human libido into overdrive with some patients engaging in intercourse up to thirty times a day. The reason is simple: rabies concentrates heavily in bodily fluids and hence any form of exchange, erotic or violent, is merely a way to pass the virus on. This may account for an odd fact that greeted Durand when he got home. Emily was asleep on the couch; the blanket she was wrapped in had slipped down to reveal one naked breast and yet he was unmoved. Having lusted after every woman he saw on the walk home, the sight of his girlfriend meant nothing. The infected male looked upon the infected female and realized there was nothing for him to do there. He shrugged and headed off to bed.

Emily awoke the next morning, feeling groggy and sick. She saw Nick's shoes by the front door and went to look for him. He was passed out naked on their bed. Quietly, she picked up his discarded clothes with the vague idea of doing some laundry today. That is when she saw the lipstick on his collar. It was not the dusty rose color of her gloss, but a bright, garish red. Her balled fists shook as she stood there and watched him sleep. She wanted to kill him. But then she remembered her outburst of the night before — she wasn't herself. Wasn't thinking clearly. So she forced herself to walk away.

Nick surfaced two hours later and while she had planned to quiz him about last night, Emily found that she was too ill to bother. The pair spent the afternoon dozing on the living room couch, with the curtains drawn. When the phone rang, the answering machine picked it up and the principal of Benjamin Franklin High School inquired why she hadn't shown up for work today. To Emily his words were mere noise devoid of meaning. She shrugged and went back to sleep.

When night fell, Nicholas went out again. Emily dressed quickly. She would follow him this time and see what he got up to. But he didn't really *do* anything. Her boyfriend wandered aimlessly, occasionally stepping off the sidewalk and into traffic. Emily was not alarmed by this, but she was disturbed by the blare of car horns as they swerved to miss him. Nick shied away from the noise too, cutting down quieter streets and alleys. In this way, the pair weaved their way through the city, until their search for dark and quiet led them to a parking lot behind a big store.

"Listen pal," a large black man was saying to Nick, "a lot of trucks will be in and outta here tonight. It's really not safe for you to be here."

He said some other stuff too, but it was all just noise in Emily's ears and more than anything she just wanted to be in bed. She was about to head home, when her man — her good and gentle man — went for the stranger's throat. She watched, open-mouthed, as the two men fought, as Nick snarled and growled like a wild animal and as the stranger hit and bit him in a desperate attempt to break free. And in that moment she was two people. What was left of Emily Hardy was shocked and appalled not by the violence, but by her reaction to it. She knew she should be frightened; and the sight of Nick attacking this man should shake her to her very core. But that was not what she felt. She wanted to join in. Nick was not getting the job done, but while the stranger was distracted she could sneak in there and …

"Oh my God," she whispered and ran. As she fled the parking lot, she too was surrounded by temptation. She saw people all around her and she wanted to get right in there next to each of them and fasten her teeth on their flesh.

"What is the matter with me?" Her voice was a sob that caught the attention of a teenage boy nearby.

"Are you ok, lady?" he asked.

She ran away before she hurt him. She knew that she was sick and yet her mind rebelled at the thought of hospitals and doctors. She could not stand the idea of being touched and poked and prodded and having bright lights in her eyes. She just wanted to be somewhere dark and alone. But it was hard to be alone in New Orleans. It was a city of 400,000 people. How did she know that? She had a vision of teaching her students that fact and she knew that if she was with them right now, she'd tear their fucking throats out. *But you love those kids,* a quiet voice inside her insisted. Love, however, was something she could only dimly remember. And then she saw the truck. She stared at it as it advanced down the street and a little smile played across her lips. She waited for her moment and then stepped off the curb.

CHAPTER FOUR

READING, ENGLAND

*"'What a curious feeling!' said Alice. 'I must be shutting up like a telescope.'
And so it was indeed: she was now only ten inches high...she waited for
a few minutes to see if she was going to shrink any further: she felt a little
nervous about this; 'for it might end, you know...in my going out altogether,
like a candle. I wonder what I should be like then?' And she tried to fancy
what the flame of a candle is like after it is blown out, for she could not
remember ever having seen such a thing."*

Lewis Carroll, <u>Alice in Wonderland</u>

*"I was continuing to shrink, to become ... what? The infinitesimal? What
was I? Still a human being? Or was I the man of the future?"*

Scott Carey, <u>The Incredible Shrinking Man</u>, (1957 film)

Janet Howarth gave up waiting on the doctors at the local hospital
and returned home. The Accident and Emergency Department
of the Royal Berkshire had been absolutely heaving. A monitor on
the wall had informed her that, due to unusually high demand, there
was a five and a half hour wait. That was ridiculous even by normal
standards.

Yet as she rode the bus home, she wondered if she'd made a mistake. Her limbs were heavy and she was desperately tired. She was running a fever and each jerk as the bus braked for traffic made her feel sick. And she was inexplicably uneasy. It made no sense. She'd had flu before and had never rushed off to bother her GP with it. She'd just bought some Lemsip Max and let her own body fight it off. Hence, she could not understand why she had gone to A&E this time. She didn't want the doctors to think of her as some sort of hypochondriac. And they would, you know. Apparently they had little codes that they wrote on your chart and, if you bothered them with trivialities, you could be branded a TBP or 'total bloody pain.' And yet, despite her repugnance at making a fuss, she had gone to hospital and that decision was made, not by the sensible part of her brain, but by something nameless, some vague instinct that this illness was different. While her symptoms weren't exactly new or earth-shattering, she could not shake the feeling that there was something really wrong with her.

For some reason her mind kept going back to little Henry Milne. She looked after the neighbor's boy twice a week while his mum went to work; and last week the child had not been well.

"He's been poorly ever since we got back from holiday," his mother had said. "I don't know if it's jet lag or the antibiotics making him queasy or what." And Claire had launched into a tirade about some nutter at a parade. She showed Janet the boy's bandaged arm with exclamations of "She *bit* him! She *actually bit* him!" Then Claire, who was looking tired and oddly pale beneath her Caribbean tan, quickly ran out of steam.

She left Janet with spare bandages and some Calpol and the rest of that afternoon had been very quiet. Henry was tired and listless and hence very easy to look after. Janet just popped a *Thomas the Tank Engine* DVD in and curled up with him on the couch.

The trouble arose when she tried to get Henry ready to go home. The boy fussed and kicked his feet obstinately when she tried to put his shoes on him. By the time this task was finally accomplished, Henry had thrown himself on the floor and was mewling at her — a whining cry that grated on her ears.

"That's enough!" she said sharply and held out her hand to help him up.

And he bit her. Right on the hand. She told him off and marched him home in disgrace.

Days later, as she sat on the bus on the way home from the hospital, she scratched absently at the small wound on her hand and her head thudded in time with the beating of her heart.

Once home she made herself a cup of weak tea, slipped on her pyjamas and went to bed. She drifted in and out of sleep, her fevered dreams populated by monsters and a rolling blackness that kept pulling her under. At one point, Janet opened her eyes, surprised to find that her room was dark. She flicked on the bedside light and checked the clock — four-thirty a.m. She had slept for hours and hours but it hadn't done her any good; she was still exhausted. The fever burned through her, causing her to kick off her duvet. The next moment she was gripped with a chill so profound that she lay there shivering. And her head, dear God her head, pulsed with such pain she felt like she was being physically hit. She rolled over onto her side and tried to think about something else.

Her mother's old dresser took up most of the wall in front of her and on it were all of the things that her husband had bought her while away on business trips. It was an eclectic collection of souvenirs, but it was precious to her. Even when they were apart, he'd still been thinking of her. Could it be that now, though cancer had separated them irrevocably, he thought of her still? Was he somehow aware of her, watching over her, waiting for her?

The nearest item on the dresser was a set of five Russian dolls that George had brought back from St. Petersburg. The biggest doll was beautifully, yet subtly painted. Her body was yellow — not overly bright or jarring, but a mellow shade topped with a light brown kerchief. In her hands, she clutched a bouquet of three tulips and her face wore an expression of calm serenity. Janet could see why he bought the set, she was a lovely piece of folk art. However, he had failed to inspect the smaller dolls that nested inside her and these had been painted with a clumsier hand.

The artist had used a completely different pallet for doll number two. Her headscarf was a bright red and her coat was green. It was not a sickly shade — not a pea soup color, but it was not pleasant either. It was a dark and somewhat dirty hue that was only lifted by a yellow flower where each of her arms should have been. The doll's face had changed too. She still had the same pink bow of a mouth, but her expression was less serene.

Her eyebrows had been drawn with a thicker black line that made her look annoyed and maybe even a little afraid.

Doll three was in the same dark outfit, but again her face had changed. The light blush that had been applied to the second doll's cheeks was absent here, making her look waxy and sallow. She glared at Janet malevolently. The old woman had never noticed before that the doll looked seriously pissed off and just a little bit crazy.

The artist had dabbed pink onto the fourth doll's cheeks, but instead of a healthy blush, the rough circles of color looked more like fever spots. Her eyes were hooded, sunken and unutterably weary. It was the same look, Janet realized, that she had seen on her mother's face the day before she died — that "I'm already gone" look of the terminally ill.

Doll five was tiny and her dark green coat was unbroken by any adornment. Her face was all red lips and livid eyes that glared at Janet with strange, demented rage.

Her eyes grew heavy again. She slept and dreamt that the Russian dolls weren't actually five different girls rendered in painted bits of cheap limewood. Instead they represented five stages of decline in the life of a single woman. And *she* was that doll. At every step she got smaller, sicker, and darker. And like Alice in Wonderland, she was afraid that soon there would be nothing left of her at all, just a great absence, a candle flame that had been snuffed out.

CHAPTER FIVE

NEW ORLEANS

"Death is not the greatest loss in life. The greatest loss is what dies inside us while we live."

Norman Cousins

Within psychology there is a concept known as "soul murder." In his book *Halo in the Sky*, psychoanalyst Leonard Shengold defines this as killing another person's identity. It is often the result of severe abuse or neglect. Yet there are other things that can smother a human soul. Take New Rabies, for instance. The virus engages in a classic example of soul murder. It abuses its victims with a range of torturous symptoms and then it drives them on — uses them as vectors whose sole purpose is to spread the disease. Meanwhile the needs of the host are wholly neglected. To facilitate its spread, New Rabies damages the memory centers of the brain — the infected forget who they are. The virus also ravages the amygdala (the neural center for emotional processing) and, by destroying a person's ability to feel, it effectively wipes out his conscience. That is the only way that Otis could have done what he did.

The night he went missing from Whole Foods Market, he wandered aimlessly through the streets of New Orleans. He had forgotten about Nola; he no longer knew his own name. Into the vacuum left when Otis

Hudson departed, there settled the Great Need. It took the wheel and steered him in the direction of a barking dog. The animal went crazy when he approached, but the Otis-thing felt nothing for the dog's distress. The German Shepherd snarled and growled at him and yet Otis came on, heedless of the danger, ignoring the pain as the dog sank its teeth into his arm. He tried to bite the dog, but the animal's thick fur was an obstacle and before he could tear it away, the creature wriggled out of his grasp and ran off into the night. He did not register the pain of his bleeding arm or any disappointment that his prey had escaped; he merely rose and walked on. That is when he saw the man.

Alan Tisono was tipsy, but not so drunk that all judgment had left him. He knew he shouldn't drive home from the party and so he pocketed his keys and decided to walk instead. It was December; the night was chilly but not freezing cold and he liked the streets when they were quiet like this. As he strolled along London Avenue Canal, a man appeared ahead of him on the sidewalk. The stranger padded along in an oddly jerking way, like a marionette having its strings twitched. The two men met under a streetlight and Alan stared at the man's gaunt face, hollow eyes and the torn, bloody sleeve of his shirt.

"On your way to a zombie walk?" Tisono laughed. "They're coming to get you, Barbara."

He'd expected a laugh, a high-five or a good Shaun-of-the-Dead-style zombie impression, but the stranger just looked at him blankly. In another instant, he lunged for Alan, digging his fingernails into the startled man's arm to get a good grip. Once fastened on, Otis bit and bit him — on the face, on the hands he threw up in defense, on the chest. Alan screamed and writhed until he managed to break free and then he was running. But he was drunk and injured and clumsy and the lunatic was gaining on him. He dove through a gap in the flood wall that lined the canal, hoping to put thick concrete between himself and his attacker.

And that is where Otis caught him. Unmoved by Alan's pleas, Otis buried his teeth in the man's throat, relinquishing his grip only after the last feeble twitches of Alan's legs ceased. For the first time in days and days, Otis Hudson felt good.

The following day he was still on the move. The Otis-thing did not like the heat and glaring light of a New Orleans afternoon. But the Need did not concern itself with Otis's comfort. It ordered him on, and he robotically obeyed. The next person he zeroed in on was seventy-six-year-old Lance Jessop. The old man was working in his front garden when Hudson approached him and in a fit of unprovoked rage punched him in the side of the head. Jessop staggered backward but Otis closed the gap and sank his teeth into the old man's liver-spotted arm. He ripped off a chunk of flesh. Lance was screaming now as pain and panic blurred his vision. As he collapsed to the ground, the last thing he saw was a large black man standing over him chewing on the strip of skin (*my skin!*). He passed out.

Otis never got to finish his meal. Jessop's neighbor, alerted by the old man's cries, ran over, picked up a shovel and brought it down hard on Otis's head. He crumbled to the ground.

"John? What's going on?"

John lowered the shovel, prodded Otis to make sure he really was out for the count, and called to his wife, "Call the police, Jenny. And tell them to get an ambulance out here."

She disappeared into their house and John booted Otis one more time and not too gently either. "Sick bastard," he muttered and then knelt down to help his stricken neighbor.

It was breaking news in New Orleans. As Tammany visited one sick friend after another, she saw the video clip of Otis — covered in blood and screaming from the back of a police cruiser — played again and again on her clients' TVs. Earnest-faced reporters recounted the details of the horrific attack on Lance Jessop and Tammany kept trying to reach Nola. No answer.

Later though she did receive a text: *At hospital. Otis is bad. Can you come?* Tammany wrapped up her work as quickly as she could and made a beeline for the University Medical Center. By the time she arrived, Otis was dead.

Tammany was exhausted by the time she got home. By far the worst parts of being a mambo are those moments when there's nothing at all you can do. Confronted with a suffering she couldn't fix or even alleviate, she just held Nola and let her weep. When Nola's daughter arrived, Tammany gave the family their privacy and cried all the way home. She cried for Nola and for Otis and she wept because she was deeply afraid. She did not understand any of this and that ignorance made her feel like a little child again. She sat trembling in her favorite chair and prayed for strength and guidance. And at some point in the midst of her prayer, she fell asleep and began to dream…

Tammany is in St. Louis Cemetery Number One. It is night and somewhere, in this little city of crypts, music is playing. She follows the sound to find a man dancing in the moonlight. He is a couple of years older than her, but still handsome with strong arms and a lithe body.

"Hello Landry," she says quietly. This is the husband she had loved so dearly, the father of her son Dempsey, and the coward who ran away. Years ago, he convinced himself that she was casting spells on him, using voodoo to control him. He'd become so paranoid about it that he would eat nothing she cooked. For Tammany this was the greatest insult. Only the wicked use magic to harm or manipulate others. But he could not get the idea out of his head and so he abandoned them — her and their child.

"Don't look so grim, mambo. I am *not* your no-good husband," the man says and this is true. Landry is wearing a black undertaker's coat and matching top hat. Resting on his nose is a pair of dark glasses with the right lens knocked out to reveal one baleful eye. And that voice isn't the deep, soothing bass that used to sing to her, it is higher and more nasal in quality.

"Greetings, Ghede."

He is a loa of death, but not a fearsome spirit. Death is a natural part of life and Ghede is there to help souls pass on when their time comes. He is actually quite nice: funny (although a bit crude in his humor), amorous (he loves the ladies), and a great connoisseur of cigars and rum. At the moment he is puffing on a Cohiba cigar with a look of intense satisfaction on his face. Tammany can smell it: the aroma of cedar and spice with a hint of dark chocolate is very pleasant. And the music that's playing is upbeat, although patently ludicrous.

As the Upperclassmen sing *Cha Cha with the Zombies*, Ghede puts his cigar down on a nearby tomb and dances toward her. With one hand on his stomach and the other raised by his head, he looks like Ricky Ricardo dancing to Cuban Pete (Boom Chicka Boom). And in another moment he slips a hand around her waist, pulls her close and leads her through the steps.

"So, what's a nice girl like you doing in a place like this?" he whispers in her ear.

"Ghede, what happened to Otis?"

He spins away from her, the cha cha steps of his dance becoming more flamboyant. "Why do you want to talk about such depressing things when the night is young, the moon is full and I am so incredibly attractive?" He throws in a little Michael Jackson moonwalk just for the hell of it.

"I need to know."

"I need to dance."

"Ghede..." Tammany loves and reveres the loa, but she has had a rotten day and she needs answers.

"Always so serious. Remember all work and no play makes mambo a dull girl."

"Ghede!"

"*What?*" The music stops.

"Why won't you tell me?"

"Because!" he shouts and Tammany is taken aback by the mixture of rage and grief and fear that plays across his face.

"I know that something's very wrong and you're upset," she says gently. "Please, let me help. Just tell me what to do and I'll do it."

The loa's expression softens. He picks up his cigar and sinks down onto the weathered old tomb with a heavy sigh. "Otis is here now," he gestures to the graveyard, "finally."

"What do you mean: *finally?*"

"You think he died today. I tell you he died *days* ago."

"I don't understand."

"Soul death. To obliterate the soul while the body still lives — what does that sound like to you?"

"Zombies."

He nods, "And slavery. It's like they all have chains around their ankles. They are no longer fully alive and yet they cannot come to me and cross over. They just continue on ... in darkness."

"B-but," Tammany was stammering now as her mind tried to wrap itself around all this. "What's *causing* it?"

He leans forward and blows smoke in her face. Tammany coughs and splutters. It is different. Gone is the beautiful aroma of a $100 cigar. Now the smoke smells sharp and dark and unhealthy. As she breathes it in, it irritates her nose and seems to suck the moisture out of the back of her throat. But for all that, the scent is not unfamiliar. She stands there for a moment trying to identify it. There is a hint of licorice and a sweet, yet woody mix of pine and lemon that she eventually realizes is frankincense. Then she picks up the nutty aroma of sweet flag. She has it now and doesn't have to stand there sniffing to know that there would also be Master Root and Devil's Shoestring in the mix. It is the smell of Bend Over Oil — one of the most dangerous substances in her world. It is used to bend another person's will to your own and that is an evil thing. God gave us free will, an absolute essential if our actions are to have any meaning. To strip that away from someone is the ultimate violation.

"Slavery," she murmurs, then looks again at Ghede. "But what enslaves them?"

He beckons her to lean in as if he is about to share a secret. "You aren't going to believe this, but —"

The loa's mouth is still open in speech, but what comes out is a ringing noise.

Tammany's eyes snapped open. The telephone was ringing on the little table beside her and she glared at it.

"Fuck me," she hissed. "Of all the fucking, stupid, asinine, fucking luck, I've had it … Hello?" She barked this final word into the receiver, ready to tear into whoever the hell interrupted that dream.

"Tam…" The voice was quiet and trembling as if the speaker was crying.

"Who is this?"

"It — It's Gerry."

"Geraldine? Are you all right?"

"No, I'm not. Can you come?"

"I'll be right there." The tone of that voice was enough. Tammany grabbed her purse, picked up her keys and ran to her car.

Geraldine Navarro was eighteen years old when she first came to Tammany. She'd been having dreams, she said, that the loa were calling and calling her name.

"So you want to become a mambo." Tam was dubious. "Do you have any idea, child, what you're taking on? It will take years to learn and when you have, what will your life be like?"

"I don't know."

"Well let me enlighten you. You'll never be off duty. The phone will ring at all hours of the day and night. Every time you decide to take a little time off for yourself, someone will have a crisis and desperately need you. You will not make money out of this. Oh sure, if you sell the loa and charge $100 to read nine cards, you can cash in. But the loa are not yours to sell. There will be a reckoning. Other mambos and houngans — you think they'll form a community of mutually supportive friends? Think again. The competition in this business (because too many treat it just like a business) is ferocious. If you become successful, they will undermine you, bad-mouth you and throw every hex that you can imagine your way. And do you imagine that, in exchange for all you do and all you sacrifice, that at least your personal life will be right?" Here her voice broke. She and Landry weren't fighting so much anymore. She could have handled the fights. But she could not take the silence and his unwillingness to look her in the eyes. He stayed away more and more now.

"Mambo," Geraldine had interrupted these thoughts. "The loa call me in my dreams. I have to do this. I *wanted* to do this with you."

"Why?"

"Because you'll teach me how to do it right."

"And what is your definition of 'right'?"

"To serve. Both the loa and the people who need my help. To learn what practices are safe and effective."

"How will you feed yourself?"

"This job will pay."

"Not enough."

"I know," the girl said, "which is why I have this!" She fished a piece of paper out of her pocket and presented it to Tammany with a flourish. It was an acceptance letter to the Aveda Institute.

Tammany shrugged and brushed it aside. "Never heard of it."

"It's a beautician school," the girl looked a little crestfallen. Then she flashed Tam a bright smile. "I'm going to be an esthetician!"

The child's enthusiasm was infectious, but Tammany kept her face neutral. "How do you feel about doctors and psychologists?"

"I know this one already! Sometimes the loa want us to send people to doctors and shrinks because that will help them."

Tam looked at her for a long moment then nodded. "See you tomorrow."

And so began a friendship that lasted thirty-six years.

When Tammany arrived at Geraldine's, she ran up the front steps and was about to let herself in when she stopped short. Gerry had painted a long, thin red cross on her door. The cross had two little hash marks at both ends of each line and a small circle around the point where the horizontal and vertical met. It was a sign that Grandma Eula had taught her about — a warning of rampant disease: stay away. The mambo barged right in.

"Gerry?" she called.

"I'm here." Sitting on the couch in the dark, Geraldine Navarro did not rise to greet her.

Tammany switched on a lamp. "What's going on?"

Gerry sat forward and, to Tam's surprise, started unbuttoning her blouse. There was a large square bandage on the upward slope of her right breast. She peeled it away to reveal a small, round, angry-looking wound.

Tammany leaned in to inspect it. "That's a bite," she said. "A human bite." *And the man who attacked Otis tried to bite him and he in turn bit that old man.*

"It's from Marie Dias's little boy. He was running a high fever and she wanted me to take a look at him." Geraldine paused and looked vaguely around the room for a minute and then started to laugh. "You know that scene in *The Lost Boys* when the little vampire boy goes all feral and one of the Frog brothers says, 'Holy shit! The attack of Eddie Munster!'?"

"Yes," Tammany mumbled. She replaced the bandage and covered her friend up.

"That pretty much sums it up. He bit me, he bit his mother, he bit the family dog."

"Where is he now?"

Gerry shrugged. "Don't know. He ran out the backdoor and before we could get hold of him, he was gone. Fast little guy."

Tammany pressed her cheek against Geraldine's face. The old woman's hands had been toughened by years of hard work cleaning office buildings to make ends meet. She couldn't press them up against a person's forehead and tell if they had a fever. But her cheek was much more sensitive and through it she could feel that Gerry was burning up.

"I know I've got a fever," the woman swallowed and winced as if in pain, "... just like the Dias boy. But Tam," she gripped her friend's arm hard, "we're not the only ones. You have no idea how many people I've seen with fever. It's all over the city."

CHAPTER SIX

GLOBE-TROTTING

"The spirit to venture, that I should go forth
To see the lands of strangers far away."

Author Unknown, Anglo-Saxon verse, "The Seafarer"

Riga, *Latvia*. Ivars Balodis sat on the floor in the upstairs hall with his back pressed against the wall. Numb with horror and despair, he stared at the closed bedroom door that shook on its hinges every time the girl flung her body against it.

It was hard to believe that, just a few hours ago, he'd been happy. Things had been so good lately. His daughter Anita, unable to get any significant time off from *Toy's Planet* over Christmas, had booked a holiday in early December — off with her girlfriends to the Caribbean. While he hated seeing her go, she was so excited as she dug her beach towel and sunglasses out of her closet. And it's not like he would have been around much anyway. He was helping to run the Francisco de Goya *Los Caprichos* exhibition at the Art Museum Riga Bourse. It was an incredible opportunity for him and the graphic illustrations were complex, fascinating works of art. It was what he needed. To be occupied, to be riveted on a subject that kept him from thinking too much. And so it was a contented man who went to pick his daughter up from the airport.

She'd left a smiling, bright-eyed nineteen-year-old and she'd returned a ghost — pale and remote. There had been trouble on her little island paradise and she was nursing a terrible bite mark on her shoulder.

The next day he'd knocked on her bedroom door and, at her incoherent mumble, entered the room. It was eight a.m. and Anita was still in bed.

"Saulītē, you have to be at work in half an hour!"

"I'm not going in today."

"I told you to come back earlier so you'd have time to get over the jet lag."

"It's not jet lag, tēvs. I really don't feel well."

He felt her forehead; she was running a fever. "Maybe you picked up something on the plane. They say the germs just circulate through the cabin till everyone's sick."

And so she remained home while he left for the museum. Today he would guide a group of local dignitaries around the exhibition.

It all went beautifully and his well-rehearsed speech was in full swing. He pointed to image Number 19 and the group dutifully stopped to examine it. "The title is *Todos Caerán*."

"What does that mean?" asked the mayor's wife.

"It means 'Everyone will fall.' What is interesting about this picture is not the three human figures here at the bottom, but these hybrid creatures we see here in the air. They have birds' wings and bodies, but human heads. I believe that these hybrids represent the human soul and the freedom of the human mind to rise to new heights of enquiry and understanding. They are purely free creatures and the horror of this piece lies in the fact that they are the ones who will fall. As you can see here, one of them is already in the clutches of the three women at the bottom of the picture. They have already plucked his feathers and are preparing to consume him. Despite this rather barbaric image of them impaling the bird-man so they can roast him on a spit, the people are not depicted as extraordinarily evil figures. They are merely visceral rather than spiritual and cerebral beings. They feed the belly, not the mind or soul. They crouch on their knees in the shadows, in the earth and wait for their prey to be delivered unto them. It seems a grim inevitability."

"It's something out of a nightmare," one of the women shivered.

"Oddly enough, before he named his collection *Los Caprichos* (meaning whims), de Goya had called it Los Sueños ... dreams."

"Excuse me," Dace, his secretary, had appeared at the edge of the group.
"Yes?"

"Your daughter is on the phone."

"Please tell her I'll call her back."

Ivars turned and was about to lead the group on to the next image when Dace said in a firm voice, "Sir, you need to take this."

Anita was inconsolable on the phone and babbling that something was "Ēd prom pie manis!" — eating away at her. He had never heard his daughter sound like that. Forgetting about the tour, the mayor, and his big opportunity at the museum, he left without a word to anyone and raced home.

He found her standing in the living room, wrapped up in a blanket that covered her head and shrouded her face. The random thought came to him that she looked like the figure in another Goya image: *Que Viene El Coco* (Here Comes the Bogeyman).

"Anita, saulīte, how are you?"

She slowly raised her head, looked at him for a moment and then suddenly rushed at him. Her outstretched hands were hooked into claws. He was bigger and stronger than her and tried gently to deflect her. Yet she would not stop. She came at him again and again, forcing him to retreat up the stairs.

She was hurting herself now in her fervor to get at him. She fell once and he heard her ankle snap. The sound made his stomach roil, and he rushed to help her. But she did not acknowledge the broken bone. Instead she darted forward on her hands and knees and, in her scrabbling attempts to get hold of him, she hit him in the groin. White stars of pain exploded in front of his eyes and his whole body jerked protectively inward to shield the offended area. He managed, just, to stay on his feet. It did, however, stiffen his resolve that this dumjš had to stop.

She stood up — sort of. Her right ankle bent at a sickening angle and to put any weight on it must have been torture; and yet she hobbled forward. With a cry of confusion and pain, he grabbed her, flung her into her bedroom and slammed the door shut.

That had been three hours ago. His first instinct had been to call an ambulance, but then he thought of his mother. As a five-year-old boy, he'd watched as men in white coats dragged her kicking and screaming out of the house. That image had haunted him all the days of his life. And now he had to call the men with the butterfly nets to come and take his Anita away? No. He couldn't bear it. He'd give her time to calm down. He could talk her around, he knew he could, if she would just sit down for a minute and listen. But for the past three hours, she had not stopped throwing herself at the door. Why didn't she just open it? It wasn't locked; all she had to do was turn the handle and pull.

As the thudding on the door continued with maddening regularity, Ivars Balodis began to sink into himself. He had been happy for a little while. And then the hammer fell as it always did, as it did one day when a five-year-old boy playing with his trucks was suddenly forced to watch his mother descend into madness. Just as it did when he got the job at the museum and practically skipped home to tell his wife the good news. But Lucia had news of her own: cancer. Life was like the fucking Grim Reaper. It let you skip merrily along, waited until you were warm and happy and secure and then it tapped you on the shoulder with one skeletal hand — "Boo." And suddenly, any joy or certainty was ripped out from under you and don't you feel foolish having trusted in those things?

Sitting there he realized that he didn't want anymore of this ... this life. It was an endless battle and it was time for him to surrender. Slowly the distraught father reached up and turned the knob on the door. Anita suddenly went quiet as if she was crouched on the other side, waiting. He gave the door a little push and it swung inward an inch or two.

Then he sat back and watched as bloody fingers wrapped themselves around the door and pulled it open.

Miami, Florida. Eugene Redford felt awful. After a couple of days of the flu, he should be rallying by now. But he wasn't. He was ... *sinking* — that was the only way he could describe it. The fever rolled over him in wave after hideous wave that made his stomach churn and his head pound. If he'd been thinking more clearly he would have called an ambulance. That thought did, briefly, flit through his mind; but when he looked at his mobile, he couldn't remember what to do with it. He wanted to get moving anyway — it was important to move for some reason and so he dropped the useless phone, grabbed his car keys out of habit and attempted the drive to the Mount Sinai Medical Center.

His route led him north out of downtown Miami and onto the MacArthur Causeway. He'd almost made it across, but the sun glaring off the surface of Biscayne Bay sent his headache into orbit. He pulled over (grinding the side of his hatchback into the concrete wall of the bridge), opened the door and fell out of the car. The pavement was hot, an affront to his fevered body, so he scrambled quickly to his feet.

Move, his mind was telling him, but it gave him no indication of direction. Looking vaguely around, he chose a path at random (one that took him back the way he came) and began the long, staggering trek across three miles of hot concrete. As he walked he removed items of clothing in an attempt to cool off. By the end of the second mile, he was naked and that should have horrified Eugene. He'd had the stereotypical dreams of being out in public in a state of undress and had always awakened from these nightmares with a pounding heart and a sense of dread. Now, however, he was completely unaware of his nakedness — a pre-Fall Adam in a concrete Eden. He was equally unconcerned about the damage to his feet. In his bid to cool down, he'd kicked off his shoes and his bare feet had stepped in melted tar and on broken glass. But none of that mattered so long as he moved. He covered the final mile and, as he reached the on-ramp, his efforts were rewarded by the sight of a scrawny, grey-haired man resting in the shade below the ramp.

In his aimless wanderings, this finally was a goal. He knew now what he'd been looking for. His tottering steps became purposeful, his speed increased and a rage that seemed to come from nowhere and everywhere propelled him physically into the man. The body slam sent his victim toppling and knocked him senseless. Then Eugene got down to work. He bit into the man's cheek and tore away a strip of flesh and muscle. As he sat there chewing contentedly, a voice (commanding and yet high with agitation) ordered him to "Freeze."

Redford turned slowly to face the young cop who stood, feet apart and gun drawn, three yards away. He suddenly felt very protective of his prey. He would not let anyone else have it and so growled a low, feral warning at the officer. By now he'd finished his mouthful. He turned and bit into his victim's nose.

Eugene's body jerked with the impact of a bullet from the cop's .40 Smith and Wesson, but he merely grunted and continued to gnaw at the nose until he ripped it free. With a cry of horror and disgust, the officer fired again.

The Island of Cáscara. Dr. Edwin Caldwell surveyed the reports compiled by his colleagues. They had traced every one of the tourists who had passed through Cáscaran immigration in the last month. Thankfully, the vast majority were fine (as confirmed by the raft of medical tests ordered by Caldwell). However, not every visitor had managed to leave the island unscathed. Nine tourists had been injured by Juanita Pimental on the twelfth of December. Lab results confirmed that she was infected with the new strain of rabies. Like the other patients who tested positive for a lyssa infection, she was plagued with intensified, but nonlethal symptoms. In short, he had an isolation ward full of rabies patients who would not die. And now, because the tourists went home carrying the virus with them, he had clusters of the disease popping up around the world…

There was the incident in Miami. Eugene Redford had been shot and killed by police while attacking a homeless man. Emergency admission records at Cáscara General Hospital confirmed that Redford was treated for a bite wound on December twelfth and he is listed among the key witnesses to the Our Lady of Guadalupe attack. While he no longer posed a threat, his victim had bitten an ER nurse at Mount Sinai and her whereabouts were unknown. Miami police were searching for her as a matter of urgency and a CDC team was on site. In addition to their more practical duties, they had to calm the panic stirred up by the media. Newspaper headlines screamed "Causeway Cannibal Eats Man's Face" and "Miami Zombie Attack." Conspiracy theorists were coming out of the woodwork, insisting that Redford had been the victim of a secret government experiment to test a weaponized "Rage Virus." There were grim predictions that this was just the beginning of a *28 Days Later* scenario that could easily go global.

Next there was a report from Reading, England and another from Riga, Latvia.

A fourth tourist was traced to Kenora, Ontario. In a brutal, animalistic attack that shocked the local community, Liam Morin had clawed and bitten his wife and four children — two of whom were now missing.

Nathan Carlson, an apparent authority on native legend, cited the many parallels between this incident and the myth of the wendigo — an angle that reporters were quick to jump on. The following quote by Carlson appeared in three separate news articles: "Even in today's fast-paced world, with our technological marvels … when circumstances dictate it, it does not take long at all before our minds swing back to the paranormal-themed fears and superstitions of cultures and eras long gone."

The problem, Caldwell knew, was not the supernatural or paranormal. The problem lay in our technological marvels — the high speed, readily available transportation that allowed an infected individual to carry the virus anywhere in the world. Hop a plane (tourists five and six) and voilà there is an outbreak in Bedburg, Germany, and another in Beijing, China.

The seventh tourist on his list hailed from Nairobi and they were currently trying to locate him. The last two travelers (a young couple) had returned home to New Orleans. The woman was dead (an apparent suicide involving a Mack truck) and Caldwell was waiting on the autopsy report to confirm whether or not she had been infected. Her boyfriend, Nicholas Durand, was missing and probably spreading the disease.

Every boat that had left Cáscara had been tracked and found to be clear of infection, save one. The *Maria Celestina* had failed to arrive at its scheduled destination of Trinidad and Tobago. Instead, it ran aground on a beach in Parnaíba, Brazil. One man was found on board, the victim of a self-inflicted gunshot wound to the head. He was covered in bite marks — rat bites. The rest of the crew had gone AWOL. One witness swears she saw figures wading ashore on the night of the wreck. Edwin did a quick google search for Parnaíba. It boasted a population of 170,000.

He closed his laptop and rubbed his tired eyes. He had sent teams to every site with orders to identify and isolate any cases that emerge; but he felt sure this would not be enough. They still did not have a cure. And, since the standard rabies vaccine provided absolutely no protection against New Rabies, they had no viable way to protect the uninfected. The situation had all the hallmarks of a burgeoning pandemic. The question was: how many people would they lose before they got it under control?

CHAPTER SEVEN

NEW ORLEANS

"One eye-witness weighs more than ten hearsay — seeing is believing all the world over."

Titus Maccius Plautus, <u>Truculentus</u>

"Extraordinary claims require extraordinary evidence."

Carl Sagan, <u>Encyclopedia Galactica</u>

"I need to get you to the hospital." Tammany was trying to coax Geraldine to her feet.

"There's no point. They can't help."

"How do you know that?"

"Agata Roche, you know, my friend from high school ... she's an RN at the University Medical Center ... she told me. They've been swamped today by cases just like this. The CDC is setting up isolation wards, but can't keep up with demand. I'm on *a list*."

"There's a *waiting list* for quarantine?"

"It's hit so fast, they just don't have the beds yet."

"*What* has hit so fast? What the hell is it?"

Geraldine massaged her temples. "Don't know."

A little battle raged within the old mambo at that moment. She was so tired and frustrated and scared that she really thought she might lose it. Truly she wanted nothing more than to launch into a good, profanity-laden rant about the absurdity of all this bullshit. With long-practiced restraint, she held her tongue.

"Fine," she said quietly. "If they can't help right now, then let's see what we can do here."

And hence began the mammoth effort you see when a mambo pulls out all the stops. First she had recourse to John George Hohman's *Pow-Wows or Long Lost Friend*, a nineteenth century Pennsylvania Dutch text that combines ardent Christianity with mysticism. It had originally been brought to New Orleans by traveling merchants. Vodouisants — with their appetite for different ideas — had assimilated it. Hence, Tammany carried a copy of Hohman's little book in that huge purse of hers. She used its prayers in an attempt to banish Geraldine's fever. Likewise she gave her friend a mix of dittany, St. John's Wort and whiskey to combat her headaches; she tried oil of cloves in a tablespoon of white wine for the nausea. But she was only fire-fighting — just treating the symptoms. And so she tried to hit upon a *Geri Tout*, a cure-all to treat the illness. She tried Gypsy Water and Four Thieves Vinegar. Nothing gave the suffering woman any relief.

In fact she was getting worse. The vomiting was so violent that Gerry wet herself during the uncontrollable retching. She cried out in pain and despair and Tammany wept at the sound and pleaded with the 911 operator to send an ambulance. Her friend needed morphine and she needed it now. But all of the ambulances were tied up and it could be "some time." Meanwhile Geraldine slipped in and out of a fevered delirium and all Tammany could do was rub her down with lukewarm water to try and lower her temperature. Finally, at about four a.m., the stricken woman slept and the old mambo, sitting in a chair by her friend's bed, felt her eyelids growing heavy. She sat up with a jerk, a lightning bolt of anxiety shooting through her.

"To sleep, perchance to dream," she muttered. She didn't want another cryptic nightmare filled with omens and foreboding and there *were* things she could do to prevent it. However, she didn't dare. Any information from the loa could be vital to Geraldine. And so she settled down to sleep and prayed for the answers she needed.

She is at home and Grandma Eula is there, sitting in her living room. Tammany wants to rush to her and wrap her arms around her, but she dare not. She has spotted a small yellow canary sitting placidly in the woman's cupped hand. This is not Eulalia Trudeau, her beloved grandmother; this is Gran Ibo, a loa so old that her origins are said to be "beyond memory." She is a kindly spirit, patient and wise. She knows the help that can be derived from her "little sisters" — the healing plants of the forests and swamps where she makes her home.

"Pull up a chair, child."

Tammany disappears into the kitchen long enough to grab a chair and positions it next to the loa who is seated in the recliner.

"I took a look at Geraldine today," Ibo says. "Did you notice her complexion? Her skin has gone very gray."

"I know," the mambo says quietly.

"I was thinking about cowboy movies — how the outlaw always wears a black hat and the hero wears a white one. You know, of course, that in our world the meanings are reversed. White is the color of the dead and black is the color of the living."

"I know."

"And yet Geraldine is so grey. That, child, is because the carriers of this disease fall in between; they are neither completely dead, nor wholly alive. And the cause of it … I know that question has been driving you crazy … comes from a clean, white room, fashioned by men in white coats."

"A lab?"

"Yep."

"Is there a cure? Can the little sisters help?"

Gran Ibo shakes her head sadly. "No. All you can do right now is get out of its way."

"How?"

The ancient loa shrugs. "Take as many as you can and run."

"But where is safe?"

"Lots of people today talk about 'finding themselves,' but in this case you really should."

Tammany is on her feet now, rummaging through her purse until she finds it — her Rand McNally Easy to Read Map of Louisiana. She spreads it open on the floor and kneels down to examine it — too excited to mind the pain in her knees.

"Find yourself," she mutters. "Myself. It can't be my home address because it's time to run. So where?"

Looking at the whole state is too much to focus on and so she flips the sheet over and studies the detailed maps on the back.

"New Orleans and Vicinity. Where is safe? It would have to be remote, yet within striking distance." She glances up at Gran Ibo and the loa smiles encouragingly.

Then the mambo sees it and laughs out loud: St. Tammany Parish. And there, accessed by the Pearl River, is Honey Island Swamp.

Tammany folds up the map and begins to list on the blank red spaces of its cover the names of everyone she must call. She writes in tiny letters so that she can fit as many names on the map as possible.

"That's a lot of people."

When the mambo looks up, Gran Ibo is gone and sitting in her place is her son Dempsey. This of course is not Dempsey, but the only clue to the identity of this loa is his right arm. It ends in a healed stump just below the elbow.

"St. Marron?" she asks.

"Give the lady a kewpie doll."

St. Marron is a legend in New Orleans. An escaped slave, he fled to the swamps where he led a community of other fugitives. He is the archetypal freedom fighter whose rebellion cost him his arm and eventually his life.

"It is a bad thing, this," he says. "The closest thing to pure slavery I've seen since the old times. Those are all the people you wish to take with you?" He nods toward the map.

"And more, if I can."

"That will take time. Wouldn't it be safer just to grab your family and run?"

"I suppose."

Marron leans forward in his chair and looks Tammany in the eye. "Consider your options carefully, mambo. You can take Dempsey and the kids and run. Or you can send them on ahead and stay behind to help the others. But it is a big thing that you ask: to save so many."

"I know."

He holds up his stump. "Do you understand, woman, that freedom costs?"

Tammany's first call was to her son Dempsey. His mother had been upset lately and not making a whole hell of a lot of sense and so he answered with a wary, "Hello?"

"Right," Tam's voice was different. She didn't sound agitated anymore, but firm and decisive. "I've got to the heart of it now."

"Mom, what are you talking about?"

"The illness that's here."

"The flu that's been going around?"

"It's not flu. It only looks like that at the beginning."

"Ok…"

"You need to see what it becomes."

"Why?"

"Because you have to see it to understand it. And if you don't understand it, how can you protect your children from it?"

"Mom, this is sounding crazy."

"I don't give a fuck how it sounds. Now I need you to come over to Geraldine's right now!"

"I'm not a little boy anymore. You can't just order me around."

"She's dying," Tammany croaked.

"What?"

"If you have anything you want to say to her, you'd better say it now, because in a couple of hours she isn't gonna know who the hell you are."

"Mom, if she's sick call an ambulance!"

"They're busy."

"What?"

"Too many people are sick."

"Shit."

"That accurately sums up the situation, yes."

There was a long pause. "We'll be right there."

"Just you and Catarina. Don't bring the kids."

"I'll ask Mrs. Astier in 3B if she can look after them for a while."

"For God's sake, Dempsey, tell her to keep them inside."

The next call she placed was to Amos Burel, a long-time client.

"Tammany! How are you?"

"Well, not so good to be honest. I have a huge favor to ask."

"Hey, you helped get my boy sober, you ask for whatever you want."

"Are you still living out on Pearl River, near the swamp?"

"Yeah, why?"

"I need you and Della to meet with me. There's something you need to see."

Her phone calls made, she continued her vigil over Geraldine. When the woman finally stirred, Tammany rose to check her temperature, groaning as her back and knees protested.

Gerry smiled at her wanly. "You should make a voodoo doll of yourself and give it a back rub." Her laugh was so weak and pitiful.

The mambo plastered a smile onto her face. "At this point, I think I'd just soak it in rum."

"Ah, a pickled mambo — that would be effective." Geraldine's attempt to look bravely chipper dissolved as a stabbing pain arced through her skull. "I used to bitch about getting old," she panted. "It doesn't seem so bad now."

"Don't worry, we'll have you back to complaining in no time."

"No you won't. I'm right about that, aren't I?"

Tammany's eyes filled with tears. She nodded and cleared her throat. "I can't stop what's happening to you, honey. But I can keep it from happening to other people."

"I know that look. You're planning something."

"Yeah. But I need your help."

Dempsey and his wife Catarina arrived, both looking harried.

"The mood is getting ugly out there!" Cat said as she embraced her mother-in-law.

"Are more people taking ill?" Tammany asked.

"No. Haven't you been watching the news?" Dempsey asked.

"What news?"

He handed her his phone and she quickly scrolled through the News Feed. The headline read, "Unarmed man shot by police!" followed by a sketchy article on how Nicholas Durand was shot and killed during an apparent mugging in downtown New Orleans.

"That's the second black man to die in police custody in the last twenty-four hours," Dempsey explained. "There's protests ... the riot cops are out..."

A knock on the door interrupted him; Amos and Della had arrived. Tammany poked her head into Geraldine's bedroom. They heard her murmur, "Are you up for this, honey?" but didn't hear the reply. Tammany turned and looked at them.

"You all know Geraldine Navarro, the mambo I trained. Well, she's got something to tell you."

Gerry lay in bed, trying to focus what was left of her dying mind on this, her last and most important work as a mambo. This could save a lot of lives, but first they needed to be convinced of the danger. Well, she was going to convince them all right. She nodded to them as they shuffled into her room.

Her story began simply with a recap of how little Jacob Dias took ill and then bit her and his mother. She listed her symptoms. She told them what Agata Roche said about the hospital being swamped and the CDC being involved and the fact that they had no cure for this new illness that was spreading through the city. The facts were disturbing. But this was the internet age — people were bombarded with disturbing facts every day. What they needed, she knew, was a punch-in-the-stomach-kick-you-in-the-crotch dose of what those facts really meant.

"It huuurts." And her voice was almost that of a small child. Tears welled up in her eyes. "I feel like someone is at my head with a hammer and chisel and every time the hammer falls, another part of my mind crumbles away. *I want my mother* ... but I can't ... I can't remember her name! And I'm afraid. I don't want to lose who I am but it is all slipping away. And I don't want to hurt anyone. But I *do!* I've never been so angry." She raised her hands and feet just a little off the bed to show them the restraints that bound her. "I *asked* for these because I was afraid I'd hurt Tammany. You'll see. It won't be long now and you'll see ..."

Her prediction was correct. Within half-an-hour she turned and it was as if a bomb went off in that bedroom. She shrieked incoherently at them through foam-covered lips and tugged at her restraints with such violence that the flimsy bed bucked and creaked with her thrashing. As the ropes bit into her flesh, her wrists began to bleed and yet she did not notice. They tried to speak to her, but that only made her worse.

Wiping the tears from her eyes, Tammany stepped up to the bed. She held her wrist just out of range and Geraldine snarled and snapped at it like a rabid dog. "Does anybody have any questions?"

"It's like a mother-fucking zombie virus," Amos said.

The mambo nodded and ushered them out of the room. The five of them stood near to each other in Gerry's small living room. Dempsey and Catarina were in tears, Amos was shaken and Della looked like she might be sick.

Amos looked at Tammany. "Have you spoken to the loa about this?"

"Yes, they led me to Honey Island Swamp."

"Would it be safe there?" Catarina asked.

"It would make a good refuge," Della said. "We've got quite a bit of space at ours."

The mambo nodded. "And your boy rents those houseboats out to tourists. They would give us even more room."

"Our neighbors would take people in, I know they would," Amos said.

"And there's the Cajun village that you can only get to by boat. Yeah," Della was nodding her head, "we can make it work and just let all this blow over."

"Yep," Tammany said. Although, personally, she didn't think it would.

"But if it does drag on, what are we going to do for food?" Catarina asked.

"I can fish," Dempsey said.

"And we hunt," Amos wrapped an arm around Della and she leaned into him. "There are alligators, wild boar, waterfowl, deer."

"Good," Tammany said. "In the next twenty-four hours, we've got a lot to do. Catarina, stay inside with the kids and start calling folks and telling them where to meet us and what to bring. Pack up everything you'll need for the twins for a good long stay. Amos and Della — call your neighbors and ask your son about the boats."

"I wanna pick up some more ammo and some extra fishing gear too," Amos cut in.

"That's good. Dempsey and I will stock up on the essentials and …"

"I have a question," Della interrupted and nodded toward the bedroom door. Geraldine had gone quiet and that was almost worse than her yelling. It made the hair stand up on the back of your neck.

"They don't have a cure," Amos said quietly.

"No," Tammany agreed, "but they might find one. We'll give her a chance."

Tammany phoned the police and told them about Geraldine's condition, that she was infected and dangerous and needed to be transferred to CDC quarantine.

"What if they shoot her like that Durand guy?" Dempsey asked as they left the house.

"We have to risk it. It's either that or shoot her ourselves. At least this way there's some hope."

CHAPTER EIGHT

POSTCARDS FROM OVER THE EDGE

"I see the world being slowly transformed into a wilderness; I hear the approaching thunder that, one day, will destroy us too. I feel the suffering of millions."

Anne Frank, *The Diary of a Young Girl*

"Everything hurts now and nothing makes sense."

Carrie Fisher, *Postcards From the Edge*

Cáscara. "All right," Edwin Caldwell was saying. "I think it's clear that this virus is not the result of biowarfare." He scrolled through the report he'd received from colleagues in Bangor, Maine. It contained details of Rachel's death and also copies of the research proposal Pickman submitted to Harvard.

"The road to hell is paved with good intentions," Sheriff Manolito murmured. "Whether he was working on a weapon or a cure, the result is the same."

"True." Caldwell closed his laptop and thought for a minute. "That's all we know about Aaron Pickman, but what about his assistant, Montgomery?"

"I can sum him up in three words."

"Yes?"

"Booze, broads and blow."

"Charming. But there's got to be more to him than that. He obviously knew what was going on at the lab and would have known what alterations Pickman made to the virus." An idea struck him. "Can I see his personal effects?"

Manolito brought out the boxes. There, among the ghastly assortment of Hawaiian shirts and a general collection of juvenile tat, they found the journal.

New Orleans. Tammany was packing her bags when the knock came at the door. She opened it cautiously to find Daniel Wade standing there.

"I'm here for the interview!" he beamed at her.

"Oh crap." The mambo glanced nervously up the street and ushered him quickly inside.

"I'm sorry, did I get the time wrong?"

"No, no. I forgot all about it — it's been so chaotic here."

"What is all this?" Daniel gestured to the suitcases and boxes.

Ignoring the question she asked, "When are you leaving New Orleans?"

"Tomorrow, why?"

"Go tonight. Now, if you can."

"What? Why?"

Tammany sat him down at a kitchen table stacked with crates of food and voodoo supplies. She told him everything about Otis and the dreams and Geraldine, but in the midst of her narrative she stopped. She could tell by the look on his face that he didn't believe her.

"You're not buying this, are you?"

"It is far-fetched."

The mambo nodded. He believed in her faith, the way you believe in the existence of, say, Mount Everest despite the fact you've never seen it with your own eyes. He believed that Voodoo exists in its own right. But he was not a *believer*. His academic interest in the faith was respectful and tolerant but also steeped in its own sense of analytical superiority. He indulged Tammany's belief in mystic dreams and improbable truths in the same way you'd humor a child's belief in Santa Claus. At any other time,

Tammany thought, it wouldn't matter. But now it could be his undoing. She decided to take one more shot.

"Well, Mr. Wade, it was lovely meeting you." She rose; he took the hint and stood too. "I wonder if you might humor an old woman and carry this to protect you on your travels?"

She handed him the *gris gris* — the charm she'd prepared for him.

"Thank you."

"Sew it into your clothes or keep it in your right pocket. To recharge it, soak it in whiskey every Friday."

"Ok." And there it was — the disbelief again.

"Be well, sweetheart." She kissed him on the cheek and showed him out.

As he walked back to the bus stop, he looked thoughtfully at the red flannel bag tied with twine and decorated with a blue bead. He teased the bag open and peered inside, but couldn't make out the contents. And so he emptied them into his hand. It was quite a collection: ashes, a tiny bone, a few hairs (although he didn't know what or who they were from) and a small piece of a snake shed. There was a toadstool top and some white powder that smelled of camphor. He shook his head and carefully returned the ingredients to the bag. He liked the old woman for her honesty and kindness. He was determined to represent her faith on its own terms, giving it all of the respect it deserved. But he simply could not buy into it. This pouch was important to him because it represented Tammany's friendship and was an excellent artifact that would no doubt give him inspiration while he wrote. However, it had no more power to protect him than the Odor-Eaters in his shoes. At the bus stop, he popped the bag into his briefcase and thought no more of it.

"St. Michael, Archangel, defend us. Be our protection against the wickedness of those who prowl about the world seeking the ruin of souls. Amen." She only had time to recite this truncated version of Pope Leo XIII's prayer and then it was time to say goodbye. The first boats were loaded with the friends and neighbors she was able to convince to go to Honey Island.

"Mom, just get on the boat, *please*." Dempsey felt like he was going crazy. He needed to get his wife and children away, but to leave his mother…

"Sweetheart, you know I can't. I have a responsibility to the people here that I can't run away from. With us all living on top of each other, we could give another fifty people refuge at the swamp. The minute I get my fifty, I'll be on the boat. I promise."

"But..."

"Your responsibility is to the family you've made. Now get 'em outta here. I love you, son."

The sight of her boy crying on the deck of that boat almost broke her. She nodded her thanks to Nola as the woman hugged him tight. Then Tammany walked resolutely away.

The drive home, however, gave her more than enough to distract her from sad goodbyes. New Orleans was in turmoil. Police and ambulance sirens blared constantly and the streets were crowded. Two black men had died in police custody in quick succession — one involving the shooting of an unarmed man. Fearing a repeat of the Stephon Clark and Terence Crutcher killings, people had taken to the streets to protest. Tammany moaned aloud as she piloted her little Chevrolet toward home. More people in the street would only mean more people infected.

Suddenly she tugged on the wheel and pulled the car up to the curb. Rolling down her window she shouted, "George! Hey George!"

The old homeless man turned and smiled broadly at her. "Hey! How are you?"

"I need to talk to you! Get in!"

He paused and looked at her uncertainly. Sleeping on a park bench and bathing only occasionally didn't earn you many lifts from people and he was a bit taken aback to be offered one now.

"Will you stop gawking at me and get in?"

George noticed for the first time just how tired and stressed the mambo looked. He obeyed. "Tam, what's going on?"

"Oh do I have a story to tell you."

George didn't take much convincing. A life on the streets had provided him with a front row seat to the changes that were taking place in the city.

"I'll talk to the others — a lot of them, I think, will come."

"How many, George? I need numbers."

He sat for a moment and started ticking off names on his fingers. "Eighteen including myself."

"Wonderful. Make sure everyone knows where we're meeting and get `em there on time."

Tammany spent the rest of the evening calling everyone she could think of. Friends and clients varied in their responses. Some were prepared to take Tam at her word. Some had seen things that supported her story. And some thanked her politely and said they'd be in touch. The mambo did not argue with them — she did not have the time it would take to change all those minds. By the time she went to bed, she had managed to convince thirty-one to come with her. Including herself and the eighteen George would gather, she had gotten her fifty.

As she lay in the darkness listening to the sirens, she remembered Marron's words: "Do you understand, woman, that freedom costs?" And he'd brandished his stump at her just in case she was under the illusion that the price would be low.

So the question remained: what would she be required to pay?

The following morning Daniel Wade slept in and just managed to get himself organized to make the 11:00 check out required by his hotel. He would have an early lunch and then head off to the airport. Hence by 11:45 he was dining al fresco with a bottle of beer in his hand and a calzone on the way. He looked at the label on the bottle and an ugly multi-colored skull grinned back at him. The waitress had assured him that this beer, *The Ghost in the Machine*, was the top-rated Louisiana brew and a local favorite. He sipped it experimentally. It was nice: biscuity with hints of pepper and citrus and pine — a very civilized way to start the day.

It was at that moment that life, with its endless taste for irony, interrupted these thoughts. Someone screamed. Daniel dropped his beer which sloshed liberally over his trousers. He hardly noticed because a man had tackled a woman literally right in front of him.

"What the fuck?" he hissed, as he rose and grabbed hold of the attacker.

The man, middle-aged and wearing an expensive suit, turned on him then, snapping his teeth in Daniel's face. As the two men grappled, they lost balance and fell to the ground. The businessman landed on top of Wade and knocked the wind out of him. As Daniel gasped for breath, some of the foamy drool that hung from his assailant's lips hit him in the face, in the eyes, in the mouth. It took every ounce of strength in his younger, fitter body to keep those teeth from sinking into his flesh. And then suddenly, the man was being hauled off him as two police officers intervened.

Daniel hopped up and made a beeline back to his table where he used every spare napkin and half a bottle of Pure Hand Sanitizer Gel to wash his face. He had a terrible taste in his mouth and looked for his beer. The bottle lay on its side on the ground, the skull grinning up at him, while *The Ghost in the Machine* drained away.

Cáscara. The island of Cáscara had fallen. The number of infected swelled, overwhelming the hospital in a scene right out of the 2008 remake of *Day of the Dead*. Across the island the scales had tipped with the sick outnumbering the well by four to one. The CDC was pulling out and as his team drove in convoy to their extraction point, Dr. Caldwell typed feverishly. The SUV jerked along, swerving and breaking to avoid the infected who were crowded in the streets. Edwin had a difficult time holding on to his laptop, let alone getting anything coherent down in the email he was sending to his boss. His vehicle slowed to avoid an infected child. Three screeching men threw themselves at the car, cracking two windows and bowing Caldwell's door inward. Janine screamed for their driver to move and the car lurched forward, swiping the child and sending her flying onto the sidewalk.

Three SUVs departed from Carite, but only two made it to the extraction point — the abandoned runway at Pickman's lab where a helicopter would evacuate them to the USS Gerald R. Ford. While he waited for the chopper, Caldwell continued to type:

> *Attached to this email you will find a document with all of the details of Pickman's research. While it does not provide a cure for the disease, it will refine your understanding of the virus.*

With a queasy lurch of his stomach, Caldwell realized that he was typing this message as if he was about to die. He pushed that thought aside and continued...

> *I believe that the quickest route to bringing the infection under control is not in establishing a cure, but in the development of a vaccine. We*

know that the standard PEP injections for rabies are ineffective against the new strain. However …

A shrill, inhuman screech echoed through the forest nearby. Janine was on the radio urging the helicopter on.

… with the information contained in Pickman's notes, it should be possible to develop a vaccine specifically engineered to fend off the New Rabies.

The question left in Caldwell's mind was one of logistics. The incubation period was so short, would they be able to manufacture and distribute a vaccine in time to stem the tide?

He could hear the chop of helicopter blades as help approached, but the infected were emerging from the trees now. Dr. Edwin Caldwell had just enough time to click on the paper airplane icon and send the email. Then Abran Manolito plowed into him with enough force to send the old doctor toppling backward onto the cracked pavement. Somewhere beneath three of the infected, Janine was screaming. The rest of his team were dying around him — or worse, surviving to become one of *them*. As Manolito bit into him again and again, Edwin opened his mouth to scream and … nothing. It was precisely like one of those dreams where you try to cry out but can't make a sound. Sobs wracked his body and stole his voice. Half-blinded by a spray of his own blood, Caldwell's last view of the world was of a gaping mouth full of teeth.

New Orleans. The night of the final exodus arrived and Tammany stared in amazement at the number of people gathered at the dock. Word had spread rapidly and, when the mambo did a final head count, she realized that nearly three times the expected number had shown up. They were families mostly, just desperate to get their kids out of harm's way. From the haunted looks on many faces, they had seen for themselves what the new illness could do.

She and Amos stared at each other for a long moment.

"How can we leave any of them behind?" she asked.

"Tammany, where are we going to put them?" He turned to look at his vessel — a large, flat-bottomed boat that would sink under the weight of all those people.

"I don't know, but we'd better think of something. I —"

At that moment a scream sliced through the twilight and everyone froze. A group of infected, drawn by the crowd, converged on the dock. It was actually happening — the nightmare scenario of a mass attack, that essence of zombie fiction, made bloody and real. And the crowd surged forward as people jumped onto every boat moored there. As trembling hands floundered with dock lines, they were overrun.

Tammany grabbed a nearby child and handed the shrieking toddler to Amos. She picked up another and another and soon people were shoving their children into her hands and her back groaned as she lifted each of them onto the boat. As the enraged screams of the infected rose around her, every instinct told her to hop aboard NOW. She managed to keep herself calm by counting each child she handed over. Ten, eleven, twelve. The fighting was nearer now and Tammany grabbed a teenage boy by the scruff of his neck and shoved him toward the boat. A pregnant woman came and Tammany held her hand to help her step into the craft. Then more children … twenty-one, twenty-two, twenty-three. She looked around and there was George carrying one child over his shoulder with another under his arm. She stepped aside so he could hand them across. The fighting had reached the boat now and something slammed into her back hard, driving the old woman onto her hands and knees. From this new vantage point, she could see a young mother, crouched beside a nearby bench, clutching an infant to her.

"Hey!" Tammany called. "Come on!" And she reached her hand out to the girl.

That is when it happened. A foam-slicked face darted forward and buried its teeth in her arm. Tammany screamed. A man who was running for the boat tripped over her attacker who fell sideways, taking a chunk of Tam's flesh with him. The world swam in front of her eyes as pain shot through her. It took her breath away. But there was no time to stop.

"Come on," she gasped and reached again for the baby.

The mother handed the child over just before a woman in a police uniform fell on top of her and went for her throat. Tammany, her left arm next to useless, almost dropped the baby. She pressed the infant to her, struggled to her feet and ran. The boat was pulling away.

"Amos!" she screamed.

But Amos was piloting the craft away. It was his son Leonard, the boy she'd helped sober up, who stepped up to the port side and yelled, "Go on! I'll catch him!"

With a scream of agony, Tammany tossed the child. It took an unbelievably long time for that tiny body to arc through the air. The mambo held her breath, her muscles pretzeling in on themselves with the tension. And then the bundle was in Leonard's hands and Tammany exhaled.

"Fifty-nine," she smiled.

Sirens blared nearby and with the arrival of police (new, uninfected victims), Tam was able to slip through the crowd and make it back to her car.

She was doomed; that was clear. But she was not finished yet. There was still something she needed to do.

New York. He made his flight — just. By the time he gave his statement and details to the police, it had been a mad dash to the Louis Armstrong International Airport. Just as they were making the final boarding call for his Delta flight to JFK, Daniel Wade hopped onto the plane. Shaken and upset by the attack — and unable to get rid of the awful taste in his mouth — he ordered three of those little bottles of vodka and drank them straight. The alcohol calmed him, masked the taste and made his lips feel tingly — a sensation he always found pleasant. He opened his laptop. As always, work would be the best distraction.

He needed to type up his notes. It was a real shame that he didn't get that interview with Tammany, but he had spoken to other mambos and houngans and had a lot of material to organize. The plan now was to delve into the thriving Voodoo culture in New York City and then compare and contrast it to what he'd seen in New Orleans. It would be good, he thought, especially if he could give his descriptions the intensity and immediacy that had made his first book a success. With this in mind, he typed furiously for the duration of the three-hour flight.

New York was fucking freezing. After the mild temperatures of the Big Easy, it was quite a shock to step out of the airport and get hit with an icy blast of snow. All he wanted now was to get to his suite at the Mandarin Oriental and take a long hot shower before Francesca arrived.

According to the website for GFE ("the ultimate Girl Friend Experience"), Francesca was twenty-six years of age and had the perfect 36-24-33 hourglass shape. She was a commercial model, but there was "more to her than just stunning good looks." Apparently, she was cultured, well-read and warm-hearted ... and, judging by the way she busted out of her bikini top in one of her photos, seriously enhanced. All of that, he knew, was just shinola. What he wanted was to curl up next to a warm body and listen to a gentle voice speak to him about ... well, anything really.

Tammany had been spot on about the PTSD, of course. He'd suspected for some time that he suffered from a raging case of the disorder, but had always resisted seeing anyone about it. He didn't want to be branded as crazy. Besides, the prospect of having to unpick all the tangled mess inside his head was just too daunting. And so he sought comfort where he could find it. Some people turned to drugs, for some it was binge eating and he turned to the Francescas of this world — that and a nice Chardonnay.

When she arrived hours later, she was a vision of loveliness — tall, blond and dressed to the nines. He'd specified in his email that they would be dining at *Per Se*. However, despite having missed his lunch (thanks to that lunatic in New Orleans), he really wasn't hungry. A micro-expression of disappointment flitted across the girl's face for the briefest moment, and then she was all smiles. He did have such a lovely room and evenings in were always so "cosy." Surprisingly her voice grated on him. The tinkling stream of her words was, it turned out, not what he wanted after all. He kissed her to shut her up.

But her silence was not his only aim. For some reason, he felt compelled to taste this woman, to forcibly worm his tongue into her mouth.

"Ow! You bit me!" she cried and pushed him away.

And he had — hard enough to draw blood.

As she held a handkerchief to her lip, she mumbled through the fabric, "What is the matter with you? And what is that *taste?*" She rushed to the bathroom to rinse her mouth out and that is when she saw the teeth marks just beneath her lower lip. That was going to take a shit-ton of makeup to cover.

The date ended quickly after that. Francesca relied too heavily on her looks to chance an encounter with someone who bit. She had a lunch date tomorrow afternoon and another in the evening and so she had better get home and put some ice on that lip. And, she decided, she'd get that son of a bitch banned with the agency. Idiot.

After she'd gone, Daniel sat there with her blood still on his mouth. The taste of it was comforting somehow, and he thought about his first book on modern vampire culture. For the first time he could see the attraction of that lifestyle. He curled up in bed with his laptop to watch *The Kiss of the Vampire* and soon fell asleep.

He was back in that closet as the house burned around him. He could hear his father shouting. He wanted to cry out to him "I'm here, I'm here!" but when he opened his mouth, nothing came out. He was so scared he could not move. The heat was unbearable and Daniel pressed himself back against the wall in an attempt to get away from it. God, it was so hot.

He jerked awake and kicked the covers off. He was burning up and the room seemed to sway around him. It must be that flu that was going around New Orleans.

His go-to maneuver for any discomfort, however, was close at hand. He grabbed his laptop and brought up the notes he'd typed on the plane. At first the document was a blur — it might have been typed in a 'wingdings' font for all the sense it made to him. Gradually the gibberish resolved itself into words. He scrolled to the bottom of the document and began to type: "The fundamental value of the Voodoo religion lies in its ..." His mind went blank; the word he'd been about to add skittered away and the whole point he'd been about to make went with it. He lay propped up in bed for a long time frowning at the screen, but nothing came to him. He set the laptop aside, but felt too ill and uncomfortable to go back to sleep. He was suddenly restless and agitated, though surely that was nothing new. Any PTSD sufferer will tell you that the anxiety keeps your stress levels thrumming along in fifth gear. For some reason, however, it was different this time. Usually when he got anxious, he withdrew. He sat at home, turned his phone off and worked. Why then did his agitation urge him to get up and get dressed and go out? He had to move and the urgency to do so made his fingers tremble as he tried to button his shirt. The result was not confidence-inspiring. His shirt was askew leaving a flap with a few unused buttons dangling at the bottom.

This at least disguised the fact that he'd forgotten to zip up his fly. He slipped on a pair of loafers with no socks and that is how he ventured out into the snowy December night.

New Orleans. In Voodoo a zombie is made by first incapacitating someone with toxins so he appears to be dead. Once he has been buried, the bokor (someone who practices black magic) will dig him up. Through the use of poisonous herbs and dark ceremony the magician extracts his victim's *ti bonanj* (his soul and that which gives him free will and identity). This he stores in a small clay jar. What is left is an extremely malleable shell that can be used as slave labor, doing only his master's will.

As Tammany sat in her recliner, she reflected on the fact that this new and terrible virus functioned very much like a bokor. It seemed to hollow you out, effectively killing the person you are and turning you into a slave to serve its own ends. She was not a trained nurse, but she understood sickness. And she knew that diseases were compelled to reproduce. They could only achieve this through transmission to new hosts who would in turn pass the virus on. That, essentially, was what the chaos at the dock had been all about. The infected had to spread the disease and hence were drawn to the great crowd of people trying to escape. And now, she looked at her bandaged arm, she was turning into one of those— what was the word they used in that TV show *Helix*? — vectors. That would be her fate unless she did something to stop it.

She rose, went to her bedroom closet and started rummaging around. At the very back was a beat up old cardboard box that held the only things she had left of her mother. Cecile Trudeau had never settled down in this life. She was the quintessential wild child who eloped with thirty-nine-year-old Clement Lanuit when she was just eighteen. Their one child, Tammany, might have saved them. Nothing makes you grow up faster than having a child of your own, but somehow the vital link was never made. When Cecile looked at her baby, she did not feel that desperate love that binds a woman to an infant. She saw an obstruction, something that would keep her in at night while Clement went out and got up to who-knows-what. It drove her insane to think of him off screwing around while she was stuck at home playing Mary Poppins to some mewling creature that never stopped crying. And so Tammany was handed to Eula. As the years passed, the girl saw her mother only a few times: she'd breeze in, stay for a day or two and then depart, always with kisses and protestations of love.

"Stupid," Tammany muttered as she surveyed the sad collection of relics in the box. There was a phone number scrawled onto the back of an envelope — but no name attached to it. There were two earrings, one with the stone (a faux emerald) missing. There was a cassette tape of Jimi Hendrix's *Electric Ladyland* and a bottle. The label read Amobarbital; she poured the contents into her hand. There were enough of the little oblong pills to do the job.

And now for the rest. First she allowed herself one good cry. She knew she was old and that she had led a full and happy life. More than that, she knew that she'd made the right choice. Fifty-nine children: that's how many she managed to put on the boat while everything went crazy around her. Fifty-nine. Could she really ask for a better legacy? And so what if she didn't get to go to Honey Island and watch her grandkids grow up … ah, there it was. That thought really got her going. What she wouldn't give to hold them one more time or to see her son's face. But at least they were safe. She'd come to look upon Honey Island as a sort of promised land (or at least a promised swamp) where the people she loved could be free. But Moses didn't reach the promised land and he'd worked for it his whole life. How could Tammany complain? And still she wept. Even people of great faith are allowed their moments of trepidation when the end comes. She let herself weep until the headache and the fever told her it was time to get moving.

A scream cut through the night and Tammany peeked out through a gap in her front curtains. She couldn't see anything, but she knew what it meant. And that old William Butler Yeats poem came to her, the one that began with: "That is no country for old men." And it wasn't. Younger, stronger people would have to fight their way through this. She put on a vinyl record of Fats Domino's *Hey, Las Bas Boogie*. Las Bas translates to "over there" and is sometimes used to refer to Papa Legba — "Papa-over-there" who sits at the crossroads where the human world intersects with that of the spirits.

"Will you come?" she asked aloud as she popped the top off a bottle of *Grace and Grit* beer and settled into her recliner. Then slowly, methodically, she swallowed one pill after another until they were all gone.

She said her prayers and recited Psalm 23. "Yea, though I walk through the valley of the shadow of death, I will fear no evil, for …" she paused and a mischievous grin spread over her face. What was that line from *Deep Blue Sea?* "Because I carry a big stick and I'm the meanest motherfucker in the valley!" She laughed. LL Cool J was a comedic genius.

Suddenly it grew very cold in her little house. She shivered and considered turning up the heat, but she couldn't remember where the thermostat was. She reached for her beer and her hand clumsily knocked it aside.

"Not long now," she said.

It was getting hard to breathe and she struggled to keep her eyes open — which was important because there, in her living room, stood a very old man with a cane.

"Legba."

He held out a hand and helped her up. "Come, my dear."

And she felt so warm and so loved and so … what? Done. Completed. She felt like a symphony that had written itself and now, that the last note had been played, she could finally rest.

PART THREE

STARS

CHAPTER ONE

ON THE ROAD

"I was surprised … by how easy the act of leaving was… The world was suddenly rich with possibility."

Jack Kerouac, <u>On the Road</u>

"…the strangest moment of all, when I didn't know who I was… I wasn't scared. I was just somebody else, some stranger, and my whole life was a haunted life, the life of a ghost."

Jack Kerouac, <u>On the Road</u>

Tanya Morin grabbed her little brother's hand and ran. She had to get out of that house, had to run from the screaming and the chaos and the blood. It was not a conscious decision made, but the instinct to take flight, the instinct of deer when wolves prowl through the valley. But it did not save her.

She'd come home after a date with Jeff and had, in fact, expected an ugly scene. She was rolling in an hour past curfew and was ready for a guilt-trip, a lecture, and the final pronouncement of "You're grounded." But what greeted her when she opened the door… Her mother lay in the hallway, blood from a jagged wound on her shoulder pooling on the beige carpet.

157

"Mom!" Tanya ran to her.

Clinging to consciousness by the barest thread, Marjorie Morin blinked up at her daughter. "*Run*," the word came out in a hoarse whisper and the effort required to give it voice tipped the woman back into blackness.

Tanya pulled her mobile from her jeans pocket and dialed 911. A calm voice asked: "Emergency, do you need police, ambulance or fire?"

"Ambulance! My mom!" And she rattled off her address.

"It's ok, an ambulance is on the way, but I need you to tell me what's happening."

"I — I don't know — I..." At that moment she heard a low moan coming from the living room. "Hang on," she whispered.

While the dispatcher tried again and again to elicit details from the girl, Tanya rose and stepped robotically up to the lounge door. But it wasn't their living room — their living room was white. Her mother, sick of the constant clutter of a family of six, had gone minimalist and, ridiculously, decorated the family room in white: white carpet, white sofa and chairs, white paint on the walls. But these walls were red, the furniture crimson, the deep pile rug a whole spectrum from pink to red to brown. And there in the most colorful patch was her father.

Liam Morin, the fourth tourist on Dr. Edwin Caldwell's list, was presently gnawing on his ten-year-old son's arm. Mitch screamed and writhed in his father's grip. Amy, his twin sister, lay nearby bleeding out from a gash in her throat. And Tommy, the seven-year-old, cowered in a corner, his face a white mask of horror beneath the smears of blood that streaked it.

Tanya screamed and that was a mistake. Her dad's head jerked up and he snarled at her like a wild animal. Only then did she heed her mother's words; she ran. But she did not make a beeline for the front door, instead she dashed over to Tommy and was gathering the child up in her arms when her father collided with her. The 250-pound man barreled full bore into the 115-pound teenage girl and Tanya felt like she had been hit by a train. The impact drove the side of her head into the wall, denting the plaster. She collapsed on top of Tommy, but was unaware of the fact. She was confused, her vision was blurred and the pain in her head was monumental.

Liam's teeth fastened onto her ear and tore it away. And *that* pain was enough to cut through the haze. The girl screamed and kicked and flailed until she managed to wriggle free — her attempt aided by the fact that her father was currently choking on the silver hoop earring that had come away with her ear. She struggled to her feet.

Tanya grabbed her little brother's hand and ran out the back door. Her father — with the earring still stuck in his craw — pursued, driving the pair away from the road and deeper into the woods. Tanya reached the shore of Black Sturgeon Lake and didn't even pause; the lake was a solid sheet of ice now, especially around the shallow edges. Dragging Tommy behind her, she fled along the ice and took refuge beneath an old wooden dock where she pulled Tommy out of the moonlight and into the safety of the shadows. From there they could hear their father bellowing and crashing through the undergrowth and they could also hear the more hopeful sounds of sirens approaching.

"I'm cold," Tommy whispered, but the fog of her concussion was settling over Tanya's brain and she did not comprehend that the child wore only a pair of Spiderman pyjamas and had lost his slippers somewhere in the woods.

"Just need to rest for a minute," she murmured and passed out.

The incubation period for rabies varies from one case to the next. The distance from the bite to the brain, essentially how far the virus has to travel to reach its objective, often determines how long it takes before the patient is symptomatic. New Rabies adhered to this principle as well and with a bite on her ear, it was not long before Tanya Morin sickened with the disease. The headache of concussion blurred into the headache of infection. The confusion of a brain injury segued into the delirium of the virus. When she finally walked away from the dock and the little blue body curled up beneath it, she no longer cared about the pain in her head, nor did she comprehend that she had suffered any great trauma or loss. She felt only the Need. She had to move, to search — for what she was unsure, but she'd know it when she saw it and she had to get moving.

And so it was that she came to be on the side of the road when Lester Jeffrey passed by. He saw the girl standing out in the snowstorm along a lonely stretch of highway and pulled the rig over to give her a lift. The girl came straight to the truck, but had difficulty with the door, so he hopped out to help her.

"What are you doing out on a night like this?" he yelled over the wind. "Are you all right?"

He was a father and always picked up young hitchhikers so that he could drop them somewhere safe. There were too many crazies on the road and he had nightmares about these kids ending up dead in a ditch. He could not see the girl well in the dim light, but she was slight in build and looked like a strong gust of wind might blow her away. He reached out to open the door for her. And that was when the little thing grabbed his arm in a surprisingly strong grip. Her head darted forward and her teeth fastened onto his bare hand. Lester cried out in pain and surprise and tried desperately to shake her off. She would not budge. No matter what he did, no matter how he flailed or hit at her (and yes, he did eventually resort to blows), she would not relinquish her grip. It reminded him of a pit bull — he'd heard those dogs "lock on" when they bite and can still hold on even after death. The longer she held on, the harder he hit until finally one of his blows connected with her jaw. Tanya went reeling backward. She paused only a moment and then came at him again, but Lester was no dummy. As soon as his hand was free, he scrambled up into his truck and slammed the door shut. The girl hit it head on, fell back and ran at it again, all the while uttering a terrible, haunting wail. Lester, with his hand hastily wrapped in a hanky, got the hell outta Dodge. He only paused to bandage the wound properly when he had put a few miles between himself and that lunatic.

"No good deed goes unpunished," he muttered as he dumped peroxide on his hand and wrapped it in clean gauze. The bite hurt like a son of a bitch, but he'd had worse. And it could certainly wait until he finished his run. He was hauling a shipment of games from Everest Toys in Ontario down to *Go! Games and Toys* at the Monroeville Mall in Pennsylvania. Little did he know that he was also transporting something else now. The virus was again on the move.

CHAPTER TWO

ZOMBIEBURGH

"STOP THE UNDEAD IN THE ZOMBIE CAPITOL OF THE WORLD: MONROEVILLE!"

Zombieburgh Lazer Tag Website

"When there's no more room in hell, the dead will walk the earth."

George A. Romero, <u>Dawn of the Dead</u>, 1978

Louella Bernhard pulled into the parking lot of the Monroeville Mall. Her grandson Sam wanted a guitar for Christmas, a (she looked at his wish list again) "Faith Electroacoustic Guitar — Hi Gloss Saturn Cutaway." She had one on layaway at The Guitar Center, but first she had other errands to run. She hit Bath & Body Works. Her daughter Peg liked that Cucumber Melon gift set that they do. And then it was on to Macy's. Peg and her husband had gotten their little girl a Victorian dollhouse from Santa. It was an expensive purchase so, to help with the cost, Lou offered to buy the furniture that went with it. Standing in line at the cash register, her stomach began to growl. She had a lot to do, but surely she could take half-an-hour to grab some lunch. She paid for her purchases and headed for the food court.

OF STARLIGHT AND PLAGUE

Outside, at the far end of the parking lot, there sat a truck with an empty trailer. The cab — a Kenworth Sleeper — was dark and the windows were fogged with condensation. And in the bed behind the driver's seat lay Lester Jeffrey. Since making his delivery, he'd come down with a hell of a bug: high fever, roaring headache and nausea. He laid down two days ago and didn't get up again. He drifted in and out of consciousness and dreamt of the hitchhiker, the girl he'd tried to help. But in the dream she wasn't a girl, not completely. She had a wolf's maw filled with long, sharp fangs and she followed him wherever he went, matching him step for step. The dream held him and he managed to fight his way to the surface only a few times over those two days. He'd take a drink of water, grimacing at the jagged pain in his throat, and then he'd be sucked down again into a nightmare of claws and teeth. On the third day he rose again, hungry for the first time in ages, and went out in search of food. He left the cab door standing wide open and staggered toward the mall — no coat, no shoes and with the rock salt that had been spread in the parking lot sticking to the bottom of his socks.

Turns out the mall was the worst place for him. It was too bright and the mix of human chatter and music was a din in his ears. And dear God he felt bad, like 200 pounds of walking roadkill. He spotted the Food Court and, more importantly, an empty chair where he could sit and rest for a while. But there was no peace to be had. There was a crying baby and two women laughing and someone dropped a tray. *It hurt.*

"Shut up shut up shut up," he moaned and clamped his hands over his ears.

Louella looked up, aware for the first time that this raggedy man was clutching at his head and rocking back and forth in his seat. He must have felt her eyes on him, because he looked at her then. He went very still and stared at her. The look reminded Lou of George Nuss. As the town lecher he used to look at her like that when she was younger and still had a discernible waistline. It was an unsettling look of interest without empathy. With a glance old George could make you feel like a piece of meat. And here it was again, repeated on the face of this stranger; but she was old now, and chubby, and should be past all that. The man made a sound then, like the one a dog makes when it chokes itself straining against its leash and a line of saliva ran down his chin. She pushed her half-eaten lunch away, gathered her bags and pocketbook, and rose to leave.

The man stood too.

He was between her and the exit, but there was an escalator behind her between Bourbon St. Cafe and Charley's Grilled Subs. She'd take that to get away from him. The Food Court was growing quiet now as more and more people stopped to gawk at this man with his stringy hair and feral eyes. Thick ropes of foam caught in the stubble on his chin and soaked the front of his shirt.

"Excuse me, sir. Can I help you?" A man, in a black ranger-style hat and with a security patch on his sleeve, stepped in between the stranger and Lou.

Lester looked at him, a ghastly smile pulling his lips back to show his teeth, and then he lunged. His head darted forward as if he was going to steal a kiss. Instead his teeth fastened on the corner of the security guard's mouth and he ripped the flesh away. The guard screamed and that was the cue: panic erupted. In a society primed for terrorist attacks and mass shootings, you run at the first sign of trouble and Louella was caught up in the stampede. She was jostled and swept along with the crowd as she reflexively clutched her bags to her and struggled to stay on her feet. They surged out of the Food Court as more security guards fought to get in. As the herd reached the main and much wider corridor of the mall, they encountered greater chaos. Instead of one group moving one way, they collided with many fractured gangs of confused people, panicked by the shrieks and dashing in all directions. Louella was swept left toward Macy's. And all was a blur as she ran.

A large man shoved Lou out of his way, slamming her face-first into the glass front of a store. She found herself looking up into the face of a zombie. His green visage was framed by a shock of black hair, his eyes were blank, his mouth a gaping hole dotted with jagged teeth. It was a painted mural with the words "Zombieburgh Laser Tag" etched beneath. She stared at the zombie picture for what seemed like a long time. That's right. This is where Romero filmed *Dawn of the Dead* and there used to be a clocktower and a bridge over an artificial pond where she tossed pennies and made wishes as a child. And in the movie the zombies took possession of the mall. They tottered through the shops to the chipper xylophone notes of Herbert Chappell's "The Gonk." How did it go again?

"Ma'am?" a woman behind her asked.

Louella spun around and looked at her vaguely.

"Are you ok?" The woman was middle-aged, nicely dressed and wearing a Macy's name tag.

"Uh, yeah," Louella answered.

"We're asking everyone to come into the store. They want us to lock all the shops down until they've resolved …" a banshee-like shriek echoed from the Food Court, "… that."

"He bit him," Louella whispered.

"What?"

"He bit that man in the face!" Louella's voice was rising in pitch.

"Come on." The woman took Lou gently by the arm and led her into the store. She let the last few stragglers in and then locked the plexiglass security doors.

Standing there amidst the wide-eyed crowd, Louella noticed that there were dark flecks on the backs of her hands. She rubbed at them and they left red smears on her skin. Blood. She wondered briefly if she was bleeding, but then realized, no. It was from the security guard. Her stomach lurched as she headed for the ladies' room. There, in the diffuse yellow light, she stared dumbfounded at what she saw in the mirror. There was blood on her face, in her hair and on her coat. Louella scrubbed at herself with the coarse paper towels until her skin was raw. The soap — she'd heard once that it was supposed to be "cherry-almond scented" — had a thick, cloying smell that did nothing to help her stomach and yet she used up a whole dispenser's worth in an effort to clean herself up. With the distraction of the blood gone, she began to notice other things: the ghastly pallor of her face, the bruise blossoming on her right cheek, and below it the split lip that was swelling up fast. That must have been from when she hit the glass. She let out a long, slow breath.

"What the fuck was that?" she asked her own reflection. The Louella in the mirror had no answer.

It had been an animal attack. Human violence was different — it was all guns or knives or fists. But this was tooth and claw, bite and rend. And it should have been her. If the security guard had not stepped in when he did, it *would* have been her. Dear God. Her hands shook as that "You've-just-dodged-a-bullet" relief flooded through her, and yet why? Why should she be spared and the guard not? It was all so random, so arbitrary, so damn ridiculous. And she saw it again in vivid detail. The teeth, slick with drool, had fastened on the man's flesh and tore his bottom lip away. And the blood flew and the guard's incisors lay exposed down to the gum-line and then there was the crowd, running, driving her along and she was afraid that she'd fall and be crushed under all those panicked feet. She'd hit the glass front of that laser tag place like a bug hitting a windshield and the whole side of her face throbbed from the impact. She dug through her purse and dry-swallowed two Extra Strength Excedrin. And then, because there was nothing for it, she took one more deep, steadying breath and went out to face the world.

The woman sitting opposite Officer Vince Miller looked like a refugee from a war zone. Given her age, the bruises on her face and the visible signs of shock, he'd already requested that a paramedic come take a look at her. While they waited for the medic, he took her statement. They were still within that "Golden Hour" — the time period immediately after an event when a witness's memory is at its best. And the old girl was absolutely clear about what had happened.

"Did he say anything to you?" Miller asked.

"No," Louella shook her head. "At one point he *was* talking. He kept saying 'Shut up' over and over again."

"To who?"

"No one. He just sat there with his eyes closed and his hands over his ears. He was rocking back and forth. I wondered if he was hearing voices in his head."

"Then what happened?"

"He was coughing and drooling. He looked," Lou broke off and shook her head again.

"Go on," Vince said gently.

"He looked like the rabid fox we had on the farm two summers ago. He was so sick. Thing is: it didn't even occur to me that he needed help. That I should call an ambulance for him."

"Why not?"

"Because I was afraid of him."

And she had been — immediately and without question. He looked absolutely wretched and yet this evoked no pity in her. She didn't hover over her duty to help him. As he stared at her, her heart raced and every instinct screamed at her to get away from that slathering mouth.

She pushed these thoughts away and told the cop everything about the incident that she could remember. Then she sat down — on the low bench in the Macy's shoe department to wait for the paramedic. It was a nuisance. She just wanted to go home. But Officer Miller brought her a cup of vending machine hot chocolate and she sat nursing the drink, letting it warm her. The attack and the panicked run through the mall had taken, oh, maybe five minutes in total. But it was utterly transformative. It had taken her from the glow of Christmas lights and the gentle refrain of *Silent Night* that had played over the tannoy, to what Herman Melville called the "damp, drizzly November in my soul." That line was from *Moby Dick* and Ishmael's response to that feeling was to "quietly take to the ship." Louella's response was similar, an innate need to go to her place of solace. For her it was her farm, quiet save for the conversations of chickens and the lowing of her cows when their udders were full and it was time for milking. She just wanted to go home.

Finally given the all clear, she walked back to her car, letting the cold air revive her and the snow and grit clean the blood off the soles of her shoes. Nat King Cole crooned *The Christmas Song* to her when she started the engine and she pulled her mobile from her purse and changed the playlist. It was a two-hour drive home and she needed something a little more rousing. Soon there was the steady beat of drum and cowbell and Def Leppard's Joe Elliot advised that it was better to burn out than to fade away. And the music bucked her up enough for the journey ahead.

She drove the back roads home, finally passing the old covered bridge on the outskirts of Midwood. When she was little, she was convinced that that was the bridge Washington Irving talked about in *The Legend of Sleepy Hollow*. She could picture it all too clearly: the headless horseman pursuing a terror-stricken Ichabod Crane through the nighttime woods. Somewhere along the way, her child's mind had tangled the Headless Horseman up with the Four Horsemen of the Apocalypse that she learned about in church. They would come at the end of days and bring famine and death, war and pestilence. The association was so strong that she used to be terrified of that old bridge, certain that it symbolized the end of things. It did not take a huge imaginative leap. It was only four-thirty in the afternoon of a December day and already shadows had settled on the bridge. It was unlit and the interior was eerily dark. A cold nothingness. An abyss.

At that moment, a tree branch raked the passenger door of her pickup truck. She'd gotten so carried away with her thoughts that she'd drifted too far to the right.

"Dammit, woman, wake up," she said aloud.

She made herself go slow and safely all the way out to the farm. And it was only as she turned into the drive that she realized: she'd forgotten to pick up Sam's guitar.

CHAPTER THREE

SOMETHING WICKED THIS WAY COMES

"One thorn of experience is worth a whole wilderness of warning."

James Russell Lowell

"She had witnessed enough calamity in her years upon the earth ... she knew that another storm was coming, even if she didn't understand it."

Max Brooks, <u>World War Z</u>

The incident at Monroeville Mall took place on the twenty-second of December — one day after Otis Hudson was attacked in the parking lot of Whole Foods Market and one day after Emily Hardy stepped in front of a truck. Louella did not know about these other events and was soon caught up in the final preparations for Christmas. There was all the cooking and baking to be done. She had to rewrap one of Peg's presents — the gold woven basket containing the bath products had gotten crushed in the stampede. And her friend Fletch drove her back to the mall to pick up the guitar. He even kept it at his house so that Sam would not spot the tell-tale shape and guess the surprise.

She was surrounded by twinkling lights and gaily wrapped presents and Yogi Yorgesson singing *I Yust Go Nuts at Christmas* on WHMD. And in truth, she felt like crap. The bruise on her cheek had come up a deep purple and she had a fat lip. And she wasn't sleeping well. Granted, her nights would have been disturbed anyway. She'd read an article once about how, as you age, hormonal changes in your body adversely affect your sleep. But this was different. She dreamt of Monroeville every night, jerking awake to find her covers in a knot and her nightgown drenched in sweat. The nightmares were so bad, she dreaded going back to sleep. And so she sat up, watching old *Frasier* reruns with the sound turned down so she wouldn't wake Sam.

More than anything, she was just sad. The world could be such a brutal place and it took so much energy to absorb it all and still wrap presents and make a honey roast ham and bake cookies and pretend she was excited about the holiday. And, unfortunately, it was about to get worse.

A week later Louella began to realize that the attack at Monroeville was not an isolated incident. As she listened to the news of Otis's assault on Lance Jessop on the twenty-ninth and how Nicholas Durand was shot after biting someone on the thirtieth, she suddenly felt very cold. That was three similar attacks in just over a week. What on earth was going on? As Christmas gave way to New Years, she tried to ignore her growing sense of unease. She told herself that it was a coincidence and that people — quite a lot of people in fact — were nuts. Drugs, mental illness — anything like that could have prompted the attack she'd witnessed. She knew that. It was just common sense. But for the first time in her life, her good, old-fashioned common sense was being shouted down by something else, some instinct that goaded her. And she was afraid. A drop in barometric pressure could irritate an arthritic joint and so her wrists ached before every rainfall. But this … *this ache* went deeper and she felt sure: a storm was coming.

Her daughter Peg, who ran the Carnegie Library in town, was surprised to find her mother waiting at its entrance when she went in to work on January second. Louella loved the library and came often, but to be camped out in the cold before opening hours…

"Is everything ok?" Peg asked.

"Yeah, I just want to look a few things up."

"A half an hour before opening time…"

"I knew you'd be here," Louella gestured impatiently at the door. Once inside she made her way to the internet terminals and switched one on.

Peg watched her, confused. Her mother was going to surf the net? I mean, yeah, she knew how; but she rarely did. "Can I help with something?"

"Nope," Lou mumbled distractedly. That typing course she'd had in high school held her in good stead because her fingers flew over the keyboard. "I'm fine here, honey. You go do what you have to."

Margaret (Peg to family and friends) certainly had enough to be getting on with. She gathered up the books from the "Featured" shelf. These catered to the pre-Christmas period: recipe books, craft books in case you wanted to give homemade gifts, tales by Dickens and Clement C. Moore. She replaced them with books on dieting, exercise and how to stop smoking. Her patrons, she knew, would have New Year's resolutions to keep. When their enthusiasm waned — in roughly two weeks time — she'd replace the dieting books with novels set in tropical locations and nature books that focused on spring (all to fight the winter doldrums).

She paused in her work for a moment and looked at her mother. The old woman was hunched over the keyboard with a strawberry Twizzler dangling from her mouth. Uh oh. Louella's Twizzler compulsion only emerged when she was stressed. But Peg didn't have time to ponder this. She had to run a "Babies and Books" session in forty minutes and the library would soon be full of squealing toddlers. She put the coffee on and got back to work.

In *The Zombie Survival Guide*, Max Brooks lists six things that could indicate an impending zombie outbreak. These include murders, disappearances, cases of "violent insanity," riots, and the spread of disease. While Louella had never read the book, she gravitated toward these topics and it was amazing what her internet search revealed. The first article to come up when she typed in "Cannibalistic Attacks" was by Christopher Ingraham of the Washington Post. The headline read: "Americans bite each other literally all the time, data shows." It noted that in 2012 there were 42,000 assaults in which one person bit another.

"Holy smoke," Louella muttered.

The article broke it down: that equates to approximately 114 bites per day or one every twelve minutes. To put it into perspective though, in a nation of roughly 350 million people, biting attacks made up just 0.03 percent of all ER admissions. The statistics seemed to suggest that, while uncommon, the attack at Monroeville had simply been part of an established pattern. However, the article went on to mention that most bites (86% of them) were inflicted during bar fights. "Late night alcohol-fueled aggression," particularly over the weekend or on public holidays, accounted for most of the injuries.

That wasn't what happened at Monroeville — a weekday lunchtime attack. And, come to think of it, that's not what happened in the case of Lance Jessop, who was out one afternoon working in his garden when Otis Hudson took a chunk out of his arm. And so she refined her search still further, looking for atypical attacks that involved bites. She began to find multiple examples of these clustered around certain areas. In Miami Eugene Redford, aka the "Causeway Cannibal," ripped a man's cheek open with his teeth. Was it another example to be placed in the same category as Monroeville and New Orleans? Maybe, maybe not. Redford could have been on angel dust or PCP — who knows? BUT his victim went on to bite a nurse at the hospital. She was missing and shortly after her disappearance, an elderly couple were attacked outside their home in a Miami suburb. Both sustained multiple injuries including bites.

Then there was Reading, England. Claire Milne entered the flat of her fifty-nine-year-old mother, Victoria Reinland. Finding her in the bath, she proceeded to attack her mom, biting her repeatedly on the legs and hand. During the altercation, she managed to sever Victoria's thumb and was seen to chew and swallow the appendage. The following day police in the Reading area were called to a primary school to break up a mass brawl among the children. An article entitled, "School children beat up cops" outlined how thirty youngsters in school uniforms attacked the officers, seriously injuring two of them and leaving four others with minor injuries that included bites to their faces and hands. There were similar outbreaks of violence in Latvia, Ontario, Germany, China, Kenya and Brazil. A rabies outbreak was followed by another cannibalistic attack on the Caribbean island of Cáscara. And a Qantas flight from Berlin to Sydney descended into chaos when a man reportedly "ran amok" in the cabin, biting fellow passengers. In every case the violence seemed to be preceded or accompanied by an outbreak of the flu. The CDC or World Health Organization had been dispatched to all of these incidents. That was the most frightening thing. Those organizations did not involve themselves in trifles. So what exactly was this 'flu' and how was it linked to such outrageous violence?

Next she pulled up *The Monroeville News* website and was shocked to learn that the security guard, Jonathan Herridge, victim of a brutal assault at the mall, had died — an apparent suicide. The article cited his long battle with depression and friends speculated that the attack had been the "last straw." The paper then recapped the details of the incident and noted that several of his colleagues had been treated at Forbes Hospital for bites and other injuries. It was an attack, the reporter noted, "that Romero himself would have filmed at the mall." Another item, much smaller and further down on the website, reported on a local flu outbreak and urged the elderly to get their shots.

She printed out each of these articles. She saw them as beads on an abacus and slid one over with the addition of each new fact. She did not like what it was adding up to. And there was more. Within the affected areas, the local newspapers recorded an abnormal number of animal attacks. They were bizarre: a chihuahua savaged a coyote, a deer crashed through a family's picture window and bit a man who'd just been sitting on his couch watching TV. And a pack of dogs — most with collars and tags — rampaged through a zoo biting the animals caged there.

Louella totted up all the beads on her mental abacus and had only one thing to say. "Shit."

A woman seated nearby cleared her throat and when Lou glanced up, she was met with a disapproving look. Louella was surprised — not because someone objected to her swearing loudly in a library, but because there was anyone present to be offended. She glanced at her watch, it was past noon. She'd been at it for three hours. But those three hours had been enough to convince her that she was right: a storm really was coming.

That night she called a family meeting. "Family" in Louella's mind was a broad term. It encompassed kin and close friends alike and so a small group of people crowded around her kitchen table. There was Peg and her husband Alec (their daughter Mae watched *Scooby Doo* in the living room). There was Sam, the grandchild she'd raised after her son and his wife died in a car accident. Her brother-in-law, Levi, was there (although his daughter Patience — the town sheriff — was on duty. His son Wyn was looking after his mother who couldn't yet manage on her own since the stroke). And Fletcher came, of course, as well as Arnold and Bib Grissinger and Effie Dietz.

"You guys know what happened at the mall before Christmas. It's just that …" Louella wasn't sure how best to state her case. "I don't think it was an isolated event. In fact, I think we're going to see a lot more of it before too long."

"What do you mean?" Arnold asked.

Louella produced the stack of articles she printed out at the library. She enumerated each one and passed them around.

"The same pattern seems to be repeating itself all over the world. There are vicious, unprovoked assaults. There is also an increase in animal attacks from both pets and local wildlife. And it's all accompanied by the outbreak of some flu-like illness. Each of these locations represents a 'cluster' and," she'd saved the article on Jonathan Herridge until last, "I think we have a new cluster brewing just up the road."

She fell silent then and listened to the rustle of papers as they read through the articles. *They're going to think I'm stupid … or crazy,* she thought glumly. Hell, she was starting to think that herself. She chewed on a thumbnail.

Fletcher Landis read carefully through it all and then looked at her appraisingly. He and Louella had been friends for going on sixty years (since kindergarten class at Midwood Combined Elementary and Senior High School) and he probably knew her better than anyone. She was, in the words of Kerouac, "my girl and my kind of girlsoul" — soft and maternal, but surprisingly tough. And she was smart. He was a writer often praised for his imagination and the meticulous research that went into his novels. Yet there were times when that woman, with her high school diploma, a baby on her hip and cow shit on her boots, made him feel like an idiot child by comparison. And that is why he knew that trouble was coming to Midwood.

"So on the basis of this, you …" He left the sentence open-ended and waited for her reply.

"I want to start stocking the farm up with supplies. And you all might want to consider coming out here to stay for a while."

Effie spoke up. "I'm sorry, honey, but this is ridiculous."

Louella had expected that response and was ready to challenge it. "Why?"

"Because … it is! This is Midwood! And you're worried about things that are happening in Nairobi?"

"It happened in Monroeville," Louella said quietly.

Levi's voice was the next one heard. "I know that was rough, Lou. But it's a helluva jump from that to 'let's barricade ourselves in at the farm.'"

Louella nodded. "I know. I *know* we're not in trouble yet. But I think before too long we will be and this time is our grace period — the only time to really prepare before …"

"Before what?" Bib asked.

"Before you all get an eyeful of what I saw at the mall."

Effie rose with an exasperated sigh. "Sorry, Lou, but I've got more important things to worry about than made-up crap."

"I'm not making this up! I didn't write these articles."

"No, but you are interpreting them to suggest that armageddon is right around the corner and I don't buy it. Look," Effie softened her tone because she really didn't want to hurt her friend's feelings, "you're upset about what you saw. Anyone would be. Just give yourself some time to get over it before you start ordering MREs from Amazon."

"Yeah," Louella nodded, trying not to let her face betray the fact that she had cleaned Amazon out of their supply and had 144 Meals Ready-to-Eat winging their way to the farm as they spoke.

Effie leaned in, kissed her friend on the cheek and left.

"I know you all think I'm nuts," Louella said quietly.

"No," Peg shook her head and gestured toward the stack of papers. "It's a compelling argument…"

"…but?"

Peg sighed. "But it sounds like a movie."

"I know that too. I am also well aware of the fact that we're all going to look pretty stupid if I'm wrong. It would be embarrassing to buy into the ramblings of an old kook."

"I didn't say that."

"No, but that's what other people will say," Louella said gently.

Fletch interrupted mother and daughter. "So then surely the solution is that we prepare, but we don't broadcast the fact. We quietly stock up, we keep an eye out for any sign of a growing … *cluster* in Monroeville and plan to meet out here if there's trouble. If you are being overcautious, Lou, then nobody needs to know about it, do they?"

"It's not a bad plan," Peg nodded.

"If you're wrong," Fletch continued, "then what's the worst that can happen? We all end up with well-stocked larders. It's not exactly a hardship."

This was met with silence as each of them thought it over. Louella felt appraising eyes on her and rose to empty the dishwasher. Seven people watched her stack dinner plates in the cupboard. She was smart, no doubt about that, and she was tough. She'd lost a son and a husband and had soldiered on to run the farm and raise Sam on her own. It took more than trifles to rattle her and she *was rattled*. That much was clear. But to buy into all this… Peg was right, it sounded like something out of a movie. You'd have to be crazy or stupid to …

In the end, Louella came away with assurances of support — made, not because they were convinced by her theory, but simply because they were a close-knit group used to backing each other up. As Ann Landers once said, "Love is friendship that has caught fire. It's loyalty."

Later that evening, with Mae finally in bed, Peg sat in her daughter's room, rocking in the old chair and mulling things over. She had her mother's logical mind and hence was doing some mental arithmetic of her own. First off, she trusted her mom implicitly. This was the woman who had always been there for her and who loved her without condition. This was the woman who gave her sound advice and comforting hugs and financial help — the undisputed matriarch of the family. And she loved her so much.

But then there was her theory: the idea that Midwood would be hit, well let's just say it, by something akin to a zombie plague. It scared her, and not because she expected to see blood-soaked neighbors shambling down Main Street. It scared her because it called her mother's mind into question. Was this a sign of dementia? Or was it just paranoia born of a hard life? After losing dad and Eben, she'd understandably be afraid of any more loss in the family. Maybe *that's* why her mom was seeing the world as a Romero flick.

But what about all those printouts? They weren't the product of Louella's mind, that was stuff taken straight off the internet. While the net wasn't always reliable, those articles had been gleaned from reputable sources like the BBC, The New York Times, Canada's Globe and Mail. The facts in those reports were indisputable. The only remaining question was one of interpretation. Effie clearly believed that each of the incidents represented some of the random crazy of this world. With 7.2 billion people on the planet, of course there was going to be lunacy... But there would also be pandemics. It wasn't that long ago that the Chief Medical Correspondent for CNN predicted that "The big one is coming, and it's going to be a flu pandemic." Wasn't flu one of the elements that mom identified within each of those clusters?

"Oh balls," she sighed.

"Honey," Alec was a darker shadow in the dim outline of the doorway. "I think you'd better see this."

The TV in the living room was on. Alec turned up the volume just as they played a video clip — an arial shot of what appeared to be a riot. People were running around, tackling each other to the ground as more and more people came piling in. It was, and this thought brought Peg up short, just like something out of a movie.

The scene then cut to a tanned reporter who explained, "These are the only images we were able to obtain from the island of Cáscara."

"Cáscara — wasn't that one of the places your mom..."

"Shh," Peg cut him off.

The reporter was saying: "It would appear that an outbreak of sporadic, yet terrible violence has swept the island with many here in neighboring Puerto Rico fearful that the chaos will spread."

An anchorman in the studio asked, "What do local authorities have to say, Jeff?"

"The police and local government here have no further information at this time. We do know, however, that the CDC sent a team to Cáscara to deal with a flu epidemic on December twenty-ninth and that the island was subsequently placed under quarantine by the U.S. Navy."

"Is there any link between the flu outbreak and the violence we're seeing?"

"The CDC has not commented on that. They did, however, issue a statement earlier today announcing that they were pulling their doctors out of the affected area."

"Actually, Jeff, we have that clip in the studio now."

The scene shifted to a press conference. A spokesman for the CDC, a Dr. Ellis Cheever, stood at the podium. He explained that, after the outbreak of a novel virus, the island was under strict quarantine and that all recent visitors to Cáscara had now been traced.

"Have any of them been exposed to the disease?" a voice off-camera was asking.

"Unfortunately, yes. We have identified isolated pockets of the infection at several different locations around the world. Each of these is now under the management of either the CDC or the World Health Organization."

"And what about the outbreak of violence on Cáscara?" another reporter asked. "Is that hampering your efforts in dealing with the flu?"

"Local violence has effectively brought our efforts to a halt and today we've taken the decision to evacuate our personnel. It is, sadly, one of the hazards we face in trying to tackle global infections. We've seen it before — in the Congo in 2018. In that instance, we had to pull our Ebola experts out of the worst hit areas due to fighting between local factions."

"Dr. Cheever!" A woman with a press badge waved at him for his attention. "Here's the big question: how worried should we be?"

"About the spread of the infection? Right now, all of the facts indicate that we can contain the disease to the affected areas."

"Have you found a cure?"

"Not yet. But we are working on the development of a vaccine."

With the press conference over, it was back to the anchorman. "In other news tonight, riots in New Orleans. After the shooting of Nicholas Durand, the second unarmed black man to die in police custody in twenty-four hours, there have been mass demonstrations throughout the city. We go now to Nikki Ford reporting from New Orleans. Nikki, I understand that one of the protests turned into a riot …"

A pretty blond reporter spoke earnestly into the camera. "That's right, Steven. I'm standing in Jackson Square where a protest is currently in progress." The camera swept over the crowd with their Black Lives Matter signs held aloft. "As you can see, things here are peaceful and orderly. But at seven o'clock this evening, a riot broke out at a public dock on Lake Pontchartrain. Local authorities are still trying to get the situation under control, but early reports confirm multiple casualties."

Alec said quietly, "And New Orleans …"

"...was another cluster," Peg nodded as she switched off the TV. They looked at each other for a long moment. Finally Peg broke the silence, "We'll let Mae sleep here one more night and tomorrow we'll move her out to the farm."

By the time Levi got home, Ginny was already curled up in bed. And he was glad. He didn't want to tell her about Louella's theory. His wife's recovery from the stroke had been slow and painful and she didn't need any further upset. What was he going to say to her? That Midwood would soon turn into the *Night of the Living Dead*? What the hell was Lou thinking?

She'd always been so sensible — someone you could count on. Like after Ginny's stroke: Louella had sat vigil at the hospital; she'd come in every week to clean the house and had stocked the fridge with enough food to feed an army. And he'd loved her for it. Which was why, of course, he hadn't given her any grief tonight. All that shit at the mall had clearly upset her and, if by agreeing to stock up on canned goods and pasta, he could set her mind to rest, then so be it. But he couldn't buy into it.

More than anything he was just sad. He had reached the age of decline — not only when his own body creaked like a rusty spring, but when all his friends were starting to go too. His brother James had died of a heart attack. His best friend Aldis Schmidt was battling prostate cancer and then Ginny had her stroke. Now Lou was ... what? Going soft in the head? And he looked at a faded picture on the wall — a family trip to Rehoboth Beach all those years ago. His kids, Patience and Wyn, stood beside Louella's Peg and Eben. They were young and brown-skinned from the sun. And behind them, laughing at something off camera, stood Ginny and Lou in bathing suits and beach cover ups. James had one muscular arm wrapped around Louella's waist and they looked beautiful. And healthy. And now Eben was dead and James was dead and Ginny had trouble feeding herself and Lou... He shook his head and, having had enough of these thoughts for one day, went to bed.

Louella's grandson Sam was heading up to bed too. His mind reeled. If there had been any doubt about grandma's theory, the evening news had laid that to rest. But at the same time, she was *right*. And he was hit with an odd mix of relief and worry. On the one hand, his faith in her remained unshaken. He'd watched the disbelief, the expressions of pity and indulgence flicker across Levi's and Bib's and Arnold's faces. And it had scared him: the idea that grandma could be so confused. She had been the bedrock of his world for as long as he could remember and bedrock was not supposed to crumble.

But she was right — right and sharp as ever — and that in and of itself was horrifying. He tried to imagine those scenes from Cáscara playing out on the streets of Midwood. Again he hit a mental roadblock: Midwood was too quiet, too boring. He tried to imagine the little Norman Rockwell town suddenly turning into something out of *Revenge of the Living Dead*. It seemed impossible. But at that moment his grandmother was sitting at the kitchen table making lists of everything they'd need to get through the trouble. Because the trouble was real.

He flopped down on his bed and stared pensively at the posters lining his walls. There was a Midwood High School "Go Bears!" pennant and a poster of Marvin the Martian saying, "I will give up my Illudium Q-36 Explosive Space Modulator when you pry it from my cold, dead fingers." There was a picture of the *Lion King* with the caption "Hakuna Mafuckit." And a drawing of a zombie. It held a severed human hand that was itself flipping you the bird. It read, "Someone has issues…" He looked at the zombie for a long while — the gray face, the bared teeth, the sunken eyes — and wondered if this was the future.

CHAPTER FOUR

AND SO IT BEGINS...

"There are all kinds of emergencies out there that we can prepare for. Take a zombie apocalypse for example. That's right, I said z-o-m-b-i-e a-p-o-c-a-l-y-p-s-e. You may laugh now, but when it happens you'll be happy you read this, and hey, maybe you'll even learn a thing or two about how to prepare for a real emergency."

CDC Website, Public Health Matters Blog — Preparedness 101

"I keep looping back to PREPARATION being the key to dealing with any situation... By the way, the reference to zombies, while adding a bit of levity, refers to the inevitable event of a very lethal, highly contagious pandemic breaking out. It has happened regularly in history and it will happen again. It is not a matter of if, but when."

Bob Mayer, *The Green Beret Survival Guide*
for the Apocalypse, Zombies and More

The sun rose the following morning to find Louella still sitting at her kitchen table surveying her night's work. This consisted of page after page of lists. Her grocery list was a mile long: food, personal hygiene items, cleaning materials and first aid supplies...

"And Aleve ..." she muttered as she wrote. "Antacids, Aspirin ...what else?" She thought for a moment and then added 'Booze and Cigarettes' to the list. She'd once caught an episode of *Armageddon Outfitters* on the National Geographic channel. On it they advised that, in the event of social breakdown, you'd be wise to stock up on coveted items that you can use for trade.

"What else?"

She went through James's tool collection last night and found it to be complete. She had plenty of feed for the animals and seed for wheat, alfalfa and corn ready to plant in April. She'd start her vegetables in February and transplant them out to her garden after the last frost. She needed more batteries, gasoline and firewood. She'd have Rich Ziegler come out to inspect the well for mechanical issues and recheck the water for coliforms and nitrates. She'd stock up on spare filters, water softeners and chlorine. She'd had the wind turbines (that provided the farm with power) serviced in the fall and they were fine. And she needed ammunition for James's guns.

At four o'clock that morning, she had walked around and around the house, making notes of every vulnerable point they'd need to fortify if things got bad. Their best defense really was their location. Her farm was situated in a remote valley, away from the potential chaos of towns and cities. But even so, by sunrise she had sketched a few basic plans. Would reinforcing the doors and windows be enough? Just how bad could it get? Would it become necessary to wall in the area between the house and the barn to create one large compound? The idea of such huge changes made her feel stupid again, like she was overreacting.

"God, I'm really losing it, aren't I?" she mumbled as she rubbed her tired eyes.

She'd talk to Alec. Her son-in-law owned *Pioneer Construction* and maybe he could interject a little sanity into all this.

She looked at her lists again. "So what am I forgetting?"

As if in answer to that question, her rooster crowed in the barn.

"I'm forgetting to do my damn chores." She rose, slipped on her black rubber boots and went to see to the animals.

The news that morning was full of the New Orleans riot and the "unrest" on Cáscara. However, Midwood barely took notice. Pushing her cart up

181

and down the aisles of Sage Foods Grocery, the snippets of conversation Louella overheard were mundane — the gossip, local. There was a great deal of discussion about the mayoral election. The filing deadline for the primaries was in early March, and incumbent Mayor Albitz had yet to confirm if he would run for re-election. Jill at Flare Clothes Boutique was planning Midwood's first ever fashion show to model the new spring lines. And Patience had pulled over Rick Kaesemeyer last night on suspicion of drunk driving and had spotted an ounce of weed in his car.

Louella couldn't believe it: not the bit about Kaesemeyer — of course he got busted, he was an idiot — but the fact that Kaesemeyer and Albitz and this year's collection of lightweight culottes occupied their attention so. By all accounts, Cáscara was a bloodbath and New Orleans? It was the site of a cluster — she was sure of it. A new disease with no current vaccine had just gained a foothold on American soil. She was in the toiletries aisle now, stocking up on shower gel and toothpaste when she paused, Value 5 Pack of Colgate in her arms, and realized: Of course they don't care. Until this moment, who the hell had even heard of Cáscara? In fact, where *was* Cáscara? Somewhere in the Caribbean. It seemed to be a little patch of rainforest and one rustic town in the middle of nowhere and yes, it was sad to hear that they were having troubles. Pastor Kulp would no doubt suggest a church fundraiser to support the victims of the disease and the good folk of Midwood would give generously. They would say prayers and the pastor would probably trot out his "No Man is an Island" sermon. It was the standard homily he used when trying to get his insular flock to engage with the wider world. He'd open with Romans 14:7 — "We do not live for ourselves only, and we do not die for ourselves only." And the congregation would acknowledge, on a comfortable, cerebral level, that it had a duty to help. But Cáscara was too far away to grab them by their guts. They knew none of the victims. The violence depicted in those grainy aerial shots was hundreds of miles away and that is where plagues always happened — *away*. In poor countries with exotic names and brown-skinned women to wail over the dead.

And New Orleans? Big city. Far away. And wholly divorced from the quiet valley where Midwood reposed in the snow.

But Louella had seen the virus up close, had seen it go to work on Jonathan Herridge's face. And she wondered if that terrible event — which to her had felt like a kick in the teeth — would actually prove to be a blessing in disguise. Perhaps God had shown her that for a reason. She knew what was coming and therefore could protect her family from it. As she wrestled her shopping cart with its wonky wheels up to the register, people looked at her in surprise. The cart was crammed full and piled high.

"Good Lord, Lou," Katie Boehler laughed as she started to ring it all up. "Are you feeding an army?"

Every child in Midwood has, at one time or another, heard the story of "Bloody Bones." It is not an intricate tale with a complex plot or characters; it consists only of a low voice saying, "Bloody Bones, I'm on the street outside. Bloody Bones, I'm on the porch. Bloody Bones, I'm at your front door …" and on and on. With each sentence, Bloody Bones comes a step nearer — inside the house, on the first step and up to the second floor. Then Bloody Bones is at your bedroom door, in your room and by your bed. Closer and closer he comes until the narrator, usually an older sibling, screams "Gotcha!" He grabs you and you (hearing this for the first time at, say, the age of seven) just about wet the bed. Why is such a thin story so memorable? Because Bloody Bones is never defined and never described. Is he alive or dead, skeleton or flesh? Don't know. He could be anything or all things that bump their way through the night. And he is coming. He is fate. But what fate exactly? What will happen when he reaches you? It is never said. But the dread you feel is real enough as onward he comes and there is nothing you can do to stop it.

Perhaps it was the dim recollection of Bloody Bones that played on people's minds in Midwood. Because the nightly news soon felt like a recitation of the old story. The "flu" epidemic was revealed to be in fact a mutated strain of the rabies virus. And it was spreading. Bloody Bones, I'm in New Orleans. Bloody Bones, I'm in Atlanta. Bloody Bones, I'm in New York. Bloody Bones, New Jersey and Philadelphia and Pittsburgh. And suddenly New Rabies wasn't an "away" plague anymore, but one that seethed just up the road. It was in places with prosaic names like Monroeville and the women who wailed over their dead wore the same clothes as you and spoke in the same tongue.

New Orleans started to implode on the fourth of January. There were too many infected to confine to the treatment centers and the army was forced to withdraw to the city limits in one final attempt at containment.

NOPD Officer Darren Wazseki had been on duty for thirty-six hours when he walked casually up to the quarantine line, pulled his service revolver and shot himself in the head. A harried-looking anchorman commented, "The death of Officer Wazseki is, sadly, not an isolated incident. His is the third suicide we've seen among law enforcement within the last twenty-four hours." He paused and sighed. "I'm not reading the autocue for this. Let me give it to you straight. What we are seeing here in New Orleans is reminiscent of Hurricane Katrina. Police numbers have dwindled. Many are stricken with the virus, still more are unable to reach work because of the chaos in the streets and some are so exhausted and overwhelmed that they have simply given up. We've had an unconfirmed report of one officer chucking his police badge out of his cruiser window as he left town. Those officers still on duty are fighting valiantly to restore order but, frankly, they just don't have the manpower. The military presence here in New Orleans has also suffered heavy loses and has been ordered to pull back and maintain the quarantine at the city limits." He leaned toward the camera, eyes haunted. "That makes sense, yes, but you have effectively trapped thousands of uninfected people in here ... with *them*."

Them. People who were terribly, wretchedly sick, were no longer seen as victims and patients; they were now the enemy who had to be gunned down. In St. Paul, a self-proclaimed "Zombie Hunter" opened fire on his neighbor's house, nearly killing the man inside because he had "symptoms." Those symptoms proved to be an allergy to his girlfriend's new cat. In Carson City, a group of vigilantes stormed a hospital where three of the infected were being kept in isolation. They shot every patient on the ward. The pyre used to dispose of the bodies reminded Louella of the cattle culls when Hoof and Mouth Disease ripped through England back in 2007. In other words, it looked to her like a vision of hell.

All around the country other groups (some made up of law enforcement, some of private citizens) began to euthanize the infected. Often they waited until sick people "turned." But not always. There was one harrowing scene caught on camera of an elderly man standing at his front door, refusing to admit the local patrol. "She hasn't got it, it's just the flu!" he yelled and gripped the doorframe in an attempt to stand his ground. They dragged him away, kicking and screaming, and a muffled shotgun blast was heard within the house. As Fletcher watched this particular horror unfold on his Samsung 52-inch, the old man's bellowing sobs made his hands shake. If he watched any more of this alone, he'd soon be back on the sauce. He'd go to Louella.

As the number of infected multiplied, the survivors themselves began to turn on each other. Scapegoating, it seems, is a time-honored tradition that goes hand in hand with plague. Take fourteenth century France for example: the outbreak of the Black Death was viewed in quite a paradoxical fashion. While many believed it was God's retribution against mankind's sins, they also harbored the illusion that the plague must be due to some human agency. Someone must be to blame. In Languedoc in 1321, the rumor circulated that the disease came from poisoned wells. Every leper within the province was burnt for the offense. The year 1348 saw mass executions of the Jews in Provence, Narbonne, and Carcassone after the same allegations were made. And a sort of witch hunt that would have made Cotton Mather proud took place in Chillon, with tortured Jews being forced to name their "co-conspirators" in the plot to poison the town.

During the New Rabies pandemic, the United States was also gripped by scapegoat-mania. It was the same old impulse, only the targets had changed. Some evangelicals declared it to be the end of days brought on by rampant sin: homosexuality, abortion, immigration, Islam. And Pat Robertson's words were trotted out again: Sure, as Christians we should love our Muslim neighbors, "but be aware that they're trying to kill you." Ten mosques were burned to the ground, two of them with their congregations still inside. Seven imams were murdered, with one poor man dying horribly from his injuries after he was tarred and feathered. To wear the hijab was to make yourself an automatic target and people's homes were vandalized — their windows smashed with hurled rocks and the slogan, "Ragheads go home" spray-painted on their front doors.

At one point the rumor spread that New Rabies was really like AIDS and hence a homosexual disease. This led to the mass lynching of twenty gay men in Texas. Gallows had been hastily erected at the foot of the Davis Mountains and black vultures had gone to work on the bodies that hung there. None of them still had their eyes. A sign had been left by the killers — spray paint, after all, is the bigot's best friend. It read in big pink letters: "Priscilla, Queen of the Dessert."

The hardest hit, however, were the Hispanics. The disease had originated (had it not?) on the Latino island of Cáscara. And so the tensions that had been simmering over immigration swiftly came to a boil. Miami saw the equivalent of gang warfare as white youths attacked Hispanics, who then banded together to fight back.

"It's like the Sharks versus the Jets." Peg stared at the television in wide-eyed disbelief as a kid, who could have been no more than twelve, smashed a brown-skinned man in the head with a brick. "It's an absolute cluster-fuck!"

In some communities, anyone with a Spanish-sounding name was run out of town. They were the lucky ones. No one knows how many Latinos were killed throughout the country in both individual homicides and larger, more organized culls. One group calling itself "America for Americans" set up "Border Bunny Hunts." On their website, they featured a cartoon drawing of Elmer Fudd brandishing a shotgun and posing with his foot on a dead Mexican (you could tell he was dead because his eyes were X's). The caption read: "It's wabbit season."

Then in Pittsburgh, one infected family rampaged through a school playground during recess. Twenty children and six teachers were bitten. The people of Midwood could pretend no longer (*Bloody Bones, I'm just up the road*). The infection was on their doorstep and so at a town meeting on the fifth of January, Mayor Anthony Albitz suggested that they quarantine themselves.

"But we don't have the infection," a woman in the front row said.

"We quarantine the town not to keep the infection in, but to keep it *out*."

"So what are we talking about here, Mayor?" Issac Stahl, owner of Country Cobbler Shoes, asked.

"There are, as you know, five routes in and out of town," Albitz said. "I suggest that we restrict people entering the town at those points."

Patience, as town sheriff, spoke up: "What the mayor wants to do is to place signs that divert traffic away from Midwood. And," she shifted uncomfortably in her seat, "he wants to post armed guards at every point of ingress into the town."

"Isn't that going a bit overboard? I mean, who's gonna come here?" Joseph, owner of Mueller's Office Supplies, laughed.

"What about people from Pittsburgh?" Albitz asked.

Town councilman, Donald Eck nodded. "We know that the infected become extremely violent and with that chaos breaking out — what? — an hour and a half up the road, we are likely to see either," he held up his thumb to indicate that this was his first point, "the infected showing up here in town or," he added his index finger for point two, "refugees fleeing the violence."

"Shouldn't we help them?" Katie Boehler spoke up.

Mayor Albitz removed his glasses and rubbed his tired eyes. "My first priority is to keep this town safe. And I don't know how else to do it."

"I appreciate that, Mayor," Pastor Kulp of St. Matthew's Lutheran Church stood up. "But let me run this scenario by you. What if a refugee, just some guy trying to get his family to safety, shows up at the town limits and won't be diverted? What if, in desperation, he tries to drive into Midwood? Are we going to shoot him?"

"Hell yeah—" a voice came from the back.

Pastor Kulp pressed on. "Are we going to shoot his wife? His kids?"

Patience was staring hard at the mayor. "Answer him," she said quietly.

"We might have to ... to protect the town."

There was a general uproar over this. While some of the townsfolk expressed their horror at the idea, others shouted that the safety of our own children should come first. We should do whatever it takes.

"Are you telling me," Katie shouted, "that the only way to protect this town is to shoot everyone who comes near it?"

Patience rose and people fell silent. "That is the point I want to make. There are plenty of nonlethal ways to defend Midwood. Tire spikes, barricades, check points..."

"So then what?" a voice from the back piped up. "What do we actually *do* with the people who come here?"

"You get someone from the hospital to check them for symptoms," Doctor Rhoads entered the fray. "We could quarantine all newcomers for twenty-four to forty-eight hours to see if they develop a fever."

"And when the food runs out?"

Louella rose. "On that point, I assume that you'll want help from the farmers. None of us are located within the town boundaries; so if you want my crops and Arnold's meat ..."

"And our dairy," Everett Weller added.

"... then there will need to be some traffic in and out of Midwood anyway," Louella finished and sat down.

"That's right. Surely it's possible to protect the town without turning this place into a scene from *Mad Max*," Katie said.

"And surely," Fletcher's quiet voice rose, "the first step to controlling Midwood's destiny is to control our own fear."

And so the people of Midwood set up their defenses. At every point of ingress, they staggered obstacles — school buses, delivery trucks and fitch barriers. These created a chicane to slow approaching traffic. Cars that slalomed through would then come to armed checkpoints where the occupants could be screened for symptoms.

Louella no longer felt that her concerns were stupid. Therefore construction at the farm was well underway. Alec came in through the back door and stomped the snow off his boots.

"It's finished," he said, blowing on his cold fingers.

"The walls?" Lou gazed out the back window to see. The new walls enclosing the farmyard between house and barn were covered with long strips of green tarp. "Are you planning an unveiling?"

"No, we're getting some pretty strong gusts of wind down off the mountain. I needed to cover it until the mortar cures." He flopped down on one of the kitchen chairs and Peg handed him a cup of coffee.

While he drank it, he looked over the plans he'd drawn up.

"As far as the front of the house goes, I can take out the windows," he said, "and brick up the gaps."

Fletch, who was still trying to defrost after helping Alec lay bricks all morning, sat hunched over a copy of Dan Spencer's *The Castle at War in Medieval England and Wales*. "You should leave gaps that we could shoot through if necessary."

Alec thought for a minute. "It's doable. And I can attach a removable plate over each hole to keep the draft out. What really worries me, though, is the front porch roof."

"What about it?" Louella asked.

"If I brick up the second-story windows, then this place is going to be really dark and really stuffy. I was wondering if it would be better to install metal shutters that we can close if there's a threat or open to get some light and air in."

"That would also give us elevated firing positions," Fletch nodded.

"Yeah, but those shutters won't be as strong as the brick I'm putting in downstairs. That porch roof is essentially a platform leading right up to the most vulnerable points on the front of the building. I think it needs to come down."

Louella sat for a moment, massaging her temples. *My house. My beautiful house*, she thought glumly but said only, "Ok."

"We can take the sheet metal from the porch roof and use it to reinforce the front door on the outside. Honey, you said Patience had an idea for securing the door?"

Peg nodded. Mae was sitting on her lap coloring so Peg grabbed a blank sheet of paper and a blue crayon to sketch it out. "We secure it with three removable cross beams as well as a security bar that slants at a forty-five degree angle from the door to a bracket set into the floor. She said that that kind of setup could withstand a battering ram."

"That's really good," Alec said. "And that just leaves the back door of the barn."

Fletch shrugged. "Can't we reinforce it the same way as the front door?"

As the two men talked, Peg watched Louella. They were discussing major changes to her home and yet she said very little. "You all right, mom?"

"Huh?"

"You've been pretty quiet through all this. What are you thinking?"

Louella had been thinking of the porch they were about to tear down. On their wedding night James had scooped her up, carried her up the porch steps and in through a front door which would soon be heavily barred. She remembered summer evenings sitting out there with James, drinking iced tea and watching the kids run through the sprinklers to get cool. And she'd always sit on the front steps shucking corn to boil and freeze. And while she worked the sun would set in brilliant purples and oranges over the fields and she'd take a deep breath and know a moment of exquisite peace.

She'd been so caught up in these thoughts that she had missed the question. "Huh?"

"I asked what you thought about all this," Peg said gently.

"I think that what I want and what we need are two different things." She looked at Alec. "Do it. All of it. I just can't watch."

And so everyone made ready. It made them feel empowered, you know, to actually be *doing* something. Sitting at home, watching the news, had an almost soporific effect — you could sit there in your cosy living room and foster the illusion that what you were watching was mere fiction — a made-for-TV movie, perhaps — and everything was normal and ok. But then you switched off the tube and the movie was still playing. Everyone was talking about the infection and there's your son's school bus parked sideways on the bridge and men with guns patrolled the roads. So you rolled up your sleeves and volunteered for guard duty. You filled sandbags and pulled on a pair of thick gloves so you could help string up barbed wire. And it made you feel better, more in control. But then your shift at the checkpoints would end and you'd shuffle — exhausted and half-frozen — back home and that's when the doubts started to whisper in your ear. *Was it enough? Would anything ever be enough? And, even if Midwood survived unscathed, then what? With the rest of the world descending into chaos, what future could you really hope to have? What life for your children?*

You never asked these questions out loud. The people of Midwood (you included) were bound and determined to remain calm and sensible and controlled. But everyone around you laughed a little too heartily at bad jokes and their tight smiles were more like grimaces. And everyone in town talked in low voices, the way you'd talk at a funeral, and really that was apt. Not only were people dying, but your whole civilization seemed to be gasping out its last breath. The whole world right now was a fucking funeral and the people of Midwood were grieving. It was no longer possible to ignore what was happening and so they swiftly passed out of the denial stage and settled comfortably into the next one: anger. You could point to a thousand tiny examples of how it flared up — parents clashing with their children, couples arguing more frequently, the odd snipe between neighbors, but in no case was it more pronounced than in that of Imelda Zimmerman.

She was a deeply discomforting figure within the town. Her story was tragic. She had tried for twelve long years to have a baby and finally fell pregnant at the age of thirty-eight. And then one stormy night, she went into labor when she was only about twenty-four weeks along. The delivery was a stillbirth and, because her womb wouldn't contract and close off the blood vessels, she began to hemorrhage. To save her life, doctors at Midwood Medical Center had to perform an emergency hysterectomy.

Later, as she cradled the child, a nurse came in to try and coax the body away from her. Imelda looked at her, smiled and asked, "Is it time for her bath?"

Imelda Zimmerman was never the same after that. She became a gaunt, hollow-eyed figure who haunted Main Street, asking random youngsters, "Are you my Melanie?" The town's children were terrified of her, believing her to be a kidnapper or a witch. And then she started picking other women's babies up — right out of their buggies without so much as a 'mother-may-I.' It is damn hard to be easy around someone who does that.

Yes, she hadn't hurt anyone so far. But she was putting her hands on other people's kids and she clearly wasn't stable. Her husband Frank, Doc Rhoads, Patience, her friends and neighbors — all tried to get her to accept the help she so clearly needed. And she'd try for a time. She'd attend counseling sessions at the hospital and get her prescription for antidepressants filled at Holliger's Drug Store. But no attempted solution would stick. Eventually Frank Zimmerman threw up his hands in defeat and ran off with Deborah Scharf, a waitress from The Pilgrim Tavern. Apparently they'd moved to Fresno.

Shortly after he left, Imelda became "creepily religious." The town of Midwood was made up of a mix of devout Lutherans and Baptists. Everyone of them knew their Bible and most had a cross displayed somewhere in their homes as a reminder of who they belong to. But Mrs. Zimmerman had festooned her disintegrating house with crosses. It was like she was trying to ward off vampires. There was a particularly ominous cross on her front lawn — cheap wood covered in black creosote — that looked like a grave marker. That, along with the sagging shutters on the windows, the peeling paint, the leaning porch roof and the tangle of thorns that spilled over onto the sidewalk to nip at your ankles as you passed by, all combined to make the Zimmerman place look like a stereotypical haunted house. It was the ultimate dare among children to walk up to that porch on Halloween night. The bravest would stand there (under the glare of a badly rendered crucifix that made Jesus look demented), they'd ring the bell, yell "Trick-or-Treat!" and then run as if all the demons of hell were on their heels.

And all that was before the pandemic. As you can imagine, the stress of the plague did nothing to improve Imelda Zimmerman's mental health.

One day, Clara Jung walked into Holliger's Drug Store to pick up some diapers for baby Callum. As she hunted for the right size of Pampers on the shelf, she suddenly heard him scream. She spun around to see Imelda standing there by his buggy holding a clear syringe with a bright yellow plunger (the kind you used with Children's Tylenol).

"What did you do?!" Clara shouted as Callum coughed and spluttered.

"I ... I helped her," Imelda stammered.

Clara launched herself at the woman, grabbing her by the jacket and slamming her into a display of formula milk. "What did you give him?! I'll kill you!" Old Holliger managed to peel the two women apart. He took Clara and her baby up to the hospital to get him checked out. Patience, after an hour of trying to coax some sense out of Zimmerman, was finally told, "It was just Children's Tylenol ... to protect her from the virus." And she was telling the truth, but that did not improve people's disposition toward her.

Compared to other places, Midwood was safe, protected and infection-free. But it wasn't right. It was "on the turn" — like milk starting to curdle — as people became more tense and irritable and prey to irrationalities. The town's cumulative anger, which had been vague and diffuse without a target, now bulls-eyed in on Zimmerman. From a psychological perspective, it made a twisted kind of sense. People were afraid but impotent; you can't really fight microbes spreading through a country. You just had to sit and wait for it to arrive. But then Imelda unsettled them even more and here, at last, was an enemy you could square up to. A tangible something to fight. She became the town boogeyman. Her house was egged by teenagers and a vicious rumor spread. A few folks had read Max Brooks's *World War Z* and remembered that some of the characters in it engaged in "mercy killings." Basically, they slaughtered their kids to spare them the horror of the apocalypse. That sounded like just the sort of half-assed conclusion that Zimmerman might come to. What if she decided that the best way to "help" the children of Midwood was to kill them before the infection hit? No, she hadn't poisoned the Jung boy. But she easily could have done. She could have put anything in that syringe. Less than forty-eight hours of chewing on that image was enough to convince quite a few of the townsfolk that Imelda Zimmerman was a homicidal maniac in embryo — "a ticking time bomb just waiting to go off." And a petition with over 2,000 signatures was presented to Mayor

Albitz. It demanded the immediate expulsion of Imelda Zimmerman from Midwood.

And then Judge Huber cut her loose. He gave her a court date in a month's time to answer charges of assault on the Jung boy and sent her home. Patience was apoplectic when she walked into the station to find Imelda's cell empty. She got on the phone to Huber.

"Sir, that is *not* a good idea," she said, struggling to control her tone.

"She isn't a danger to the public — you and I both know that. So how can I hold her?"

"Yeah, but what about *her* safety?"

"Heavens-to-Betsy, this is Midwood. What do you think is going to happen?"

"On a normal day, nothing. But these aren't normal times. Everyone in this town is twitchy and under a helluva lot of stress. The mood is ugly, Bill. I'm telling you right now this is a mistake."

It was to no avail. The troubled woman was released from the town lockup and at four-thirty the following morning, someone dowsed that wooden front porch and its hideous crucifix with gasoline and struck a match. Oblivious as always to the harsh realities of life, Imelda Zimmerman sat in her rocking chair in the nursery, quietly singing lullabies to a child who wasn't there.

And so in the midst of a viral pandemic, Patience Bernhard found herself embroiled in a murder investigation. Normally she would have called in the experts from the Pittsburgh Bureau of Police Arson Squad, but that was impossible now; and so she sifted through the debris with only a deputy to help her. It was clear where the blaze had originated and it was equally clear that Imelda had sat in the upstairs nursery without making any attempt to flee. The nursery window overlooked her backyard and she could easily have stepped from that window onto the roof of the back porch and dropped down to safety. Instead she just sat there and died. What was not at all clear was whodunit. The neighbors had all been asleep when the fire broke out and by the time they awoke and called in the Volunteer Fire Company, there was no sign of the arsonist.

An accelerant had been used and had destroyed all fingerprint and fiber evidence. The blaze had melted the snow, so Patience didn't even have a boot print to go by. She considered what she knew about the people of

Midwood. They were generally a quiet bunch, committed to maintaining the beauty and peace of the town. And so the arson attack would not have been some mass act of destruction. There would have been no villagers with torches besieging the Zimmerman house. This was the act of one or two individuals. But who? Was it motivated by fear or did some sadistic prick simply use the crisis as an opportunity to have a little fun? She had to find out. Now more than ever law had to prevail or else what would become of them? What she didn't know, what she couldn't have known, was that soon it would all be a moot point.

CHAPTER FIVE

DEVIL IN DISGUISE

"Things fall apart; the centre cannot hold;
Mere anarchy is loosed upon the world,
The blood-dimmed tide is loosed, and everywhere
The ceremony of innocence is drowned…
And what rough beast, its hour come round at last,
Slouches towards Bethlehem to be born?"

William Butler Yeats, *"The Second Coming"*

"His barking roused the bats… They wheeled and swooped in the darkness,
their membranous wings sounding like small pieces of clothing – diapers,
perhaps – flapping from a line in a gusty wind… Cujo became frightened.
He didn't like their scent or their sound; he didn't like the odd heat that
seemed to emanate from them."

Stephen King, <u>Cujo</u>

In nearby Laurel Caverns, between Roland's Dig and Durgoon Falls, there is a large subterranean chamber known as the Bat Room. It was empty. In early January that cave should have been full of hibernating bats. Yet the colony was gone. They were the latest victims of "white-nose syndrome" — a contagious fungus that strikes them when their immune systems shut down for winter. According to a theory devised by scientists (known as the "Itch and Scratch Hypothesis"), the fungus disturbs the bats' hibernation, driving them out into the cold, the snow, and the daylight to spread the disease. And this year, it drove them out into the world of New Rabies. Through contact with other animals, the colony soon picked up this second infection. The two illnesses, working in tandem, drove them on and they bit every warm-blooded creature they encountered along the way. They attacked as they sickened and died. They bit even as their wings, thinned by the fungus, tore like tissue paper.

At the Weller Dairy Farm, where the milch cows sheltered in the barn from the biting wind, the bats descended. Silent as ghosts, they hopped from one beast to the next. It was a moment of terrible irony. The infection had finally come to Midwood, not with a bang, but with a whimper, not with the shriek of ravening hordes, but with the papery flutter of wings and a plaintive lowing in the byre.

Two days later Rick Kaesemeyer and Abel Nuss, who'd signed on at Weller's as hired hands, came in for the evening milking.

"So what did she say?" Rick asked as they herded the cows up to the carousel.

"She's meeting me at the Tombstone tonight and," Abel pointed his fingers at Rick in the shape of two cocked pistols, "she's bringing a friend."

"Oh shit, you're not setting me up with some dog, are you?"

"I don't know, is Cindy Wilson a dog?"

"Cindy Wilson? … Cindy Wilson?" And Rick cupped his hands in front of his chest to suggest enormous boobs.

Abel smiled and nodded. "You're welcome." He bent down behind a cow to attach the milk claw to her udders. "OUCH!"

"What is it?"

Clasping a hand to his shoulder, Abel backed away. "Bitch kicked me!"

The son of George Nuss was an apple that had not fallen far from the tree and so out of sheer spite, he planted a vicious kick on the cow's rump. It was the first of many kicks and slaps that evening. The stock, usually placid and cooperative, were obstinate as hell. It took twice as long to get them hooked up to the machine. Of course it would be this way: with Candace and Cindy waiting for them at the bar, *of course* these fucking cows would have to act up.

"What the f—"

"What is it now?" Abel called over to Rick.

"This one sat down!" Rick pointed to a black and white Holstein that was drooling heavily.

"Don't be dumb. Cows don't sit."

"Look man, she's on her ass!"

Abel joined Rick to gape at the animal. He hated this fuckin' job, but he knew what was normal and what was not. And this shit just wasn't right.

"Well," he stared at the cow uncertainly, "get her up and let's get this over with."

Finally every tit was hooked up to its tube and they could hear the clicking toggle of the machine as it sprang to life. The milking machine is a wonderful invention. It used to take half an hour to milk one cow. Multiply that by the thirty-two head in the herd, each needing to be milked twice a day, and you can see just how much manpower it required. With the machine, however, you could milk them all in three minutes. And it was a good thing too; the old girls stamped and pawed at the ground. Despite the fact that their udders were full and milking should have been a relief, they did not want to stand still for it and kept trying to back away from the carousel. Normally quiet, they uttered low, rattling sounds that sounded more like moans than moos. In this tense atmosphere, three minutes seemed like a very long time indeed.

As he pulled the suction tubes off of the final cow, Abel said, "Hurry up and settle them down, I wanna get outta here."

Habitually the two men split the jobs. Rick guided the animals back to the barn, replenished their hay and topped up their salt and mineral feeders. The water tank heater was on the fritz again and so he'd have to take an axe and break up the sheen of ice on the water trough so the cows could get a drink. Meanwhile, Abel was supposed to put the milk through the pasteurizer and start sterilizing the equipment. He fiddled with the controls on the machine. The boss wanted UHT milk because it would last longer. That suited Abel just fine because it took all of three seconds to do. The problem with doing a job you hate is that you're not overly particular about doing it right. The setting for ultra-high temperature milk is three seconds at 290°F. He programed the time in all right, but flubbed the temperature. Barely looking at the display, he set the pasteurizer at just 110°F with a few indifferent taps of his fingers. That's only a little warmer than the milk was when it came out of the cow. The men cleaned up the equipment, stored the milk for next day's delivery and then headed into town. Candace and Cindy would be waiting.

In the early part of the twentieth century, the cattle ranches of Brazil were hit by *peste de cadeiras* or "the plague of chairs." Farmers found their cows sitting in the fields. The cause? Rabid vampire bats. They fed on the cattle, thus infecting them with the virus. As the disease took hold, a sad paralysis set in. Their hind legs collapsed beneath them, forcing them into that unnatural sitting position. The paralysis then spread, working its way up the body until the poor brutes could not even draw breath. Thousands of animals died that way.

New Rabies had a similar effect on livestock populations and so within a few days, there wasn't one cow on the Weller farm that was still up on four hooves. And the unpasteurized milk? That was the real ticking time bomb. It was loaded with the virus which, at its current storage temperature, had an active shelf life of about a week. It was delivered to the town and distributed amongst its people.

By the thirteenth of January a lot of people in Midwood had come down with the flu. Obviously this caused quite a stir. John Wyndham put it well in *The Midwich Cuckoos* when he said, "I've never worked in a fireworks factory, but I know just what it must feel like. I feel at any moment that something ungoverned and rather horrible may break out and there's nothing one can do but wait and hope it doesn't happen." The first cough, though not particularly dramatic as coughs go, sounded like a death knell to the townspeople. The first rise in temperature on a thermometer's digital display, although only by a degree or two, was enough to take your breath away with fear. Old Doc Rhoads took the bull by the horns and summoned every person with symptoms (no matter how minor) to the hospital. Then he and Mayor Albitz called a town meeting.

Smiling on the assembled company, the doctor said, "Midwood's got the flu — normal, mundane, seasonal flu. It is *not* the New Rabies."

There was an audible exhalation of relief from the crowd.

"But how do you know that?" Katie Boehler asked, her eyes damp with grateful tears.

"Because the disease doesn't just spontaneously occur. You have to catch it from somewhere. No one here has been attacked. I've looked over every patient and there isn't a mark on any of you — not a bite, not so much as a scratch. How could you have gotten it?"

"There are other ways to get it," a voice from the back piped up. He cleared his throat awkwardly, "Sexual contact, that kind of thing."

"I have a patient in traction with a broken femur and four kindergarteners who have the same symptoms. They're not sleeping around. You have to understand that I fully expected to see a lot of you in with just these symptoms because *it is* cold and flu season. Hell, I've got a touch of it. So please set your minds at ease. You all know the basic things to do while we wait this out. Everybody should try to get some rest and up your intake of Vitamin C. For those of you with asthma or other respiratory conditions, keep an eye on it. If you feel like the bug is settling on your chest, come and see me. Does anybody have any questions?"

There were none — that pronouncement of normal illness was all they needed to hear.

"As you can see," Mayor Albitz chimed in, "nothing in this town has changed."

Patience stared glumly at her boots thinking of the burnt-out Zimmerman place. A helluva lot had changed in Midwood. But no one else was thinking of that now. They were just happy to be in the clear. As the townsfolk shuffled out, coughs echoed from every corner of the hall.

After the meeting Louella popped over to Levi's house. She hadn't visited Ginny in a while and had a couple of hours before she needed to be back at the farm. Levi's wife, Virginia, had suffered a stroke seven months ago and her recovery had been slow and difficult. Gradually, her balance and coordination had improved. She could swallow now and, more or less, had regained control of her bladder. But she was never quite the same and she knew it. She was on Fluoxetine antidepressants and seeing a counselor for that talking therapy to try and come to terms with it all.

When Louella arrived, Ginny grasped her hand. "I heard what Doc Rhoads had to say."

"Yeah," Louella nodded. "It's good news."

Virginia shook her head. "Doc Rhoads isn't Doc Rhoads." The woman's grip, though still weak, tightened as she clung to Louella. She looked, Lou realized, absolutely terrified.

"Honey, it's ok," Louella soothed.

"No it's not. The doc and the mayor and Katie and all the rest of them — they're not who they are."

"Lou, can I speak to you in the kitchen for a minute?" It was Virginia's son, Wyn, the veterinarian who looked after Louella's animals.

"I'll be right back, Ginny." Louella wriggled her hand free. "We'll sort it out, ok?" She joined Wyn in the kitchen, "Wha—" she began, but Wyn raised a hand to silence her until he could shut the door.

"All the craziness lately is really taking it out of her," he said quietly.

"It's a strain on everybody."

"Yeah, but she's convinced that our friends and neighbors are … I don't know … like pod people."

Louella could think of nothing to say to this.

"I took her up to the hospital this morning and they've diagnosed Capgras Syndrome."

"What's that?"

"It's a delusion where you start thinking that the people you know have been replaced by imposters."

"She's hallucinating again," Louella nodded glumly. She vividly remembered visiting Ginny in the hospital shortly after her stroke. The poor woman was shouting at imaginary cows in her room, distressed because they were bumping into the equipment and tracking mud onto the nice, clean floor.

Wyn sighed and rubbed the stubble on his chin. "It should decrease over time, but it is just horrendous to watch her regress like this."

"Ah hell, so much of life is two steps forward, one step back." Louella gave the man a big hug. "We'll get her through this."

"Listen, I have to hit the pharmacy to pick up her meds. Do you mind sitting with her while I go?"

"Not at all."

And so Wyn kissed his mother and she smiled at him as he searched for his car keys. When he was finally gone, she sighed in relief.

"Right," she turned to Louella. "They don't believe me, but you will. You saw this coming so you'll know," she was nodding hopefully at Lou.

"What, honey?"

"I'm not crazy. This isn't like before."

"Ok," Louella nodded. "Lay it out for me. Why do you think that Doc Rhoads isn't Doc Rhoads?"

"I've been getting out more, seeing more people lately, trying to get back to normal. Well yesterday, Levi took me to Kacee's for lunch. As hungry as I was, I couldn't eat. There was this ...*rancid smell* in the place, like spoiled meat. It damn near made me sick. But Levi didn't smell a thing! So then I thought, ok, maybe my nose was acting up again."

"Your nose?"

"Yeah, right after the stroke everything smelled like burnt rubber. That lasted about a week."

"But it went."

"Yeah, but ever since I've been really sensitive to smell. God, Patience came over the other day and wanted to use our Scotchgard to treat a new pair of shoes and the smell, Louella, was just overwhelming. She sprayed them outside, but the smell through the open back door was so ..." she struggled to describe it. "I couldn't breathe."

"So your sense of smell has returned to normal; I mean you're not smelling things that aren't there. But every scent you do come into contact with is just really, really strong?"

"Yeah, like right now you smell like you've got way too much perfume on."

"Sorry."

"Don't be. Anyway, I've wandered off the point here." Ginny shook her head as if to clear it. "I was in Kacee's and there was this terrible smell of ... rot. And then I realized that the smell wasn't coming from the food, it was coming from the *waitress*."

"Which one?"

"Barbara Yeakle. She smelled really ill, the way you'd expect ... I don't know ... an animal with gangrene to smell. Louella, you smell like you — a more intense version of you, yes — but you're you. Barb didn't smell ..." She paused.

"What?"

"... *human*." She sat silent for a while. "And she's not the only one. The town is full of that smell now."

CHAPTER SIX

THE FALL

"Ring-a-ring o' roses,
A pocket full of posies,
A-tishoo! A-tishoo!
We all fall down."

Traditional Nursery Rhyme

"hard be hard'nd, blind be blinded more, that they may stumble on, and
deeper fall."

John Milton, "Paradise Lost"

In truth Louella wasn't certain if Virginia's brain altered her perception of reality or if she really was picking up on an objective difference in people. Either way, Ginny was clearly terrified and living in a sort of carrion world that was patently horrible. The medicine that Wyn went to fetch seemed to help. It was an antipsychotic drug called clozapine and it made Ginny very drowsy. But whether it banished her fears or just knocked her out so she couldn't talk about them anymore, Louella didn't know. So what should she make of the information Virginia had given her?

202

Peter Diamandis noted that "Once we start believing that the apocalypse is coming, the amygdala goes on high alert, filtering out most anything that says otherwise." That pretty much described Lou's state of mind. She was hyperalert for any signs of trouble and Ginny's assertion that Midwood smelled of rot did nothing to calm her down. But then later that same day Mae came to her in tears. The child asked if all her friends who had the flu would turn into monsters and try to hurt them. Honestly, what the hell do you say to that? *Sure, honey. Yeah, it might just be the flu, but the world is such an incredible cluster-fuck right now, I wouldn't be at all surprised if they turn into raging cannibals and try to eat us. Really, how long can our luck hold out?*

Instead Louella scooped the girl up in her arms and repeated what Doc Rhoads had said: that lots of people get the plain, normal old flu this time of year and that you need to have some contact with the infected to get New Rabies.

"But the town is sealed off. No one has brought the infection in," she soothed.

The doctor's logic was indisputable. New Rabies doesn't just magically appear — it follows a traceable chain of infection. And it made perfect sense. The trouble was that Ginny's idea tapped, not into those circuits of the brain that processed logic and facts, oh no, it went straight for the limbic system. That primitive part of our brains helped us survive when the world was "red in tooth and claw" and it was screaming at her now. But should that voice be heeded? Should she listen to the ramblings of a woman with significant brain trauma? It was then that Louella's own logic kicked in: she was internally debating something that was not hers to decide.

"Quite a few teachers at the school are off with the flu," she later told Peg. "They've asked me to come in and help with Mae's class. The question is: do you want her there at all?"

Peg bit her lip. "What Ginny said is disturbing, but there's no reason to think the infection has actually gotten in."

"No, there hasn't been one reported attack."

"So then the question becomes: do we go with the logic or the fear?"

"I know," Louella nodded. "I know that there *should* be nothing to worry about and yet I'm paranoid as hell."

"And yet is it right to pass that paranoia on to a five year old? Shouldn't we try to give her as normal a life as possible?" Peg considered the matter a moment and then said firmly, "She should go into kindergarten on Monday. But you'll be with her, right?"

"Oh yeah."

Two days later Louella drove into Midwood. The town was quiet. There were far fewer cars on the road than you'd expect for a Monday morning and there were plenty of places to park on Main Street. Bernhard's Auto Repair and Filling Station (Levi's garage) was brightly lit and had an air of business as usual. But Prudential Insurance, Country Cobbler and the Law Offices of Kohr and Myer were dark with "Sorry, We're Closed" signs hanging in the windows.

Mae sat in the back of Lou's pickup, singing along with David Seville and the Chipmunks — "The Witch Doctor" song. Every time the damn thing ended, the girl chanted, "Again! Again!" and Louella would hit the back arrow on the CD player. *If I have to listen to "Oo-ee-ting-tang-walla-walla-whatever" one more time,* she thought, *I'm gonna have a frigging aneurysm.* Sam, in the seat next to her, dealt with the annoyance by listening to thrash metal through his earphones and drumming absently on the dashboard. Finally they arrived at the school and Louella hopped gratefully out of the car.

"Don't forget your bag," she smiled at Mae as the child unhooked her seatbelt. She handed Sam his lunch and watched him head off to class.

Due to high levels of student absence, Principal Snyder had decided to combine the morning and afternoon kindergarten classes into one session. Out of the fifty-two kids in Mae's year, only nineteen showed up. Louella spent the morning doing arts and crafts with them while Edna Hinkle, the first grade teacher, popped in at regular intervals to see if she needed any help.

As the morning drew to a close, Louella sat them all down on the carpet for story time. She grabbed the book of poems that was propped against the leg of her chair and opened it to the marked page. Today's offering was "When the Green Gits Back in the Trees" by James Whitcomb Riley.

"This is a good poem," Louella said. "It's all about spring. Who here can't wait for warmer weather?"

Hands shot up from the assembled children.

"Yeah, me too," she nodded and began to read of the green months when "the sap it thaws and begins to rise/ And the swet it starts out on/ a feller's forred."

Outside a frozen wind blew. At the Midwood Medical Center, just across Fifth Street from the school, the flu patients who'd been hospitalized would have welcomed a blast of cold air. Their fevers hovered around the 104°F mark and their sheets were drenched with sweat. In his bed near the window, Eli Geissle quietly died. The disease had whittled away at him for days, carving away at his mind until he could not hold a coherent thought and no longer knew his own name. As Louella settled the children down for story time across the street, the last gasp of Eli's dying soul sent a shudder through his chest and an exhalation of air through his trembling lips. He lay still. His body cooled. While his heart still beat, the man was gone. And then slowly a subtle warmth originated in his stomach and began to spread. At first it felt good, like a sip of brandy taken to banish the chill. But soon it intensified, cramping his stomach muscles painfully. Eli sat up suddenly and drew his knees up to his chest; oh, it hurt and he let out a low moan.

Angela Clemmer, one of the nurses on duty that morning, rushed to him. "Eli? What is it?" She grabbed a nearby basin. "Are you going to be sick?"

She stood close to him, her hand on his back. He bristled at this. His skin prickled with a needling oversensitivity and the smell of her perfume irritated his nose. But underneath that smell he caught a hint of something else. It was more basic — the elemental scent of sweat and flesh. His stomach, which had been unable to abide food of any kind for the last two days, suddenly growled. His spasming abdominal muscles relaxed. He sat up straighter and looked at her. It was a curious expression, the sort you wear when an elusive answer finally becomes clear. And then he grabbed her.

Angela gasped and stumbled backward, but he had such a vise-like grip on her arms that he came right with her. An IV line tore from the dorsum of his hand and his catheter ripped free as the two of them toppled onto the floor. In another moment he was on top of her, pinning her beneath his weight. He buried his face in her neck and a hard, sharp pain tore through her. She had all of seven seconds before she passed out — not enough time to truly register the fact that she was dying.

She felt only that she was falling backwards, in darkness. The other patients on the ward, however, were watching intently. Their shattered minds took in every detail with a keen attention that they had not been capable of in days. They watched as the blood pooled around Angela and Eli. They listened as the nurse's right shoe drummed convulsively on the tiles and as Eli sucked noisily at the wound he'd made. But it was the smell — that dank, faintly metallic musk of spilled blood — that roused them.

At first as they moved through the halls, doctors and nurses ran to help them. They were too ill to be out of bed and the Chief of Medicine had visions of some of them collapsing and smacking their heads on the way down. But these thoughts were banished when the first medic, an intern by the name of Hartwell, was grabbed and brought down hard by an eighty-six year old patient with mobility issues. Once on the ground the crowd swarmed over him, tearing at him with their teeth. His screams jumped an octave and then ended abruptly as a spray of arterial blood arced across a nearby wall. The rush to help the stricken patients became a panicked retreat.

Across the street, just as Louella read the line "a-gitten down/ At the old spring on his knees," the door opened making her jump. But it was just Edna Hinkle.

"Time to go, guys," she announced. "What do you say to Mrs. Bernhard for coming in to help today?"

This was answered by the singsong "Thank you, Mrs. Bernhard" you get from small children when prompted.

Louella chuckled. "You're welcome."

"I'll take them out and hand them over to their folks," Edna said as she herded the class toward their pegs.

Louella helped Mae wriggle into her puffy pink jacket. She grabbed the child's Scooby Doo backpack and they followed the class out into the watery January light.

As Mrs. Hinkle caught sight of a parent, she'd tap the corresponding child on the head as a signal to go. It was during this exchange that the front doors of the hospital flew open and an orderly, Mitchell Fuhrmann, pelted out into the snow. He hit a poorly gritted patch of ice and fell. Before he could regain his feet, Mayor Albitz (in bare feet and a flapping hospital gown) dove on top of him, clawing at him like a wild animal.

Mitchell screamed, actually head-butted the Mayor and pushed him off. As he struggled to his feet, two more people plowed into him.

This was the vanguard of the pajama-clad army that flowed into the streets. For a moment everyone outside the school froze … and then the crowd broke apart with people screaming and dashing in all directions. Louella grabbed Mae's hand and ran. It was only a short distance across the parking lot to her car, but it took forever to get there. The journey, for the most part, was a blur. But there were moments — usually accompanied by a physical jolt — that focused her attention on some detail. When her boots hit a patch of ice and her ankle twisted painfully under her, she skidded to a temporary halt and there was Elsie Benfield clinging desperately to her son, Caleb. Dr. Rhoads tore the child from her grip and bit into the boy's scalp with tooth-shattering ferocity. Louella picked up her screaming granddaughter and ran. But Mae was heavy and the old woman felt as if her lungs would burst. The car was in sight now, straight ahead. But at that moment Denny Latshaw staggered in front of her. He was clutching his daughter, Anna, and still attempting to run in spite of the two people who clung to his jacket. They finally managed to bring him down. As he fell, he literally threw the child away from himself, screaming, "Run!" Anna, God bless her, tried. She took off as fast as her little legs would carry her. Josh Heffley, a boy in Sam's class, gave chase. He ran with all the nimbleness of youth and didn't even slow down as he scooped the girl up and carried her off. Louella dodged these obstacles, her eyes on her Chevy, her teeth gritted with the exertion and with Mae's shrill cries spurring her onward. And she almost made it.

Suddenly she was yanked backward by the hair. Still clutching Mae to her, she fell heavily onto her rump. She looked up and there was Josh Heffley again, high school track star extraordinaire and, apparently, the most prolific vector for the infection currently in play.

"Josh … *please*," Louella gasped and then the teenager was struck by another body. It was Sam. Her grandson came in low, his chin level with Joshua's gut. On contact, he brought his hips and arms forward in one smooth movement, hoisting Josh off his feet and slamming him into a nearby car. It was a perfectly-executed football tackle and then Sam had Louella by the arm.

"Here!" she screamed, passing Mae to him. "Go! Go!"

The boy clutched his little cousin and took off like he was going for a touchdown. Louella ran after them. She pressed the button on her car key and the Chevy's doors unlocked with a cheerful "blip" just as Sam reached it. He dove into the back seat with Mae and slammed the door shut.

In another moment, Louella joined them. "Are you ok?" she gasped. "Mae? Sam?" She leaned over the front seat to look at them. "Are you bleeding?"

Panting heavily, Sam shook his head. "We're fine."

"Get her strapped in and get your seat belt on." Lou turned around and started fumbling for her inhaler, but her few seconds of respite were over. Joshua was on his feet again. He charged at their car, colliding with the back window on Sam's side, cracking the glass. Louella stomped on the gas pedal. Her wheels spun briefly, then gained purchase on the grit and the car shot forward.

The quickest way out of town would have been to turn left out of the parking lot, take Fifth Street for one block and then follow River Road to the Third Street bridge. However, that way was blocked. The street was a chaos of crashed vehicles and the swarming infected. She veered right and headed out to Lincoln Avenue. It was the second widest street in town, running perpendicular to Main Street and while there were accidents here too, she had room to maneuver around them. She made decent progress until old George Nuss ran out in front of her with the mayor's wife hot on his heels. He stopped, turned to face his pursuer, and raised a little Beretta .22 bobcat. As Irene Albitz plowed into him, he pulled the trigger. The impact, however, knocked his arm to the side and the bullet shattered one of Louella's headlights. George was blasting away now and as the bullets flew, Louella yanked the steering wheel to the left and careened down First Street.

She was going too fast and clipped parked cars and mailboxes as she went. Farther down First Street, a pickup truck had T-boned a Ford C-Max and in their panic the drivers had abandoned the vehicles. There was no way through. Feeling like a cow being funneled down a cattle chute at a slaughterhouse, Louella was forced to turn right onto Bugler Avenue. She could have taken the narrow alley to get to Main Street but that too was blocked — this time by a minivan. A crowd of about eight infected had shattered its windows to get at the people inside. Louella veered away from the carnage and found herself in the parking lot behind First Federal Savings and Loan.

She skidded to a halt and sat trembling at the wheel. The parking lot was empty and blessedly quiet.

"Gran?"

"Huh?"

"What are we going to do?"

"There's only one way out of this lot. We have to go back the way we came."

Louella turned in her seat to face them. In doing so she accidentally hit the radio control that Levi had installed on her steering wheel. With a sudden crescendo, there was David Seville and his fucking chipmunks "Walla-Walla-Bing-Banging" again. The absurdity of it was too much. She and Sam burst into hysterical laughter.

Collapsing weakly back into her seat, she wiped tears from her eyes. "Need to focus," she muttered.

The boy unbuckled his safety belt, leaned through the gap in the seats and hit the Media icon on the MyLink screen. He tapped the listing for "Sam's phone" and a different song began to play. The first thing Louella heard was a throbbing drumbeat. In her mind's eye she saw again Dr. Rhoads biting into little Caleb Benfield's head and at that moment a low voice on the radio commented, "Oh shit." Oh shit indeed. She glanced up into her rearview mirror and looked into the white, terrified faces of her grandchildren.

"That's not going to be you," she said.

"What?" Sam asked.

"Put your seat belt back on."

Down with the Sickness by Disturbed is not a relaxing, easy-listening song to play in day spas or elevators; it is a wailing ode to utter insanity. And oddly enough, it calmed her. She sat for a moment gathering herself, hardening herself for the task ahead. She didn't care, frankly, if she got infected and she didn't care if she died. But those two kids were getting out of here. No matter what.

Calmly, deliberately, she put her glasses back on. "Hang on," she said and hit the gas pedal.

There was only one way to go. She had to backtrack just to keep moving. But there, like a recurring fucking nightmare, stood Josh Heffley at the corner of First and Lincoln. She hit the brakes. The two of them stared at each other for a long moment. This was the boy who used to come over to the farm for sleepovers with Sam. This was a child who loved Spaghetti-Os and Teenage Mutant Ninja Turtles. She'd bandaged his skinned knees and gotten him a weekend job at Levi's garage. She could still see that boy beneath the smears of blood on his face. But as he looked at her, there was no recognition, just the same black indifference you see during Shark Week: a Great White eyeing up a grey seal.

"Just go, just go, please Joshua, pick any other direction," she whispered.

But then he screeched — a shrill, unholy sound that brought gooseflesh out on her arms. He ran full pelt at their car. With a choked sob, Louella stomped on the gas. She hit the boy while going about forty-five and on impact he buckled at the waist, his head and outstretched hands slamming onto the hood of her car. She hit the brakes and he flew backward, out into the intersection to land in a bloody heap. She maneuvered around him and sped off toward Main Street.

At the corner of Lincoln and Main, she had to stop. In front of her there was a line of stationary traffic who waited, horns blaring, for their turn to nip past the barricades at the far end of the Main Street Bridge. The people of Midwood seemed to have decided en masse to get the hell out of Dodge. But it was very slow going. Two old school buses and more sandbags than she'd seen during the last flood created a chicane that cars had to weave through at little more than a crawl. It would be the same at every exit. As Louella considered her options, a cacophony of shrieks and screams sounded behind her.

"Oh shit!" Sam's voice was hoarse as he stared out the back window.

The infected surged up Lincoln Avenue behind them. Louella leaned on her horn and waved frantically at the owner of the Jeep Cherokee that was blocking her path onto Main Street. He took one look in the direction she was pointing and kicked his Jeep into reverse. It collided with the car behind and pushed it back a little. Next he rammed the car in front, shunting it ahead. Back and forth he went until he could clear no more room for himself and then with a grinding of metal he made a sloppy U-turn and headed back away from the bridge. In an instant, Louella shot into the gap he'd made. But she wasn't quick enough. Mae screamed as Doctor Rhoads appeared at her window. He hammered so hard on the glass; Lou was sure that, broken hand or not, in another minute he'd be inside. She jerked the wheel to the right, grinding the man's body between the side of her Chevy and the front bumper of a car that was trying to force its way forward. The doctor screamed and flung out a bloody hand to leave its print on her windshield. And then he fell and she felt her back wheels skid over him as she accelerated away. She turned right, away from the bridge, and darted up another alley and onto Cemetery Road.

This led to the old covered bridge and again the road was thick with traffic as people tried to get past the barricades on their way out of town. But Louella had already decided to bypass that mess. She turned into the cemetery itself. She knew it well — hell, she was down here every other week tending the graves of her husband and her son. She knew precisely where she needed to go. At the back of the graveyard, there lay an impressive mausoleum that belonged to the Ott family. Josiah Ott, Midwood's version of Mr. Magoo, had once occupied a sprawling mansion on private woodland just behind the cemetery. For convenience sake, he'd paid to have his own private entrance to the boneyard there, next to the family mausoleum. But no one had lived in the Ott Mansion for over forty years now and it had fallen into ruin. So had that old gate. It was pure rust. Louella suspected that the chain that had been threaded through its bars to lock it shut was actually sturdier than the old hinges that connected panel to post. She meant to try those hinges now. As she revved her engine, she muttered quietly to herself. At first Sam couldn't hear what she was saying, but then he caught a phrase: "dei nohma loss heilich sei" — "Hallowed be thy name." She was reciting the Lord's Prayer just as her old Pennsylvania Dutch grandmother had taught her.

That made sense. Because this, he realized with chilling clarity, was the moment of truth. If they couldn't get out this way, they would not be getting out at all.

He joined her. "Dei Wille loss geduh sei /uff die Erd wie im Himmel." (Thy will be done on earth as it is in Heaven).

And then Louella hit the gas. With another squeal of tires (she was turning into quite the drag racer today) she barreled into the gate and sent the left panel flying.

They emerged onto the old country road just past the barricades and darted over the bridge. Sam whooped and clapped at their escape. But as they emerged from the cover of the trees, sunlight struck Louella's windshield and the bloody handprint on it glowed a warm red. *Doc*

Rhoads, she thought. *The hands that delivered my children, that gave me a sedative the night James died, that set Eben's broken arm when he fell in the barn.* She pulled over, hastily unclipped her seat belt and hopped out of the car.

"Gran? Are you ok?" Sam asked, but Louella could not respond. She stood, hands on her knees, being violently sick. *I killed him,* she thought, *and Josh. Oh God.*

She returned to the car, wiping her mouth on the back of her hand.

"Gran?"

"I'm fine. Let's just get moving."

CHAPTER SEVEN

DAY ONE

"So long awaited that its coming was a shock."

Mohsin Hamid, <u>Moth Smoke</u>

"Today is the first day of the rest of your life."

Abbie Hoffman, <u>Revolution for the Hell of It</u>

Throat and nose still burning from being sick, Louella stopped at the Grissinger Farm on her way home. It was the first chance she got to hug her grandkids. Little Mae climbed into her arms and clung to her like a limpet and even Sam was reluctant to leave her side.

"Bib? Arnold?" she called in a hoarse voice — she'd really done a number on her throat with all that retching.

The front door banged open and Arnold appeared carrying a shotgun. "Is it just you?" he asked scanning the road. Bib, also armed, appeared behind him.

"Yeah. Look, you've gotta get outta here. It's all kicked off in town and you are too damn close."

"Oh we know." Bib, her face ashen, nodded to the left of her front porch and Louella noticed for the first time the stiff forms lying there

213

covered by a coarse, brown stable blanket. Two pairs of feet stuck out from underneath — one clad in work boots and one bare, dark and swollen with frostbite.

"Who?" Louella asked.

"The Wellers," Arnold shook his head. "They came charging up to the house like they were fucking possessed. Jeanie punched through the window and got my Niamh by the hair. I had to … I …"

"You did what you had to do to protect her," Louella nodded.

"What the hell happened to you?" Bib was looking at Lou's car with its dents and crimson splashes of blood.

"The infected hit the school." Just saying it out loud made her cry.

"Jesus," Bib whispered and the two women, with Mae in between them, clung to one another. Bib sniffled loudly, "You all get out ok?"

Louella nodded and wiped her eyes. "So are you coming? Bib, you can see Main Street Bridge from the top of that hill." She pointed to the snow-covered hummock behind the house. "It's not safe to stay here."

"We're way ahead of you." Their daughter Niamh appeared in the doorway carrying a box of canned goods. "Do you have room for this in your truck?"

Throughout that afternoon they came. Some with cars full of supplies, some with only the shirts on their backs. In the end, there was Louella and Sam, Peg, Alec and Mae. Between them Levi and Patience had managed to get Ginny out. She was absolutely reeling — she just kept shaking her head and muttering, *That smell.* Wyn, his wife Josie and their twelve-year-old daughter Emma arrived and looked vaguely around Louella's living room as if none of them could quite understand just where they were. There was Arnold and Bib (tearful at leaving her house) and Niamh and that young fellow Owen she brought home with her from college. And Fletcher made sixteen.

For a while, a sort of inertia took hold of the group. Once they sat down they didn't want to get up again. Shock and sorrow had left them cowed; and they sat in front of the TV clutching mugs of coffee that they forgot to drink. And the news did not help. They were running this mesmerizing, scrolling list of every city that had fallen to the infection — including Atlanta. From there a spokesman for the CDC announced that they had developed an effective vaccine to keep people from contracting the disease. However, with the breakdown in infrastructure, there was at present no way to manufacture and distribute the drug on a wide scale.

"We will work tirelessly with the army to reestablish supply lines and get the drug out there," the man was saying, "but there will be significant delays. Therefore any community that is able to develop its own stock of the vaccine is encouraged to do so at the earliest opportunity. The instructions on how to do this are as follows…"

Peg dove for the control and pressed "record." Louella rose, went out front for the umpteenth time and stared down the road. *Where was Effie and her family? Surely they'd be here by now.* And Lou wasn't the only one with worry twitching her strings. Owen called his parents in Minneapolis again and again and got no answer. And Patience sat in the kitchen trying desperately to get hold of Marie.

"I thought she'd be with you." Her brother, Wyn, stood in the doorway.

"No. She, um, went to get her parents. Allentown was still clear but she didn't want to leave `em that close to Philly."

"Pat, I'm sure she's all right."

"No she's not." Patience ran a hand over her tear-stained cheeks. "How can she be? Out in the middle of all this … with nowhere to go."

Wyn wrapped her in a hug. "Why don't you come on in? They're talking about how to make the vaccine on the news. It looks like we could beat this thing yet."

It was great news — the first positive thing all day. *A vaccine.* From what they were saying, you could employ the same method that Louis Pasteur used when he created the original rabies shots. However that was easier said than done. Niamh, who was pre-med, pointed out that the method required daily contact with infected animals. They would have to capture and keep them. They would then have to expose generation after generation of healthy animals to New Rabies in order to develop the most virulent strain possible. Then they would have to extract it, attenuate and test it. And that was only after they managed to gather all the needed equipment and set up a lab secure enough for the job. No, there would be no vaccine today or tomorrow or next week or even next month. And in the meantime, there were more fortifications to build and they had to keep the farm going.

Speaking of which, Louella thought, *I'd better get on with that.* It was five o'clock and the sun had set. She needed to get the chickens in the coup and milk the cows. She pulled on her old boots, a body warmer and a knit hat that read "MHS Bears" (a hideous pom pom affair sold by the Football Booster Club last October). Despite the fact that night fell early this time of year, the moon reflected off the snow giving her enough light to see by. The air was crisp, the yard quiet. The chickens, a mixed brood of eleven birds each named after a character in *To Kill a Mockingbird*, had already gone into the barn and hopped onto their perches. She checked the thermometer to make sure they'd be warm enough and she shut them in for the night.

She had two cows. It was Louella's habit to separate them from their calves every morning so their udders would be full by evening. Although the sixteen people at the farm did not know it, these old girls had saved them from the infection. They had provided them all with untainted milk. She called Rickie to her. The heifer — named for Def Leppard's Rick Savage (Lou had eclectic tastes) — came to her and nestled her snout into the woman's chest. Louella spoke to her gently, slipped a halter over her head, and tied the end of the rope to a post. She'd just sat down on a low stool and was about to give the udders a wash when Rickie tossed her head.

"What are you fussing for?" Lou asked. And then she realized: she'd put the halter on upside down. The chin rope rested on the cow's forehead, pulling the knot right up into the animal's eye. What the hell had she been thinking?

She undid the halter and went to put it on again. Again she got in a muddle. By the light of the bare bulb she flicked on, each section of the harness looked the same. Louella had done this everyday for the last forty-three years and yet for some reason she could only stare in mute confusion at the tangle of rope in her fists. She slumped down heavily on the stool and was surprised to find that she was trembling. Her breath came in hitching gasps. And she saw Josh's face again and that bloody handprint on her windshield. Dropping the rope, she buried her head in her hands and pressed the heels of her palms into her eyes as if that would banish the images. But they would not go away. She'd killed two people today. One old man, one little more than a child. One who took care of her and one whom she'd cared for — perfect bookends for her past and future and she wiped them out within ... what? ... ten minutes of each other? She was crying now, so hard that she could not utter a sound and she could not breathe and her chest felt like it was on fire. As the terrible, racking sobs spasmed through her, she sank onto her hands and knees and all she could think was "I'm sorry. I'm so so sorry."

The good news about this type of episode is that it takes a hell of a lot of energy and hence, is difficult to sustain. In a little while, she sat on the concrete floor, utterly spent, while Rickie looked down at her with wide, questioning eyes. She pulled herself to her feet and went to wash her face at the tap. As she settled back down to her work (she'd finally managed to get the damn halter on right), she remembered a passage she'd once read in a book. It was *The Return* by Walter de la Mare and in it he'd said something about how God had fashioned our brains to work slowly. The human mind took a hit the same way your skin does. First the blow, then the bruise. Something to that effect. She'd taken a hell of a hit that day and her hysterics were simply the mental bruise blossoming purple and black and sore. It was not her first. She also knew that it didn't matter one iota that she'd been driven to her knees. She'd been there before too. What mattered was what you did next.

If she thought logically about it, then it was perfectly obvious what she *should* do. First milk the cows, put the calves in with their mothers, and lock up the barn. Then she'd take her two pails in, strain the milk and get it on the stove. Then she'd start dinner and then… Then what? Just what were you supposed to do with a mess like this?

Over the years Louella had developed a theory; she called it the Delta Theory of Life and it was a pretty good one. People had a tendency to get obsessed with big moments — it was that 1988 Summer Olympics "One Moment in Time" vibe. And don't get me wrong, those moments are important. Take motherhood, for example. After giving birth, when the doctor delivered her babies right onto her bare stomach — those were two of the most powerful, shining moments of her life. Even now the recollection took her breath away. But the relationship with her children was not made and set in those brief minutes. It was cemented by thousands of days, millions of tiny actions and words and hugs and kisses. These built up like the silt that forms a delta giving them firm, dry land to stand on. And it was fertile ground; it had produced a lifetime of good memories and of love.

And so, if the big shining moments were not the be-all and end-all of life, then neither were the big tragedies. They could rise above this and the simplest way to do it would be to silt it up with something else — something better. That was her theory, anyway. Not expertly wrought, but solid. L.R. Knost put it much more eloquently when she said: "Do not be dismayed by the brokenness of the world. All things break. And all things can be mended. Not with time, as they say, but with intention. So go. Love intentionally, extravagantly, unconditionally. The broken world waits in darkness for the light that is you."

As she bustled around the kitchen, Louella listened to the conversation in the living room. Peg and Alec were discussing ways to augment their fortifications. This was met by a harsh, mirthless laugh and then a voice that Lou didn't immediately recognize: "It doesn't matter how many boards you nail over the windows, we're screwed." It was that boy, Owen.

Both Emma and Mae started to cry at this and then many voices were talking at once. The mothers comforted their little ones; the fathers swore at Owen for his lack of tact; Patience weighed in and said that they all had an excellent chance of keeping safe at the farm and Owen maintained his opinion that "We're fucked."

Through all this, the group had not registered the familiar sounds of someone making dinner. But when Louella started frying bacon, the smell reminded them that they hadn't eaten since breakfast and were actually quite hungry. They filtered into the kitchen.

Peg asked, "What are you making, mom?"

"Chicken, Potato and Corn Chowder."

"Can I help?" Bib volunteered.

Lou nodded. "We need to set the table and put out some bread and butter and there's stuff for a salad in the fridge. Sam, that milk will be done in a minute, will you…"

"Got it."

A quiet bustle filled the kitchen. Louella worked quickly, deftly adding green onions, red pepper, white wine, and thyme to the main ingredients of her stew.

"We're not fucked," she said matter-of-factly. "We've got bacon!" And she flashed the others a toothy grin. "Alec, would you fish that out of the skillet and drain it on some paper towels, please? Anyway, what was I saying?" She glanced at Owen. "Oh yeah, about being fucked. Nah. We have a stocked larder, fresh water from the well, our own power source, seed to plant, a barn full of animals and Arnold has how many pigs in my storage shed?"

"Twenty."

"Which means even more bacon. What's that saying you have about pigs, Bib?"

"That you can use everything but the squeak," her friend said as she laid places at the table.

"And yes," Louella finished, as she ladled the chowder into bowls and crumbled bacon on top, "we are safe enough here that we can sit down and have something to eat."

The mood lifted somewhat over dinner. For all the lofty thoughts, the philosophies, the ideas and theorems and creativity of the human mind, when it comes right down to it, we are creatures ruled by our stomachs. The state of your belly, whether empty or full, will determine your mood, color your outlook and affect your concentration. That is why Louella hit them first with chowder and then with ideas. From her seat at the head of her crowded table, she could see an old wooden sign hung on the wall by the refrigerator. James gave it to her for her birthday one year. The words "Hatching Plans" were painted over the silhouette of a chicken.

"I saw it and it just reminded me of you," he'd said at the time and gave her a squeeze. "Does your mind ever switch off?"

The answer was no, not really. And it was time to kick it up a gear.

"Alec," she said between bites of butter bread, "what's left on our list for the Stage 1 fortifications?"

"As you know, I've bricked up the front windows and walled in the yard between the house and the barn. I still have to tear down the front porch roof, reinforce the door and hang the brackets for the crossbeams."

"Ok then, that's tomorrow's job. In the meantime, we can barricade the door with furniture and post guards for the night."

Niamh, who hadn't registered the changes they'd made to the house, stared in shock at the bricked up kitchen window. It really hit her in that moment that her mom and dad and Lou didn't expect all this to blow over. "You really think we'll be here for a long time?" she rasped because her throat had gone painfully dry.

Louella nodded. "I think things are in a hell of a mess and it's going to take time to sort it all out. In the meantime there's stuff we can do to get through this."

Fletch was smiling at her knowingly. "What do you have in mind?"

"We divvy up the jobs. Wyn, I need you to get your mother settled. And then I'd like you and Niamh to go over our medical supplies and make a list of what else we're going to need. Peg, Mae, Josie and Emma, would you find everyone a bed or a mattress or cot to sleep on and start thinking about long-term accommodation. Alec, Patience, Fletch and I will go over this place and map out what fortifications we need to work on next. On that point: building materials…"

"Doc Rhoads had contracted me to build his retirement home. It's just," Alec jerked a thumb over his shoulder, "over in the next valley. I've got everything we'll need at the site."

"Ok," Louella was nodding. "We draw up the plans tonight and hit the site tomorrow morning for supplies."

"What do you want me to do, Gran?" Sam asked.

"I need you, Bib, and Owen to take an inventory of all the food we've got and then start calculating how long it's gonna last us."

"And me?" Levi asked.

"I'd like you and Arnold to sort our weapons and ammo out and," she nodded toward Mae, "make certain it's all out of reach of little fingers."

"I should tell you now that I won't be here to take that inventory," Owen said.

Everybody at the table gaped at him.

"Why?" Niamh asked.

"I'm going home — I'll pack up and head out after dinner."

Niamh laughed nervously. "That's — that's ridiculous! You can't!"

"I have to go check on my parents."

"You're parents are in Minneapolis! Didn't you tell me that's like a thousand miles away?"

Louella leaned her elbows on the table and massaged her temples. A thousand miles. This afternoon she barely managed to drive six blocks to get out of Midwood. A thousand miles was just…

"That's suicide," Arnold spoke her thoughts out loud.

"I'll be fine."

"In that ancient Volkswagen Jetta of yours? Are you kidding me?" Levi asked.

"Listen, this is my decision and I don't think that things are nearly as bad as you …"

"I shot two of my neighbors today," Arnold said quietly. "How many did you have to go through, Louella, just to get the kids out of town?" Arnold looked at Louella hoping she'd chime in. She didn't answer; she just went slightly green and pushed the remainder of her dinner away.

The boy continued, "I appreciate what you're trying to do, but I'm going. I'll load up the trunk and ..."

"With what?" Louella asked quietly.

"Huh?" Owen looked at her, confused.

"What are you planning to load into your car?"

"Supplies."

"Supplies," the old woman nodded. "From my farm?"

"Well, I ..."

"Has it occurred to you that maybe I want to keep that here to help us survive?"

Owen blushed furiously, but he plowed ahead anyway. "Surely you can spare ..."

"What?" Louella snapped. "We don't even have a complete list of what we've got yet."

"If I stayed, you'd feed me, right? You'd end up giving me more than I'm asking for now!"

"Yes!" she shot back. His tone was getting her riled and it actually felt good to get mad. She went with it. "If you stay, I'll feed you. I just have a slight problem with taking a trunk-load of food and throwing it the hell away!"

"How is giving it to me throwing it away?"

"Because you're going to die out there and the supplies will rot."

"Oh I'm gonna die?" He was on his feet now. "And you base that on what?"

Louella crossed her arms and leaned back in her chair. "If you have car trouble, do you know how to fix it?"

"What?"

"Do you know how to siphon gas? Or use a gun? If you have to go off road, do you know how to navigate? Do you possess any survival skills at all? It's the dead of winter, can you even make a fire? And yes, Owen, are you prepared to kill people in order to survive? If you have any illusions about what it's like out there, then go and take a look at the blood that's splattered all over my truck. That blood's from two of my friends who were trying to eat my grandchildren!"

"Who?" Peg whispered.

"Josh and Doc Rhoads."

The whole table gaped at her, but Louella ignored them. Here was another child — a kid not that much older than Josh and maybe she could save this one. When she spoke again, she was calmer, quieter. "And so let me recap my day for you. I watched a town full of people get ripped to shreds — *literally* torn apart. I killed my friends, threw up on my shoes and had a nervous breakdown in the barn. Are you up for a thousand miles of that shit?"

"But my parents…"

She looked at him pityingly. "Today I didn't care if I died or got bit or muddied my own soul, I just wanted them to be ok," she pointed to Sam and Mae. "I'm pretty sure your parents feel the same way about you. They'll want you safe and this *is* the safest place for you right now. So no, I'm not giving you the supplies. I have enough blood on my hands for one day — why on earth would I help you kill yourself?" She signaled the end of the discussion by rising abruptly, scraping her leftovers into the dog's bowl and starting to tidy up the kitchen.

Owen glowered at her back for a moment. The argument had been humiliating — it had made him feel stupid and inept and worst of all, she'd been right. But even if it *was* stupid, he wanted to go. Except for Niamh, these people were strangers and he wanted so desperately to be home. Problem was: he'd just barely mustered up the courage to go when he thought they would give him food and medicine and a gun and a map. Without their help, his courage failed. He rose, took his plate and slung it into the sink in front of Louella and then walked out of the room.

That first, long day ended late. Inventories were taken, plans were made, guards posted. Many decided to eschew the beds and cots that had been set up for them and instead curled up together by the fire in the living room. Later on they would probably be sick of the sight of each other, but that night no one wanted to sleep alone.

Fletch joined Louella on the couch. "You ok?" he asked.

She was just about to say no when Mae came over.

"Come on then," she said, inviting the girl to climb up on her lap.

The child asked, "Can I have a song?"

Louella, as a mother and grandmother, knew lots of lullabies. But the melodies she favored were not the stereotypical ones. She liked to take her favorite songs, the songs from her youth, and sing them slow. And so she broke into a delicate, quiet rendition of *Crazy Crazy Nights* by Kiss and watched the little girl's eyes close. Mae's breathing settled into a gentle, steady rhythm. Louella looked at her — at the smoothness of her cheek, at the long eyelashes and wisps of hair that smelled of Johnson's Baby Shampoo. Despite all the chaos and hell of the day, she smiled, knowing intrinsically what Lao Tzu said over 2,000 years ago: "Being deeply loved gives you strength, while loving someone deeply gives you courage."

CHAPTER EIGHT

BROWN SUGAR AND CHEDDAR CHEESE

"It is not the strongest of the species that survives, nor the most intelligent, but the one most responsive to change."

Attributed to Charles Darwin

"We are going to be all right, because we constantly get to tell the whole world who we are. We constantly get to define ourselves — that journey never stops… We, who are a week into wondering what the hell just happened, will continue to move forward. We have to choose to do so. But we will move forward, because if we do not … what is to be said about us?"

Tom Hanks

The Boy Scout motto is "Be Prepared" and the people at the farm pursued that state with compulsive fervor. They had seen what comes of complacency, of resting on the assumption that everything will be ok. And so they stripped the Rhoads building site of, well, everything. It was like construction-obsessed locusts had descended and picked it clean.

If Stage 1 fortifications concentrated on the ground floor, Stage 2 saw them go up a level. They installed metal shutters on the upstairs windows and erected scaffolding inside the newly-built walls out back. It created a second story where they could post guards and fend off attackers. And that was just the beginning. They had plans to fence in a wider area around the main compound. This would protect the tractor shed, the parking area and Arnold's pigs. When the ground softened they'd dig a trench around the perimeter and set traps that would hopefully snare the infected before they even got close to the house. Eventually they'd build guard towers and they wanted to bring in big, heavy obstacles to create a chicane along the road. If other survivors came barreling up *Mad Max* style, they wanted to slow them down so they couldn't just plow into the fences.

All of that was good. Unfortunately, the denizens of the farm did not rise every morning and commence work with a merry "Hi-Ho!" like the dwarves in *Snow White*. After a night of disturbed slumber and hideous nightmares, they hauled their exhausted asses out of bed and went to toil outside in a Pennsylvania winter. While the fortress around them grew in strength, its occupants, in big and small ways, began to buckle. They were traumatized by what they'd seen, but there was no psychiatrist with a leather couch and prescription pad to mitigate the universal state of PTSD at the farm. They had all lost loved ones, but an apocalypse allows you no time to grieve. They were living on top of each other and so everybody knew everybody's business. They all knew that Niamh and Owen were fighting and that he hated being here in this "podunk hell right out of *Deliverance*." When Emma used the last of the hot water just before Sam could get a shower, well, you'd think she'd just kicked his sainted mother in the teeth based on the strength of his reaction.

At one point Bib realized that she didn't have some ingredient she needed — brown sugar to make barbecue sauce. She made a mental note to pick some up at the ... What? At the store? Yeah, like she'd just nip to the grocery store for her weekly shop. But there was no "just nipping to the store" anymore, was there? If they didn't have it, couldn't grow it or make it, or didn't risk their lives to find it, then it was totally, irrevocably out of reach. The realization took her breath away.

When Louella came in, expecting to be greeted by the smell of Bib's World-Class BBQ Chicken, she found her friend sitting at the kitchen table, staring into space.

"Bib?" No answer. She tried again and got the same response. Lou shook her gently by the shoulder. "Honey, what's the matter?"

"I — I couldn't make barbecue sauce."

"Well, that's ok."

"No," Bib shook her head and there were tears in her eyes. "It's not. We don't have brown sugar and we can't just go and get some and it's like we're on some sort of island and..." She began to weep.

Louella held her until she quieted down. "If we can't get anymore brown sugar, is there something else we could use?" she asked.

Bib thought for a minute. "Molasses. That would do the trick."

Louella smiled at her. "And that is why you are the master chef here. Will you show me what to do?" Bib joined her at the counter and the two women made dinner.

It was funny how little things seemed to spark big realizations at the farm. A deficit of brown sugar or hot water highlighted just how much things had changed. And a debate between Louella and Peg over cheddar cheese centered around the biggest question of all.

It started because the cows were producing well and Lou had extra milk. She could, in the space of half an hour, make some mozzarella and be done with it. Although it would be nice to have, they'd need to use it up within the week and they had plenty to eat right now. What worried her were the lean months — periods of scarcity that would inevitably come. If she devoted the time now to making cheddar (which lasts ages) then they'd have it later on when perhaps food wouldn't be as plentiful. Cheddar, however, is a time-consuming job: it takes hours to get it started and so she asked Peg for help.

Peg, who'd been washing dishes, didn't look up. "Why don't we just make egg cheese ... It'll be quicker and we'll have it today."

"We have enough food today, we might not have enough in six months time."

"It's a lot of work, mom."

"I know."

"And, likely, a huge waste of time."

"Why?"

Peg glanced out the back window. Mae and Emma were playing tag in the enclosed garden — out of earshot. "Who exactly do you think is going to be around to eat it?"

"We will."

Peg laughed bitterly and shook her head. "You saw what it's like out there. The whole country, hell the world, is collapsing in on itself. And even if the infected don't find us — which is pretty freakin' unlikely — do you have any idea how much more precarious life is now? Wait until people start getting sick and dying of things that we used to be able to treat with a pill. Wait until we start losing people to accidents or they just decide to eat a bullet because the world *has* ended and no amount of bacon or cheddar cheese can fix that. I won't say it to the others, but we *are* fucked. We just haven't figured it out yet."

Louella stared at her open-mouthed. "Margaret Florence Bernhard," she said and Peg blanched. Her mother had used her full Christian (and maiden) name and that was never good. "You've got a kid, so you damn well plan for six months' time and a years' time and five years' time because … well, you just have to. That cheese is stored calcium for next year. Even if we lose the cattle, she'll still have a shot at healthy bones and teeth."

Peg laughed, a hysterical laugh, and tears welled up in her eyes. "Healthy teeth! Why? All the better to eat you with, grandma!"

"What's the alternative?"

"What do you mean?"

"If we don't plan for the future — if there *is* no future — then what do we do? Sit here, get drunk and wait to die?"

"Mom…"

But Louella didn't let her finish. "Because those are your two options, Peg. Give up and die or fight on. And if you're going to choose death, why wait? Why not do it today — right now? Let's just eat a bullet … oh wait, I guess we better shoot the kids first and *then* cap ourselves. Or maybe we should all hold hands, walk back into town and get bit."

"Stop it."

"No. You've got to hear this. Because you're a mother and you don't have the luxury of giving up. We've been given a real chance here, so you grab it with both hands!"

Gripping the edge of the counter, Peg stood sobbing.

"It's gotten on top of you today," Louella said.

Peg nodded. It took a moment before she could speak. "The last TV broadcast stopped."

"When?"

"There was snow on every channel when I got up this morning. We really are alone, aren't we?"

Louella thought for a moment. "In the time before — when you could just take it for granted that our world had billions of people in it, I still had moments when I felt entirely alone. There were times I felt that I couldn't count on anyone to do anything for me and if I wanted to see something happen, then I'd have to do it myself. Did you ever feel like that?"

"Yes."

"What did you do?"

Peg shrugged. "Got down to work."

"Good plan," Louella nodded. "Oh look: here's some work for us." She held up a bottle of rennet and gave it a shake.

Peg laughed and wiped her eyes. "How is this not affecting you?"

"What do you mean?"

"You're so damned positive about everything!"

"Honey, I take too much Aleve and cry into my pillow at night."

"You do?"

"Hell yes. It's the only indication that I'm still sane."

Peg laughed weakly. "How does the saying go? 'If you can keep your head when all about you are losing theirs…'" and her mother recited the end with her: "'it's just possible you haven't grasped the situation.'"

Louella hugged her daughter tight. "I'm going to start on that cheddar. Will you help me?"

Louella had just added rennet to the milk and left Peg to stir it. She slipped on her boots and went to fetch the eggs in from the barn. She barely recognized the farmyard anymore. The walls and scaffolding made it look less like a rural paradise and more like a permanent construction site. Fletch, who'd been working beside Alec all morning, was using his coffee break to paint something on the front of the barn. It was a four-pointed star that connected up with words scrawled beneath it.

"Camp North Star?" Louella asked.

Fletch shrugged. "We need a name for this place."

"Yeah, I guess. But why that one?"

"We have a lot of good people working hard and hence, this place has real potential. It could be a beacon, a light in the darkness, a shining example of how things can be."

While Louella agreed with the sentiment, she looked at her friend suspiciously. He was a writer who hated hyperbole. His style was streamlined, direct and at times brutally sparse. So why was he laying it on so thick?

"Hang on a minute," she said. "North Star. Wasn't that the summer camp full of misfits in the movie *Meatballs?*"

He grinned at her. "Which is why the name is doubly fitting."

"You're an idiot."

"But you love me."

"Yep," she said as she turned to go.

"I heard what you said to Peg just now."

Louella stopped mid-step and turned back to face him. "Was I too hard on her?"

"No. She needed to hear it." He downed the last of his coffee. "You're doing a good job, Lou."

She nodded her thanks. The chickens had clustered around her ankles hoping that she'd brought treats. Reaching into the pocket of her body warmer, she pulled out a little Tupperware container full of sunflower seeds. She scattered these around her and stood for a moment, watching the flock peck merrily at their snack. And Fletcher watched her. He had an idea that he meant to raise at dinner that night. It was necessary and it was right. And she was going to hate him for it.

CHAPTER NINE

LEADERS

"If your actions inspire others to dream more, learn more, and become more, you are a leader."

John Quincy Adams

"The world is looking for leaders to step up and serve in extreme conditions with unconditional love."

William T. Chaney Jr.

The cheese was out of the press and stored in the cellar, away from the heat, where it could be left to mature. Louella taped a note over the kitchen sink to remind her to go down and turn it everyday. She'd cleaned out the chicken coop and mucked out the cattle stalls and, while she was at it, fed Arnold's pigs (he was busy helping Alec to reinforce the upper level of the scaffolding while Bib was on guard duty). And then it was time to milk the cows and get dinner on. She seemed to have spent her whole day in either the kitchen or the barn. She sighed as she mixed together enough flour, sugar and Budweiser to make several loaves of beer bread. With that in the oven, she started on her homemade spaghetti sauce, dumping cans of Hunt's diced tomatoes into a pot to simmer. As she added ingredients and the good smells of garlic, onion and oregano wafted from the kitchen, people started to trickle in, half-frozen and ravenously hungry.

"Get some hot food in you," she said as she served it up.

"Ooh, what are we having?" Fletch called from the backdoor as he struggled out of his boots.

"Spaghetti and *meatballs* tonight. Where'd I get that idea from?"

It was quiet around the table — the silence of hungry people too tired for small talk. Conversation only returned when their bellies were full.

"So apparently we're Camp North Star," Alec said. "I guess that's as good a name as any."

Louella dropped her head into her hands. All she could picture when she heard that name was Bill Murray wearing a ridiculous spaceman helmet with blue lightning bolts on the sides and spindly little antenna sticking out the top. She could hear him over the tannoy: "I'm Tripper Harrison, your head counselor. I'll be coming at you every morning, about this time, hoping to make your summer camp experience the best available … in this price range."

Interrupting these thoughts, Fletch said, "I've been thinking a lot about sorting us out as a group. The first order of business, surely, is to establish a leader. We haven't talked about that."

"Well, it's Louella's farm," Bib said. "Shouldn't she be in charge?"

"Oh no no no," Louella answered. "I can tell you when the seed needs to go in the ground, but that does not qualify me to lead us through a friggin' apocalypse."

"Well, technically, no one here is qualified to do that," Peg said.

"No," Fletcher conceded. "And yet someone still has to. Lou, it should be you."

"Fletch," her tone was a warning.

"You're the one who rallied us on that first night, divvied up the jobs and got us moving. You were the one who picked the team to go to the construction site."

"I wondered about that. Why didn't you send me?" Wyn wanted to know.

Louella shrugged. "As a cop, Patience had to go and keep the team safe. If I send one of Ginny's children out there, then the other has to stay behind. If something went wrong and she lost you both… I don't wanna think what that would do to her."

"Which is why you insisted that I stay," Peg nodded. "Alec needed to go and so …"

"You had to stay behind for Mae. Josie could go because Wyn would be here for Emma. Arnold could go, but Bib had to stay behind unless Niamh went too. If all three of you rolled the dice together, that's your choice. But if two of you go out and don't come home, what the hell would the third one do?"

"You see, I didn't even think of that," Fletch said.

"It doesn't mean I'm right for the job," Louella shook her head.

"You've been *doing* the job."

"Will you at least consider another …"

"I have. And I keep coming to the same conclusion. We need somebody tough — you got the kids out of Midwood when it fell. We need somebody strong — you've buried a husband and a son and still kept the farm going. We need somebody smart — you saw this coming before any of us. And we need somebody who loves this group — you cared enough to make sure that Ginny would still have a son and Emma a father."

"Fletcher Landis…"

"Using my full name is not going to shut me up."

"But I don't want this!"

"Which is another reason why you should have it. If you wanted the job, well, there'd be something seriously wrong with you."

Louella looked at the others desperately. "Will somebody else say something?"

Alec did. "All in favor?"

Hands were raised, the motion passed and Louella was left sitting there, wondering what the hell just happened to her life. With an inarticulate groan, she rose and walked out the back door.

Fletch gave her a few minutes and then joined her in the barn. He found her sitting on the floor of the cow stall. Joe, her Milking Shorthorn, had laid down next to her and rested its head in the old woman's lap.

"I know her name's Joe," Fletch said. "Is it short for Josephine?"

Louella stroked the animal gently. "That's what I tell everybody, but really I named her after Joe Elliot, lead singer of Def Leppard."

"You're a weirdo, you know that?"

232

"Not weird enough, apparently. If I was truly bonkers you wouldn't have elected me to be your Grand Poobah or whatever the fuck you decide to call me now that all this shit's my responsibility."

"I know you're mad …"

"I'm fucking *furious*. What the hell were you thinking?"

"That you're the best person for the job."

"Stop saying that!" She wanted this conversation to be private so she was whisper-yelling at him. "Tonight when I was making dinner, I went to take the sauce off the stove. The arthritis in my wrists … both joints just gave way and I damn near spilled the whole boiling mess down the front of myself. That's me, Fletch. An uneducated, asthmatic, can't-lift-a-pot-off-the-stove old woman. And you think I'm going to what? Lead you all to the promised land? I mean, what the fuck?"

"I think you're going to make Camp North Star the best it can be. And you're going to do it because you love the people here."

"And what if I screw it up?"

He shrugged, "You can only do your best."

Louella looked at him and he was surprised to see tears in her eyes.

He knelt down in front of her. "Before you were a mom, did you know how to be a good one?"

"No, and don't even try to make the comparison. This is a hell of a lot more complicated than raising a couple of kids."

"How so? Planning for people's future, providing for their needs, setting down rules, protecting them — are you gonna tell me that that job description doesn't ring any bells with you?"

Louella let out a long sigh and buried her face in Joe's neck.

"I suggested that you lead us because it's a job you've spent the last forty-odd years learning how to do. And you're good at it." He rose and offered her a hand up.

Joe moaned a low protest when Louella wriggled free. She let her friend help her up and he gave her a hug.

Her face was buried in his shoulder, her voice muffled when she said, "You really are a prick, you know that?"

"Yeah, but a lovable one."

"Which is the only reason you're still alive." And with that they headed back to the house.

Back in September, Bethany Adams walked into her first day of eighth grade science class and realized that the only remaining chair was next to Abigail Williams. She cursed herself for not getting there earlier to get a better seat. Abigail, with her tatty clothes and greasy hair, was the class outcast. She was visibly dirty and her breath was diabolically bad. CariAnn, one of the most popular girls in their year, had made up a song about it (sung to the tune: *Oklahoma!*). "Haaaal-itosis, when the breath comes sweeping down the plains!" But it was more than just the hygiene issues. She was slow in school and hence had collected the inevitable label of "retard." She lived in a ramshackle house on the outskirts of Crucible, PA, and her family was pure white trash. Her father was the town drunk, collecting his unemployment checks and food stamps and blowing the lion's share of it on *Old Crow Bourbon*. And her mother, who had five kids by five different men, had run off with boyfriend number ... oh, who the hell can keep track?

Trash, retard, scumbag — these were the monikers used by people who never bothered to learn Abigail's name. And Bethany Adams now had to share a table with her, probably for the whole year. The old taunts of "cooties" that had been hurled at Abby in Elementary School resurfaced in Bethany's mind and she nudged her chair as far away from the girl as she could.

And then class was underway. As Mrs. Hemmingway described the earth's water cycle, Bethany grabbed her brand new Trapper Keeper and the pens she'd picked out at Woolworths. The desk in front of Abigail remained empty. Bethany started to take notes, but her eyes kept wandering back to the blank laminate tabletop in front of her neighbor. She tore a sheet from her notebook and slid it across to Abigail. She looked sadly at one of her new pens and then pushed that over as well.

Abby looked at her wide-eyed, then slowly took paper and pen and started to copy (badly) the diagram Mrs. Hemmingway had drawn on the board. As the girl wrote, the sleeve of her shirt hitched up and there, on the child's forearm was an old bruise. Bethany stared at it. It was massive and a deep greenish purple. Beside it there were five small circles: two were healing, sort of, and were crusted over with dirty white scabs. The other three, however, were newer — a swollen, bright, angry red. *Holy crap*, Bethany wasn't listening to the teacher anymore, *are those cigarette burns?* At that moment Abigail caught her looking and hastily pulled down her sleeve. Bethany sat there, her heart racing. *What the fuck? I mean ...* but words failed her. Quietly, she reached into her bag and took out her spare notebook. She slid this and half of her pens over to Abby.

As the kids packed up their gear at the end of the lesson, Abigail handed the stuff back with a quiet, "Thanks."

"No, you can keep it," Bethany said.

"Oh." Abigail stared in wonder at the nicest gift she'd ever received.

It would be lovely to say that that was the beginning of a redemptive story — that through Bethany, Abigail was welcomed into the fold and found love and acceptance. But it was never going to be that simple. The girl was so starved for attention that she latched onto Bethany with a smothering desperation. It was less like the natural evolution of a friendship and more like a drowning man pouncing on his rescuer in order to stay afloat. And Bethany, who was jumping through her own hoops in an effort to fit in, found that her association with the class pariah weighed on her like an anchor. Case in point: Tobey Wilson, a really cute boy in her Social Studies class, came over to her locker one day. "The gang" was going bowling on Saturday and did she want to ... but then Abigail bounded up to them and Tobey beat a hasty retreat. And the other girls were a nightmare about it. All through that fall, they teased her about her new "BFF" (Best Freak Forever) and asked her why she was "slumming it." As Christmas approached, there were so many things she wanted to be part of. Lena was having a sleepover and they were going to order pizza and stay up all night watching horror movies like *Silent Night, Deadly Night* and *Krampus* and Stephanie was even going to swipe her older brother's copy of *Bikini Bloodbath Christmas* which was almost like porn. And for New Year, CariAnn was having a party and Tobey was going to be there. If Bethany wanted to be a part of any of it, then she had to shake Abby off. It was a horrible thing to do, but maybe, just maybe if she did it slowly, if she quietly eased Abigail out of her life, then her feelings wouldn't be too hurt.

And so Bethany became very busy — projects due, doctors' appointments, family commitments. Then one evening she was sitting in Moretti's (the local pizza joint) with Stephanie and Tobey, and CariAnn, Jake and Lena when she happened to look up to see Abigail standing at the window, staring in at her. She'd told Abby that she couldn't hang out because she was grounded. She'd been lying so much lately and now finally, she'd been caught. Bethany felt sick — she knew exactly what she'd just done, but the feeling was tempered with a guilty relief. It was over. She was free to choose her own crowd and her own path and not have to carry someone when she could barely sort out her own shit.

In another moment, Abigail was gone. And it was during her long, cold walk home that she encountered the dog. And it bit her.

She got sick — really sick — and too weak to get out of bed. The fever rolled over her in great dark waves. Occasionally, she'd drift to the surface, literally gasping for air and you'd think that these moments of awareness and light would be a reprieve. But no. The first time she surfaced it was to the recollection of Bethany sitting there, laughing with all those bitches who'd made Abigail's life a misery. With their jokes about her hair and clothes and shoes — they had a seemingly infinite capacity to find things to make fun of. And now Bethany was one of them.

This hurt Abigail more than the cootie jibes, the ostracism, and the fact that, except as the butt of many jokes, she was invisible. Because this time someone had seen her — actually *seen* her — only to turn away. This time she had dared to hope. Proverbs 13:12 reads, "Hope deferred maketh the heart sick." And that is correct. Truly, it pained her more than the virus that raged through her scrawny body.

Another wave of delirium rolled her under and she thought no more of this. That was the supreme irony of New Rabies as experienced by Abigail Williams. The disease was preferable to her life. The next time she awoke, her father was in her room, rifling through her drawers, looking for her hidden stash of money. He obviously needed another bottle.

"Where is it?" he demanded.

When she didn't answer, his temper flared. But the wave rolled over her again, pulling her away from him and down into a darkness, safe and quiet and still.

In this key aspect, her experience of New Rabies was different to that of most victims. The horror people felt as the virus whittled away at them — that didn't trouble her. The reason? It had already been done. While her father was unfamiliar with the psychological concept of soul murder, he had effectively accomplished it with his daughter. He had stripped the child of all pride and potential. Other people were so attached to themselves, to the capital "I" of their being, but Abigail's identity was based on negation. It was not about who she was or what she needed or who she could be. It was about what she could not be a part of. It was based on rejection and neglect. There was nothing about herself or her life that she was particularly attached to; there was nothing about herself that she was proud of. She had been raised to believe that she was worthless and stupid and unwanted. And so who cares? So what if the virus strips you of your identity? It could not take what she did not possess. Instead, it offered her an escape — a glorious, black oblivion and the chance to lie back and float, dizzy and giddy, on the wave.

Her final coherent thought came at three a.m. the following morning. She sat up in bed with a sudden urge to go find her father. She rose and shuffled into the old man's bedroom.

He awoke the moment her teeth fastened on his throat. But no matter how much he thrashed and flailed, he could not shake her off. If someone had been present to observe this last act of violence in the Williams' house, they would have been struck by an odd sense of déjà vu. The scene that played out in that bedroom was not a human act of murder. It was like something out of *Mutual of Omaha's Wild Kingdom* — oddly reminiscent of the way a lion brings down a cape buffalo. When a lion takes down large prey, it will fasten its teeth on the neck, crushing the windpipe. Unable to draw breath, the buffalo suffocates.

The human trachea is less than one inch in diameter at the front of the throat. Abigail bit through the thyroid cartilage and fastened onto the windpipe. And she simply did not let go. While the man felt all the animal panic of having his air supply abruptly cut off, the girl experienced a moment of power, of control. The blood in her mouth sent a rush of euphoria through her. And for the first time in her life she was a being without pain or fear. Hope deferred may maketh the heart sick, but (as the Proverb goes on to say), "*when* the desire cometh, *it is* a tree of life." In this case: a new life born out of New Rabies.

With the bite delivered, Abigail strolled casually out of the room and never thought of her father again. She reached the bottom of the steps, fumbled with the lock on the door, and stepped out into the wide world. In Crucible, there was a section called "the patch" where most of the houses were clustered, and these were now under assault by the infected. Abby joined in. As a large man ran past her, she stuck a foot out to trip him.

She leapt onto his back and bit and clawed at him until he was finally able to buck her off. She lay in the snow then — panting and sated as he fled.

Soon, however, that feeling of repletion began to fade. Eager to restore it, she rose and recommenced the hunt. And she did get some good bites in — there was a woman trying to run in slippers. Abby tore out her calf. And there was a chubby kid she chased down and killed in her fervor. But she was kept on the periphery of the fighting by the sheer violence of the main protagonists. The biggest, strongest and fastest of the infected were on point and the battle they waged as they tore through that neighborhood was so far beyond her capabilities that she was shunted aside.

She found herself standing outside a house. Screams echoed inside, but the crowd of infected at the door was so dense, she couldn't get in. She looked down at herself — at her gray sweatpants and snow-encrusted socks. All her life she had cleaned and bandaged her own wounds and looked after herself. It was an ingrained, programed response to any moment of violence and so she turned and walked into one of the houses that had already been hit. A man, still clutching a shotgun, lay in the front hall. His throat had been torn out and he'd been disemboweled. She knelt by his feet and began to tug at his boots. They were laced up and she had quite a job getting them off because she'd forgotten that a simple pull on the laces would untie them. Her exertions began to attract attention as more and more of the infected stopped to investigate what she was doing. Had she found more prey? Apparently not and still they were intrigued. They watched as she finally yanked the shoes off and put them on her own feet. Standing with her new boots in the man's spilled guts, she pulled a coat off the rack by the door.

There were eight infected peering in the doorway now, looking at her as she stood there in her too-big coat with sleeves that flapped down past her hands. They saw her turn and walk quietly down the hall and into the living room. They followed. The room was empty and they were just about to leave when Abigail approached the couch. Her head cocked first to one side and then the other. And then with one swift movement, she wedged her fingers under the sofa and heaved it up. The couch was old — the seat cushions were supported by wire mesh and springs below which there was a gap where crumbs and loose change collected against a thin bit of fabric stapled at the bottom. That fabric had been cut away and, in the gap between wire and floor, there lay a thin boy in his early teens.

Abigail had used the same trick to hide from her dad once and now she smiled down on the boy as he cried and begged her to leave him alone. But it doesn't work that way — it never works that way and so Abigail tore into him and the others followed suit.

As the sun rose in Crucible, she ambled from house to house followed by a growing contingent of the infected. Walking through the rooms, she checked every possible hiding place and delivered another dozen people to the waiting horde. She may not have the brute strength needed for the sort of melee she saw last night, but she had spent a lifetime hiding from beatings and that instinct had survived in her when everything else had been burned away. She'd been prey for so long, she knew precisely where prey would hide. And so Abigail emerged as the undisputed leader of the horde.

CHAPTER TEN

ROLLER COASTER

"There are no great people in this world, only great challenges which ordinary people rise to meet."

William Frederick Halsey Jr.

"The horror no less than the charm of real life consists precisely in the recurrent actualization of the inconceivable."

Aldous Huxley

To begin with, being the leader of Camp North Star wasn't too bad. Everyone started calling Louella "Chief" and really, she just carried on doing what she would have done anyway. She hatched plans. They were simple and logical:

1. Complete the fortifications on the main part of the complex — the farmhouse, enclosed garden and barn.
2. Extend the security fencing to protect the outbuildings and keep Arnold's drove of pigs safe.
3. When their basic security needs had been met, she suggested they divide each day into three parts:

   A. Continued work on improving defenses and running the
      farm.
   B. Training.
   C. R and R.

The assembled company sat quietly, waiting for her to elaborate.

"I saw a program a while back on the old west. The pioneers who thrived were the ones who constantly worked to better their situation. And that's what we're gonna do here. When we aren't tied up with planting and the harvest, we need to keep improving this place — adding more defenses, hell building more accommodation so we can all have more privacy and space. And we've got to set up the lab so Wyn and Niamh can get started on the vaccine."

"We don't have the equipment we need for that," Wyn said.

"Which is why we need to start training. We have to learn how to carry out raids. I'm not sending anybody out for that equipment until they know how to handle themselves."

"Louella," Alec laughed, "you're looking at a room full of hunters."

"Yeah, but when was the last time a buck tried to eat you?"

"She's right," Patience nodded. "We need tactical training before we go — how to work together as a team, how to sweep an area ..."

"And you're going to teach us that," Louella told her. "Congratulations, Patience, you are the new Head of Security. When we go back out into that mess, I want us functioning like a frickin' SWAT team."

"It all sounds good," Bib said quietly. "I ... I'm just having a hard time picturing that."

"And that's what we have to change. We have to stop thinking that we can't do these things and just get on with doing them. And the only way to do that..." Lou gestured toward Patience.

"... is to learn how," the sheriff nodded.

Louella continued: "Which just leaves point number three — Rest. We have all been working around the clock to get this place fortified. It was necessary. But now, everyone is going to have a break everyday — take a nap, read a book, watch a movie, have some *fun*. Peg, you double majored at college ..."

"Yeah, Library Science and Psychology."

"I want to put that psychology background to use which is why I'm putting you in charge of morale."

Peg's face clouded over. "So I'm … what? Julie from the *Love Boat?* Entertainment director for Camp North Star?"

"No, you're the person with the psychology degree who can help us deal with the PTSD epidemic that we're likely to see here. Whether it takes counseling or giving us all coping strategies or organizing some fun, I don't know. But I know we need to do something. It's the apocalypse. And the question I'm posing to you is how do we stay sane?"

Peg went pale and slightly green as the full ramifications of her new job became clear to her. As she wrapped her head around the idea, Louella delegated other areas to the "experts."

"Wyn and Niamh, you are our medics."

"Whoa, I'm only pre-med," Niamh said. "You said experts and I'm not one."

Louella shrugged. "So become one. Wyn is the best vet in the area so he can help you and," she looked at Peg who was still looking a little nauseous, "you snagged a bunch of medical books from the library, right?"

"Huh? Uh, yeah. There's a ton of information there."

"There you go," Lou said to Niamh. "Alec, you obviously are in charge of the development of the site. Arnold, I'm putting you in charge of the animals." He opened his mouth to raise an issue, but Lou cut him off. "I'm not saying you have to do all the work yourself; I'm saying that you're in charge of that area." When he nodded his agreement, she continued: "Fletch will manage the guard schedules and patrols. Now that we have fences, we need to inspect them everyday to make sure they stay intact and that nothing is digging under them to get in. I also want you to help sort plans for additional defenses. Bib, you're managing our provisions and planning the meals. Sam, it's now your job to maintain the weapons and teach gun safety. Levi, you've got the motor pool. And Josie, you're better with a needle and thread than anybody I know. I need you to keep us clothed and I want you to start thinking about armor."

"Armor?" Josie asked.

"When we do leave the farm, we're going to need protective clothing to keep from getting bit."

"Hoo boy," Josie sighed.

"Sucks to be given a job, doesn't it?" Louella's voice was jolly, her grin wide.

"Ah, sweet revenge," Fletch muttered.

"No. I'm not doing this to get you back for making me chief. I just don't have all the answers and I'm hoping that, if we put our heads together, we can figure this out."

Louella had outlined her plan decisively and confidently, but it was a confidence she did not feel. In truth her head was pounding. She'd always been prone to migraines and they had gotten worse and a lot more frequent since becoming chief. Take today, for instance. Delegating was the right thing to do. She'd read a zombie book once, *The Cost of Living* by David Moody, in which a family barricades itself in against the ravening hordes. To Louella's mind, the main character had one fatal flaw: he tried to shoulder everything. At the time, she'd called it the "One-Man-Band-Syndrome." Not only had it overtaxed him, but it deprived his family of the ability to exercise any control over their situation. And so, with that example in mind, she had decided to give people their own domains — something they could put their minds to. She hoped it would empower them, give them a greater sense of control and provide an intellectual distraction from the horror of recent events. But what if it backfired — what if it was too much? What if, instead of thriving in these roles, everybody worked themselves into the ground or cracked under the pressure? Because that was Louella's greatest fear for herself. When she was just making suggestions and helping people settle in at the farm, she was ok. But now she was in charge. Whatever happened, happened on her watch; and so while her workload hadn't really changed, the pressure on her increased tenfold. She was eating NSAIDs as if they were M&Ms.

"Lou?"

The chief looked up. It was Niamh. "What is it, honey?"

"What about Owen?"

"What do you mean?"

"Well, it seems like everybody has a job except him."

Just the mention of Owen made Louella's head throb harder. "I'll tell you what: when he can be bothered to drag his ass to the table for a meeting, then I'll give him a job."

Niamh looked hurt at the response, but only nodded and walked away. The old woman leaned back in her chair and watched her go. Owen was another problem she'd soon have to address. The kid was depressed; that much was clear. He had trouble hauling himself out of bed — it was like he couldn't face the day. But that meant that he was always the last person to join in and help with the work. It didn't make him popular. He rarely spoke and when he did he was caustic. All in all, people thought he was a douche. So what the hell was she going to do about it? Nothing immediately occurred to her. She reached into her apron pocket for her bottle of Aleve. What was the joke by John Barrymore? "America is the country where you buy a lifetime supply of aspirin for one dollar, and use it up in two weeks." Truer words were never spoken.

Human perceptions are intrinsically skewed by what psychologists call "negativity bias." From our earliest days in the caves, our brains had to become finely attuned to potential dangers — we had to be hyperaware of the bad things in our lives. That is how we survived as a species. This instinct became so ingrained that, even today, we automatically react more strongly to negative stimuli than to positive. For instance scientists have calculated that, within our relationships, one insult cannot be counterbalanced by one compliment. It takes no less than five positive comments to neutralize the hurt feelings caused by one snipe. Why? Because we fixate on and remember the bad far more clearly than the good.

At Camp North Star there were quite a few good and productive days. However, these were easily undermined by the problems that arose. Yes, security fences now enclosed the outbuildings giving them more space. Yes, Louella was bringing her seeds on for the vegetable garden and by summer they would have more produce than they could eat. The surplus they would blanch and preserve and put by for next winter and that was good. But the hope they derived from these improvements evaporated with the arrival of Mared.

Mared Dietz, Effie's daughter, drove up to the gate one grey morning in late February. Louella recognized her goddaughter's car, but could barely recognize the wild-eyed creature that emerged from it. Her clothes were soiled with blood and feces. Her hair, which had been her pride and joy, was a matted, filthy rats' nest. And she was drooling. Saliva gathered thickly at the corners of her mouth.

"Lou," she called as she gripped the fence. "Let me in!"

"She's infected," Fletch muttered to Louella as they approached the fence.

"Hi honey." The chief plastered a smile on her face. "What happened to your arm?"

Instinctively Mared hid the bloody limb behind her back.

"If you're bit, you don't have to hide it. Now tell me what happened."

"It — it was mom!" the girl stammered. "But she didn't mean it, she's sick. And I thought that maybe you could help her and — and this." She held up the arm with its torn skin and exposed bone. "It hurts so much and I couldn't get to you and …" Finally overcome, she sank to her knees and cried.

All the people of the farm were out on the scaffolding now, watching this exchange. If the revelation that Effie was infected had shocked or pained the chief, she did not show it. Instead she sat down on the ground across from her goddaughter. And they heard her say, "Did you see the CDC report? The one where they gave us instructions for the vaccine?"

"I — I can't remember."

"They told us how to make the cure."

The woman looked up, her eyes big with hope. "Really?"

Louella's face was beatific, that of an angel. "Really. Everything's gonna be ok."

"For my mom too?"

"Yes."

"Oh God, I — I…" Mared started to say, but suddenly she went rigid and fell over on her side. Her eyes rolled back, her jaw clenched and her whole body started to twitch.

"She's seizing!" Niamh shouted and ran toward them.

Louella bellowed "Stop!" so fiercely that the young medic skidded to a halt and stared at her wide-eyed.

When Lou turned back to face Mared, she saw that the muscles in her neck were pulled taut, her lips were blue and her mouth and nose were streaming.

Louella rose and unlatched the gate. As she pulled it open, she heard a dozen guns cock behind her. She went to the stricken young woman and knelt beside her.

"It's ok," she soothed. "You'll be all right in a minute."

She drew a little .22 Rimfire out of her pocket and shot Mared in the head.

The dull crack of the shot was swiftly followed by a second. Patience had taught them to double tap a target — just to be sure. And then Lou rose unsteadily to her feet. Fletch reached out to her, but she batted his hand away.

"Close the gate," she ordered.

The others had joined her on the ground now. From the level of her eyes, it looked like she was talking to their belly buttons. "I want full protective hazmat clothing for the cleanup team. There's a spare tarp in the shed, wrap her up in that. And then we need to build a pyre. I want guards on the ground and at elevation to cover the cleanup crew while they're outside the fence. I don't want anything to see the smoke and come looking. So we'll pray over her and burn the body after dark." She finally raised her eyes. They were red and raw. "Go on now."

As she walked back to the house, she passed Owen. "Yet more Christian charity from our fearless leader?" he asked.

Her fist shot out from her side and connected with his crotch. He moaned and dropped to his knees. Leaning down into his face she spat, "Wrong. Fucking. Day." As she continued on her way, she shouted over her shoulder, "Owen's on cleanup."

Once inside, she made a beeline for the bathroom and knelt there waiting to see if she was going to be sick. Nothing happened so she doused her face with cold water and studied herself in the mirror. She was ghastly pale, slack-jawed, and wide-eyed. So that's the face of a killer, huh? And she heard her father in that moment, back when he was minister of St. Matthew's Lutheran Church, as he recited the Liturgy for Infant Baptism over Mared.

"Do you promise to share responsibility for this precious child?" he'd asked her. "To pray for her, and walk with her in the way of Christ to help her take her place within the life of the Church."

And she had answered, "With God's help, I will."

So what about today then? Every moment she delayed in pulling that trigger was another moment of needless suffering for Mared. She knew that. She knew her goddaughter could not be saved and they would have to put her down. She also knew that there was no one on the farm she could have delegated *that* job to — it was too much to ask. She wanted to tell herself that she *had* done right by Mared, because Mared was now at peace. But all these thoughts brought her no comfort and *my God*, her head was an all-encompassing throb so excruciating that it made her pant. She rummaged through the medicine cabinet and knocked back four aspirin and two Tylenol and then sat down on the bathroom floor and waited for the painkillers to kick in.

She became aware that something was jabbing her in the side. She pulled the gun from the pocket of her body warmer. The Walther was squat, uniformly black and a comfortable fit for her small hands. She had just shot Mared with that gun to spare her further suffering and for one moment that verged on insanity, she wondered whether she should extend the same mercy to herself. Instead she pocketed the gun, rose, and went to sweep out the barn.

The sun set at five-fifty that night and Mared, who had been laid out on wood, covered in hay and doused in petrol, was set alight. If the people of the farm thought that it would smell like cooking meat, they were mistaken. There is a quality to burning human flesh that *is* innately human. You can say that people are just thinking animals and you can say that elementally our bodies are made of the same stuff as the cattle and the deer. But burn a human body and you will never forget it.

It was not an odor that people wanted to keep company with and so they retreated into the warmth and light and clean air of the farmhouse. Only Louella lingered with Fletch at her side. As she watched the flames consume the shrouded figure, she asked, "What must they think of me?"

"Well, the general consensus is that you have brass balls the size of Detroit."

"I killed her."

"You gave her peace. And people were just relieved that someone else did the job."

"Who could I have asked to do that?"

"I would have done it for you."

Louella looked at him. He was staring straight at her and there was such kindness in that gaze. She leaned against him and rested her head on his shoulder.

"It was hilarious when you hit Owen in the nards."

Louella laughed out loud and then clamped a hand over her mouth. "I shouldn't have done that."

"He got off lightly. If he'd pulled that shit with Alec or Levi, we'd be sweeping his teeth up with a dustpan and brush. It does raise the question, though: What are we gonna do about him?"

"I was thinking about that today while I was sweeping out the barn. I've got an idea ... finally."

"Care to share it?"

"No, too tired now."

"You know pretty soon things are gonna come to a head with that boy."

"I know," Louella said matter-of-factly. "That's what I'm counting on."

She didn't have to wait long. Mared's death, hell the condition she'd arrived in, had unnerved the group. That, combined with the horrible job of cleaning up the mess (the blood, the shards of skull) and burning the body (it took so long to render Mared down to ash) ... well, everybody at the farm was pretty raw.

And so, when Owen failed to report for guard duty at the appointed time, people had had enough. He managed to appear for lunch and Peg glared at him.

"So you can come down for food, but not for guard duty, huh?" she asked.

"Maybe we should make a new rule," Wyn said, looking up from his sandwich. "If you don't work, you don't eat."

Owen's mouth twisted into a nasty grin. "Well, that would allow us to get rid of your mother."

"What?"

"She's barely gotten off her ass the whole time we've been here."

"She's sick!" Patience stared at him in disbelief.

And it was true. Ginny's recovery from the stroke had been knocked back by the stress of the outbreak and the abrupt cessation of her healthcare. She was frail, had mobility issues and suffered from post-stroke fatigue. It was a tiredness that did not get better with rest. She still had difficulty swallowing and her vision was impaired.

"She's not contributing anything to the farm," Owen shrugged. "But she's eating and taking up a lot of time and for what? So we can convince ourselves that, despite the fact that we shoot women in the head, we really are good people because, look, we're taking care of the resident vegetable?"

Levi, Wyn and Patience were on their feet, but Owen did not heed the warning. "Hey chief," he called to Louella. For some strange reason, she was filling a canvas shopping bag with food. "You're the one who's so keen to blow people away, why don't you do us all a favor and ..."

Levi's fist connected with Owen's jaw before he could finish that sentence. The kitchen erupted then with some people swinging at the boy, while others tried to break up the fight. Mae screamed and clung to her mother, who hurried the children into the living room. Cutlery flew and dishes shattered in the general flailing of arms and legs as Owen was ejected out the back door. He landed on his ass, rose and kicked one of the chickens out of his way. The bird squawked in pain and hobbled off dragging a wing behind her.

Louella's reaction was immediate. A skillet came hurtling out of the kitchen door and clanged onto the frozen earth at his feet. "Listen up, you little bastard, you do not mistreat my people or my animals."

Wyn appeared beside her at the kitchen door. He was trying hard to get himself back under control and his voice still trembled with rage. "Her wing's broken, but I can fix it."

Owen said shakily, "See, she'll be all right."

"Yeah," Lou nodded, "but she isn't going to lay tomorrow or the day after or the day after that. How many mouths do we have to feed? You know what?" She handed him the bag of provisions. "I've changed my mind. You'll do great on the road. Get out."

"What?"

"You heard me, get the hell out."

"But you said that if I left here I'd die. If you do this, it's murder."

"Nope. It's suicide. Because if you can be handed all of this," Louella gestured wildly at the farmyard, "and still manage to fuck it up, then you have no one to blame but yourself. Now git!"

And with that he found himself outside, clutching a bag of food and the keys to his ancient Volkswagen with its half tank of gas. He stood there, the loneliest man in the world, and admitted to himself that he had no idea how to get home. And he had no idea how to fit in here. And he had nowhere in this world to go.

Meanwhile, Louella had a quiet word in Fletcher's ear. "Take a rifle, head up to the scaffolding and cover him. Make sure nothing gets near him, ok?"

"Is this part of your plan?"

"Yep."

"You are one crazy-ass broad."

"Flattery will get you nowhere," she said as she stooped to clean up the mess.

"I'm sorry, Lou," Niamh helped her tidy up.

"Your boyfriend's a real asshole," Peg said as she chipped in.

"I'll go talk to him."

"Niamh, with all due respect, whether you patch up your relationship is secondary to whether or not I let him back in here," Louella said quietly.

"Seriously?"

Lou filled a bucket with soapy water. There was so much food on the floor that it needed a good mopping. "You ever read any zombie novels?"

"No."

"They're interesting. All about surviving at the end of the world. In them there's usually some idiot who works against the group. I'm not wasting time with that. We've got too much to do. We have to work on this place, defend it, raise the crops, tend the animals, raise the kids, and sort out this vaccine business — all while trying not to go nuts. We don't have time to argue with an asshole. He toes the line or he's out."

Dusk fell and still Owen remained. He sat in his car, turning it on periodically so he could get a little heat. Louella had seen, well actually heard, of this happening before. Her father was rebellious during his younger years and after one particularly nasty argument with his dad, he had been told to hit the road. He made it as far as the mailbox. There he realized that he had precisely nowhere to go and still he could not swallow his pride enough to go back to the house. In the end, it was his mother who broke the stalemate.

Dinner at the farm that night was hamburgers and Louella wrapped two of them up and went out to Owen's car. She hopped into the passenger seat and handed him a burger.

"I just want to go home," his voice was thick; he sounded bunged up like he'd been crying.

"You know I would help you if I thought it wouldn't get you killed."

"I know. And I'm sorry. I'm just ..."

"What?"

"I'm just so angry all the time."

"It's not surprising. It's the apocalypse and that's a tad upsetting," she said dryly.

"It isn't just the outbreak. You guys *have* each other. I can't turn around without tripping over somebody and yet I've never felt so alone."

250

"You know, if you spoke to them a little nicer, shared the work a bit more, you'd have them too. No one here wants to see you isolated, but we don't know how to get close to you."

"I've been wondering if I'm just too different. I'm from a big city and you …"

"Are from a 'podunk hell right out of *Deliverance*'?" She laughed and bit into her burger. "None of that matters anymore. Republican or Democrat, Black or White, gay or straight, town mouse or country mouse — who cares? We're just trying to survive." She paused while she formulated the idea in her head. "Actually, we can do more than that."

"What do you mean?"

"We have an opportunity to really do something here. We've got such a good set up, the sort of place survivors will gravitate to. And we can make a sustainable life for them, but we'll need to establish some sort of … I don't know … *society* to do it."

"Establish a society?" he laughed. "Look, I'll admit that the group's doing well, but we're not exactly a bunch of George Washingtons and Ben Franklins."

"I've got the gray hair and dentures." She smiled at him and shrugged. "I'm just saying that if we want a future, we're going to have to build one. You're pre-law, aren't you?"

The question threw him. "I was a Political Science major and, yeah, I was going into law. Why?"

"Because I want you to start thinking about how we're going to draft laws for this place. We need a constitution that sets out how decisions are made, how we're going to function, what rights people have. We need to define what is and isn't acceptable to the group and also establish how to replace a leader who's become dangerous or ineffective."

He looked at her for a long time. "Fuck me, you're serious."

"Don't get me wrong — the law's meaningless if we all starve to death or get overrun; so we still need a young man like yourself to help with the jobs. But while you work, this is something you can think about. It's something that'll challenge you and maybe take your mind off being so homesick. And it's something that would make you indelibly one of us."

"But why…," Owen found himself getting flustered, "… after today. With the way you feel about me…"

"You have no idea how I feel about you. Yeah, we clashed today and you made me so freakin' mad I could've …" Louella didn't finish the sentence. "But I also posted guards to make sure you didn't get hurt while you were outside the walls."

"You did? I thought the guards were there to keep me out."

"Nope, they've been watching out for you this whole time." She turned to him. "You've made some mistakes. Join the club. The question is do you want to be the guy who storms out of here and is just a bad memory? Or do you want to be … I don't know … the legislator for a new society?"

He stared at her in disbelief. He knew he'd behaved horrendously and a part of him was surprised that it had taken this long for the old woman to crack and finally kick his ass out. And yet here she was offering him a chance to reinvent himself, to become so much more than he ever dreamed. To do something important.

"All right, you're on." He felt a little giddy.

She got out of the car and he followed her. "I want you to draft the law, but keep it simple. The people here aren't stupid, but no one is going to want to sit and read a lot of legalese. When you have a rough draft, I'm going to open it up to everyone to question and debate. That way they'll all be involved in the process. When the amendments are made, we'll all sign on to it."

"All right. I'll get started on it tonight."

"After you apologize to Ginny's family. There are a lot of ruffled feathers in there." She smiled at him wryly. "You dirty rotten chicken-kicker."

"I'm sorry, Lou."

"It's done."

"And you really think that this is the start of a new world?"

Louella shrugged, "Why not? Human civilization didn't begin in the cities. First came the hunters and then the farmers. Where else is it going to start if not with us?"

CHAPTER ELEVEN

INTERLUDE

"None of us, including me, ever do great things. But we can all do small things, with great love, and together we can do something wonderful."

Mother Teresa

"Alone we can do so little; together we can do so much."

Helen Keller

If life on the farm was a movie, this is where the work montage would go. There'd be scenes of people rising to the challenge, innovating, prevailing. We'd see, for instance, Alec directing the building projects and laboring in the noonday sun — shirtless, sweat glistening on his muscles — while Joe Esposito sings *You're the Best* in the background. We'd see the group engaged in weapons training — they'd start off clumsy, a band of misfits with no hope. But to the synthesized momentum of Survivor's *The Moment of Truth*, they'd improve until they became frankly awesome with even Louella's round frame capable of ninja-like prowess. Bananarama's *It Ain't What You Do It's the Way That You Do It* would make a perky accompaniment as Niamh and Peg hit the books or you could just accompany all of it with Roxette's *Stars* to underscore their sense of hope.

The reality is always different. Alec, dressed in filthy jeans and a flannel shirt, was freezing his ass off every day as he worked on the fortifications. To the left side of the house there was a paved area with three outbuildings: a storage building (now a pig sty), a tractor shed and a grain silo. He'd already plugged the gaps between these with security fencing and now he planned to extend the fence to the right side of the house to give the cattle more free-range pasture to graze. Then he'd build guard towers — elevated firing positions to counter attacks coming from any direction.

Normally, he found work therapeutic. The most relaxing thing in his life had always been to work outside with his hands. It was like that old saying: "If you love what you do, you'll never work a day in your life." But now, the stakes were so high. He was responsible for creating a safe haven for everyone and therefore he worked like a fiend. It was Mae, most of all, who drove him. The five-year-old had been so pale with brown shadows under her eyes; she talked less, laughed less. But with each addition he made to their defenses, she slept better. And the color was returning to her cheeks as her dad built her "a castle" to keep her safe.

Likewise, Fletcher was obsessed with the security of the base. He'd read a lot of history books while researching one of his novels and hence had a wealth of ideas on how to protect the farm. The difficulty for him lay in the tension between compassion and logic. Take, for instance, Francis Galton's survival handbook for Victorian explorers, *The Art of Travel*. In it Galton describes how to make "pitfalls." These were small holes dug into the ground with sharpened stakes embedded at the bottom. They could then be camouflaged on top to look like the surrounding turf. The idea was to dot these holes randomly all around the farm; that way if the infected approached, they would likely run afoul of the traps. Just stepping into one of those holes was probably enough to break a man's ankle, but Fletch meant to truly hobble them. Hence, he recommended that the wooden spikes be baked in hot ashes. Apparently that would keep them strong and sharp despite seasonal wear and tear. If the infected managed to yank themselves free of the stakes (and, let's face it, they'd sure as hell try), then they would be slowed down as they crossed "the killing field" — the bare ground between the pit traps and the fences. In essence, they would be a lot easier to pick off.

All of that made logical sense. But to set those traps... The people most likely to step into them were his friends, people he'd known all his life, the Mareds and Effies of Midwood. He was under no illusion about the pain and damage he would cause and it kept him awake at night. While he prided himself on his talent and intellect, he felt — no he *knew* — that what must ultimately define a man was his compassion. And now he was … what? Actually recommending that they put hardened *spikes* in holes in the ground so that when Katie Boehler or the Mayor came trundling along, those stakes would punch up through the bottoms of their feet. Hell, if they hit it just right, the spikes could penetrate right up into the ankle. How the fuck had he changed from a man who would not throw a punch into this?

But it was a different world now and it was changing all of them. Louella was an old softie and she'd been forced to mow down two people just to get the kids out of town. If circumstances could turn the Louellas of this world into combatants, then it really was time for the gloves to come off. Still, those spikes …

He mentioned this to Peg and was disappointed when she did not have an immediate answer for him. She would only say, "I've been thinking about that. We'll talk about it tomorrow."

The following day, Patience split the group into two. One half would stand guard and keep to their tasks while the other had a training session. And then they'd swap. She was covering the main principles of retreat — how, if you had to run for it, you should not look back over your shoulder.

"You know they're coming," she said. "That's not a fact that requires constant verification. And every time you look back, you take your eyes off where you're going. Is there anything ahead that'll trip you up? Are there more infected approaching from the front? To keep looking back is a fear response and it means that you are not concentrating on your goal. I'm going to keep drilling that into you because, if you have to run for your lives, you need to do it effectively. Any questions?"

Bib raised a hand — it's funny how the old habits from school never die. "Where do we run to?"

"On every mission, we will designate a fallback position where we'll meet up if things go sideways. Everyone will know at least three routes to get there. If there is a problem here and we have to evacuate, well, I'm going to talk to Louella about designating rendezvous points. And Lou was thinking about setting up a 'Site B.'"

"What's that?" Niamh asked.

OF STARLIGHT AND PLAGUE

"Another fortified, well-stocked location that we can retreat to if we lose the farm."

There were no other questions and so Patience moved on. "In a minute, Niamh is going to talk us through first aid ..."

Fletch cut in: "You mean whisky and duct tape?"

"But first," Patience continued, "I want to turn things over to Peg."

Everyone was confused by this. It was a defensive training session, so why was the cop handing it over to the librarian?

Peg answered that question with her first statement. "We need to talk about killing people." They all gawked at her. "That is what all this training amounts to. To defend ourselves and the farm, we will have to shoot the infected and perhaps other survivors. And these are likely to be people we know."

They were sitting at the kitchen table for this and she shuffled through the papers in front of her.

"This is an assessment of how New Rabies affects the human brain. It was submitted by Dr. Edwin Caldwell and a colleague posted it on the CDC website shortly before the internet went down. It reads:

I have spent a significant amount of time interviewing infected patients before they lost their capacity for speech. Without exception, they speak of their diminished mental faculties. They find that the virus erodes their memories. Not only do they forget significant people in their lives, but they also experience extreme difficulty in holding on to who they are. One patient remarked that the fever seemed to be "burning her out," destroying her sense of identity and cauterizing her emotions in the process. It is true that emotional responses such as compassion, mercy and regret are wholly absent from patients once they have fully succumbed to the disease.

I believe that this mental destruction is a mechanism employed by the virus. Traditional rabies ramps up aggression in animals and makes them more likely to bite and hence spread the disease. Likewise New Rabies also increases aggression while simultaneously attacking the areas of the brain responsible for memory and moral reasoning. In short, it turns its victims into vectors. It rids them of all impediments to violent action. Then it propels them out into the world to look for *people to infect. Within nature this is not a new phenomenon. The virus's only aim is survival and to survive, it must reproduce — in this case it must spread. To achieve this end, it reduces complex human beings to the level of puppets with the disease twitching their strings.*

Some mental vestiges remain. Patients have been observed opening doors and using tools (such as sticks and rocks) to break windows. However, the similarity between the infected and the rest of humanity ends there. There is nothing left to reason with. No communication is possible. And they no longer possess a conscience that is capable of pity or remorse. We talk about zombies in movies and books. This virus has given us a medical example of what a zombie might be. While their cardiovascular functions continue unabated and hence they are technically "alive," the person — the soul — is dead. What remains is an empty, and highly dangerous, husk.

"Dr. Edwin Caldwell was the lead investigator from the CDC assigned to the initial outbreak on Cáscara. He's the one who managed to determine the nature of the disease and he gave us the name 'New Rabies.' Therefore, I believe it is safe to say that he was one of the few experts on the disease."

"Was?" Bib asked.

"He was killed by the vectors on the island. In fact the whole team was lost. But this assessment," she waved the paper at them, "is the word of one of the few authorities on the subject. So when he says that the infected have lost everything that made them human, that the person you knew and loved is dead and what is left is an empty shell, then you should believe it. If you have to shoot any of these husks, then understand it is not an act of murder. It's an act of mercy."

"Which is why Louella shot Mared," Fletch nodded.

"Yes," Peg said. "I know that just the thought of it feels wrong and wholly alien to who we are. But that business with Mared ... it's a prime example of what we're dealing with here. The infection was killing everything that made Mared ... well, Mared. We have no way to halt that process once it's begun. And with Mared gone, the virus could hide behind her face and use her body to spread the disease. When mom pulled the trigger, she was killing the virus, not the woman. And it cost her. I hadn't seen her look like that since dad died. And that is why I'm introducing two things. The first is simply a word. Up until now, we haven't given a name to the infected. That's odd, really, because every work of zombie fiction does it. Walkers, stenches, ghouls, living dead, Zeke, dark seekers, dead heads, and skulls as well as 'puppies and kittens.'"

"Puppies and kittens?" Niamh asked.

"That one's from *Z Nation*. Anyway, the name is important. It is a reminder that when you pull the trigger, you're not shooting Effie or Clarence or Bob. You are shooting…"

"A puppy?" Fletch asked.

"I thought we'd use Dr. Caldwell's term and call them 'husks.' It is apt given the circumstances."

They thought it over and there was a murmur of assent.

"The second thing that I wanted to introduce was this." She pulled out a thick leather bound journal and handed it to Fletch.

"What's this?" he asked, flipping it open.

"It's our story and you're going to write it. Everything we do, every contribution we make, will be recorded in that book including those moments when we have to fight. As we saw with mom, it is a sacrifice to pull the trigger. You lose some equilibrium, some peace of mind. But you will be honored and remembered for that sacrifice. And we will love and support you. On that note: I'm making counseling and therapy sessions available for whoever needs them."

Niamh spoke up. "It's a nice idea," she nodded at the book, "but who's going to read it?"

"Future generations," Fletch murmured.

Peg nodded. "Yeah. You know how we used to sit in school and try to imagine what it was like for George Washington and Paul Revere? Well, someday people will look back on us and wonder the same thing. That," Peg pointed to the journal, "will be the story of Camp North Star's founding mothers and fathers."

Less than fifteen miles to the north, another group was banding together. Abigail's growing horde was now 163 strong and they had discovered a group of survivors holed up in the old elementary school. Crucible Elementary had closed in 1992 and was in a state of advanced decay. The ceiling had fallen down in several places and internal doors hung crookedly from their hinges. The place, even before Abby arrived, looked like something out of a horror movie. That, actually, was intentional. Since its closure, the building had been used by local organizations to raise money as a Halloween Haunted House. Therefore, the twenty-three survivors who'd taken refuge there were surrounded by fake cobwebs and disturbing graffiti. There were "bloody" handprints on the walls and slogans that read "Devil" and "Mad Surgeon," a hastily scrawled ad: "Body Parts for Sale" and the rather cryptic "Stubbie Never Came Back." Who Stubbie was was anybody's guess.

The set dressing was not the problem. The problem lay in the dozen or so points of easy ingress. The external doors were wooden with glass windows and the huddled survivors, during a hushed conversation the night before, debated what to do about them. They could try to barricade them, but it was a big job to do in the dark with no tools. And the noise of it might attract attention. Therefore they opted for silence. They would retreat to a classroom on the second floor, block the door and hide. If they were lucky the horde would pass them by.

However they did not factor Abigail into their calculations. She had no particular instinct about the school. She had just gone systematically from house to house, building to building all through the night. By morning, she had reached Rices Landing and the derelict school. Before the search commenced, she left a group of infected outside to field anyone who tried to flee. And then the horde moved in. Upstairs the survivors pressed themselves against the walls, hugged their knees and listened to the shuffling footsteps below. There was the crunch of glass breaking underfoot and the clatter of a kicked chair. Two of the infected clashed briefly and they could hear the screeches as a body was slammed through a door, shattering the wood. At this Dina Winslow started to sob — too loud — and she pressed her hands against her mouth to stifle the sound. Robert Grimes hastened over to her and placed his hands on her shoulders. Looking her in the eye, he kept mouthing "It's OK. We're going to be OK." And everyone else held their breath.

The moans and heavy footsteps were louder now. They were on the second floor, milling through the rooms, getting closer. Then finally it happened. Something collided lightly with their door. It did not swing open as the others had done and so the figure on the other side hit it again more forcefully. Still it would not budge and with a screech of rage the thing out there threw itself against the wood. The door shook on its hinges as men ran and threw all of their weight against it in a desperate attempt to keep it closed. But you cannot bar a door once it has ceased to exist. A constant onslaught of the infected literally bashed the door to pieces and then they were in the room and there was nowhere left to run. The screams of the twenty-three echoed through the empty halls and more bloody handprints were pressed into the walls.

If life were a movie, a savvy director would not shoot that scene of carnage. What we imagine is always so much worse and so he would merely let you listen to those screams and then fade to black.

CHAPTER TWELVE

THE LOST BOYS

"Teenager: (noun) Someone who is ready for the zombie apocalypse, but not for tomorrow's math test."

Internet Funny

"There is a saying in the Neverland that, every time you breathe, a grown-up dies."

J.M. Barrie, <u>Peter Pan</u>

Winter gave way to spring and the vegetables in Louella's garden were coming on full and green. She'd planted mint and nasturtiums around the broccoli to keep the pests away and bedded cabbage alongside cucumbers and beans because they were compatible neighbors. Her garden would provide them with ample food for summer and plenty to blanch, freeze and preserve for the colder months. In the meantime she picked dandelion greens when the plants were young and tender and served them up in salads with hot bacon dressing and thick slices of bread. The wheat, alfalfa and corn went in in April and there was a general feeling of hope and growth on the farm.

Everything, however, was not completely idyllic. One of the obvious targets on their list was Sage Foods, the big grocery store and pharmacy out on the highway. It was an ideal first raid — far enough from town that they hoped to pick it clean without encountering too much trouble. But the thought of sending her people out, away from the safety of the farm, unnerved Lou. When Patience picked her team and Louella did not make the cut, she insisted on going anyway.

"But…" Patience faltered. It was her domain. Technically, she had ultimate authority over how their missions would run. However, she had to respect the chain of command and the chief had spoken.

Watching this unfold, Fletcher spoke up. "The leadership of the tribe has to remain consistent in order to be effective."

"What?" Louella asked.

"You told me that just a few days ago. I was keeping that journal for us and I asked you what your views on leadership were. You said that it's a lot like parenting: you have to be consistent."

"Yeah."

"So how exactly do you provide consistent leadership if you go out and get yourself killed?"

"I'm not going to get myself killed."

"I tried that argument once," Owen said quietly. "It did not work."

"Fletch, a good leader doesn't order people to risk their lives while she sits at home on her ass. If you all go out there, I should ante up as well!"

It was a decent argument, but Fletch was unmoved. "We all have jobs to do — you designed it that way. Your job is to lead and you have that job because you're good at it. But you are *not* suited to go on missions. You are not fast or agile or the strongest pair of arms or the best shot. You have asthma and arthritis. You're exhausted and you suffer from constant headaches. And if you go out there, you're going to get yourself killed."

Louella opened her mouth to speak, but Fletcher barreled on. "Patience is in charge of this operation and she's picked her team. You shouldn't second-guess that. It undermines her authority. And how, exactly, would it work having two leaders on one mission?"

"But…"

"Why did you decide not to send Bailey along?" Fletch changed direction so fast it caught her off guard.

"What does Sam's dog have to do with this?"

"Levi asked whether taking the dog was a good idea and you said no. Why?"

"You know why."

"Tell me again."

"It made no sense," Louella sighed. She could see where this was going and she was not happy. "The dog isn't trained to deal with the infected and hence, he'd be unpredictable. He might bark at the wrong moment and give our position away or attack and bite one of the husks. In which case, he'd get infected too and we'd have to put him down."

"You said that it would be the waste of a resource. The dog had one fight and one fight only in him. And so to send him on missions was effectively to throw him away. But here at the farm, he could be our early warning system if anything came near the compound. And he would last for years. Do you see what I'm getting at here?"

"Sure I do," Louella snapped. "So far you've compared me to a dog and made me feel like an errant child while at the same time telling me how old and decrepit I am. Is there anything you wanna add before I shove my boot up your ass?"

"Only that I'm asking for a group vote. Who thinks the chief should stay here?"

Louella didn't have to count hands to know she'd lost. It was the first time they'd overruled her and it hit her like a slap across the face. She rose from the table.

"Mom," Peg spoke up, "you're so worried about being fair and honorable that it's clouded your judgment. You…"

"I get it." And with that Louella turned on her heel and walked out the back door.

She stood in the barn taking deep calming breaths and wiping away angry tears. Fletch was such an asshole — treating her like a child that needs to be sheltered and cosseted. What the hell was she supposed to do? Sit on the couch eating bonbons while her people were out risking their lives? She couldn't do that. And in her mental rant she was just about to start whining that it wasn't fair when she caught herself. How infantile. Damn it. She slumped down on the milking stool. North Star needed a leader who was sensible and clear-headed and she had just stormed off like a petulant child. And worse, she'd undermined Patience. It was up to Pat to chose her team and lead the mission. And Louella had basically implied that she had no confidence in her Head of Security. But that wasn't the point. She didn't doubt Patience; she just had no faith in life. That was the wild card she couldn't trust. Because life was an absolute bitch. It let you carry on thinking everything was ok, and then one night you're babysitting for your son so he can take his wife out to dinner for their anniversary. And then Patience is at the door with tears in her eyes. And she's telling you that Eben swerved to miss a deer and hit a tree and they have to identify your boy by his dental records because the impact ruptured the gas tank and there was a fire. That was life. Life was your husband going into hospital for kidney stones and then Doc Rhoads tells you that James had a heart attack in the night and they did everything they could but… That was life. Life had somehow conspired to bring the infection into Midwood despite all their work to keep it out. And life wasn't done with them yet. And so yes, she wanted to go along so that she could protect them all. And she isn't Wonder Woman and she can't fight or run with the rest of them but, damn it, she was *responsible* for these people. So what was she supposed to do?

Louella stopped short. If anyone at the farm had asked her that question, what would she have said to them? *What am I supposed to do?* The answer was obvious: your job. She was not a soldier. She was not built for it. She was a thinker, a planner, an organizer, a mother … a leader. How ironic that such an exulted position should make her feel so impotent, and ashamed.

For his part, Fletcher was absolutely miserable. He hated seeing her hurt and yet he wanted to utterly crush that impulse to be a hero. And he admitted to himself that he hadn't done it because he was worried about Pat's authority. No, his motives were infinitely more selfish and impossible to deny. He needed to keep Louella safe.

Louella had been his friend for the last fifty-six years. She'd been his comfort during all the years he'd looked after his manically depressed mother who'd wanted him to be nurse, companion, father and provider all in one and all at the age of fifteen. And when his friends and teachers asked 'How are you?', he smiled and always said 'Fine.' After all, so much of life is deceit — polite lies of omission, the brave face we put on things, all those excuses we make. But to Lou he could say anything. He could say that he was scared and the rent was overdue and his mother refused to talk about it because she just couldn't deal. And now he'd have to quit the school paper and take on extra hours at the Dairy Queen. He could tell her that his situation felt like a huge ravenous dog that devoured everything — his youth, his sanity, his future. And he was tired, so exhausted that once he'd leant his head on her shoulder and wept. He could tell her that he hated his mom for her weakness and self-absorption. He wondered, given her lack of empathy for her son, if she was just a psychopath in flowery pajamas and a pink housecoat. And Louella listened to all of this without judgment. She was the only person with whom he could just be himself — no filters, no censoring, just his unadulterated self. The times he spent with her — those were his moments of truth and they kept him sane. And here they were, two golden oldies at the end of the world, and all he needed to keep going was for that woman to be ok. Without her, he'd probably eat a bullet.

Louella spent the rest of that wretched evening (after she'd apologized to Patience, of course) checking and rechecking the plan and chewing her fingernails down to the quick. Patience had gone on two recon missions to scope out the area. There was no sign of anyone. On her second trip, she discharged her weapon to see if anything came running. Nothing. From her scouting expeditions, she was able to show the team photos and she drew them a map of the area. They all knew the lay of the land. They all knew their specific jobs. They had drilled again and again on how to approach the target, secure the area and post guards so the scavengers could collect and load up the gear.

Josie had cobbled together the toughest fabrics she could find to provide them with protective clothing. They had boots and gloves and hoods. They'd wear goggles and dust masks to shield their faces from any infected material that might spatter back at them if they had to fight. Louella had kitted them out with weapons, bottled water, MREs, flashlights, walkie talkies, first aid supplies and highway flares. And still Lou could not shake the horrendous feeling that she had forgotten something vital. Therefore, when she wasn't poring over plans and rechecking kit lists, she was praying to God to deliver them home safe. And then there was nothing for it. She had to let them go.

Peg was on the team for this mission, and in retrospect she should have known that something was amiss the moment she stepped into the store. There was a discordant note there — something wrong. No, that's not quite right. Something that should have been wrong was not. At the time this was only a vague notion picked up by her subconscious. But it needled her as she swept the aisles looking for any husks that might be hiding there. It wasn't until she hit the produce aisle that she realized what the problem was: the air was clear — it did not smell of rotting food.

She grabbed her walkie talkie. "Pat, someone's here. They…" She never finished that sentence, because at that moment she heard the unmistakable double click of a shotgun being cocked behind her.

Every member of the team soon realized that they were in someone's crosshairs. They had trained for this contingency and knew exactly what their options were. It was a choice between immediate action and forbearance. Yeah, if you didn't hesitate, you could run for it. It is very difficult to hit a moving target. And unless the enemy understands and has practiced "forward allowance" — basically aiming in front of you as you run — then the odds of hitting the bullseye are pretty low. They decrease even further if you start shooting; if your assailant is ducking for cover, he can't take aim. But this constitutes immediate escalation and you might get nailed anyway. The alternative? Put your hands up and try to talk it out. Yes, you're being held at gunpoint, but that might simply be a defensive act. Open the lines of communication and you may find some allies — maybe even future members of Camp North Star. On the other hand, if you put your hands up, you could be surrendering to God knows who. They had all seen the post-apocalyptic movies and TV shows where survivors ended up as sex slaves or food for cannibals. And there was the rub. The chances of sexual slavery or ending up in the stew pot were probably minute, but human fear doesn't give one damn about the odds. Hence they were ready — as one — to shoot first and ask questions later. That is until they saw who they were dealing with. They were children — every single gun was in the hands of a Midwood child.

"Hello Peter," Peg said quietly as she turned and raised her hands. "It's me, Mrs. Gebhard, from the library."

Peter Eckert was a twelve-year-old boy who came into the library sometimes — usually in a panic with a class deadline looming the next day and very little work done. And on more than one occasion, he'd asked her for help.

"I know who you are. What do you want?"

"Well, we had come here looking for supplies."

"Everything here is ours," Curtis Ziegler said, with his .22 still pointed at Levi.

"Ok," Patience said. "We're not here to steal what's yours. But do you think you could lower those guns for a minute so we can talk?"

"No," Peter said. "Now get out."

Peg had been scanning the faces and there was not one adult among them. And so she simply said, "No" and sat down on the floor in front of him.

"What do you mean 'No'? I have a gun in your face. Get the hell out of here."

"Not until you stop for a minute and talk to me." She leant back against a salad dressing display, crossed her feet at the ankles and folded her hands in her lap.

"Look, if you're hungry we can give you some food…"

"I'm not hungry," Peg shook her head. "I just wanna talk to you."

Peter sighed. "Fine."

They were seated back in the staff room — all of them together, although the kids still kept hold of their weapons. It was quite a motley assortment: a 12 gauge shotgun, a little .410 bird gun, a .22 hornet, a Red Ryder BB gun, a slingshot, a Louisville slugger, and a broom handle with a carving knife duct-taped to the end. Peg looked past the gun barrels into the faces of the children. She knew them all. There was Peter, of course, and next to him stood Steven Wannemaker. He'd earned the nickname Pigpen around town, because that boy could not stay clean. It used to drive his mother crazy, especially on Sundays. Steven had an angelic voice — not yet changed — and hence he was a fixture in the church choir. Zoe had battled valiantly to keep her boy clean before he stood up to sing. But Zoe wasn't around anymore to polish his cheeks with her handkerchief and a little spit. Peg's fingers twitched — she wanted to tidy him up herself.

Then there was Thomas Gerber, a small, bookish little boy with delicate features and big glasses. He used to come into the library every Sunday and spend hours choosing what he'd read next. Niles Kaufmann stood by the door; he was the class clown who left whoopee cushions on the stuffed leather chairs in the Adult Fiction Section. Curtis Ziegler held the spear, but try as he might he could not look intimidating. Curt was perhaps the most beautiful child Peg had ever seen. With curly, blond locks, big blue eyes and long eyelashes, he looked like a Botticelli angel. But appearances were deceiving. Curt was the biggest hellion in the school — always in trouble, always in detention and always grounded. His crimes ranged from tacks on the teacher's chair to bubble gum in girls' pigtails to spray painting the word "Fart" on the Carnegie monument. The Bausman twins were present too, although Peg wasn't sure which one was George and which was Ezra. They looked pale and tired. And finally there was Isabella Rhyne — a tiny waif of a girl. One of the boys had obviously tried to plait her hair for her and the two fraying braids stuck out at wonky angles from the sides of her head. Altogether their faces wore one of two expressions. Their eyes were either dull and hollow and wore the disinterested look of prolonged shock or they were over-bright, too intense and angry. They were, however, all pale, their mouths drawn in permanent downward arcs and they each looked unutterably weary.

"So why won't you come with us back to the farm?" Patience was asking.

"Because this compound you keep talking about – it won't last," Peter said.

"And you know that how?" Patience was starting to lose, well, her patience. They were supposed to be out here on a scavenging expedition, not wasting their time having a ludicrous argument with a bunch of kids. She could not fathom why they were so hesitant to come to the farm.

Peter shrugged. "Why would it? Midwood was protected and that didn't last."

"But we could protect you," Patience insisted.

"That's what our parents said," Tom's voice was quiet.

"Yeah," Curtis nodded. "We've done pretty well on our own. Why should we go with you?"

Peg nodded, "I get it. This is working for you and, if it's not broken, why fix it? Let me guess how it happened. When Midwood fell and all the adults ran for cars that just ended up stuck on Main Street, you took to your heels. You're young and fast. You know every back alley, every shortcut through Midwood, every hiding place. You never realized that all those games of hide-and-seek were preparing you to run for your lives. Am I close?"

Peter gave her a curt nod. There was a hell of a lot more to it than that: his father held off three of the infected while Peter took his brother's hand and ran. The screams echoed behind them as his dad was murdered and little Billy cried so hard that Peter had to clamp a hand over the boy's mouth as they hid.

"Ok," Peg nodded. "You've got skills we don't have. You can run and hide in ways that make us look old and clumsy. But let me ask you this: if you come with us, will you lose those skills? No. If it all falls apart and you need to run again, you still can. But you'll be in a better position to do it. You'll be well-fed and stronger."

"Well-fed? We live in a supermarket."

"Yeah, but sooner or later, the food here will be gone. Then what? We live on a farm with a vegetable garden and three crops in the ground — two for people and one for the animals."

"Animals?" Isabella piped up.

Peg smiled at her. "Pigs, cows, chickens, and a dog who wants you to scratch his belly all day long."

Peter replied: "That's nice, but..."

"It means we have fresh meat and milk and eggs. We have hot showers. We have people training as doctors..."

"Midwood had all of that!" Peter yelled. "It didn't make any difference! It didn't save my family!"

"You know you're sitting ducks here, right?" Patience said quietly.

"How?" Curtis asked.

"This supermarket is an obvious target."

"From looters?" Curt looked skeptical. "We got the drop on you all right."

This time Levi spoke up. "The only reason we didn't start shooting was because you're kids."

"And what exactly were you hoping to accomplish with a BB gun and a baseball bat?" Sam had a Beretta in one hand and a Timber Classic Marlin in the other.

The kids were wavering and so Peg kept pushing. "With us, you'll have access to better weapons and training on how to use them. And you'll be able to sleep at night knowing that someone else is on guard."

Peter, however, was still unconvinced. "And when it all goes to hell? Then what?"

"Every man, woman and child has a bug-out bag full of survival gear. This summer we are going to set up caches — hiding places with spare supplies in case of emergency. And, after the harvest is in, we're going to set up a place where we can go and be safe if we lose the farm. Peter, if you have to, you can still run."

"Pete," Tom said, "I think we should go."

"But this is working for us!"

"I'm twelve years old, Pete. She's seven!" He pointed to Isabella.

Peter closed his eyes. He remembered the time before. Riding his bike over to Wannemaker's house to play video games or heading down to the swimming hole on a hot August day. The biggest concerns he had were a failing grade in English and how to shake off his little brother so he could go have some fun. Billy had followed him like a shadow and he'd hated the lack of space and freedom. He'd told himself that when he grew up, he'd finally be able to do whatever he wanted, whenever he wanted. But it hadn't turned out that way. He grew up fast after the fall of Midwood and his new found maturity did not set him free. It heaped responsibility on his shoulders and pressure and fear and guilt. And so, yes, he would give anything to go back to being twelve. And here they were, offering it to him on a plate and he was afraid.

Patience waited for an anxious moment while the boy deliberated. She knew that, if he said no, she was going to give the order to take the kids in anyway — kicking and screaming if necessary.

"All right," Peter said and there was a collective sigh of relief.

As they loaded up the contents of the pharmacy, the little band was spotted. Shuffling along in his Carter's Snowsuit, Billy Eckert quickened his pace. But the trucks were full and pulling away and he could not reach them. He shrieked in frustration. Peter knew that sound and turned to stare out the back window of the Chevy. The boy, clad in his navy snow gear with its bright red zipper, stared hungrily back; and Peter groaned. He should have shot Billy when he had the chance. He knew that. But he couldn't — he just couldn't. It wasn't Billy anymore and he knew that too. But that raging, snapping creature still wore Billy's face and so Pete had run. And, as always, Billy followed. He may be lost, but he was still his brother's shadow.

All through that day, the trucks hauled supplies from Sage Foods back to the farm. But Peg did not join in these runs. She had so much to do at home. The kids were offered hot showers and clean clothes (although most of these had to be rolled up at the sleeves and cuffs). They were given the first hot meal they'd had in months. And as she watched them eat, her mind raced with ideas. They would need toys and Louella had an excellent collection in the attic. But where would they put them? They were already tripping over each other without having Lego scattered all over the floor and plastic tea sets underfoot. But maybe they shouldn't bring the toys down at all. If they cleared everything out of the attic except kid stuff, then they could turn the loft into a sort of clubhouse for the children. They could use that space for lots of different purposes. It could be a boys' dormitory, a kids' play den, and a schoolroom. They'd have to move the Christmas decorations and other stuff out to the storage shed; and they'd need to put lamps and a couple of portable heaters up there, but it could work. They could fix the room up real nice and that would help the children settle in. And that idea about the school — that was something she'd been thinking about more and more lately. Sam and Emma's educations were incomplete and Mae's had barely begun. And now with so many new children at the farm, school had to be a top priority. Knowledge was power in this new world and the kids needed to know how to access it. She grabbed a notepad and, like her mother, started making lists.

In the old Crucible school, in the room where the massacre had taken place, they slept. Abigail was in the middle of the huddle, warm and protected as the others snored and fidgeted around her. And then a noise, soft at first but growing in volume, roused her. Multiple footsteps. A warning growl from Abby woke the others and the horde was soon up, crouching on all fours, ready to spring. Six came to the door and when Abigail approached, they cowered and hunched submissively. And Abigail sniffed them and recognized their scents. It was not just the familiar mix of sweat and vomit and blood that you smell on a rabies patient; she knew them. She had no recollection of the names Stephanie, Tobey, CariAnn or Bethany. And the irony of the fact that *they* wanted to be in *her* group now was not something that her mind was capable of appreciating. They were young and strong and their injuries did not hinder their ability to keep up with the horde. And so they were in. The virus was so much more egalitarian than the old society had been. It was the great leveler:

rich and poor, black and white, popular kid and outcast — all were one in the New Rabies. And all were united by the one supreme goal — to spread the virus, to bite. The horde moved on — south, toward the town of Carmichaels.

The people of Camp North Star made one trip after another to Sage Foods, never realizing they were being watched.

Roger Silsbee, a man in his thirties who still looked like the boy next door, lowered his binoculars. "They seem pretty well organized," he said.

"Yep," Bishop said. "They look healthy, well-equipped. I'd say they must have a pretty good setup somewhere."

"Follow them," a voice behind them said. "I want to know where their base is."

There were four men camped out at the Mohawk — a cheap motel on the highway just down the strip from Sage Foods. In the time before, Silsbee had spent his days on his knees, measuring people's feet for minimum wage at Country Cobbler Shoes. He'd smile and flirt with the town's ladies and hence picked up a lot more in commission than Mal Prentice, the other salesman. Louella had bought a pair of Sporto boots from him last fall, but the transaction had left her feeling flat. The boots were great and he'd been nice enough, but the man himself rubbed her the wrong way. He was charming and flirty and complimentary and she couldn't bring herself to warm to so much blatant bullshit. She hated it when people tried to play her — it was insulting. So no, she wasn't a fan.

The second member of the Mohawk group was Blake Turner. He was a huge man, locally known as "The Mountain." Yet he had the intellectual capacity of an eight-year-old child. He had lived out on Cemetery Road with his mother, Gladys; and when Midwood fell, he'd carried her through the chaos, eventually ending up at the Tombstone bar. The Tombstone was a dive situated across the street from Midwood Cemetery (hence the name), and as he ducked inside and slammed the door behind him, there was Roger Silsbee pointing a gun at his face and telling him to "get the fuck out."

"Hang on a minute." This was said by a man Blake didn't know. He was tall and had a buzz cut. His thick eyebrows and the thin line of beard that underscored his chin stood in sharp contrast to his pale skin. A cigarette dangled from his mouth and Blake didn't like that: he knew that smoking's bad for you and the smell made his throat tickle.

"So you're The Mountain," the man was saying. He looked at Silsbee. "That's right, isn't it? He's the big retard?"

"Yeah."

"What's the matter with her?" The stranger nodded toward Gladys.

"Mama's hurt." Blake laid her down gently on the pool table.

The old woman had had her throat ripped out and now Roger could see that what he thought was a red blouse had originally been a pale yellow.

"Dude, she's dead," he said.

"No! No, she's not!" Blake began to cry and looked to the stranger. "She's not dead! Why is he saying that?"

"Shhh," the stranger wrapped his arms around this weeping boy who was the size of a WWE wrestler. "A lot of people have died today. Your mom too."

"No…"

"What's your name?"

"B-Blake."

"Blake look," the stranger wriggled free of Blake's grasping hands. He walked over to the pool table and lifted the cadaver's arm. He released it; it thudded heavily back onto the green felt and sent the 8-ball drifting toward the corner pocket.

Dropping to his knees, Blake began to wail and the man sat on the floor next to him, cradling him and rocking him.

"It's going to be OK." His voice was low and soothing. "*You're* going to be ok."

"I can't … I just can't," Blake sobbed. "Not without my mom."

"It's OK. I'll look after you."

"But … but who are you?"

"My name is Leon."

A fourth man came to the Tombstone that first day. Wilford M. Bishop was your quintessential pillar of the community. On Sundays, he ushered and took collection for the morning service at the Lutheran Church. He was a member of the local rotary club, sat on the town council and volunteered every year to collect items for Christmas boxes so that struggling families could receive food and gifts for the holidays. He earned his living as a teacher at the high school, tenth grade Civics and Economics, and he'd been at the blackboard when the first scream ripped through that quiet winter's morning. At first, he stood with his class at the window, staring dumbfounded at the carnage just outside. But then he remembered the lockdown drills they'd practiced. The drills were intended to respond to an "active shooter" incident, but they were applicable now. He pulled the blinds down, locked the door, and turned off the lights. He yanked a poster off the wall (it had a drawing of a mobile phone with a big red X over it under the caption, "Just pretend it's 1995"). He stuck the poster up over the door's window, hiding the students from view and deepening the shadows in the room.

"All right," he said quietly. "I want everybody back against the far wall."

"Is it New Rabies?" Terence Brandt, a pimply kid with a B- average, asked.

"Yeah, I think so," Wilford said. "Listen, our best bet is to hunker down, keep quiet and let them pass us by. So please, everyone just sit down and I don't want to hear a peep out of any of you."

It wasn't long before the infected gained entry into the school. They could hear them running through the hall, hurling themselves at the doors to other classrooms. They heard a nearby door give and then a cacophony of shrieks from the students inside.

Mr. Bishop's own students were crying now and he was frantically trying to shut them up. One girl, Lisa Medford, was too loud. Her high pitched little girl sobs and frequent exclamations of "Oh my God!" would give them all away.

"Lisa," he hissed, "be quiet."

From the classroom next door, the last scream cut off abruptly and was followed by an ominous hush. Lisa sat with her hands clamped over her mouth and tears streaming down her face as the handle on their door slowly twisted. It was in need of a little WD40, so it actually creaked in an eerie, horror movie sort of way. When the door would not open, the handle began to twitch more violently. And then the first thud fell on the door's glass window. Lisa cried out and the sound spurred the thing on as it pummeled the glass with its fists.

That's ok, Wilford thought, *it's tempered glass. It'll hold.*

There was a shriek of rage and then the sound of rustling leaves and the thud of a heavy terracotta pot hitting the floor. In another moment the big ficus that the guidance counselor had placed outside her office came hurtling at the door. The tree itself was not the problem, but the decorative stones that covered the soil were. One hard, sharp little pebble was all it took to punch a hole right through the window. The poster tore but still hung on, and so Wilford did not see the cracks spread as the glass shattered. And then the thing was inside the room. It was a bloodied, maniacal Pastor Kulp.

Chaos erupted as students screamed and ran — most of them right into the teeth of the infected that piled into the classroom. The teacher picked up a desk chair and flung it through a nearby window. Lisa Medford saw this and felt a surge of hope. Mr. Bishop would save them. He'd get them out! But he did not even pause. He tore the blind aside and scrambled through the gap himself.

She dashed to the window and flung a beseeching hand toward him. "Mr. Bishop! *Please!*"

He looked at her. The moment lasted only a few seconds, but in Lisa's mind it seemed to stretch out for an eternity. Then he turned away and ran and hands were fastening onto her, dragging her backwards. She died screaming his name.

The APA Dictionary of Psychology defines the self-preservation instinct as "the fundamental tendency of humans and nonhuman animals to behave so as to avoid injury and maximize chances of survival." Sigmund Freud paired this with the sexual impulse under the name "Eros" — the life instinct. And Nigel Nicholson, in a Harvard Business Review article, stated: "Homo sapiens emerged on the Savanna Plain some 200,000 years ago, yet according to evolutionary psychology, people today still seek those traits that made survival possible then… Human beings are, in other words, hardwired. You can take the person out of the Stone Age … but you can't take the Stone Age out of the person." But perhaps Yann Martel said it best in *Life of Pi*, when he observed: "When your own life is threatened, your sense of empathy is blunted by a terrible, selfish hunger for survival." That is why Robert Carlyle's character abandoned his wife in *28 Weeks Later*. He was simply trying to save his own skin. And Wilford Bishop wasn't running away from anything as important as a wife. The snot-nosed kids in his class, who laughed at him behind his back and called him Mr. Blobfish (look it up if you want to fully appreciate the insult), really meant … well, nothing to him. Yes, he was their teacher. But that didn't mean he had to die for them.

And so he ran. He took one look at the chaos at the bridge and realized that no one would be getting out of Midwood that day. The only option was to hole up somewhere. But the town was in a state of absolute mayhem. The infected were swarming up Lincoln Avenue and bullets were flying. He had to get somewhere safe. He tried to force his way into one house but the owner, assuming that Wilford was "one of them," threw all his ample weight against the door, slamming it on Bishop's hand. The impact shattered the metacarpal bones of his right hand and he screamed, reeling backward as the door shut. Once again he was running. On Main Street, he was nearly mowed down by a jeep that had just pulled a U-turn and was speeding away from the bridge. He dove out of its way and landed on his ruined hand. He was in the snow, sobbing now, but did not allow himself to stop. Leaning on his left arm, he got to his feet and staggered up Gallows Hill Road. It was a dead end alley that skirts the east side of the cemetery. And there, in front of him, was the Tombstone bar.

Roger Silsbee was confused. He and Leon, if they happened to run into each other on a Friday night, would have a beer or two, maybe shoot the shit for awhile, but the two men were not exactly friends. Roger got the impression that Leon didn't have friends. He was notorious for his temper and once had shattered Rob Hunsecker's cheekbone over a card game. He'd done time for that one. Then there was his suspended license and a string of DUIs, two drug convictions and a rape charge in NYC that'd been dropped on a technicality. No, Leon Shaw was not a kind-hearted, virtuous soul. And yet now, as all hell broke loose in Midwood, here he was taking on every charity case that came down the pike. Wilford Bishop had shown up with a badly broken hand. The guy was right-handed and guess which one got smashed — hence he was useless. And Blake Turner? What the actual fuck? Not only did they not need to be saddled with a moron right now, but what the hell was all that hugging crap? Sitting on the floor, rocking the big guy like a baby? He watched this, silently wondering if Leon had lost his mind.

On the contrary, Leon Shaw was thinking clearly and planning ahead. In order to survive this mess, he'd need other men to back him up. Roger Silsbee was all right, but he wasn't exactly Rambo. And then Blake Turner came stumbling in. His brain — permanently stuck in the third grade — had been hit simultaneously with the loss of his mother and a zombie apocalypse. He arrived at the Tombstone a lost and broken child. But a friggin' huge child, powerfully built and strong as an ox. And all Shaw had to do to have that strength at his disposal was to wrap his arms around the big man and tell him that everything was gonna be OK.

And then there was the poindexter, Wilford. He showed up, sobbing from pain and exhaustion, with a bum hand that couldn't hold a gun or pull a trigger. But he was smart and that could come in handy. He was desperate for their help and that could come in handy too. And so, for the price of an Ace bandage he'd gotten from the first aid kit behind the bar and a bottle of Jack to numb the pain, Leon had just bought himself another ally.

As darkness fell, the four men bedded down for the night. Leon was sprawled out on the long, padded seat that lined one wall of the room. On the floor in front of him, curled up like a faithful dog, slept Blake. Roger had tried to fold his long legs into one of the booths, but he couldn't get comfortable. He gave up and stretched out on a pile of old coats behind the bar. And Wilford Bishop curled up in a corner and closed his eyes. He'd been nursing that bottle of Jack for the last two hours, and while the alcohol had made his lips numb and his stomach queasy, it had not taken the pain away. He had to keep loosening the bandage as his hand swelled and as he rewrapped it, he stopped to marvel at his rotated index finger and the blue and purple bruise that mottled his skin. His hand was balloon-like — swollen to look like Mickey Mouse's paw and he couldn't bend his fingers.

It was awful luck — to get hurt like that on the first day of the outbreak. But, in a perverse way, it was helpful too. The mess he now called a hand made him feel vindicated. He had begged the man in that house to let him in. But the guy forced Wilf back out into the carnage, shattering his hand in the process. And then the man in the Jeep almost ran him over. Why? For the same reason that Wilford Bishop had left his students to die. They were just trying to save their own asses. It was the survival instinct, a biological imperative, that drove them and so what if he was no different from the rest?

He had as much right to live as anybody else. Take Lisa-oh-I-broke-a-nail-Medford. She was a child in his care. She'd begged him for help and he'd abandoned her. But why should her life count for more than his own? Why was he obliged to sacrifice himself for that blond-haired bit of fluff? Because she was young? So what? She was a fatuous slave to Instagram, Maybelline and Justin Bieber. Oh yeah, that was worth preserving and surely outweighed his degree, his public office, his respected position within the community. Or was he obliged to die for her because she was a girl? Or because her gormless parents would be sad or because …

"Because she was your responsibility," he said quietly to himself. And while he felt shame at his actions now, at the time his duty to her had not mattered one bit. When it came right down to it, survival had been paramount for all of them — for everyone who'd tried to claw their way out of Midwood that day. And so it was OK. It was OK to be a coward, because the cowards were the only ones left alive.

And yet still he struggled with the knowledge that he had behaved like an absolute shit. It was hard to wrap his head around. He'd always been so good. But then being good was simple when all it required was putting on a suit and passing the collection plate at church. Or sitting around a table making a few inconsequential decisions for the town. Or throwing some canned goods and toys into a box and slapping a bow on it. He'd received praise for all of those things.

But really they were easy. He risked nothing by doing them. And today, when he'd been called upon to risk it all to do the right thing … he'd refused. That, surely, counted more than all of the Sunday mornings and toy drives put together. Oh, but that's dangerous thinking; it threatened to sink him into a despair so deep that he might never emerge. And so began the mental gymnastics people use to justify their actions to themselves. First he had recourse to that time-honored excuse: "Well, everybody else was doing it too." An action was somehow justified if other people engaged in it also. In court you are tried by a jury of your peers, but if your peers were committing the same crimes, then surely they could not pronounce you guilty. He knew, of course, it was a juvenile argument. No matter how much you pointed your finger at other people's behavior, it did not excuse your own.

Therefore he swiftly moved on to rationalization. It was "survival of the fittest." But again, he hit a snag in logic. He couldn't exactly describe himself as "the fittest." He was a middle-aged man, with a middle-age spread, sedentary in his lifestyle and overly fond of bacon cheeseburgers.

Yes, he was smart, very smart actually, but brains had not saved him; he had survived only through dumb luck.

And then there was his hand. It was useless. It would take at least six weeks to heal and, in a collapsing world, six weeks might as well be a lifetime. And yet, for all his sins, he had landed on his feet. He was alive and uninfected and safe. These men had taken him in. And it's not like they were prime specimens either. Blake was a moron. Silsbee was a bit of a suck up. And Leon Shaw was the town's most notorious scumbag. So they were all freaks really — each in their way. And maybe that, in and of itself, was telling. The *nice* people, the meek, had in fact not inherited the earth. It had been left for the cowardly, the dishonorable, and the degenerate. Why? Because it was that kind of a world now.

A virus so tiny that it could only be measured in nanometers had effectively expelled God from Midwood. That was a hell of a statement to make, but when trouble comes and everybody looks out for number one, what does that tell you? Sure, God had resided in Midwood in moments of peace and on drowsy Sunday mornings, but He had been wholly absent in the town's chaos. The virus had made Him irrelevant.

And so began the alliance. It did not take long for Shaw to emerge as the undisputed leader. Bishop was too weak to do the job and Blake was too dumb. And Roger? Well, after what happened, he saw the advantages of toeing the line.

It all coalesced in this way: the group barricaded itself in at the Tombstone and carried out short raids on nearby houses for supplies. They were raiding Katie Boehler's place when they found Robby Hunsecker. He was holed up in the basement, living off cold tinned food; and Leon greeted his old enemy with a knock out punch to the jaw. They scavenged his cans of Campbell's soup and spam, found his stash of Oxycodone, and took his gun and Buck knife. Yet when it came time to go, Shaw insisted that they take Rob with them.

Roger looked down at the unconscious man. "Why?"

"I have an idea" is all that Shaw would say and so they dragged him back to the Tombstone. Hunsecker was bound and gagged and left until later that day when he finally came to.

"All right, Shaw, what are you planning?" Silsbee asked.

Leon leaned back in his chair. "You're going to kill him. All of you."

The three men gawked at him.

"What?" Roger asked.

"Think of it as an initiation into the gang."

"That … that's insane." Wilford Bishop was on his feet and attempted to cover his agitation by strolling to the bar to pour himself a drink.

"No it's not. It's how a lot of groups are."

"In the ghetto, maybe, but …"

"Where do you think you are?" Shaw was up now too and looking belligerent. "The ghetto's a fucking weekend in Vegas compared to this shit," he said, gesturing towards the heavily-barricaded door.

"And so killing him accomplishes what?"

"It proves to me that you're fit to be a member of this group."

"Oh I get it," Wilford nodded. "I read an article on this once."

Roger rolled his eyes thinking, *Dude, don't. He doesn't want to hear about your fucking article.*

But Bishop plowed on. "In violent neighborhoods, people form gangs for protection. But in order to join, they have to prove that they're tough enough to help defend the group. Which begs the question: why don't you kill him yourself? Or don't you want to get your hands dirty?"

Wilford leaned back and crossed his arms, confident that his argument would put this nonsense to rest. But Shaw crossed the room, leaned up against the bar, and smiled.

"I already have," he said quietly.

"What?"

Roger had joined them now. "Who?"

"That Zimmerman bitch. Who do you think started the fire?"

"No you didn't." Even as Bishop shook his head to deny all of this, he was starting to see the truth. "Why?"

Leon shrugged. "I'd never done it before. I wanted to know what it felt like." He said this as casually as he might have said, "I just tried a cup of Oolong tea" and the smile on his face was so placid. Never before had Roger seen anyone look so calm and yet so irretrievably insane at the same time. It sent a shiver through him and he backed off.

"You killed her out of," Bishop groped for a word, "curiosity?"

"Yep. Surely *you* can understand that."

"Why me?"

"Oh come on! All this self-fucking-righteous-I'm-a-pillar-of-the-community bullshit … doesn't it ever get on your nerves?"

"I don't know what you mean." Even to Bishop's own ears that sounded priggish.

"Yes you do. All that time spent doing good works and what does it get you? Getting your ass beat by Albitz every four years in the mayoral election and your wife off banging some jock. She and that gym teacher … they live three doors down from you, don't they? That's gotta be fun. Your students think you're a joke, Mr. Blobfish — yes, the whole town has heard that one. Don't you ever want to be bad? Just to say 'Fuck you all' and go and take what you want?" Leon asked.

"Yes, but this," Wilford pointed at Hunsecker, "is not what I want."

"Don't you want to survive?"

"Yes."

"Well, you're going to have to kill to do that. It's a dog-eat-dog world, friend. Here's your chance to practice."

"But my hand…"

"Your feet work, don't they? Let's cut the shit," and now Leon was addressing all of them. "I'm happy to do whatever it takes to survive. But I need men with me who are willing to do the same, 'cause I'm not gonna carry you people. Make no mistake about it: if you don't have what it takes, you're out."

Blake went over and clutched at Shaw's arm, but Leon shook him off. "Nope. I said I'd look after you, but I need you to look after me too. Now you show me you can do it."

Trembling, the big man walked over to Robby who stared up at him with wide, pleading eyes. He took a deep breath and then punched him in the face. It was a clumsy, unpracticed punch, but it was hard. Hunsecker grunted with the impact and started to cry.

"That's good," Leon said, "keep going." He turned to Bishop. "It's this or the door, man."

And Wilford chose. He landed a kick to Rob's side and it was as if some dam within him broke. The seemingly endless string of humiliations. His wife Catherine leaving him for Jeff Burgess — a *jock*, for fuck's sake. The town had gotten months of juicy gossip out of his divorce and not one woman he'd invited to dinner afterward had accepted his invitation. And then there was all the shit he swallowed being nice to people who never appreciated him and never gave him his due. He'd run for mayor five times and lost *five times*. His most successful campaign in the last twenty years had only landed him an embarrassing twelve percent of the vote. All the rage of being disrespected and marginalized. All the insufferable tedium of having to do the right thing, the polite thing every fucking day. People's judgments and expectations had clamped shackles on his ankles. But the chains fell away now as he delivered kick after kick, to the head, to the body, to the groin. And this spurred Turner on, who was now punching more enthusiastically. Robby Hunsecker started screaming — a muffled sound around his gag.

Shaw walked over to Silsbee. "You too."

Roger shook his head. "I can't."

"Roger, how far do you think you're gonna get on charm and a winning smile? That may sell shoes, but it ain't gonna cut it here." Leon produced a switchblade. "Finish it."

Roger backed away until he was up against the door. He knew in that moment that if he didn't play along, he would be out that door in a heartbeat. The thought terrified him. He needed Shaw. Leon was the only fighter, the only real badass in their group and without him ... Roger sighed, defeated. *Without him I'm dead.* There was no doubt about it. And come on— was he really the weakest member of the group? Even that cream puff Bishop was able to do this. He took the blade and clumsily went to work on Hunsecker.

On subsequent raids, Leon noticed something important about the infected. They seemed to be sensitive to light. There were a lot less of them out during the day, especially when the sun glared so brightly off the snow. Therefore, his group scavenged in the mornings. On one such raid they ventured onto Main Street and Roger kept suggesting places to hit. There was Pilgrim's Tavern which used to serve food and so would have a well-stocked kitchen. And across the street from that there was the police station, which was bound to have weapons. But Leon passed on both of these and made a beeline right for Holliger's Drug Store.

"Listen, boss," Roger said, "I know you're almost out of oxy, but shouldn't we get guns first and drugs second?"

Shaw wasn't listening. Holliger's would have everything he needed to keep steady: OxyContin, Percocet, Vicodin and ... he stopped abruptly and stared in surprise. There were *people* in there, waving at him as they pulled away a large shelf unit that had been used to block the door.

"Thank God!" Old man Holliger said as he ushered them inside. "We didn't think anybody else was left!"

Leon answered this statement by shooting the old man in the face. A woman screamed and another man opened fire. He managed to squeeze off a few badly aimed rounds before Silsbee took him down with a bullet to the gut. The woman ran to his aid and Wilford Bishop said in an eerily calm voice: "Hello, Catherine." He nodded to the wounded man, "Jeff."

The Tombstone bar was a squat brick building with a leaky roof. On the front, on either side of the heavy wooden door, there was a small window. In the time when zombies weren't taking over the world, those windows had held neon signs: one for Budweiser and one for Miller High Life ("the champagne of beers"). But zombies were taking over the world and so the gang had boarded them up. Now, however, Turner was given a claw-hammer and told to pry the boards away to reveal the scene outside. There, in the parking lot, tied up between the Dead End sign and a telephone pole, stood Jeff Burgess. And night was coming on.

A road flare had been lit to help guide the infected to him and indeed they came in droves. They hated the light; it hurt their eyes, but here was prey served up on a platter and they could not resist. And so they'd clamp their eyes shut and dive in for a quick claw and bite and then retreat from the hateful glare of the light. The way they did that, circling around him to bite and then backing away, reminded Leon of a documentary he'd seen on Shark Week. It was all about a feeding frenzy. And with each strike, Jeff screamed and cried and strained against the ropes. For thirty minutes that flare burned and smoked. And all the while Catherine, who had to be held up by Turner, sobbed and gasped because her gag was making it hard for her to breathe. But then the flare flickered unsteadily. Cat moaned as it finally guttered out. The infected rushed in then, coming at Burgess from all directions. The people inside the Tombstone could no longer see him amid the crush of bodies. But they could hear him, his screams high and frantic as they ripped him to pieces.

When Jeff had fallen silent, Leon nodded at Roger. "Go on, seal it up again."

283

Shaw took a long pull of *Old Crow* and offered the bottle to Catherine. "Want some?"

The sobbing woman gathered herself so she could enunciate as clearly as possible around her gag: "Go fuck yourself."

"Not quite what we had in mind," Bishop said. He grabbed her by the hair and dragged her to the pool table.

That was in the beginning, before they were able to clear a path out of Midwood and relocate to the Mohawk Motel. They had just moved into their new digs and were planning to hit Sage Foods when the North Star convoy pulled up and Leon sent his men to follow them home.

"It's the Bernhard farm," Wilford reported.

"Where the hell's that?" Shaw asked.

"We'll show you. It's a good location, fairly remote. They've got crops in the ground (I think), and the place is heavily fortified."

Roger nodded. "It does look pretty impressive."

"I bet," Leon said quietly and then seemed to reach a decision. "Let's see just how impressive they are."

And so they went to the high school. The infected, when they weren't milling around looking for prey, tended to retreat to the High School gymnasium. They slept there, huddled together, and waited for night. But as dusk fell they found a pickup truck idling in the parking lot. And in the back, hanging over the tailgate and waving, was fresh meat. With a screech they darted forward. Every time they got near, however, the truck would drive off a ways and then stop again just a little further down the road. In this way, the Shaw gang led Midwood's infected out of town, over the bridge and out into the countryside.

They reached the farm by daybreak, just in time to hear Louella's rooster crow. And as the truck drove away, the husks spotted people up on the scaffolding and heard a dog bark.

Before the guards could even see the horde, the people of Camp North Star were up and out of bed. Bailey — a laid-back Labrador — was going absolutely nuts and that could only mean one thing.

Still in her pajamas, Louella slipped her bare feet into her boots and climbed up onto the ramparts. Arnold handed her a pair of binoculars and together they watched the horde approach.

"Patience!"

"I'm here," came a voice beside her.

"Get everybody ready."

"What can we do?" Louella turned around to see Peter and the other new children, each holding a weapon.

Lou called out again: "Emma!"

The child was there in a heartbeat. "Here!"

"Patience has got you on reload?"

"Yes."

"Now you've got helpers. Show them what to do."

As the girl led the kids away, Peg (who was checking her own weapon) called, "Hey Peter!"

"Yeah?" He was walking backwards now in the direction his group had gone.

"You said you were afraid the farm wasn't safe?"

"Yeah."

"Well," she smiled at him, "watch this."

It is a little known fact that war is a mixture of boredom and hell. For all of its violence and horror, there seems to be an inordinate amount of waiting around. So it was on the farm that day. Sure enough, the husks came charging at them with all the speed they could muster. But before they could reach the compound, before even one shot needed to be fired, the infected got hung up on the traps. First there was the barbed wire. This slowed them down a bit, but was not enough to deter an army oblivious to its own injuries. They simply ripped themselves free and carried on. Next they came to a series of obstacles — a couple of 18 wheelers and an old RV — staggered in front of the farm.

Watching, hidden, from a nearby ridge, Roger commented, "The trucks aren't even slowing them down. Why did they bother?"

"The trucks aren't meant for them," Wilford said quietly, "they're there to keep us from crashing through the fences. Now *those* are zombie traps."

The infected had reached the pitfalls. As they raced across the open lawn between the road and the farmhouse, they would suddenly lurch and fall to one side. In each case the zombie had a foot stuck in what seemed to be a deep hole. They cried out. They had been pretty vocal all morning, but this sound was different. These were cries of pain and, when one of them yanked himself free, Wilford saw blood pouring out of his ruined foot. More and more of them got loose and hobbled toward the compound. In some cases the damage was so great, the zombies fell forward and crawled, pulling themselves across the wet grass.

Finally, after what seemed like an age, the husks were within range and the people of Camp North Star got a good look at them. Pastor Kulp, Katie Boehler, Clara Jung (although, where her baby was was too horrible to contemplate), Barbara Yeakle, and dozens more.

"They're empty shells, guys," Peg reminded them. "They..."

But a strangled cry interrupted her. Peter Eckert stood, clutching a scaffolding bar for support. His face was a ghastly white and tears streamed down his cheeks.

"Oh God it's Billy," Thomas, who'd stepped up beside him, whispered.

Curtis clapped a hand on his friend's shoulder. "I'm sorry, man. Do you want me to ... to deal with this?"

"No," Peter shook his head. "I'll do it."

"Do what, Peter?" Isabella Rhyne looked up at him with big innocent eyes.

Before Peter could answer, Pigpen said, "Let's go help Emma, ok?" He crouched down so she could hop up on him for a piggyback ride and he carried her away.

Louella watched this unfold, saw how the little group pulled together to look after each other. She was impressed. Peter must have led them well to forge a bunch of traumatized kids into something that solid.

She went to him. "The little one in the snowsuit — that's your brother?"

Peter nodded.

"That's not Billy, sweetheart."

"I know." He cocked his shotgun.

Louella gently rested a hand on the barrel. "You don't have to do this."

"It's my responsibility."

"No, it isn't. Look at me." She nudged the gun down so that it pointed at the ground. "The minute he came to the farm, he became my responsibility. Wasn't that one of the reasons you came here? So you wouldn't have to be responsible for everything?"

Peter nodded and swayed a little on his feet. Then Emma was there, leading him away. In the midst of his passive retreat, he stopped. His eyes were those of an old man and his voice a dry rasp as he said, "Don't let him suffer."

"It'll be quick. I promise."

Peter was not the only one who'd been rattled by the horde. Every person on that wall saw a friend or neighbor in the crowd below. And the ravages of the disease were grotesque. None of their injuries had healed well. Gangrenous arms and hands had turned black and looked more like horror movie props than actual human limbs. They were pitifully thin and their skin stretched taut over jutting bones. They were filthy and the stench that rose from them was enough to make your eyes water. But then Patience hit the play button on a portable tape player. The familiar discordant notes signaled for everyone to make ready. Then Creedence Clearwater Revival's *Run Through the Jungle* resolved into a steady beat, the order came and they opened fire.

Watching from the ridge, Leon noticed that they did not just blast away. Instead they seemed to shoot in time with the music, pulling the trigger on every fourth beat or so. This was staggered along the line; one person would shoot, while his neighbor took aim and vice versa. It was a calm, controlled and very efficient way of killing. Leon didn't know it, but Patience had gotten the idea from *World War Z*. In the book, the soldiers had actually practiced firing in time with a metronome and Patience had seized on the idea. If she could use a steady rhythm and a song to bolster their confidence, then she could keep them from blasting away in a panic, wasting time and ammunition in the process.

There was another idea the security chief borrowed from the novel. Every time someone ran out of ammo, they'd holler 'Out!' and a child would be there to hand them a fully loaded weapon and take the empty one away for reloading.

Within a fairly short period of time, the guns and music fell silent. The lawn in front of the farmhouse was littered with bodies.

"Can we go now?" Blake asked. Riding in the back of the pickup truck had been fun and all the shooting had been exciting, but he was tired now and getting bored.

"In a minute," Leon muttered. "They're not finished yet."

Sure enough, with guards covering them from an elevated position, a heavily armed contingent emerged from the compound. They were all wearing protective clothing as they walked among the bodies double tapping each one in the head. They swept the area and, once it was secure, the cleanup operation began.

As the Shaw gang crept back to their truck, Wilford asked, "Thoughts?"

"I don't know," Leon answered. "Let's think on it a while."

CHAPTER THIRTEEN

ANOTHER BRIEF INTERLUDE

Bugs Bunny: "Wait a minute, Dracula. Did you ever have the feeling you're being watched? That the eyes of strange, eerie things are upon you? Look, out there in the audience.
Gossamer: "PEEEE-PLE! Aieeeeeeee!"

Looney Tunes, "Hair-Raising Hare"

Mornings were busy times on the farm. Louella would take coffee up to the guards, get a status report and then head off to the barn. She separated the calves from the cows so there'd be milk by evening and filled their troughs with alfalfa hay and grain supplements. She let the chickens out to run, put mash in the feeders and collected the eggs. She placed fresh bedding in the nest boxes and then turned her attention to her garden. It was May and she had broccoli, cabbage, peppers and tomatoes to pick. She had a bumper crop of tomatoes this year and so, after breakfast, she planned to make a big vat of spaghetti sauce to freeze for the winter months.

While performing these tasks, she could almost fool herself into thinking that nothing had changed. If she drove into Midwood, she could pop into Kacee's Kitchen for a patty melt or nip into Holliger's for a jar of Oil of Olay. And she would see Doc Rhoads on his lunchtime run, jogging along with his shuffling little-old-man gait. This time of year Main Street would be decked out in flowers: hanging baskets of lilac impatiens and planters full of daisies and petunias. The red maple and white oak trees that lined the road would be greening up nicely, while birds sang from their branches and the mild air kissed the bare skin of your arms.

But then they'd need her up on the scaffolding as an extra spotter while a team inspected the perimeter fences. And she'd stand there with a gun in her hand and the illusion would shatter. This was usually the point when she took her first headache tablets of the day. From her vantage point, she could see the trailers parked out behind the barn. One would serve as a lab where Wyn and Niamh could develop the vaccine. They were still gathering the needed equipment for this. The second trailer was already stocked with rows and rows of cages. That's where they'd house the sick animals and they'd have to drill holes in their skulls to harvest infected brain tissue and do all manner of terrible things. Yes, Louella had lived on a farm her whole adult life and she knew how it all worked. Things lived and things died. And sometimes you'd kill an animal to feed your family and sometimes you'd put a sick animal down so it wouldn't suffer needlessly. But this procedure to get the vaccine, that was going to be a whole different ball game. It was tantamount to torture for the animals and she ached for the days when she was not called upon to do that. She missed who she used to be. She'd come to think of this new life as a hammer and chisel, chipping away at who she was, at the person she liked being. But she was still going to see that the job got done. That vaccine was their best shot at survival and she would stick at nothing to get it for them.

With the inspection done, it was time for breakfast and then everyone would see to their chores. Alec would pick his crew for the building projects; Lou and Bib would get busy making that spaghetti sauce, and the children, with their hands and faces scrubbed clean, would head up to the attic for school. At first there were vehement protests against this. And you can see the kids' point of view: *it's the apocalypse and you want us to sit through class?* But then they saw the curriculum. Yes, there was reading, writing, and arithmetic. But there would also be self-defense and weapons training, first aid, drills on defending the compound, and time spent working with the animals. They came to realize that a day at school was frankly awesome.

At first Peg was tempted to focus purely on learning and on the future and try to move the children on from the trauma of their pasts. But her reading on PTSD quickly convinced her otherwise. They had to deal with the emotions now: acknowledge them and be guided through them before the trauma became a mental and physical part, not only of who they are, but also of who they will be. And so part of each school day was devoted to dealing with the past. Sometimes, they just told stories about the time before — like the time Peter Eckert's mom went down with the flu over Christmas and his dad had to make the big holiday meal by himself.

They could all picture Michael Eckert in his hideous Christmas sweater; it depicted a brick fireplace with stockings, wreath and raging fire — all knitted in the brightest wool known to man. He dragged that monstrosity out every year and the year of mom's flu was no exception. Peter told them how Mike had pots boiling on every burner of the gas stove and he leaned over them to check the carrots at the back. Then Michael turned to his son and said, "I know you hate this jersey, but it is so nice and warm." Peter gaped at him, "Dad, you're on fire!" The hideous sweater had caught the edge of the gas flame and now burned fitfully as Mike hopped around the kitchen trying desperately to take it off. Peter hopped after him, smacking him with a pair of oven gloves which only seemed to fan the flames. Finally, in desperation, his father sprinted up the stairs, past his wife (who lay in bed, vomiting into a bucket), and into the shower, where he stood under the frigid water, cussing.

As he emerged, cold and dripping, the smoke detector started to beep shrilly. "Let me guess," Melanie Eckert croaked, "dinner's ready?"

They all laughed at that story and Peter laughed the hardest of all. He laughed until tears spilled down his cheeks. "Dad held three of them off. It was pretty amazing."

"The husks?" Peg asked.

"Yeah. I always used to think he was kind of goofy, you know. Kind of a nerd because he didn't like football and he wasn't good with cars and stuff. But when he told us to run, I looked back and it was like something out of a movie — the way he fought."

"He sounds amazing," Peg smiled at him.

"And I left him there."

"He told you to."

"I should have gone back and helped."

"Peter, you'd be dead too and if you had died, we never would have heard that story. No one would ever know how brave your dad was that day."

"I guess."

"There's no guesswork in this. You are the only physical evidence left that he existed. Without you there is no one left to remember him. His blood runs through you. You have his eyes and I can see his face in yours. He lives on through you. If you had gone back, we would have nothing of him now."

She told them over and over again that they must never feel guilty because they had lived. That is what their parents had wanted more than anything and that's why the grown-ups at the farm worked so hard. "You are the future," she told them. "You're the whole point."

These were necessary conversations, but school could not be all work and learning and group therapy sessions. They also needed time to rest and play. They needed recess. In her mother's recipe box, she had found a card written in her grandmother's spidery handwriting. It read:

For Preserved Children.

You will need:
One half dozen children
One farmyard
One sunny day
One or more dogs

Mix the children and the dogs together. Add them to the farmyard and stir in the sunny day. Sprinkle the yard with flowers. Cover with a clear blue sky and bake in the sun until brown.

And this was the recipe she followed that day and children's laughter echoed through a fallen world and made it sound like paradise. Up on the ridge overlooking the valley, a man listened and studied Camp North Star through his binoculars. Looking for a weakness ... and a way in.

CHAPTER FOURTEEN

ROCK OF AGES

"While I draw this fleeting breath,
When my eyes shall close in death,
When I rise to world unknown,
And behold Thee on Thy throne,
Rock of Ages, cleft for me,
Let me hide myself in Thee."

Augustus M. Toplady, "Rock of Ages"

"How lucky I am to have something that makes saying goodbye so hard."

A.A. Milne, Winnie-the-Pooh

The corn was getting high, but still had a way to go before harvest. The ears were thin, the kernels pale. One of Louella's fields was a sea of wheat, but there was still green on the stalks. Normally this would be the time to have Russ Johnson out to service the harvester so that it would be ready for use come July. But Russ had been shot along with the other infected who'd attacked the farm. Therefore the job fell to Levi. It was well outside his comfort zone. He was an excellent mechanic and if you'd asked him to work on a Chevy or a Ford or a

Buick, he wouldn't have batted an eyelid. But a combine harvester was another thing entirely and he had to rely on the manual to walk him through the process.

According to the literature, "The importance of replacing worn components cannot be overemphasized." This statement was followed by a laundry list of things that can go wrong and Levi worked through it systematically. Happily, the machine seemed to be in pretty good shape. It was only when he looked under the feederhouse and removed the rock trap door that he began to suspect there was a problem. The rasp bars looked different from the picture in the manual.

In the margin, his late brother James had written: "If a No.2 pencil is higher than the cleats — replace." The part did not pass the pencil test and Levi sighed heavily. Where the hell was he going to get a replacement rasp bar?

"Is it really necessary?" Ginny asked, as she sat at the table darning a pair of his socks.

"Yep," Louella answered from the sink where she was washing dishes. "A worn rasp bar won't thresh the grain properly. It'll gum the cylinder up. That'll make the engine work harder and wear out the parts faster."

"So that's a big yes then." Fletch dried a skillet and put it in the cupboard.

"But where are we gonna get a replacement? I've got nothing like it at my garage." Levi turned the part over in his hands.

"The dealership is out on the highway," Louella shrugged.

Patience shook her head. "It burnt down."

"What?" Lou was genuinely surprised. "When did that happen?"

"Don't know. But I passed it when I was scoping out *Sage Foods*. It's been completely gutted."

"Well, shit." Louella was hit again with the horrible realization that some things were just no longer available. Today it was a tractor part, tomorrow it could be antibiotics. All her life, she'd always been able to get what she needed and yet she had never truly appreciated that fact. Not until now when so much was out of reach. The thought sent its customary jolt of fear through her.

"What about Hackett's?" Levi asked. "Alistair used to carry John Deere."

Hackett's Parts and Service Center was located out on Old Mill Road. It was a great cavernous building with room for a service area, repair and overhaul bays, an office that smelled of cheap cigars, and storage for parts and machinery at the back. When the recon team first approached it, they were especially wary. Hackett had a guard dog he called Cujo and damned if the bastard didn't live up to that name. There, on the fence, was a sign with the black silhouette of a pit bull etched above the message:

WARNING
Cross the Line
Your Ass is Mine!

The dog was so aggressive that Wyn would only treat him if he wore a muzzle. And that was before the infection. If Cujo had New Rabies, then he would be absolutely lethal.

But Cujo, it transpired, was dead. They could see his carcass lying just inside the chainlink fence, his belly ripped open and most of his entrails gone. Upon seeing this, Sam relaxed and was about to open the gate when Patience shot out a hand to stop him.

"We don't have to worry about the dog," she said quietly, "but aren't you just a little worried about what killed it?" She put two fingers in her mouth and whistled.

A screech echoed from the garage and old man Hackett came sprinting out into the daylight. He flung himself against the fence, scrabbling frantically to get at the people on the other side. Patience rammed the straight claw end of a crowbar through the chainlink and into Alistair's skull. He collapsed next to his dog.

Pat was thorough in her recon work; she gave her team every detail she could to help prepare them for the mission ahead. But at the same time, they all understood that anything could happen once they left the safety of the farm. Hence, they suited up in their protective gear with its heavy, tear-resistant fabrics and hoods and goggles and boots and gloves. And while that had been good for the winter months, it was June and unseasonably warm with temperatures topping out in the high eighties. It could have been worse — Louella's grandmother had once told of a day back in 1933 when the mercury hit 107 °F — but back then no one had to venture out in hazmat gear. And so the timing of the mission suddenly became more complicated. They still had to sweep and secure the area. They had to post lookouts and find the needed part and all of that had to be executed carefully and methodically. But now there was an added time pressure. If they took too long, they'd overheat in all that gear.

The garage itself was like a sauna; it had been sealed up for winter and obviously Alistair had been too far gone to open it up and let some air in as summer came on. Hence the thermometer in Hackett's office read 95 °F. To Fletcher it was damn near unbearable. It made him feel like a damp rag that was trying to wring itself of all moisture. He didn't realize that, because of his age, he was suffering from heat stress. Anyone over sixty-five can find themselves at greater risk from high temperatures and he was now working his way down the list of common symptoms. He'd gone profoundly pale and his muscles cramped painfully — especially his stomach muscles as a wave of nausea swept over him. Most worryingly, sweat stung his eyes and blurred his vision and he kept pushing an awkward finger up under his goggles to wipe it away.

The world was too damn dangerous to go traipsing around blind. In frustration he whipped his goggles off and rubbed hurriedly at his eyes. As the details of the garage came back into focus, he spotted a flutter of movement in the corner of the room. His first assumption was that it was a bit of black tarp rustling in the breeze. But then he realized: there was no breeze, no free-flowing air in the garage at all. So just what the hell was moving over there?

"Got it!" Levi announced triumphantly and at that sound the shadow rose into the air and fractured into individual wisps of blackness.

"Bats!" Fletcher bellowed and every member of the group hit the deck. They yanked the drawstrings on their hoods tighter and pulled thick scarves up over their mouths and noses to cover the last of their exposed skin.

But Fletch was too near and too slow and the swarm hit him full in the face. There was a flurry of papery wings and sharp pain as bats latched onto his chin, his cheeks, his forehead so that they could bite and bite and bite. Fletcher screamed and flailed at them, but the attack continued until Patience reached him and literally tore the bats free. And then strong hands under his armpits pulled him up and half-guided, half-dragged him out the door. Fletcher could taste his own blood as he gasped for air. The world was a blur around him; the high-pitched voices of his team seemed to babble utter nonsense and only one thing made itself known to him with any clarity. It was a single thought. *I'm dead.*

The call came in over the radio as the team sped back to the farm. One man down, infected. Multiple bites. They had already discussed their options should the situation arise. If the bite was on an extremity, then they would apply a tourniquet and amputate the affected limb. For this reason, the team had a Black and Decker 40-volt cordless chainsaw as part of its first aid kit. It was an awful prospect, but at least you could stop the infection and save the life. When, however, the bite was located somewhere else — on the torso or face — then the treatment protocol became much more of a gamble.

Louella quickly lit a fire in the hearth and thrust the end of a steel poker into the flames. In the days before the rabies vaccine, the only logical treatment was cauterization. You had to try to burn the infection out. That is what they did in October 1831 when a rapid wolf rampaged through Arbois, France. Some of the victims went to the blacksmith to have their wounds cauterized and an eight-year-old Louis Pasteur could hear their terrible screaming. Likewise, when a young Emily Brontë was bitten by a rabid dog, the child marched straight into the kitchen, grabbed an iron out of the fire, and burned out the infection herself. As a result of that moment of incredible bravery, she survived to write *Wuthering Heights*. The people of Arbois were not so lucky. Eight members of Pasteur's community died of hydrophobia. Therefore cauterization was a crapshoot. Taking hot iron to Fletcher's face did not guarantee his survival, but it was the only shot he had.

Seated in a chair and so scared that he was literally panting, Fletch slipped a kitchen towel into his mouth and Niamh tied it firmly at the back of his head. Alec held one arm and Owen the other and Louella hugged him from behind. And then Wyn went to work with the iron. Fletcher's face was covered in bites and scratches — some ragged and inflamed and others little more than small red dots and Wyn knew he had to go deep on each of them. With the first touch of steel, Fletcher arched his back and screamed — a high muffled sound around the gag. As the iron came at him again, he yanked his right arm, pulling Alec off balance and there was a general flailing as they all tried to restrain him. Again and again, the iron was reheated and applied to the wounds and Fletch bucked and cried and Louella held on. She was not the one being tortured, but every spasm of his pain communicated itself directly to her; as she gripped him, her body was forced to writhe with his. She took every knock as he arched and thrashed and threw his head back into her chest until finally the job was done. Lou knelt in front of him as he collapsed into her arms and wept.

She gently coaxed him back onto the chair so that Niamh could clean and bandage his wounds. It was decided that he would bed down in the barn where Louella had a separate quarantine pen for sick or calving livestock. They could lock him in there and wait and see if the treatment was successful. But first Lou helped him into the downstairs bathroom, cleaned him up and brought him fresh boxers and sweats because, at some point in all the pandemonium, he had wet himself. They set up a cot in the calving pen and gave him Tramadol for the pain. And Louella had James's old easy chair carried out there so she could sit with him.

When, however, she tried to drag it into the pen, Fletcher became very agitated. "Get out! You are not bringing that in here!"

"Fletch, you're going to be fi..."

But he was on his feet now, drunkenly trying to push her out of the stall. "You are not sitting in here! Damn it, Louella!" He would not be persuaded to lie back down until she was out of the pen and had chained and padlocked the gate.

She stood there trembling, looking at him through the bars. "Fletch, if you're infected, you're not contagious yet. It's too early."

"I don't care."

"Besides, I think we got it all."

"Yeah, Wyn was pretty thorough." Fletch lay down and stared up at the ceiling. "Oh God, Lou."

She didn't know what to say to him. The man had been attacked by a swarm of ravening bats, he'd been tortured with an iron brand and now lay in a barn waiting to see if he was doomed. No words were an adequate response to that. Except perhaps "I'm here" and "I love you." But the Tramadol was kicking in now and every time Fletcher blinked, his eyes remained closed a little longer. Finally, mercifully, he fell asleep.

Ginny sat with him while Louella went back to the farmhouse.

"Is there anything else we can do?" she asked Wyn.

He could only shake his head grimly in reply.

"Right," she sighed. "I want to get a few things out to the barn, make it feel a little less like a cage and then, as bizarre as it seems, we need to carry on as usual while we wait."

"I want to post a guard on him," Patience said.

"We will *if* he develops symptoms. Until then, I'll keep an eye on him."

Fletcher was out for the count and so they were able to spruce up the pen without waking him. They placed a low bench beside his cot with books and a lamp and a glass of water. And the kids drew him pictures and made 'Get Well Soon' cards that Louella taped to the walls and bars. Bib cooked up a batch of chicken soup and Peg brought in a vase of orange and yellow nasturtiums, although these were already starting to fade in the heat. They set up a fan to keep him cool and laid a fleece blanket out in case he got a chill. It was homier, nicer, and hopefully it would cheer him to wake up and find his cell transformed into something that looked a little more normal. But all Louella could think was: "We've just given him a nicer place to die." And she reached for the tablets in her pocket.

Her headaches came every day now and it took more and more medication to beat them into submission. She found that two extra strength Tylenol and six Aleve would at least keep her functional. But as she sat and watched Fletcher sleep, the tablets did not even begin to touch the pain. And when a sheepish Levi informed her that (in all the chaos of getting Fletch out of the garage) he'd dropped the needed tractor part, Louella smiled at him kindly, told him they'd sort it out, and (as soon as he left the barn) threw up in the sink.

Fletcher had a hard night. Niamh came in to prop him up with more pillows, because apparently the burns on his face would swell more if he lay down flat. Whether the pillow trick worked or not, Louella couldn't tell. She sat and watched as the pain dragged him out of sleep again and again. Sometimes he would shift around under the thin sheet, but then swiftly pass out again. Other times he would awaken fully and remember the bats and the virus and the torture. He was sure in these moments that he was infected; he'd turn and they'd have to put him down. He wept, from pain and exhaustion yes, but also from fear. He did not want to die. It didn't matter that he was sixty-five years old and had had a good run. He wasn't ready for it all to be over. He wanted more time. In his most lucid moments, he grappled with the idea that he was running out of nexts. There had always been a next — his next meal, his next book, another spring, a tomorrow. He could not conceive of a moment from which nothing would follow on. A day would come when there would be no more nexts. No more of him. It seemed incomprehensible that he should no longer exist.

He found these thoughts hard to articulate — his mind was too blasted. Yet as he rambled on, Louella got the gist. *She* was convinced that even in death there is a next, a crossing over, a heaven. But he did not believe in such things and this wasn't the time for Sunday school. She tried a few times to go in to him, to hold his hand and hug him as he cried, but he would not let her get anywhere near. And so she sat outside the pen all through that long night.

In the morning Bib brought him some thin broth — she wanted to see if he could keep that down before offering him anything more substantial. And Wyn changed his bandages and checked his temperature which, thank God, was still normal. But even through all this, Louella was not admitted into the cage.

"I don't understand you," Louella said quietly when they were alone again. "You let the others in, why not me?"

"I'm trying to protect you."

"Oh for God's sake," she sighed wearily. "If I thought you were dangerous, I wouldn't let Bib or Wyn in there with you. Your temperature is down and you're still you. So what exactly is the problem?" She had not meant to sound harsh, but exhaustion was taking its toll and her head throbbed with nauseating regularity.

He looked at her for a long moment and then said, "Even when we were little, I loved you so much. And it took a while to understand why. I mean, I had other friends. What was so damn different about you?"

"So what was it?"

"It was you and all your dolls."

Louella couldn't help herself, she burst out laughing. "What?"

"You played with your dolls all the time. Loving them, caring for them. But if I skinned a knee or got upset, you'd put them aside and look after me instead. You were such a little mother. I think that's what you were meant to be. My mom was always so sick and remote — she barely acknowledged anything going on in my life. And yet here was this little girl doing what she couldn't. Can you imagine what a revelation it was to feel cared for … and loved? And you've been doing it ever since. I'm failing geography and you study with me. I get sick and you nurse me back to health. I can't think of what to write and you're my sounding board."

Louella shrugged. "It's always been a two-way street."

But he wasn't listening. "I have no control over any of this. But I can look after you and the only way to do it is to keep you on the other side of those bars."

"Fletch…"

"I'm infected."

"You don't know that."

"Well if I'm wrong, you can razz me about it later. But right now — you are to stay the hell out of this cage."

Fletch kept the broth down and so for lunch Louella offered him chicken soup and a sandwich. He didn't eat as much as she would've liked, but he ate some. As she carried plates back to the kitchen, she absentmindedly threw the scraps to the dog. The Labrador shied away from them. This stopped Louella in her tracks; Bailey never refused food. And it wasn't just his odd reaction that disturbed her. She came from a long line of Pennsylvania Dutch — the devoutly religious and downright superstitious descendants of early German settlers. Once, when she was a child, her grandmother told her how to predict the outcome of an illness. You take a piece of bread, rub it against the patient's teeth and then offer it to a dog. If the animal eats it, you can expect a full recovery. If not, you've got trouble. As Louella picked up the untouched scraps, she told herself that it was all just an old wives' tale. It meant nothing. But later that afternoon Fletcher's temperature spiked. It could be, she knew, from a regular infection. That was the big risk when you had to cauterize a wound — the burns could so easily become infected. And his throat might be sore from all the screaming and the nausea could be attributed to the pain. It was *not* New Rabies. Louella told herself that again and again even though Niamh and Wyn looked pale and drawn as the day progressed and Fletch's mind began to falter.

He'd been so quiet that she fell back on an old trick that always got him talking. She asked about his next book. He was endlessly fascinated by plot, character, symbolism and impelling incident. And her questions *did* rouse him. He started to tell her about a Neolithic tribe that gains immortality only to find it a curse. He would call it *Good Neighbours* and it would be packed full of history and folklore. He would get into the very skins of his characters and render their world with such clarity. He had an experimental structure in mind too, because he really wanted to do something that hadn't been done before. And Louella listened and nodded and asked all the relevant questions as tears streaked her face. *Good Neighbours* was his debut novel — his big break — and HBO had turned it into a miniseries decades ago.

Next he turned to her and asked, "So when is James having another poker night?"

Lou, who'd been hanging onto her composure by a thread, looked again at her watch. He could finally have another Tramadol and she hurriedly passed him the tablets. She knew that she shouldn't be so quick to drug him up; she should spend every moment she could talking to him. But this was unbearable. Every word out of his mouth spoke of his delirium. He might as well have said, "I am doomed" over and over again because that is what the conversation conveyed.

Mercifully, the meds knocked him out and Louella no longer had to listen as Fletch made plans to hang out with her dead husband. She dried her eyes and went to see to the animals. It was time to settle the chickens down for the night and usually by this time, they'd be congregated by the door to their coop. Her barn was an old Pennsylvania Dutch structure with three doors on the front: one led to the henhouse, another to a storage room, while the middle one opened onto the main area with its cow stalls and quarantine pen. And the chickens would go nowhere near it. They were clustered over by the house at the far end of the yard. Lou extracted the little Tupperware container full of seeds from her pocket and gave it a shake. Surely the familiar rattle would entice them. Still they hung back. Growing impatient with this performance, she tried to shoo them toward the barn; but when she nudged Boo toward the coop, the hen completely freaked out. She started clucking frantically and beat her wings. They gave her a little lift, but not enough to clear the wall. She hit the bricks hard and tumbled to the ground. Boo's foot bled heavily and Wyn had to bandage it so the poor thing wouldn't end up with bumblefoot. Louella gave up and left the hens to bed down in the yard for the night. The cows, too, refused to approach the barn. Essentially, none of her animals would go anywhere near Fletch.

All was quiet as the sun set. If you didn't know the situation, you might have mistaken the hush for an abiding peace. But there were now armed guards posted outside the barn and the children were forbidden to leave the house. All anyone could do was wait and try to get some sleep.

The following morning they awoke, not to the usual robust crow of the rooster, but to a high-pitched shriek. They ran to the barn in their nightgowns and pajamas — all armed — and there they found Louella standing just out of reach of Fletcher's grasping hands. He screamed and spat and strained against the bars in his efforts to get at her, but she just stood there and said in a quiet voice, "Wyn, Niamh. If you please."

They went immediately to her side.

"I don't know what else we can do for him, do you?" She looked at them for the first time and her eyes were red and puffy.

Niamh shook her head and Wyn uttered a barely audible "no."

"This is the New Rabies?"

"I'm so sorry, Lou," Wyn said.

A tremor went through her, but she pushed ahead with her questions. "And are we in agreement that we're out of options?"

"Yes."

"Right," she nodded and seemed to focus on a blank bit of wall over Niamh's shoulder. "I want everybody out, but guards still posted outside. The kids are restricted to the farmhouse. When it's done, I want a cleanup crew in full hazmat gear to bleach every inch of that pen — that includes the walls, the floor and the bars. Everything he touched needs to be disinfected or burnt. We'll build the pyre this afternoon and hold the service to cremate the body after sundown. I want guards at their regular posts and business as usual when it comes to inspecting the fences."

She rattled the instructions off so quickly that Niamh glanced over her shoulder expecting to see a list hanging there. The commands were clear, there was plenty to do and yet everyone seemed frozen to the spot. They just stood there staring at Louella.

"Move!" she yelled and it was a high, cracked sound that startled them into action.

Owen approached her. "Chief, let someone else…"

303

She said nothing, but the look on her face cut him off mid-sentence. Her pain and despair bordered on a kind of savagery. There was no talking to that face. He nodded and left with the others.

They stood together in the kitchen, listening to Fletcher scream and when the shot rang out, many of them jumped. Niamh was in tears and the children were crying and before her mind even registered the fact, Peg was running toward the barn and her mother.

Fletcher lay on the floor with a large hole punched through his forehead from the .357 slug. Louella stood there staring at the body, the magnum on the floor at her feet.

"Mom..."

And Lou did turn toward her; then the old woman rushed past, shouldering Peg out of the way and reaching the sink just as she started to retch. Peg stood with her hand on her mother's back and wondered briefly why her mom would be throwing up coffee grounds. Then it hit her— that was blood, old blood, churning-in-your-stomach-for-hours-as-your-ulcer-hemorrhages sort of blood and as she cried out for Wyn and Niamh, she thought her own head might explode from the stress.

And that is why it was so odd to hear Niamh calmly ask from the doorway, "Lou, just how many painkillers have you been taking?"

It took a moment before the chief could answer. "Quite a few."

"For how long?"

When Louella didn't answer, Peg gripped her arm, "How long?"

"Since Midwood fell."

"You've been cramming NSAIDs for five months?" Niamh asked incredulously. "No wonder you're bleeding. Right. Peg, help her get cleaned up and then I want her in bed."

"I have work to do."

"Screw your work," Niamh snapped. Louella gaped in surprise at this quiet, slip of a girl who was suddenly bossing her around. "I know that you're the chief and all, but I'm a medic and when it comes to health matters, what I say goes." She was rocking nervously on her feet but plowed on anyway. "Now move your ass, woman!"

Wyn kept an eye on the proceedings, but did not interfere. Despite all the stress and horror of that morning, he felt a moment's pride at how far Niamh had come along. First she double checked her books and reread the material on peptic ulcers. Then she rummaged through the meds they'd scavenged from the pharmacy at Sage Foods. The prescribed treatment for an ulcer included:

1. H2 Blockers that inhibit acid production. From their stash she selected Pepcid.
2. Proton Pump Inhibitors that block the cells that produce acid. For this she grabbed a box of Nexium.
3. Over-the-counter antacids to neutralize the stomach acid already present. Tums and Rolaids would do.
4. Cryptoprotective agents to protect the lining of the stomach and small intestine. This came in the form of a big pink bottle of Pepto Bismol.

"You are to take all of these as directed," Niamh said, handing her patient a glass of milk. "There can be no more aspirin, ibuprofen or naproxen sodium. No soda, no fried foods. You are going to rest here …"

"…But Fletch's service…"

"…is not until later tonight and I will come and get you when it's time. Meanwhile, I want you to take these." The girl handed her two 5 mg tablets of diazepam. "You're exhausted, Lou, and you need to get some sleep."

When Niamh finally left them alone, Peg sat on the edge of her mother's bed and held her hand.

"God you scared me," she said.

"I'm fine."

"No, you're not."

"Compared to what just happened to Fletch, this is hardly a big deal."

"Stop it!"

Louella looked at her in surprise. "Stop what?"

"Pretending that you're ok. You're suffering from chronic headaches that have caused you to shred your stomach lining just to keep going. You've just shot your best friend, you're hacking up blood, you …" Her voice broke and she burst into tears. Louella reached up and touched her cheek.

Louella knew that she should be crying too — hell, screaming into a pillow right now would not go amiss. But she was so tired. She'd had moments like this before, when things were so bad that it felt as if something in her head had ... *blown*. It reminded her of the way that an overloading surge of electricity can blow a fuse. And then everything goes quiet and dark. In those moments she did not have the strength to cry as she should. She did not even have the capacity to register the full horror of the situation. The last time she'd felt like that was just after James died.

"Did I ever tell you what Fletch did after your father died?"

"No."

"It's hard to say what was worse, really. Losing Eben or losing James. To lose a child, it felt like someone had hollowed out my chest, like a giant hand had reached in there and ripped out everything vital and just left me with this ragged, gaping hole. I knew I'd never be the same again. But your dad kept me going. It was always that way. No matter what sort of day I'd had, no matter what the problem, I knew that if I could just sit and talk to him about it — it might not be fixed, but it would be better. I'd feel calmer at least. Kept me sane. I guess that sounds lame, like I should have been able to sort myself out on my own."

"No, mom."

"But then I lost your father too. And Sam was — what? — fourteen years old and you'd just had Mae and I felt sure that I couldn't ... I just couldn't do it. All the things that everyone needed me to do. I couldn't. That was when I sent Sam to stay with you and Alec over Thanksgiving break, remember?"

Peg nodded.

"I was here on my own and it was three o'clock in the afternoon and I was still in my PJs and then Fletcher shows up with a video tape. He swore it would help..."

Fletcher had sat on his couch trying to puzzle his way through it. He'd always thought of Louella as being so strong, but now she was buckling. James was gone and she seemed utterly lost without him. How long had they been married? He did the math and realized it had been thirty-nine years. Then one day, quite suddenly, he died and Lou did something she'd never done before. She gave up. She sat down and did not get up again. And Fletch tried everything he could to prod her back toward life. It was all there waiting for her — Peg and Sam and Mae and the farm and her animals and her friends. But they were all so temporary, she'd said. What could any of it really mean? A life's worth of struggle and then you die.

How many millions of people just like her had lived and fought their way through and now weren't even so much as a memory? It all — always — got lost.

Hearing her talk like this made Fletch realize: she'd lost her faith. For all her logic, the thing that sustained her was belief; and after James passed, she believed in precisely nothing. He could sympathize. For him, life had negated the possibility of the existence of God. But he didn't need that faith. She did. And so the atheist tuned into TBN (the Trinity Broadcasting Network on WGTW — TV48). A cheerful voice announced, "Coming up on The Potter's Touch... " In truth he almost switched it off. T.D. Jakes and his congregation got so "into it" that he could not imagine Louella responding to the sermon. It was such a far cry from the ordered, and decidedly reserved, services that Lou's father had once presided over. No, they leaned a little too much toward the "happy clapper" end of the spectrum. His thumb was on the remote's off button, when a single phrase leapt out at him: "Don't take the presence of the storm to indicate the absence of God." Fletcher realized that that was the crux of Louella's problem. She felt utterly abandoned by God in the storm. He quickly popped a new tape into the VCR and hit record.

As he listened he thought, *Now that is good.* Not only was the sermon emotionally charged, but the argument was brilliantly constructed. It would engage Lou intellectually and, as she seemed to have gone completely numb, that might be the only way to reach her.

Later on as she watched the tape, the sermon did speak to her. It was all about Paul's shipwreck in Acts 27 when suddenly the very thing he was counting on started to break up in the storm. It was not a huge mental leap for her to equate James with the boat. She needed him so desperately and whenever times were hard, he had kept her head above water. Then he was gone, like Paul's ship, and what was she supposed to do? And Jakes, as if he had some strange insight into her thoughts, answered that not all blessings are meant to last for your entire journey. Sometimes we only have them for a season.

In the Bible story, the crew took hold of the shattered parts of the vessel in order to paddle their way to shore. And Jakes pointed out that if they had believed that the only way to survive was in a whole boat, then they would have drowned. But instead they grabbed a piece of the ship and it sustained them. Stop weeping, he said, over all you have lost and start living on what you've got left. The program ended and Louella looked thoughtfully at the bald black man that was frozen on the screen. Then she rose, showered and brushed her teeth for the first time in days, got dressed and headed over to Peg's. She had a lot left to cling to and it was time to get on with it.

"Looking back," the diazepam was kicking in now and Louella's voice was thick and drowsy, "I think there was a reason why I lost your dad. I had to be tough if I was going to be able to deal with all this. I couldn't have done it in my twenties; probably couldn't have done it before Eben and James died. No, it's only now... And I am handling it — not perfectly, this fucking ulcer — but I'm handling it. Just like I'll handle Fletcher's service tonight and the fact that we have to go back for the rasp bar and then there's the harvest and on and on it goes. So don't cry," she wiped a tear off of Peg's cheek with her thumb. "I know you're worried, but understand: I'm not drowning."

Steven Wannemaker sang *Rock of Ages* as they lit the pyre. As Louella watched it burn, she thought back to her first day of kindergarten. She was afraid to be left there with all those people she didn't know and she had clung to her mother's leg and wept. But Fletcher came over and showed her the little plastic chicken from his Fisher Price Farm set. He said that, if she stayed, he'd let her keep it. She'd let go of her mother then and spent the day with her new friend. There were summer days when she'd ride on Fletch's handlebars out to Fishing Creek where they'd perform "death-defying dives" from the old railway bridge. He had taught her how to play poker and given her her first beer. And he had introduced her to James. She watched the fire and smiled even though there were tears in her eyes; and she thanked God for bringing him into her life, even if it was only for a season.

CHAPTER FIFTEEN

QUEEN TAKES BISHOP

"Life is a kind of Chess, in which we have often points to gain, and competitors or adversaries to contend with."

Benjamin Franklin

"One doesn't have to play well, it's enough to play better than your opponent."

Siegbert Tarrasch

"God, I am so sorry." Levi looked like he might cry. "I had the damn thing in my hands and then, I don't know…"

"I know what happened," Patience shrugged. "Fletch got hurt and we all dropped what we were doing to help him."

"The minute I heard him scream I forgot all about the rasp bar," Sam added.

"And so," a hoarse voice said quietly, "we need to go back for it. Whereabouts did you drop it?"

Louella sat in an old rocking chair in the corner of the kitchen. She had visibly aged in the last few days. It pained Peg to see it, but it didn't surprise her. She'd once read an article on U.S. presidents. It featured before and after pictures of men like Washington and Lincoln and

Roosevelt. The difference in their faces was startling. They entered office so bright-eyed, so fresh-faced and vibrant; and then the weight of their responsibilities etched furrows in their brows and grayed their hair. The most notable change, however, had been the alteration to their eyes. So many of them had had smiling, quite innocent eyes. Yet by the end of their term, their eyes looked tired, in some cases infinitely sad, and most of all *knowing*. Some terrible knowledge had come to them during their time as leader. And it haunted them. That is how her mother looked now.

"I dropped it outside," Levi was saying. "Fletch stumbled and I needed both hands to help him."

Patience nodded as she formulated her plan. "So it's right there on the forecourt. That's good. We grab the part and get out of there. But I still want us covered head to toe — no gaps. Josie…"

"No problem," she said. She was already sorting through their hazmat gear.

They approached Hackett's in two cars. When they were about a hundred yards out, Patience radioed for them to stop. From there she could see the forecourt through her binoculars and wanted a quick look before they drew near. At first glance, the place looked exactly as they had left it. The gate stood open and there on the pavement lay the rasp bar. But then a flash of metallic brown caught her eye and she nudged the focus wheel to get a better look at it. Among the junkers parked to the right of the main entrance, there was a pickup truck, and not just any old pickup. It had once been Mayor Albitz's pride and joy: a fully customized Ford F-150 with a deep mahogany paint job that the manufacturer had dubbed "Caribou." It had not been there before. She was sure. Patience had helped carry the mayor's body to the pyre after the attack on North Star. So who was driving the truck now?

"Huddle," she said into her radio.

She gathered them together. "All right, guys. New plan…"

Fifteen minutes later, Patience drove up to Hackett's and parked outside the fence. From his place behind a stack of old tires, Roger Silsbee crept over to where Blake Turner sat eating what was probably his ninth Milky Way bar.

"It's time," he whispered and the big man shoved the rest of the candy hurriedly into his mouth.

They watched the woman approach, knowing that Wilford had taken up a flanking position across the forecourt. Shaw would be maneuvering around behind her. And in front of her there was only the main garage … and the bats. They had her boxed in. When she reached the bait (the odd looking part they dropped days ago), Leon gave the signal. They were supposed to surround and capture her without firing a shot. She was, after all, their ticket into that farm and hence they needed her alive. But then Blake got carried away. He'd been thinking this was some wonderful game of "Cops and Robbers" and so he started shooting. He fired the gun the way he'd seen gangsters do it on TV, moving his hand as if he was almost trying to throw the bullets. Consequently, he came nowhere near to hitting his target. However, Levi didn't know that. He knew only that his daughter was under fire and in another breathless moment he appeared behind Silsbee and Turner. He had James's Beretta semi-automatic in his hands and shot Blake three times before he could even turn around. As the big man slumped face-first into the tires, Silsbee dove to the side and managed to fire one round. It went wide and Levi didn't give him the chance to squeeze off another.

Leon found that he was taking fire from the rear and hence, dove into Pat's truck for cover. But Arnold was close now — close enough for his Colt .45 to punch through the car door and hit the man inside. Leon screamed, a high-pitched keening sound that caused Wilford Bishop to bolt back through the scrapyard, hoping to hide there among the derelict cars. What he didn't know was that Sam had climbed the fence on that side. Man and boy met next to the rusted-out hulk of a 1958 Plymouth Fury and Wilford dropped his gun and put his hands up. Sam had never shot a man in his life and this wasn't just some random guy; this was Mr. Bishop, his old teacher. He could not bring himself to pull the trigger and so accepted the man's surrender. Patience, in a panic over the one member of her team unaccounted for, raced through the yard and eventually found them. For the first time since the fall, she slapped a pair of handcuffs on a man, although for the life of her she couldn't imagine just what the hell they were going to do with Wilf once they got him home.

As the team swept the area to make sure there were no others laying in wait, Patience returned with Sam and the men gawked at their prisoner.

"Wilford?" Levi looked at him wide-eyed. "You were with them? With *Shaw?*"

"I … I got injured and … and needed help. They took me in." Bishop looked from one to the other, searching for some sign that they believed him, that they understood.

Ignoring him Patience asked, "Was that Leon Shaw who came up behind me?"

"Yeah," Arnold nodded. "He's dead. Bled out all over your car," he grimaced apologetically.

Patience shook her head and gave a low whistle. It was then that they heard a dull thudding coming from the mayor's pickup.

"Open it up, Wilford," she said quietly.

"I don't have the key."

She dug through Shaw's pockets, found the key and threw it to Wilf. "Open it the fuck up."

With his hands cuffed in front of him, he was able to unlock the Tonneau cover over the truck bed. "Listen: this was Shaw. I didn't do this. I wouldn't…" He raised the cover and stepped back.

There, tied up and lying in a fetal position, was Catherine Bishop.

Louella sat at her kitchen table, massaging her temples. "How is she?"

Wyn shook his head. "She's been badly beaten. They broke her arm, her collar bone, three ribs and her nose. I'm worried about internal injuries and …" He shifted awkwardly on his feet. "There seems to be signs, I mean I'm no expert, but…"

Niamh spoke up. "There are signs of sexual trauma."

"She was raped." Louella stared down at her hands.

"Yes."

The chief looked up. "What does she say?"

"Nothing," Wyn shook his head again. "She's been unconscious since Pat brought her in."

Louella looked at Patience now. "And what does he say about all this?"

"That he was a prisoner too. That he was forced to work for the gang and that he took no part in the assault on Catherine."

"Do you believe that?"

"No. You don't give a prisoner a gun. Besides, he had the strongest motive of any of them. His wife leaves him for another man and then suddenly all law and order evaporates. I can't believe he didn't take the opportunity to get some payback."

"Besides," Peg said, "why the beating? Why would they risk it?"

"I don't follow," Bib said.

"The world's gone to hell and we're all competing for limited resources. That's not only food and water. To an all-male group surely women would be a commodity, a resource that you don't waste. They could have incapacitated her a dozen different ways, but instead they beat her to within an inch of her life? Why risk the one female body you've got?"

"Because the beating had nothing to do with any of that," Patience said quietly. "It was an act of rage."

"Guys, I understand everything you're saying. I agree with you." Owen shifted awkwardly in his seat. He had to play devil's advocate and he knew that no one wanted to hear it. "But we have to decide what to do with him. And right now, all we have is supposition to go on. What *if* he didn't lay a finger on her?"

There was a general muttering over this. Louella put her hand up. "Enough. Owen's right. We don't know anything for sure." She thought for a moment. "I want someone in with Catherine 24/7. The minute she wakes up, ask her about Wilford's involvement."

"But Lou," Wyn said, "what if she doesn't wake up?"

"That's why we try plan B."

"Which is?" Peg asked.

Louella's head throbbed and she automatically reached into her pocket for the bottle of Aleve that was no longer there. *Frick.* "I'm going to have a little talk with our guest."

She took Owen, Patience and Peg with her to the barn. Bishop was handcuffed to the bars of the calving pen and it took an act of sheer will for Louella just to approach it. The cleanup crew had done their job well. The quarantine pen reeked of bleach and there was not one sign of the violence that had occurred there. She could still see him, though — Fletcher, foaming at the mouth, eyes wide and insane as he scrabbled at the bars to reach her. With a few deep breaths, she managed to get hold of herself and walk up to the pen.

"Hello, Wilford."

"Louella, I'm glad to see you. You can tell them."

"Tell them what?"

"That I didn't hurt Catherine. And I didn't shoot at Patience either." In a move that reminded her again of Fletcher, he clasped desperately at the bars. "Come on, you know me. I was raised in your father's church. I wouldn't do anything like that."

"Catherine is awake," Louella said. "And she's talking."

She watched him carefully. His eyes widened and before even one accusation could be made, he started shaking his head furiously. Wilford let go of the bars and backed up as far as the cuffs would allow.

"She said," the chief continued, "that you took part in the attacks on her."

"No."

"That you beat her."

"No."

"And raped her."

"No."

"Because you hated her for making a fool out of you with that Jeff from the high school."

"No!"

"We all heard it!" Lou yelled. Wilf opened his mouth but she gave him no chance to speak. "And do not say to me that it's her word against yours!"

"Mr. Bishop," Pat said quietly. "I have an assault victim with multiple broken bones and internal bleeding that we can't stop. You understand what that means? Everyone here is gonna believe a deathbed testimony." She held her gaze steady, but internally recoiled. In the old world she never would have lied during a suspect interview.

"I know." Louella sounded almost sympathetic. "It must have been awful to be thrown over for Jeff Burgess. Of course you'd hate her. She hurt *you* so badly, how natural to want to hurt her back. And I'm sure there must have been a lot of pressure from Shaw to join in, right?" When he didn't answer she cried, "Say something!"

Bishop looked at her with hollow eyes. "I was so scared. And with Shaw you have to play along to be one of the gang, 'cause if you're weak, they cast you out." He was weeping now. "You don't know what it was like. I had to!"

"Had to what?"

"Join in."

"You could have refused…"

"I'll say it again, he would have cast me out! I was injured and terrified and everything I've done, I've done to survive."

Louella nodded but her eyes had gone stony now. "So you raped and beat your ex-wife in order to survive."

"Yes."

"To be part of the gang."

Bishop nodded.

"What else?"

"Huh?"

"What else did you do to be part of the gang? Where's Jeff? Was he with Catherine when you found her?"

Again his eyes went wide. He looked desperate and panicked and the denials came thick and fast. "No! I didn't do anything else. I swear!"

There's bullshit in this barn and it's not from my cows, Louella thought. Aloud she said, "Thank you, Mr. Bishop, that'll be all."

As she walked away, he yelled after her, "What else could I have done? You tell me! You sit here in this cushy little haven — you have no idea what it was like back there!"

She spun around to face him. "I was in Midwood when it fell. I know exactly what it was like."

"Well yippee for you. You were able to get back here. I was stuck there in that hell and I did what I had to do. What choice did I have?"

She thought this over for a moment, then shrugged. "You could have died as a good man, Mr. Bishop."

"Why do you keep calling me that? It's Wilford! It's always been Wilford for as long as you've known me." But she was walking away … and didn't bother looking back.

Owen sighed, "Well there's no doubt as to his guilt, so the question is what do we do with him?"

The laws he'd drafted had been collected into a ring binder that Sam used to use for trigonometry. Every member of the group over sixteen years of age had signed the last page, hence ratifying the law and pledging to uphold it. But now it lay open to a short section entitled, *Outsiders.*

These were the laws that governed their actions toward anyone who did not belong to Camp North Star…

> *Violence is permissible only in cases of self-defense, or during those incidents when you are called upon to defend the family or the farm.*
> *Violence is strictly prohibited toward noncombatants.*
> *It is forbidden to attack a peaceful group.*
> *It is forbidden to steal from a peaceful group.*
> *It is forbidden to commit acts of torture, rape or sexual assault even against hostile strangers.*

And that was it. They had not foreseen the surrender of a hostile enemy or the need to place one on trial for his crimes. So what were they going to do?

Everyone seemed to have an opinion and they were all talking at once. It wasn't anything like a proper debate, it was just a bunch of upset people simultaneously venting their frustrations. Modern feminist fury advocating everything from castration to the death penalty clashed with old time religion that insisted thou shalt not kill. Pragmatism that identified Bishop as a threat to be neutralized butted heads with sentiment that wanted the group to preserve their compassion and their humanity. There were protracted debates about the collective soul of the group and how this was a defining moment for Camp North Star. Louella sat back and let them get it out of their systems. But all the while her head pounded and she thought: *Wait for it… wait for it…*

And then it came. Owen asked, "What do you think, Lou?"

She sighed. "It is a moral question, but it's also a practical one and we might as well deal with the two together." She sighed again. "I can only see three options open to us: imprison, exile or execute. Am I missing any?" She looked around the room, but no one had anything to add. "So let's look at option number one; let's say we keep him prisoner. That would answer both the moral dilemma and your safety concerns. We'd feel like justice had been done without having to string him up. And, if he's locked up, he can't hurt anybody. But there's a problem."

"Which is?" Levi asked.

"It would be a logistical nightmare. We're already overcrowded and yeah, we can keep him in the barn but it still leaves the question: what do we do with him?"

"He could work," Bib ventured. "He'd be an extra set of hands to help."

Lou shook her head. "No, he wouldn't. If we put him to work, someone would have to guard him. That's two people – two mouths to feed and nothing extra gets accomplished. There are no appreciable benefits to having him work for us."

"And we'd have to feed and cloth him, and treat his illnesses," Peg frowned. "That means diverting resources from the rest of the group."

"We are doing well in terms of supplies," the chief nodded. "But that won't always be the case. Sooner or later we are going to have a lean year. Then what? You gonna take food away from yourself or the kids to keep him alive?"

"I just …," Patience sighed, "I think that running a civilized penitentiary requires more than we can manage right now. And we'd be responsible for him for the rest of his life. It would have to be a life sentence because we could never trust him. And if we're not prepared to do it for that long…"

"Then why do it at all?" Levi asked.

"Yeah."

"And then, of course, there's Catherine. All logistics aside," Louella said, "we cannot ask her to live here with him in such close proximity. Seeing him everyday…"

"I really don't know, Lou, if that's going to be an issue," Niamh said.

Ginny's quiet voice asked the next question: "Maybe it won't, but do you really want him around the kids?"

This was met with a heavy silence that Louella eventually broke. "We wanted this place to be our sanctuary. How much does that change if he becomes a part of it? How safe, how good, will it feel?"

"Ok," Bib nodded, "so we drive him off."

A lot of people nodded at this including the chief. "Exile is another option and the most convenient. It gets rid of him and we don't have to do anything … unpleasant."

But even as they nodded along, people could see flaws in the idea. One person worried that "He knows our location. He could lead the infected here. Or sit outside with a rifle and a scope and pick us off." Another carried the logic even further, "Or mess with the well or wind turbine." That was their paranoia talking, but paranoia is persuasive.

"So take him far away." Bib could see where this was going and was getting upset.

Owen piped up. "You all convinced me that a long trip was too dangerous. And that was to reach my parents. Now you want to do it for him?"

"We'll ...," Bib stammered, "we'll scare him off."

"Then what?" Louella asked quietly.

They looked at her in confusion.

"Here's a man who, the minute society fell, engaged in gang rape and beat the shit out of his ex-wife. Say we let him go ... then what? You think he'll just turn over a new leaf? Find Jesus?"

"Does it matter?" Sam asked.

"Letting him go," Louella explained, "seems like the most moral option for us — we certainly wouldn't have to get our hands dirty. But if he goes out and hurts someone else, that's on us. We had the opportunity to stop him and instead we turned him loose."

"That's not our responsibility," Alec said. "Seriously guys, is that our problem?"

Louella leaned back in her chair. "You tell me. This is our defining moment."

Owen sighed. "Actually, it is our problem. In the absence of law, moral rule (whatever form it takes) will be determined by the strongest groups. That's us, folks."

"As one of the strong, I'm asking you do we or do we not have a moral responsibility to protect other survivors?" Louella's question was met with silence and so she pressed on. "Let's make it less abstract. If we pick up a survivor in the future and find out that she was raped by that man, will you be able to look her in the eye? Or can you just shrug it off and say 'Tough break, kid'?"

Bib slumped forward, elbows on the table massaging her temples in a way that announced she was working on a migraine of her own. "No," she murmured. "It would be our fault." She looked up at the others, pleadingly. "But to kill him — it's against the ..."

"Law?" Owen asked gently. "There is no civil authority, no state and federal law. That's why he did all those things in the first place. He didn't expect that there could be any consequences. But the same law that would have deterred him is also not there to protect him now. The only law we have is our own."

Bib tried one last time. "But we're not killers."

Arnold took her hand. "Sweetheart, I shot and killed Leon Shaw today."

"But that was in a fight!" She was crying now. "You were defending Patience. This is an execution!"

"I know," Louella fished a dog-eared packet of tums out of her pocket and popped two in her mouth. "Nevertheless, it is one of our three options and we need to take a vote."

There was a heavy silence in the kitchen as the votes were counted. The children watched, wide-eyed, as the verdict was announced. Death. Louella closed her eyes and bowed her head. She had expected this, hell she'd voted for it, but now she felt like she might pass out. Yet again, here was another awful job that she could not delegate. She could not possibly inflict this on anyone else. And so now, she would have to be a fucking executioner too and the realization made her want to curl up and die. But then Niamh was at her elbow, wanting her to take a stronger dose of her meds before she went out to the barn. Louella felt so ill that she followed her without question and did not notice the look that passed between Peg and the medic.

Niamh proceeded to dither about — checking her blood pressure, listening to her heart, asking questions that she already knew the answers to and still Louella was too preoccupied to realize that anything was amiss … until she heard the shot.

Out in the barn, Peg stood looking down at the man she just killed. Wilford Bishop hung from his handcuffs in an attitude that resembled prayer. She understood now. To do this kind of work diminished and hurt you in a way that could not be properly defined or truly mended. But that's why she had to do it. Fletcher hadn't been dead for a week and her mother was still sick — there was no way that she was going to let Louella walk into that barn with a gun. It was too much. And so she sacrificed a cherished piece of herself to protect her mom from this. She wiped hastily at her eyes and headed back into the house.

CHAPTER SIXTEEN

ROCK OF AGES
(REPRISE)

"There is no real ending. It's just the place where you stop the story."

Frank Herbert

"There's a trick to the 'graceful exit.' It begins with the vision to recognize when a job is over — and let it go. It means leaving what's over without denying its validity or its past importance to our lives. It involves a sense of future, a belief that every exit line is an entry, that we are moving up, rather than out."

Ellen Goodman

Lightning flashed and the rain bucketed down, effectively calling a halt to the day's wheat harvest. Therefore Louella had a rare afternoon off. She used the time to sort through Fletcher's belongings. She redistributed his clothes among the men, although his t-shirt collection raised a few eyebrows. There was his beloved *Billy and the Boingers* shirt and another that read, "Legally, it's questionable. Morally, it's disgusting. Personally, I like it." And then there was Louella's favorite: "I think, therefore I'm dangerous."

That was the easy part. Going through his briefcase was much more painful. It was filled with intimate reminders of her friend. He'd kept the receipt for his 1993 Harley-Davidson Wide Glide. That had been a beautiful bike and he'd ridden it across the country writing about all the things he saw and experienced. That book, simply called *Blacktop*, had prompted critics to compare him to Robert M. Pirsig and some had even called him the next Kerouac.

Scrunched up at the bottom of the case was a scrap of hotel stationary (from the *Fairmont Hotel and Resorts*). A phone number and the name Kate was written on it in loopy script and the woman had actually left a lipstick "kiss" on the paper. Kate was Fletcher's one big regret. They'd met in San Francisco and, by all accounts, he should have stayed there with her. But he struggled with the notion of love versus liberty. In his mind, the two were always diametrically opposed. He'd loved his mother and that had enslaved him; it had chewed up his youth in an unending slog of need and dependency. He'd grown up thinking that to love someone is to subordinate yourself entirely to their needs and desires. And so when Kate came along and yet again someone proclaimed their love for him, he bolted. He could not abide the thought of shackling himself to yet another person. It was only years later, after seeing how James and Louella's marriage had turned out, that he realized: Love, at its best, is the freedom to be exactly and completely who you are. Anything that requires the abnegation of the self, the need to be something less, is not love. He told Lou that he could have had that with Kate, but by then she had moved on — married some accountant or banker or something and they had a kid.

Louella set the phone number aside and extracted an old picture of herself, taken back in the days when she looked like a young Stevie Nicks. She lingered over this for a moment, marveling at the girl she'd been — so happy in her world and utterly ignorant of all the wonder and the horror that was to come.

Next she found his fountain pen and the lighter she'd given him when he left for college. It was a cheap thing really, but pretty in its way. It had an eagle in full flight on the front and the words, "I'm free" etched on the back. It turns out that he wasn't just keeping the lighter for sentimental reasons, because the next thing she extracted from the bag was a pack of Marlboro cigarettes.

"I knew it," she muttered, shaking her head.

Louella gave up smoking decades ago when she and James started trying for a baby, but it had not been easy. A cigarette for her had always signaled a moment of relaxation and without that prompt, she'd found it hard to switch off. She was fidgety and didn't know what to do with her hands and, in the end, just freakin' crabby. Fletch, himself an avid smoker, offered to quit with her, reasoning that it would be easier if they did it together. But Louella had always suspected that he'd never quite kicked the habit.

"And now you're busted," she said sadly and another wave of grief washed over her.

She sniffled loudly and pulled the last item from the briefcase: a battered old leather journal that contained ideas for his books. She flipped through it. Apparently he'd been mulling over an idea for a new novel — a book about a global pandemic and a group of survivors in a remote cabin. *Gee*, she thought, *I wonder where you got that idea from.* Beneath a brief outline that started with a mad scientist conducting experiments on an island (à la Dr. Moreau), he'd listed two quotes to use in the text. The first was by Og Mandino: "I will love the light for it shows me the way, yet I will endure the darkness for it shows me the stars." It was accompanied by a note about the characters rising to meet their challenges, becoming more than they ever thought possible. He wrote, *It is a fundamental irony of tragedy that the darkness is ultimately necessary. We only see things through contrast — we see the light (the brilliance inherent in human beings) most spectacularly when it is surrounded by darkness.*

The other quote, from an unknown source, read: "The situation is deteriorating faster than I can lower my expectations." Louella laughed out loud at that. God, it was true. They'd had three funerals in quick succession: Fletcher's (which had just about killed her) and those for Wilford and Catherine Bishop. Cat lasted two days at the farm before finally succumbing to her injuries. She was cremated with a full service and prayers, but no one had any words to say over Wilford. They just stuck him on a pyre, set it alight and walked away.

It had been a harrowing time for the group and was swiftly followed by a harvest that she had to bring in with the help of novices. Most of them had never done anything like it before and so it was more arduous than usual. And then, of course, there were the security concerns. To go into the fields risked contact with infected animals, and so it was a palaver of guards and guns and protective clothing. And now the weather was working against them.

That, it turned out, was not the last of the complications. When the sky cleared and work resumed, Louella was showing young Thomas Gerber how full the grain bins needed to be in order for the wheat to dry properly. Although quiet by nature, the boy was uncharacteristically silent.

"Is something the matter, Tom?" she asked.

"I don't feel so good," he said and promptly threw up on her shoes.

That was the first case of stomach bug at Camp North Star and soon it spread throughout the farm. Max Brooks touched on this idea in his novel *World War Z*. He maintained that having a fortress was only one part of the survival equation. Within those walls, illness could spread like wildfire. Imagine a beleaguered, exhausted group trying to bring in the harvest as more and more of them fell ill. Those still on their feet had to look after their stricken friends. And so, while they'd managed to get the wheat and alfalfa in, the corn harvest was delayed. When more rain hit the crop moldered. Louella soon realized that eighty percent of it was no longer food safe. And the last, salvageable twenty percent? She had to let it rot in the field because another problem reared its head.

Having gone down with the bug early on, Patience rallied quickly. Once back on her feet, she left the farm to conduct one of her regular recon missions. These were quiet sweeps of the valley to search for survivors and keep tabs on the known pockets of infected that dotted the countryside. Thankfully all was peaceful and there was no sign of any intruders near the farm. She was just about to head home when something small, a mere glint in her binoculars, caught her eye. She drove up the old jeep trail to a high ridge to get a better look. What she saw made her blood run cold. The infected. Moving in a slow herd across the farmland to the north. Using Jacob's Method of crowd counting, she estimated the horde to be 4,000 strong. And they were headed straight for Camp North Star.

Louella was just throwing a load of sheets into the washing machine (little Isabella Rhyne had gotten sick in her bed) when Patience broke the news. There were only a few members of the group present to receive it — Bib and Alec and Lou and Owen. All the rest were in bed — not dying, but certainly feeling like they were.

"What the hell are we gonna do?" Bib asked.

"We saw off the last horde," Owen said.

"Yeah, but 4,000! Can we really handle that many?"

"No," Patience said. "We can't."

Louella asked, "How long before they get here?"

"It's hard to say. They're moving slow and there's some rough terrain between them and us, but I reckon we have no more than three days."

"We could evacuate," Alec said. "Wait until they pass and then come back."

Louella switched on the washing machine and washed her hands. "People can barely make it to the bathroom before they get sick. How the hell can we evacuate them and all the animals?" She sighed. Truth be told, she wasn't feeling particularly well herself. "Patience, you've got maps in your car?"

"Yeah."

"Go get 'em."

In a few minutes, the Pennsylvania road map was spread across the table and Patience was running one thin finger in a wiggly line. "They are moving parallel to Route 88 down from Carmichaels. I take it you're thinking of trying to redirect them?"

Louella nodded. "In theory, all we have to do is give them something interesting in a different direction."

"Like what?" Bib asked.

"An explosion would be the best thing — lots of noise and fire and smoke," Patience said.

"And then once they're headed there, they'd have no reason to come back this way," Louella murmured.

"Ok," Owen said, "so what do we blow up?"

"What about Webster's out toward Garard's Fort?" Bib asked.

"It would make a helluva bang," Pat smiled.

Webster's Petroleum Products, according to their website, offered a range of services including the delivery of on-road diesel and gasoline, farm diesel, industrial lubricants and home heating oil. Everyone in the area who lived off the main gas grid, relied on Webster's to heat their homes through winter. And those stockpiled supplies would just be sitting there on a barren stretch of the T616 to the west. Pat's plan was simple: torch the place. It would by necessity be a solo mission; Owen went down with the bug that night, Bib was pale and unable to take any breakfast, and that left a grand total of two able bodied people (Alec and Louella) to stand guard at the farm.

Up on the ramparts, Louella watched Patience go. The chief had already been sick twice that morning. With so many people ill, it had gone unnoticed so she took a bucket up with her and tried to keep watch. It was an exercise in futility. For the first couple of hours, she got sick once every twenty minutes or so and she was so violently ill that her eyes streamed from the exertion. Even if the husks came waltzing right up to the fence, there was little she could've done. But she kept to her post. And in those moments (right after a bout of nausea) when the adrenalin flooded her system and her mind cleared, she prayed to God to keep Pat safe and please, *please* let her mission be a success. She couldn't imagine climbing back down the ladder to ground level, let alone packing up the farm to evacuate.

For Patience, her first act of arson was a simple enough affair. All it required was the liberal application of petrol and a match. She set light to the buildings and the tankers and then retreated to a safe distance to watch. And the result was spectacular — a conflagration unlike anything she'd ever seen. The flames and smoke could be seen for miles and the intermittent explosions as gas tanks ruptured sent echoes down the valley. Watching them through her binoculars, she saw the horde stop and turn to look. The husks seemed to be on a hair trigger — any stimulus was enough to set them running, full pelt, in search of prey. Patience laughed out loud and punched the air in triumph as they took off in the direction of the fire.

Then she noticed one tight knot of husks who had not moved. These had been at the front of the group and as the vast majority of their fellows rushed toward the diversion, this group stood motionless around one small, grime-streaked figure.

"What are you waiting for?" Patience whispered. With growing horror, she watched the girl (for it was a teenaged girl, she realized) shake her head ever so slightly and then continue walking in the direction of the farm. The others followed.

"How many? How many?" she hissed and started counting. She'd gotten to 223 when the wind changed direction and a cloud of acrid smoke obscured her view. It was time to go. She may have significantly whittled them down, but a horde was still coming. And these, it seemed, could follow orders … and think.

Louella had nothing left in her stomach and so just dry heaved every hour or so. Patience brought her some water to sip.

"Did it work?" Lou's voice was a thin rasp.

"Let's just get you to bed," Patience said, trying to pull the chief to her feet.

That prevarication frightened Lou. Her hand shot out to grip Pat's arm, hard. "Did it work?"

"Mostly."

"Meaning?"

Patience sighed. "The vast majority of them went toward the fire. It's just … there were some that didn't. They just stood there around this one infected girl and watched the others rush off and then she shook her head and carried on in this direction and they followed her."

"She was their leader?"

"That's what it looked like."

"And she stood there and made a conscious decision."

Patience nodded.

"I didn't think they could do that," Louella said quietly. "The virus — it's supposed to destroy your ability to think."

"We appear to have an exception to the rule."

"How many followers does she have?"

"Somewhere between 250 and 300."

A wave of nausea swept over Lou and she felt so exhausted, so physically wretched that for a moment she was unable to care about the mess they were in. But then she stopped heaving and asked, "When will they get here?"

"The lowlands are pretty marshy because of the rains so that'll slow 'em down. Still I'd say we have two days max."

The bug passed quickly over the next twenty-four hours. Most of the group were back on their feet by the following afternoon. They were slow and wrung out and no one was at all sure how best to receive the 300-odd guests who were approaching the farm.

"Do we evacuate?" Sam asked.

Ginny piped up. "How many were in that horde from Midwood?"

"The one we beat? That was," Patience searched her memory, "ninety-seven."

"So we're looking at three times that number," Arnold said grimly.

"Maybe we *should* bug out," Bib added.

"We have site B," Louella said, taking a sip of flat ginger ale. "But it isn't fully stocked yet and it's nowhere near as secure as this place. Sam, what was your latest count on our ammo?"

"Nearly 5,000 rounds," he answered.

"And Fletcher's traps are still in place. That'll slow them down and give us more time to pick them off," Owen added.

Louella looked at Patience. "Can we take them?"

"I think so. And to be honest, swapping this compound for something less secure makes me really nervous. I say we stay."

"All in favor?" the chief asked.

The decision was made. They'd stay and fight.

Patience, as the head security officer, was in charge of preparations for the siege. As she made her plans, Louella rose and went to check on the animals. They hadn't had their troughs and feeders replenished in the last day and she was anxious to make sure they were all right. The cows and chickens were fine — she'd put extra food and water out for them when she started feeling rough. But Arnold's pigs were boisterous in their pen, which usually meant they were hungry. She went to feed them, leaving the main compound for the wider fenced-in area that enclosed the outbuildings.

Lou was halfway to their sty when she saw the fox. It was just a russet blur on the periphery of her vision but in an instant, it had reached her. It was snarling — a low, rasping series of barks as it leapt. As Louella fought to keep its snapping jaws away from her face, she tried to cry out but couldn't. After the illness, the struggle took everything she had and she couldn't seem to draw enough air into her lungs to scream. The animal twisted in her hands and clamped its teeth down on her fingers. She lost her grip entirely then and the fox, now free, leapt at her throat. He caught her right below the jawline and bit into the loose flesh beneath her chin. There were shouts now behind her and she managed to yell, "Stay back!" Peg was screaming and fighting Alec who'd grabbed her to keep her from running to her mother. Louella dropped forward using her whole body weight to pin the fox to the ground. If she lost her grip again, it could attack any of them — Peg, Sam — and so she clung to the animal even as it bit her chest and arms and hands.

Patience quickly ushered everyone back into the main compound and took a position on the ramparts with a hunting rifle.

"Lou," she called, "you got a good grip on it?"

"Yes," Louella croaked.

"Ok, on the count of three I want you to chuck it aside. One, two, three!"

Louella threw the animal away from her and two shots rang out in quick succession. The fox lay still and Lou staggered to her feet.

She looked around vaguely for a moment. Her hearing had gone funny. She could hear her jagged breath very clearly, but everything else was muffled — the way sound reaches you underwater. And then she was moving, someone had a hand on her back and was guiding her into the main compound and into the kitchen where everything looked so normal. There were dishes in the sink and the notepad that she made her lists on sat on the table where she'd left it. She was dripping blood on the floor. *I'll need to clean that up*, she thought absently. And then she was sitting in a chair as Wyn and Niamh buzzed around her.

Everything hurt. That wasn't new. She was an old woman with an extensive collection of aches and pains. But this was on another level. It took her breath away. Wyn was surprised when she started inhaling and exhaling as if she was doing Lamaze. But it helped. The steady pattern was something to focus on while she endured.

Peg was in front of her now. "Don't worry, mom. The iron's in the fire. We'll take care of this."

Wait, Louella thought, *iron, fire. What? Holy shit, they're going to cauterize the wounds.* She stammered for a moment before she could form the word, "No."

"What?" Peg asked.

"Look at me. Do you really think you can burn it all out?"

In a rare moment of immodesty, she ripped her blouse open to reveal the extent of the damage.

Niamh leaned in with alcohol and gauze and cleaned an area just below the chief's right shoulder. "I can see your collarbone, Lou."

Peg was shaking her head, "No."

"It bit down to the bone," Wyn said quietly. He gently tilted Lou's head back. "And here at your chin too. We could try to cauterize the wounds, but... I don't see how I can get it all."

"I'll do it," Peg said quickly.

"No you won't," Louella said calmly.

"But mom! It's that or die! Come on!" she barked at the others. "Get the irons!"

They stood looking uncertainly from Lou to her daughter and back again.

"Peg, I'm sorry," her mother whispered.

"I don't want apologies," Peg hissed. "I want you to fight! This is your life — your one life! You don't just give it up!"

There was so much distress in her girl's voice that Louella almost relented — anything to quiet that despair. But then her eyes fell on the little sign that James had given her — the one with the chicken that read "Hatching Plans" — and that old light bulb in her brain switched itself on once again.

"I will fight, but I'm gonna pick my battles."

"What are you talking about?" Bib asked.

As Niamh patched her up and Wyn bandaged her ruined left hand, Louella explained. "Right now we have 300 husks on their way here. We can probably beat them, but Patience, you taught us that no matter how much you prepare, there are no guarantees. You should avoid a fight if you can."

Pat nodded, "Yeah, because you can never truly predict the outcome."

"And yet, that is our whole plan. Stay and fight and hope to win, hope the fences hold and everybody is well enough to do their job. Half of you are still struggling to tackle a piece of toast, let alone 300 rabid lunatics. So why don't we broaden our options?"

"How so?" Levi asked.

"Plan A — you don't fight. You go dark. Shut everything off. Wyn, you could tranq the animals so they don't get scared and make noise. We could make this place look like nobody's home."

"But what if they check it out, anyway?" Patience asked.

"We give them something else to go for."

Peg was sitting with her head in her hands and didn't even bother to look up. "You're going to use yourself as bait, aren't you?"

"Yep. Lead them off Pied Piper style."

"To where?"

And in her mind's eye, Louella saw the bridge — that damned covered bridge that had haunted her as a child because it seemed to suggest the end of things. A few tears ran down her cheeks and she hastily wiped them away. "The bridge on Old Mill Road."

"And then?"

"Well, they'll have to crowd around the car to try and get in at me and then..."

Peg still hadn't looked up and her voice was flat. "You'll blow it up."

Lou looked at Sam and Arnold. "James used to make his own ammo — we still have that gunpowder, right? Could you rig something?"

Sam, who'd just been asked to make a bomb to kill his own grandmother, started grasping at any other option. "But you said that was Plan A. What about Plan B? We'll take them on instead."

"Sweetheart, Plan B comes after Plan A, not in place of it."

"I don't understand."

"The aim is to reduce the size of the horde. I won't be able to get them all. But there will be fewer left for you to deal with."

"What if they won't follow you?" Ginny asked.

"Then I blow the car out front and take out as many as I can."

"Is there a Plan C?" Peg asked, finally looking her mother in the eye. "One that doesn't involve suicide?"

"No." Louella rose and looked at her people calmly. "Whether we go with my plan or not, I'm still going to end this before I turn. So you might as well let me try."

There was much to do. Levi souped up her car and filled it with gas — Louella wanted the biggest possible bang for her buck. In the meantime, Arnold, Alec and Sam filled a large plastic drum with Hodgdon Varget Gun Powder, only to be sent in search of a metal container instead. In answer to their questioning looks, Lou shrugged, "Shrapnel." They finally found what they were looking for: a 20-gallon barrel that James had used to burn trash. They duct taped the holes on the side, filled it with black powder and then started on the fuse. They tried different sorts of string and different accelerants and in the end opted for yarn coated in some of Peg's old nail polish. That seemed to burn pretty well. With the bomb complete, they strapped it into the shotgun seat of Louella's Chevy.

Patience was about to get rid of the fox when the chief stopped her.

"Burn it after the horde's moved on. In the meantime, I want you to get a thick pair of gloves and paint the perimeter fence with its blood. When the horde passes by, I want this place to smell dead."

Pat obeyed the order. It reminded her of Passover, when the Jews daubed blood on their doors so the Angel of Death would pass by, sparing those inside. She was creeped out by the parallel, but then something else caught her eye. It was a small hole dug underneath the perimeter fence and the sight of it wrung an abrupt sob from her throat. This was all her fault. She'd been so tired and strung out, that she hadn't checked the perimeter. *Oh God.* It was her job to protect this family, to train them and keep them safe. And now her mistake had cost them the chief.

She went to Louella, head bowed, ready for the fury and recriminations that she felt were her due. But Lou only shrugged.

"You forgot to check it? So did I. So did everybody. These last weeks have been one giant avalanche of crap. We're ragged as hell and no, we didn't remember to do that. So? There hasn't been a sign of anything digging at the fences for months and now a fox comes along and it just happens to coincide with one of the few days we didn't check?"

"You saying that all this is fate?" Patience asked through her tears.

"I'm saying that it is quite obviously my time."

With the preparations made and a largely uneaten dinner put back in the fridge for tomorrow, Louella sat on the living room couch with Mae asleep on her lap. Peg sat beside her with her head on her mother's shoulder and Sam curled up on her other side, holding his grandmother's good hand. Lou could feel herself tottering on the brink of a real collapse. By this time tomorrow she'd be dead — a fact that seemed frankly impossible. To cease to be — how could she even wrap her head around the concept? Yes, she believed in God and Christ's redemptive act on the cross; she believed in forgiveness and Heaven and love and light. But she was in pain and she was afraid. The storm that howled through her head was almost incomprehensible in its violence and grief. She wanted to cry and rage. She wanted God to understand that it wasn't fair; it was too soon, her work wasn't finished yet and why couldn't the Supreme Being grant her, His child, a stay of execution?

They were childish thoughts, she knew, and in her childishness she did not care. She inhaled sharply and gritted her teeth so that she would not cry out. Peg heard that intake of breath and looked up at her mother.

"Are you ok? Do you need more painkillers?"

"No, honey. I'm fine."

Her daughter's face was pale and drawn. Her eyes were puffy from weeping and that is why Louella had to be very careful about what she said and did next. It was, she realized, a damnable opportunity. Damnable because she wanted to cry and yell and frankly she had every right to do those things. But what would it accomplish? If there was ever a way to make a child terrified of death, it was to let her watch her mother face it crying and screaming. It would be awful. She knew that, for Peg and Sam and the rest of them, how they viewed their own demise would be greatly influenced by how she reacted to her own. She could leave them absolutely horrified by the concept or she could give them a chance to view it more philosophically. Therein lay the opportunity.

It took a mammoth effort, but she got a grip on herself and said: "It really is ok."

"Huh?" Sam asked.

"It's all right — tomorrow, I mean. I'm not scared."

The boy had no idea how to respond to that.

"You don't have to give us one of your pep talks, mom," Peg said quietly.

"It's not a pep talk. I've just been thinking that the one thing in life that's guaranteed is the fact that it'll end. And yet people are so afraid of dying. You spend your whole life fearing the inevitable and why? I mean, take this mess. I die tomorrow and no, I'm not doing cartwheels at the prospect, but what's the alternative? To sicken and become one of those things? To turn on the people I love?"

The others in the room were listening now as Louella continued. "As your mom, I taught you so many things. It was my job to teach you how to live. And now there's only one lesson left."

"What's that?" Sam asked.

"To teach you how to die. How to face it with a little grace. Because there is no reason why your passing has to be fearful and anguished. To step beyond the reach of all this pain and fear … can you imagine what it will be like to be safe again, and *free?* So I don't want you to worry about me tomorrow; I'm going to be absolutely fine."

Patience was up early the following morning and headed out to check on the progress of the horde. At the rate they were going, they'd be at the farm by midday. She returned home to find Bib fussing in the kitchen. The woman was cooking like a fiend: eggs and bacon and sausage and French toast and pancakes. There was talk of waffles and ice cream and that is when it really hit home — this was Louella's last meal. Lou ate some of everything that Bib offered her, but she was not hungry. Whether it was due to nerves or the fact that her temperature had spiked, she really couldn't tell. What she did relish was the view. A daughter and two grandchildren and her friends — all her people, healthy and well-fed and the kids growing strong. Even Ginny was doing better. And this home which had served them so well — Camp North Star with its band of inspired misfits. She'd done all right.

Soon, too soon, it was time to get ready. The animals were drugged; the children were ushered into the basement under the strictest orders not to make a sound. The others armed themselves and got into position and Louella stood alone on the porch. Peg hovered at the door and this was the biggest test of all. No, death was not the ultimate evil and during the night she had come to accept the fact that God did not promise her a body that would endure forever. He promised the immortality of the soul. He'd promised Heaven — that's what waited for her, right? And James and Eben and her mother and father. What will it be like? She'd often heard of an individual's own personal hell, but what about your own personal heaven? In hers she could eat whatever she wanted and still maintain the body of an eighteen-year-old. She'd live on the farm with James and the kids and her animals. The fields would be green and the air mild. And Fletch would be sitting out at the picnic table tapping out his latest novel on an old typewriter. A summer idyll — that's what her heaven would be.

It was ok to die. She'd made her peace with it and was surprisingly calm, but here was her daughter and she had to say goodbye. For all her religion and philosophy, she did not know how to walk away from this child. It took every ounce of her strength to say, "Go on, honey. Lock it up."

With a sob, Peg closed the door and Louella sagged against it, feeling like the loneliest soul on earth. Then she stood up straight and got moving. The car was waiting for her on the road with the keys in the ignition. As she walked toward it, the people of Camp North Star saw her do things that seemed at once perfectly natural and utterly out of character. She always wore her long, gray hair up in a clip. It wasn't an aesthetic choice. It simply kept it out of her face while she worked. But as she walked away from the farm, she tugged the clip free and tossed it nonchalantly over her shoulder. It looked so casual; and yet it was a calculated, almost choreographed move on Louella's part. She would teach Peg and Sam how to die with a little dignity and courage and grace. And so the grand demonstration began. She ran her fingers through her hair and let it fall across her shoulders — the way she wore it when she was young. Leaning into the car she turned on Def Leppard's *Rock of Ages* full blast and reflected with some regret that she'd never know what "Gunter gleiben glauchen globen" actually meant.

The music bolstered her up. That's when she spotted the *Jack Daniels* Levi had left on her seat. She took a long drink straight from the bottle. As she walked to the rear of the car there was actually a swagger in her step that had a curious effect on the people of the farm. Despite their grief and their fear, they were hooked, intent upon watching this play out and seeing exactly what she would do. Her next move, in fact, was to grab that pack of Marlboro's she'd found in Fletcher's case. She had rolled it up in the sleeve of her T-shirt just like the guys used to do back in high school. She lit one using Fletch's lighter, leaned against the Chevy's rear bumper and watched the horde come.

As they drew near Louella looked at them calmly, took another drag, and then flicked the lit butt in their direction. They shrieked and charged forward, but the chief just stood there, unperturbed. In another moment, she sauntered casually over to the open car door and hopped in. Still she did not drive off.

"What is she waiting for?" Peg whispered.

As the first of the infected reached the back bumper, Louella peeled away in a screech of tires and spray of gravel that peppered the husks with stones.

She led them off. While the beginning of the chase certainly looked dramatic, what followed was decidedly pedestrian. She could only go so fast or risk losing them. And so she ambled slowly toward town. However when she finally came within striking distance of her goal, she accelerated. She needed time to prepare. She crossed the bridge and there were all the cars that had gotten snarled up at the checkpoint and never made it out of Midwood. She recognized Councilman Eck's BMW, its windshield shattered, the gray upholstery of the driver's seat stained a dark brown. Tearing her gaze from this, she turned around and pulled back onto the bridge. She popped the trunk and hefted out a large jerry can of gasoline. The wounds on her chest and arms screamed as she struggled with the weight and soon she was bleeding freely again. But she didn't stop. She walked back and forth on that bridge, pouring petrol until the can was empty.

The task really took it out of her and she collapsed back into the car. She was burning up now and started the engine to switch on the air con. But when the blast of cool air hit her in the face, her neck spasmed, jerking her head back. She suddenly felt very anxious and just needed that stream of air to stop. Her trembling fingers frantically hit at the buttons. Once it was off, she sat there panting.

"What the hell?" she gasped.

She was very ill now. The infection was like some alien creature inside of her that was hunkering down, getting comfortable, gripping the wheel. The pain was a living thing with claws and teeth gouging out the inside of her skull. She had an image of being turned into a hideous jack-o-lantern, her pumpkin head scooped clean of pulp and seed and pith. Like the pumpkin the Headless Horseman used for a head. And he rode a white horse and he was pestilence. And she shivered in the early August heat. She could feel something building within her and in the midst of her torment, two words flitted across her mind that brought her some relief. *The farm.* She could go back to the farm. Her jaws involuntarily snapped shut on her tongue. Louella cried out and spat blood. Bite. The farm. Bite. God, no, please no.

"Hurry," she whispered and reached over to crank up the music.

She accidentally hit some button on the sound system. Def Leppard's *Armageddon It* was replaced by none other than David Seville and his fucking chipmunks. Oddly enough the shock of that change brought her back to herself for a moment. She cast woeful eyes skyward.

"Really?" she said aloud. "You couldn't just let me be cool. I had to have *this* as my swan song?"

Her conversation with God was brought to an abrupt halt with the arrival of the girl. She was a sad, haggard thing — filthy and battered, with wounds on her arms and face that were beginning to fester. But for all that, there was clearly something going on upstairs. She stood and studied Louella for a moment while her followers caught up with her.

"So you're the one," Lou murmured.

At that moment the chipmunks reached their refrain, which had about the same effect on the girl as it usually had on Louella. She howled in rage and ran forward. Louella hurriedly put up the windows and locked the doors, but she still flinched as one body after another slammed into the car. The driver's side door buckled from the impact. Then two more were at the passenger's side, screeching their frustration at being able to see prey they couldn't reach. Something threw itself onto the hood and then the girl — the smart little girl who led this army of maniacs — hammered on the windscreen. Now some were scrabbling at the latch of the trunk. The bridge in front of her filled with the infected and Louella popped the lid on Fletcher's lighter.

She leaned her head back and smiled. *Almost done now*, she thought and once again she recited the Lord's Prayer as her grandmother had taught her...

"Unsah Faddah im Himmel,
dei nohma loss heilich sei,
Dei Reich loss kumma.
Dei villa loss gedu sei,
uf di eaht vi im Himmel."

The windscreen cracked. Lines spider-webbed their way across the glass, but she didn't care. They couldn't hurt her now. Nothing could. She was free. As Louella uttered her Amen there was a brilliant flash. To her mind it looked like a star had gone supernova. And all was pure, white light.

ACORN

"You're gonna have to look after them," Louella had said.

"What?"

"The group, when I'm gone."

Peg had sat on her mother's bed as Louella leaned forward to lace up her sneakers. The old woman gasped from the pain.

"Here, let me do it." Peg knelt in front of her to tie the shoes.

"Ah, the classic reversal. The child becomes the parent," Lou smiled and shook her head. "Under any other circumstance that would freak me out, but it's good. You're gonna need this."

"What?"

"Your mothering instincts. It's the best way to look after North Star."

Peg sighed and looked up at her mother. "You keep talking like I'm set to be the next chief. *Why?*"

"Because I think they'll choose you."

Margaret was growing impatient with this. Her mother was about to walk out the door and never come back. The thought left her feeling like a frightened child. The last thing she wanted to hear was some crap about the leadership of the group.

Lou rolled a pack of cigarettes up in the sleeve of her T-shirt. "They'll choose you because, once I'm gone, no one will know this farm better than you."

"There's Sam."

"Sam hasn't graduated from high school yet."

"Mom, no one's gonna graduate ever again."

"He will," Louella nodded fervently. "Under you." She looked at her girl sadly. "I'm sorry to lay this on you. Truly. But after so much upheaval, they are going to want consistency and you and I are a lot alike. We *think* a lot alike…"

"Mom…"

"I'm not saying that you're my mini-me or whatever the hell they call it. We're just similar. But you — you're smarter than me, better educated…"

"*Mom…*"

"… and younger and more resilient."

Peg's chest constricted. What her mother was suggesting — she received this news the way a landslide victim receives a boulder to the gut. She did not want to think about this shit now. She was exhausted and scared and she wanted her mom. But Lou was slipping away. "*Stop it,*" she snapped.

Louella ignored her. "And you're a mother. The way you love Mae — that's how you're gonna have to love North Star. You'll have to love every single one of them as if they're your very own."

"This is crazy. I can't."

"Yeah, I tried that argument too. It doesn't work. They don't give a damn about your doubts." She rose to leave. "Just give them your best. You do that, and they'll see something wonderful."

Peg was mulling that conversation over when they heard the explosion. She locked her arms around Sam as he wept and one question cycled frantically through her brain: *What do I do? What do I do?* As the others embraced them, she saw a list beginning to form in her mind.

"Patience," she said quietly, "we need a small recon team to scout out the situation at the bridge. Do not engage and don't let them know you're there. If there are quite a few husks left, we don't want to lead 'em back here."

Patience looked at her in surprise and then said, "Will do."

"Niamh, go have a word with Ginny and the kids in the basement. Let them know that the horde's passed, but we're going to stay quiet until we know how many are left and where they're at." She handed Sam over to Bib and backed away from the group.

"Where are you going?" Alec asked.

"I want to check on the animals."

Peg walked through the kitchen and into the little back porch area that her mother had called a mud room.

I can't do this. It's too much.

She looked around for a pair of shoes to wear out to the barn and spotted Louella's old rubber boots in the corner. Propped on top of them was a leather journal — Fletcher's record of Camp North Star. A page was marked with an empty Twizzlers wrapper and there, in her mother's neat handwriting, was the message:

I know. You don't think you can do this. The job is so wide and so high — how can you ever surmount it? I felt exactly the same way EVERY FREAKIN DAY. And there is only one thing for it: forget the hand-wringing and simply get on with it. Do the best you can. I think that the world will see something truly awesome. And know that I love you. So much. Forever.

~Mom

P.S. Now put the damn boots on and go see to my animals.

↑

(Sorry, I couldn't resist the opportunity to boss you around one last time).

This was followed by a smiley face with its tongue sticking out and big wonky eyes that suggested complete idiocy. Peg laughed out loud. And cried. *Right. The animals.* She slipped her feet into her mom's old boots. They fit.

CPSIA information can be obtained
at www.ICGtesting.com
Printed in the USA
BVHW041812080921
616386BV00010B/329